Growing Up with Jane
A Jane Eyre Devotional

Quotations are taken directly from Charlotte Brontë's work, Jane Eyre, unless otherwise stated in the footnotes.

Scripture verses are taken directly from the King James Bible. Hebrew and Greek references come from the Strong's Concordance.

For information contact:
Providence Media LLC
http://www.providencemediallc.com

Book Design by Amanda Howard
Contributions by Deidra Howard
ISBN: 978-09989550-6-3
Published by: Providence Media LLC

10 9 8 7 6 5 4 3 2 1

Introduction

I owe my love and admiration for Jane Eyre to my grandmother. Jane and I did not get along right off. It took me three separate tries to become fully immersed in her life's story. I would start with the first chapter and then put it down just to move on to an "easier" read that was not as thick and intimidating.

I remember during one visit with my grandmother; she suggested watching the miniseries with Toby Stephens and Ruth Wilson. I immediately fell in love! The story, the darkness, the love, the characters; everything! It was then and there that I decided to finally read past the first chapter. The book had to be even better than the show, right?

Jane and I became great friends and Charlotte Brontë's famous work quickly made it to one of my top favorite books of all time (*a very difficult list to get on*). Since that time, I have read Jane Eyre again and again, never really going much deeper than the surface of the story and looking at it purely as an excellent work of fiction.

Jane Eyre really was one of my first deep works of fiction. Prior to that I had been reading Jane Austen, L.M. Montgomery, and the like. Though I love these authors dearly, Jane Eyre made me want to read more challenging literature. Literature that spoke to my heart while also stimulating my mind. This is where I began to fall in love with literature analysis.

As I started reading more challenging books written by a variety of incredible authors, I began to see that there was so much more beyond the surface of what we read. Not a lot of people have the time or the patience to do so but my mind craved the exhilarating task.

About a year before I began this project, I began to see a large portion of women talking about Jane Eyre in analytical settings. I was saddened to see that the majority of women dragged Mr. Rochester down into manipulative, deceitful ruin while they elevated Jane into perfection.

Now, please do not get me wrong, reader, Jane is a strong, beautiful, moral, and virtuous woman who deserves our praise. However, Mr. Rochester does not deserve our hate. In fact, there are many other characters, St. John for example, that would fit the manipulative description much better. But that is beside the point.

This took me on a journey. I knew that I had not read a different version of this story and yet everything that I was hearing from other female readers was that the relationship between these two was toxic and undesirable for any good and moral woman. How was this possible? How was it possible that I was getting a completely different perspective?

Jane took me through her spiritual growth, from childhood to adulthood. I dove deeper into the scriptures as I worked through this novel and began to realize the deeper, more beautiful details that lay beneath the surface for only those patient enough to search them out.

I reexamined the characters and became better acquainted with Helen (*Jane's only friend*), Miss Temple (*Jane's mentor*), Mr. Brocklehurst (*the tight-laced, unforgiving master of Lowood school*), Mr. Rochester (*the broken, yet honorable love interest*), Miss Ingram, Mrs. Reed and her children, St. John and his sisters, Adèle, and Mrs. Fairfax.

Unfortunately, the more I read, the more I strongly felt that this story never received its due. I saw that feminism had destroyed the deeper, more spiritual, more virtuous and moral parts of the story.

Jane begins as a self-pitying child who does whine and is bitter over her circumstances. Helen plays an important role in how Jane learns to rely on God and become a woman of substance. She learns the importance of forgiveness and turning the other cheek.

"And be ye kind one to another, tenderhearted, forgiving one another, even as God for Christ's sake hath forgiven you."
Ephesians 4:32

Mr. Rochester, though he is mysterious and misunderstood, genuinely wants to be a good, moral man. Jane is the first person, let alone woman, to say no to him. We see God working, not only through Jane's life, but also Mr. Rochester's.

Her influence changes him into the better man he so desires to be, and he eventually gives thanks to God for His guidance. It then becomes a redemption story for the both of them, not just our beloved heroine.

Feminists overlook all of this, especially the more spiritual parts. But they also overlook Jane's protection of her own virtue. She resists a most tempting offer which she almost gives in to. She trusts God and his plan for her and chooses forgiveness repeatedly.

Beyond the relationship between Mr. Rochester and Jane, we also see the love that Jane pours into others. She genuinely loves Adèle and treats her with respect, knowing that she is a human being, worthy of love, full of emotion, and capable of being hurt.

Jane also shows love and respect for St. John and his sisters as if they were her own siblings. Yes, Jane was hurt, but she decided to continue to show love and be love to those around her in spite of the hurt they may have caused.

"And now abideth faith, hope, charity [love]*, these three; but the greatest of these is charity."* 1 Corinthians 13:13

As you read, you can begin to see the finer details of how God works in the lives of the people around us as well as in our own lives.

Both characters were put through a process of growth, spiritually and emotionally so that they could ultimately grow into the people God created them to be. This growth then ends in complete joy as they finally come to a place of peace and contentment.

In the end, it is revealed throughout the whole story, how much our decisions affect our futures, and sometimes the futures of others, both on earth and in eternity with God our Father.

This is the Jane Eyre I knew and loved! This is what I read so many times. This is why Charlotte Brontë's book has a very special and beloved place in my heart. And this is what I sincerely hope that you will see as you read Growing Up with Jane.

Chapter I

"...Eliza, John, and Georgiana were now clustered round their mama in the drawing-room: she lay reclined on a sofa by the fireside, and with her darlings about her (for the time neither quarrelling nor crying) looked perfectly happy. Me, she had dispensed from joining the group..."

Jane Eyre opens as Jane is gradually introducing her "family." In only the first couple of paragraphs, we see that Jane is left out of intimate family togetherness. She is not accepted as one of the family and is told to go elsewhere.

She has no concept of what a healthy family life looks like or what it even feels like to be an accepted or loved part of a family unit. She has no father figure since her uncle has died and the only mother figure in her life openly abhors her. This sets Jane up for being defensive, feeling unloved, and always feeling unwanted.

Rejection entered Jane at a very young age, and this begins Jane's process of seeking the approval of the adults in her life. She is made to believe that she is worthless, not worth being loved, and "unnatural." Rejection then becomes part of her identity.

The Truth of Rejection[1]

Rejection establishes your value based on whether or not another human being accepts you. This goes against God.

When you begin to believe that you are not worth anything, this makes God a liar because He specifically said that our identity is to be found in Him and that He loves us.

"Having predestinated [foreordain] *us unto the adoption of children by Jesus Christ to himself, according to the good pleasure of his will,"* Ephesians 1:5

Thinking that our value must be found in other people means that we are setting them up on a pedestal as an idol. They then become God in our lives rather than our true Father in heaven. But it can also make us believe that we must first be accepted of people before God can accept us.

"Thou shalt have no other gods before me." Exodus 20:3

Rejection is a liar and a thief. It steals our relationship with God and the love He has for us.

"Be sober, be vigilant; because your adversary the devil, as a roaring lion, walketh about, seeking whom he may devour:" 1 Peter 5:8

"For the LORD will not cast off his people, neither will he forsake his inheritance." Psalm 93:14

"He that heareth you heareth me; and he that despiseth you despiseth me; and he that despiseth me despiseth him that sent me." Luke 10:16

Rejection can also make you feel that you were an accident. No matter how your conception occurred, you were never an accident or a mistake. You are here because God wants you here. He loves you and accepts you and adopts you as His son or daughter through Christ.

"What shall we then say to these things? If God be for us, who can be against us?" Romans 8:31

"For thou hast possessed my reins [kidneys, seat of emotion and affection]: *thou hast covered me in my mother's womb. I will praise thee; for I am fearfully and wonderfully made: marvelous are thy works; and that my soul knoweth right well. My substance was not hid from thee, when I was made in secret, and curiously wrought in the lowest parts of the earth. Thine eyes did see my substance, yet being unperfect; and in thy book all my members were written, which in continuance were fashioned, when as yet there was none of them. How precious also are thy thoughts unto me, O God! how great is the sum of them!"* Psalm 139:13-17

We were created with the need to be affirmed/accepted. Not receiving that affirmation of love creates a void which we try to fill with love from various places. Jane sought books to escape the reality of being in a world that did not love her. Dreams of adventure and travel pulled at her heartstrings. She strove to learn things. She did not understand that she was loved from the very beginning of her conception by a Father who would never leave her.

"With Bewick on my knee, I was then happy: happy at least in my way. I feared nothing but interruption, and that came too soon."

Enter the cruel John Reed. We have seen some, and will see more, of the emotional and verbal abuse inflicted upon Jane, but this is our glimpse into the physical abuse that Jane is subjected to. John is the only character that physically abuses her; beats her, pushes her, and throws things at her.

She lives in fear that John will hurt her in some way or other. There is no specific reason other than he has been raised without any sympathy toward any living creature. He had no love for his own kin and hated Jane. Mrs. Reed indulged him to the point of creating a spoiled, sickly, hateful, defiant child.

"Now no chastening [the whole training and education of children, cultivation of the mind and morals, correcting mistakes, reproof and punishment] *for the present seemeth to be joyous, but grievous: nevertheless afterward it yieldeth the peaceable fruit* [work, act, deed, profit] *of righteousness unto them which are exercised* [to exercise vigorously, in any way, either the body or the mind] *thereby."* Hebrews 12:11

"He that spareth [withhold, restrain, hold back, refrain] *his rod* [of shepherd's implement, mark of authority, staff] *hateth his son: but he that loveth him chasteneth* [discipline, chastening, correction] *him betimes* [to seek earnestly, look diligently for]." Proverbs 13:24

By not disciplining and by over-indulging her son, Mrs. Reed created the despicable child we see now. Unfortunately, the child then grows up and becomes a lazy, indulgent, hateful adult who dies young and alone.

If we look forward into the story a bit, we begin to understand why Mrs. Reed has demonstrated these ways to her son. She felt rejected by her husband, loving his sister more than her. If we know this about her, then we can begin to understand that John has inherited this rejection, pain, and bitterness from his mother and is acting out on it.

"'Wicked and cruel boy!' I said. 'You are like a murderer –
you are like a slave-driver – you are like the Roman
emperors.'"

Here we see how intelligent Jane is. We also see how
ignorant John is despite all his schooling and wealth of
tutors. He has no idea what she is talking about, and this
increases his anger because he will not allow her to have the
upper hand in intelligence or superiority. Thus, his temper
flares and he attacks her.

"I really saw in him a tyrant, a murderer. I felt a drop or two
of blood from my head trickle down my neck, and was
sensible of somewhat pungent suffering: these sensations for
the time predominated over fear, and I received him in
frantic sort. I don't very well know what I did with my
hands, but he called me 'Rat! Rat!' and bellowed out aloud.
Aid was near him: Eliza and Georgiana had run for Mrs.
Reed, who was gone upstairs: she now came upon the scene,
followed by Bessie and her maid Abbot. We were parted: I
heard the words —

'Dear! dear! What a fury to fly at Master John!'"

Jane lives in daily fear of being hit, flown at, yelled at, etc.
She puts this fear into words earlier on,

"...every nerve I had feared him, and every morsel of flesh in
my bones shrank when he came near. There were moments
when I was bewildered by the terror he inspired, because I
had no appeal whatever against either his menaces or his
inflictions;"

This fear overpowers every other feeling. She has been conditioned to feel this fear whenever John is around. This must be the first time that Jane has stood up and fought back. She is not thinking of the fear she has toward John but fighting for her position in the house as an equal, and I believe, fighting out of a sense of survival.

Fear tries to overpower faith. It tries to kill every hope, every bit of peace, and every bit of love in order to separate us from God. Fear is also a liar and a thief. Fear projects into the future deceiving us into thinking that God cannot or will not be our provision.

Faith is trusting God for everything no matter the circumstance. Fear does not want our faith to be strong because we are easy to take down when we are weak in our faith.

Fear exists everywhere. Fear of failure, fear of rejection, fear of death, fear of others, etc. The question then lies in whether or not you are choosing to live in that fear and accepting it as who you are, making it your identity or rejecting its influence.

Finally, we also see more rejection in the final paragraph of this chapter. The servants and Mrs. Reed blame Jane for this outburst, accusing her of flying at John. Thus, Jane is punished and sent to the "Red Room." A room which Jane is deathly afraid of, letting John off the hook for any wrongdoing in spite of the presence of blood on Jane's head.

What Have We Then Learned?

It is easy for us, as readers, to see the Reeds as bad people. We can easily see them as the villains of the story; as the villains in Jane's upbringing. We can easily blame them for everything bad that happens in Jane's childhood.

However, we must understand why people are the way they are. We are spiritual beings living in a spiritual world. Discovering that rejection plays a huge role in the lives of these people, as well as bitterness and possibly fear of poverty, helps us to better view them as what they are; human beings who have passed down spiritual iniquities from previous generations. Does this make what they did to Jane okay? Absolutely not. But it gives us a better idea of how we can better deal with and love people like this in our own lives.

"For we wrestle not against flesh and blood, but against principalities, against powers, against the rulers of the darkness of this world, against spiritual wickedness in high places." Ephesians 6:12

This is how we practice separation. We will learn more about this in detail in chapter six when Jane begins to understand what separation is and how to utilize it in her own life.

How Can You Apply This to Your Own Life?

Have you been experiencing any rejection lately?

Rejection can come from others, from yourself, and perceived rejection from God. All of it can lead to discontent and loss of identity. You have two choices:

1. You can either accept rejection as part of who you are or
2. You can recognize the rejection in your life and get rid of it in the name of Jesus Christ.

Remember, rejection is a lie from Satan to destroy our relationship with God, our heavenly Father, and others. Satan does not want us to live in peace, love, joy, and contentment.

If you recognize that you are holding onto rejection in your own life and you are ready to be free from it, here are some steps you can take to gain that freedom.

As believers, we are called to be in obedience to God the Father. God wants you to be free from rejection and be in a right relationship with Him! Knowing the Word and building an understanding of what is *of* God and what is not is important.

"But seek ye first the kingdom of God, and His righteousness; and all these things shall be added to you."
Matthew 6:33

"My people are destroyed for lack of knowledge: because you have rejected knowledge, I will also reject you, that you shall be no priest to Me: seeing you have forgotten the law of your God, I will also forget your children." Hosea 4:6

Recognizing what is not of God and not taking the next step to remove that sin, means that you are rejecting that knowledge that God has given you to recognize the sin.

This brings us to what is called, the 8 Rs to Freedom (Be in Health ®/Hope of the Generations)[2]:

1. **Recognize** – recognizing that you are dealing with something against what God wants for you (*i.e., rejection*).
2. **Responsibility** – take responsibility for the fact that you have allowed this sin to enter in and that you have participated in without accusation toward yourself.

"For I acknowledge my transgressions: and my sin is ever before me." Psalm 51:3

"If we confess our sins, He is faithful and just to forgive us our sins, and to cleanse us from all unrighteousness." 1 John 1:9

3. **Repent** – a process of actually turning away from the sin that is pulling at your heart.

"I acknowledged my sin to You, and my iniquity have I not hidden. I said, I will confess my transgressions to the LORD; and You forgave the iniquity of my sin. Selah." Psalm 32:5

"Then Peter said to them, Repent, and be baptized every one of you in the name of Jesus Christ for the remission [release from bondage or imprisonment, forgiveness or pardon of

sins, remission of the penalty] *of sins, and you shall receive the gift of the Holy Ghost."* Acts 2:38

4. **Renounce** – once you repent for the sin you have allowed in, you can renounce it in the name of Jesus. Renouncing is you making the decision to be free once and for all. The formal definition of renounce — *to give up or put aside voluntarily, to give up by formal declaration; to disown.*

"But have renounced the hidden things of dishonesty [the confusion of one who is ashamed of anything, sense of shame], *not walking in craftiness* [cunning, false wisdom], *nor handling the word of God deceitfully* [to ensnare, to corrupt]; *but by manifestation of the truth commending ourselves to every man's conscience* [the soul as distinguishing between what is morally good and bad] *in the sight of God."* 2 Corinthians 4:2

"If My people, which are called by My name, shall humble themselves, and pray, and seek My face, and turn from their wicked ways; them will I hear from heaven, and will forgive their sin, and will heal their land." 2 Chronicles 7:14

5. **Remove** – get rid of the sin permanently in the name of Jesus (*i.e., removing the rejection from your life*).

"There is therefore now no condemnation to them which are in Christ Jesus, who walk not after the flesh, but after the Spirit. For the law of the Spirit of life in Christ Jesus has made me free from the law of sin and death." Romans 8:1-2

"But if we walk in the light, as He is in the light, we have fellowship one with another, and the blood of Jesus Christ His Son cleanses us from all sin. If we say that we have no sin, we deceive ourselves, and the truth is not in us. If we confess our sins, He is faithful and just to forgive us our sins, and to cleanse us from all unrighteousness." 1 John 1:7-9

6. **Resist** – take a stand against the devil and resist his temptations to fall back into sin.

"Submit yourselves therefore to God. Resist the devil, and he will flee from you." James 4:7

"Watch and pray, that you enter not into temptation: the spirit indeed is willing, but the flesh is weak." Matthew 26:41

"This I say then Walk in the Spirit, and you shall not fulfill the lust of the flesh." Galatians 5:16

7. **Rejoice** – rejoice in your freedom that God has given you and the knowledge of how to be free, give thanks that He is restoring your relationship with Him.

"And you shall know the truth, and the truth shall make you free [set at liberty: from the dominion of sin]." John 8:32

"Stand fast therefore in the liberty wherewith Christ has made us free, and be not entangled again with the yoke of bondage." Galatians 5:1

"For by grace are you saved through faith; and that not of yourselves: it is the gift of God: not of works, lest any man should boast." Ephesians 2:8-9

8. **Restore** – share your testimony with others that they may be free as well.

"Then will I teach transgressors Your ways; and sinners shall be converted to You." Psalm 51:13

"Brethren, if a man be overtaken in a fault, you which are spiritual, restore such a one in the spirit of meekness; considering yourself, lest you also be tempted." Galatians 6:1

Footnotes

[1] Rejection by Dr. Henry W. Wright – Be in Health ®

[2] 8 R's to Freedom by Dr. Henry W. Wright – Be in Health ®

Chapter II

"'*She never did so before,*' *at last said Bessie, turning to* *Abigail.*

'*But it was always in her,*' *was the reply.* '*I've told Missis* *often my opinion about the child, and Missis agreed with me.* *She's an underhand little thing: I never saw a girl of her age* *with so much cover.*'"

In a lot of these classic novels around Jane Eyre's time, the adults always held to the idea that children should be seen and not heard. This was not Jane's nature. Perhaps early on in her history, before the reader is introduced, she did comply and was serene and put up with the beratements and beatings.

If that were so, we can easily see why the adults in this narrative are beginning to see her true self coming out. She fought against them, and her rebellious nature was revealed. Either that, or rebellion has developed in her due to the way she has been treated. In the bible, we are constantly reminded of how important children are to God.

"Take heed that ye despise [disdain] *not one of these little* *ones; for I say unto you, That in heaven their angels do* *always behold the face of my Father which is in heaven."* Matthew 18:10

"Lo, children are an heritage of the LORD: and the fruit of *the womb is his reward. As arrows are in the hand of a*

mighty man, so are children of the youth. Happy is the man that hath his quiver full of them: they shall not be ashamed, but they shall speak with the enemies in the gate." Psalm 127:3-5

"But Jesus said, Suffer [to permit, allow, not to hinder, to let alone] *little children, and forbid them not, to come unto me: for of such is the kingdom of heaven."* Matthew 19:14

Jane has never been taught that she has a Father in heaven who loves her and created her. She has never been taught that she is important to Him. She does have a vague knowledge of God, heaven, and hell. However, it was never instilled in her (*let alone a lot of others at the time*) that she is a gift and that her life matters.

When Jane is finally spoken to directly and not just spoken *of* in her own presence, she is spoken to as someone who should feel guilty, ashamed, and fearful of her own future.

"'You ought to be aware, Miss, that you are under obligations to Mrs. Reed: she keeps you: if she were to turn you off, you would have to go to the poorhouse.'

I had nothing to say to these words: they were not new to me: my very first recollections of existence included hints of the same kind. This reproach of my dependence had become a vague sing-song in my ear: very painful and crushing, but only half intelligible."

Jane has clearly been told since she was young that she should be grateful for her living situation because the alternative would be to be turned out to live in the poorhouse. This is a frightening reality to put into the mind of a child at the time. If you have ever had the pleasure of reading a novel by Charles Dickens or watched a film that represents this particular time period, you can understand how frightening it would have been to have that alternative hanging over your head. To threaten a young child in this way is extremely unfair and damaging.

As we work through this novel, we can see that Bessie (*I am not completely sure about Miss Abbot*) means well but goes about things in a very wrong way. We begin to understand how vastly different people's perspectives were at this time than they are today. The threat of the poorhouse was very real. Perhaps because of the reality, they meant well by telling children to behave well and be grateful. Instead, they caused doors for fear of abandonment to enter.

"Why was I always suffering, always browbeaten, always accused, forever condemned? Why could I never please? Why was it useless to try to win any one's favor? Eliza, who was headstrong and selfish was respected. Georgiana, who had a spoiled temper, a very acrid spite, a captious and insolent carriage, was universally indulged...John no one thwarted, much less punished; though he twisted the necks of the pigeons, killed the little pea-chicks, set the dogs at the sheep, stripped the hothouse vines of their fruit, and broke the buds off the choicest plants in the conservatory: he called his mother 'old girl,' too...bluntly disregarded her wishes; not unfrequently tore and spoiled her silk attire; and he was still 'her own darling.' I dared commit no fault: I strove to fulfill every duty; and I was termed naughty and tiresome,

*sullen and sneaking, from morning to noon, and from noon
to night."*

Jane is losing hope. More than that, she is letting anger, rage,
and bitterness tear at her heart and soul. She compares
herself to the Reed children and wonders why it is that she,
who has a good heart and wants to please, is constantly put
through such pain.

She has clearly tried for the few years she has been alive to
please and to be good without any support or words of love.
As Jane sits in solace in the Red Room, all she can dwell on
is her anger toward the tyrannical John, the unloving Mrs.
Reed, and the indifference of the servants.

This begins thoughts toward death. Jane contemplates
starving herself to death so that she will not have to deal
with any of it anymore. She felt the injustice. She did not see
an end and did not feel that her life meant much. It was
better to be done with it all.

God's Justice

Justice is a tough thing. In the worldly sense, a lot of
injustice occurs every day. We see people who get away
with terrible crimes while those who do good suffer. As long
as you continue to look through the world's lens, justice will
never come. Why does God allow bad things to happen to
good people? Does that question sound familiar?

One of my favorite quotes from the movie, Love Comes Softly[1] (*I would reference the book, but it is unique to the movie*) represents this perfectly:

"Missie [*his daughter*] could fall down and hurt herself even if I'm walking right there beside her. That doesn't mean that I allowed it to happen. 'Cause she knows, with a father's unconditional love, I'll pick her up and I'll carry her. I'll try to heal her. I'll cry when she cries. And I'll rejoice when she is well. In all the moments in my life, God has been right there beside me. The truth of God's love is not that He allows bad things to happen, it's His promise that He'll be there with us when they do."

Disobedience brings injustice and pain. This disobedience began when Adam ate of the fruit in the garden of Eden. He opened the door for sin to enter into God's perfect creation. God is love. He only brings love and good things to His children. But He also allows us to choose.

He gives us free will. If He did not, then we would call Him a tyrannical ruler. God wants us to choose Him and His ways of our own free will. When we do, that is when blessings will come. The Bible clearly states that God never changes. He is the same today as He has always been; wanting to love us and have relationship with us.

"Let no man say when he is tempted, I am tempted of God: for God cannot be tempted with evil, neither tempteth he any man: But every man is tempted, when he is drawn away of his own lust, and enticed. Then when lust hath conceived, it

bringeth forth sin: and sin, when it is finished, bringeth forth death. Do not err, my beloved brethren. Every good gift and every perfect gift is from above, and cometh down from the Father of lights, with whom is no variableness [variation or change]*, neither shadow of turning."* James 1:13-17

Unfortunately, other people's sins do fall on us sometimes. Anger, bitterness, rage, and fear are all sins in which we are tempted into daily. These temptations that affect our lives, just as Mrs. Reed's have affected Jane, can tempt us toward the same behavior. Her bitterness and envy shut out a young girl and created fear and loneliness in her. Whatever is in the heart of a person, will come out and either bless or poison those around them.

"A good man out of the good treasure of his heart bringeth forth that which is good; and an evil man out of the evil treasure of his heart bringeth forth that which is evil: for of the abundance [of that which fills the heart] *of the heart his mouth speaketh."* Luke 6:45

Our goal then, as believers, is to be aware of these temptations and rebuke them in Jesus' name and to forgive the people who have unknowingly caused their sin to fall upon us. Temptation is not sin until we agree with it and act on it. This includes the temptation to allow another's sin to damage our spiritual journey.

The best way to explain temptation is by using the story of Cain and Abel as an example. Abel gave of the of best he had to the Lord, but Cain did not. Because of this, Abel was blessed, but the Lord did not accept Cain's offerings. This made Cain downcast and envious of his brother. God saw this and warned Cain that the temptation toward sin was waiting at the door of his heart.

"If thou doest well, shalt thou not be accepted? And if thou doest not well, sin lieth at the door. And unto thee shall be his desire, and thou shalt rule over him." Genesis 4:7

Unfortunately, Cain gave into the temptation and killed his brother which completed the act of sin. If Cain had resisted temptation and turned his heart and mind toward God fully, he would have been blessed.

"(For the weapons of our warfare are not carnal, but mighty through God to the pulling down [destruction, demolition] *of strong holds;)* [castle, fortification, fortress] *Casting down imaginations* [thought]*, and every high thing that exalteth itself against the knowledge of God, and bringing into captivity every thought* [intellect, mind, evil purpose] *to the obedience of Christ;"* 2 Corinthians 10:4-5

Evil exists for all people, including Christians. Otherwise, temptation would not exist and there would not be a need for repentance.

We also know that God never leaves our side. He provides us with a way out of our sin as a good Father would and offers us a genuinely safe relationship with Him. This is what makes God a perfect Father. His love goes beyond what any earthly father could ever offer.

So often we see our earthly fathers fail to execute the example of Christ to their family. But God is not like any other earthly father, and He will never fail to cover you and be your refuge. Lay down the disappointment you may have and see God the Father as He is.

"There hath no temptation taken you but such as is common to man: but God is faithful, who will not suffer you to be tempted above that ye are able; but will with the temptation also make a way to escape, that ye may be able to bear it." 1 Corinthians 10:13

"If we confess our sins, he is faithful and just to forgive us our sins, and to cleanse us from all unrighteousness." 1 John 1:9

"These things I have spoken unto you, that in me ye might have peace. In the world ye shall have tribulation: but be of good cheer; I have overcome the world." John 16:33

Jesus has already overcome the world! I know it is hard to see justice in the world. But God's justice will come. We will be judged according to how we follow after what God has laid out for us in His word. Vengeance and judgement belong to the Lord, not us.

"And I saw the dead, small and great, stand before God; and the books were opened: and another book was opened, which is the book of life: and the dead were judged out of those things which were written in the books, according to their works." Revelation 20:12

"Dearly beloved, avenge not yourselves, but rather give place unto wrath: for it is written, Vengeance is mine; I will repay, saith the Lord." Romans 12:19

For further study, I highly recommend reading the whole of Psalm 94.

"What a consternation of soul was mine that dreary afternoon! How all my brain was in tumult, and all my heart in insurrection! Yet in what darkness, what dense ignorance, was the mental battle fought! I could not answer the ceaseless inward question – why I thus suffered; now, at the distance of – I will not say how many years, I see it clearly."

It is sad for us to see a child fighting this spiritual battle. It makes it even worse for us to understand that Jane did not have the insight into how to rely on a greater, heavenly Father for comfort and peace during this time. She was ignorant of how to overcome.

"...in his last moments [Mr. Reed] had required a promise of Mrs. Reed that she would rear and maintain me as one of her own children. Mrs. Reed probably considered she had kept this promise; and so she had, I dare say, as well as her nature would permit her;..." – *brackets added by me*

As Jane begins to reflect on how she has been treated, we see the foreshadowing of Jane ultimately forgiving her aunt for her cruel treatment. Here we see that Jane concludes that perhaps Mrs. Reed did try. Maybe not hard enough, but she did. And in her own grief, perhaps seeing this child who was so admired by her husband brought pain and reminded her of her envy and rejection every day.

If we think in this way, we can sympathize with Mrs. Reed in her pain though not in her treatment of Jane. We begin to see her as a human being rather than a one-dimensional figure of torment.

Jane begins to think of her uncle. Though she does not remember him, she believes in her heart that he would have treated her kindly and with love. This makes her loneliness more real, and Jane imagines him coming back to punish Mrs. Reed for her ill treatment of his sister's child.

We close out chapter two with Jane's imagination getting the better of her, metaphorically choking her and ultimately rendering her unconscious in her fear.

There is further injustice done before she passes out, as Jane is believed to be lying and acting so she can get out of her punishment. Rather than having pity of Jane's fear, the servants only thrust her back into darkness and terror again.

How Can You Apply This to Your Own Life?

Hopelessness is running rampant throughout our world. Every day something occurs that causes grief and hopelessness…a feeling that nothing will ever get better or change.

Fortunately, you have learned that you have a loving Father who does not want you to lose faith and hope in what He has created. We are, as believers, called to live by the fruits of the spirit.

"Now the works of the flesh are manifest [evident, to be plainly recognized or known], *which are these; Adultery,*

fornication [homosexuality, lesbianism, intercourse with animals, intercourse with close relatives, eating the sacrifices offered to idols], *uncleanness* [moral impurity, lustful, of impure motives], *lasciviousness* [unbridled lust, shamelessness, insolence], *idolatry, witchcraft* [sorcery, magical arts], *hatred, variance* [contention, strife], *emulations* [an envious and contentious rivalry, jealousy], *wrath* [passion, angry, heat, ager forthwith boiling up and soon subsiding again], *strife, seditions* [dissention, division], *heresies* [dissensions arising from diversity of opinions and aims], *envyings, murders, drunkenness, revellings, and such like: of the which I tell you before, as I have also told you in time past, that they which do* [to practice, to perform habitually, a way of life] *such things shall not inherit the kingdom of God. But the fruit of the Spirit is love, joy, peace* [security, safety, prosperity, felicity], *longsuffering* [patience, endurance, constancy, perseverance, slowness in avenging wrongs], *gentleness* [integrity, kindness], *goodness* [uprightness of heart and life], *faith, meekness* [gentleness, mildness], *temperance* [self-control]: *against such there is no law.*" Galatians 5:19-23

If we are not living in faith that God has everything under control and the He has a plan, then we are not thriving but just surviving. God wants us to thrive! He wants us to have faith and hope that humanity is not totally lost. You are to be a light in the darkness and the salt of the earth so that you may bless others.

How you respond to what is going on in the world matters more than you think. You never know who is watching you and considering in their hearts why you are so hopeful, positive, and faithful.

Does this mean that we, as believers, are to reject, shame, or be hateful or unkind to the people who *have* fallen into temptation and the sins outlined in Galatians 5:19-23? Of course not! We are called to love and be love to ALL people.

This is where separation comes into play. Separate the sin from the sinner. All people were created by God in love. But, as we discussed earlier, God gives all His children a choice to either follow Him or not. Christ died for these people as much as He died for believers.

"But God commendeth his love toward us, in that, while we were yet sinners, Christ died for us." Romans 5:8

"For God so loved the world, that he gave his only begotten Son, that whosoever believeth in him should not perish, but have everlasting life. For God sent not his Son into the world to condemn the world; but that the world through him might be saved." John 3:16-17

"For all have sinned, and come short of the glory of God;" Romans 3:23

"That we henceforth be no more children [childish, untaught, unskilled], *tossed to and fro, and carried about with every wind of doctrine, by the sleight* [deception of man, cheated and defrauded] *of men, and cunning craftiness* [false wisdom], *whereby they lie in wait to deceive; But speaking the truth in love, may grow up into him in all things, which is the head, even Christ: From whom the whole body fitly joined together* [joined closely together] *and compacted* [to

unite or knit together: in affection, to teach, instruct, and
gather] *by that which every joint* [bond, connection]
*supplieth, according to the effectual working in the measure
of every part, maketh increase of the body* [a number of
men/women closely united into one society, or family as it
were] *unto the edifying of itself* [the act of one who promotes
another's growth in Christian wisdom, piety, happiness, and
holiness] *in love.*" Ephesians 4:14-16

We cannot be like Christ if we are isolating ourselves away
from people who go against God's word. Christ went to the
lowest of the low in order to share the Gospel and His
Father's love. God wants all His children to be in heaven
with Him. If we are truly to be Christ-like, we do not have to
accept their way of life, but we must be salt and light to a
hurting and broken people.

*"Now the Spirit speaketh expressly, that in the latter times
some shall depart from the faith, giving heed to seducing*
[deceiver, corrupter, imposter, misleading] *spirits, and
doctrines* [teachings, instruction] *of devils* [evil spirit];
*speaking lies in hypocrisy; having their conscience seared
with a hot iron* [whose souls are branded with the marks of
sin, who carry about with them the perpetual consciousness
of sin]; *forbidding to marry, and commanding to abstain
from meats, which God hath created to be received with
thanksgiving of them which believe and know the truth. For
every creature of God is good, and nothing to be refused, if
it be received with thanksgiving: for it is sanctified by the
word of God and prayer. If thou put the brethren in
remembrance of these things, thou shalt be a good minister
of Jesus Christ, nourished up in the words of faith and of*

good doctrine, whereunto thou hast attained [to understand, to follow faithfully a standard or rule]." 1 Timothy 4:1-6

"Rejoice, and be exceeding glad: for great is your reward in heaven: for so persecuted they the prophets which were before you. Ye are the salt [2] *of the earth: but if the salt have lost his savour* [to be foolish, to make foolish, to make flat and tasteless]*, wherewith shall it be salted? It is thenceforth good for nothing, but to be cast out, and to be trodden under foot of men. Ye are the light* [3] *of the world. A city that is set on an hill cannot be hid. Neither do men light a candle, and put it under a bushel, but on a candlestick; and it giveth light unto all that are in the house. Let your light so shine before men, that they may see your good works, and glorify your Father which is in heaven."* Matthew 5:12-16

This does not mean that you must be perfect all the time. But really take your thoughts captive. It is a daily decision to make in your heart. Sometimes it is an hour-by-hour or minute-by-minute decision. The best first step you can make is by committing God's word to your heart. Living out the Word is so much easier when you are actively studying it and meditating on it.

Letting hopelessness into your heart feeds self-pity, despair, grief, and loss of faith. This loss of faith separates you from God and interferes with hearing the Holy Spirit. Take time to rest in God. Ask Him for the strength you need and the wisdom to know how to approach every day and every person with a positive attitude. Stay grounded in His word and meditate on it. When you feel like your hope and faith are waning, pray and read the Word.

Footnotes

[1] Love Comes Softly directed by Michael Landon Jr. – Hallmark Entertainment

[2] Salt based on the interlinear, Greek text (G217 – halas ἅλας) – salt is a symbol of lasting concord, because it protects food from putrefaction and preserves it unchanged. Accordingly, in the solemn ratification of compacts, this is a practice that continues to this day in some cultures, partaking of salt together. Wisdom and grace exhibited in speech.

[3] Light based on the interlinear, Greek text (G5457 – phōs φώς) – a heavenly light such as surrounds angels when they appear on earth. God is light because light has the extremely delicate, subtle, pure, brilliant quality, of truth and its knowledge, together with the spiritual purity associated with it, that which is exposed to the view of all, openly, publicly. Reason, mind, the power of understanding especially moral and spiritual truth.

Chapter III

After the frightening ordeal of the Red Room, Jane wakes to the comforting presence of Mr. Lloyd, the servant's apothecary.

"…I felt so sheltered and befriended while he sat in the chair near my pillow; and as he closed the door after him, all the room darkened and my heart again sank: inexpressible sadness weighed it down."

The sadness and loneliness of being cast aside and unloved weighs heavily on Jane. Even more so now that she has been subjected to such a cruel punishment from her aunt. And yet, as we read further, we see that Jane, as she is reminiscing over these events, still chooses to forgive her aunt for her cruel treatment.

"No severe or prolonged bodily illness followed this incident of the red-room; it only gave my nerves a shock, of which I feel the reverberation to this day. Yes, Mrs. Reed, to you I owe some fearful pangs of mental suffering, but I ought to forgive you, for you knew not what you did: while rending my heart-strings, you thought you were only uprooting my bad propensities."

This reminds me of when Jesus, on the cross, about to die, cried out to God and asked Him to forgive the people crucifying Him because they knew not what they did.

"And when they were come to the place, which is called Calvary, there they crucified Him, and the malefactors [criminals], *one on the right hand, and the other on the left. Then said Jesus, Father, forgive them; for they know not what they do. And they parted* [to cut in pieces, to be divided, to distribute] *His raiment, and cast lots. And the people stood beholding. And the rulers also with them derided* [to deride by turning up the nose, to sneer at, to scoff at] *Him, saying, He saved others; let Him save Himself, if He be Christ, the chosen of God. And the soldiers also mocked Him, coming to Him, and offering Him vinegar, and saying, If thou be the king of the Jews, save thyself."* Luke 23:33-37

We have already seen the torment that Mrs. Reed must be under. She has suffered loss, envy, and bitterness. All lies from Satan to tempt us into sinning against others and God.

Unfortunately, since the beginning, sin has existed, and Satan's lies continue to deceive us. He is the master deceiver because he does not want us to be in relationship with our heavenly Father.

Satan used the Jewish leaders and their envy and pride to convince their followers that Jesus was a problem and needed to be quieted and removed completely. Even though they were leaders in the church, they were still ignorant of scripture and did not listen to Jesus and His wisdom. Instead, they believed their own, human wisdom raising it above the Son of God's.

"My people are destroyed [cut off, perish] *for lack of knowledge* [discernment, understanding]: *because thou hast rejected knowledge, I will also reject thee, that thou shalt be*

no priest to Me: seeing thou hast forgotten [cease to care, ignore] *the law of thy God, I will also forget thy children. As they were increased* [become many or great]*, so they sinned against Me: therefore will I change their glory* [reputation, riches, abundance, dignity] *into shame* [disgrace, dishonor]. *They eat up* [literally eat, slay, destroy] *the sin of My people, and they set* [to desire, long for, exalt] *their heart on their iniquity.*" Hosea 4:6-8

"The thief cometh not, but for to steal, and to kill, and to destroy: I am come that they might have life, and that they might have it more abundantly." John 10:10

Thankfully, Jesus knew the importance of separation between the person and their sin. He knew that they were acting on the deception of Satan. They chose to agree with the temptation of pride, envy, bitterness, and anger and that decision led them to sin, and ultimately to the death of Jesus Christ by their hands.

Even though Jesus knew that He was meant to be the sacrifice for our sins, He still knew that the people themselves mattered more to God than what lies they were allowing into their lives. His grace and mercy then became apparent when He asked God to forgive them in their ignorance.

They rejected knowledge, which would heap coals upon them in the day of judgement. However, many came to know the Father through Jesus and turned from their wicked ways even after He was resurrected and taken to be with His Father. To further reveal the mercy of God, we see throughout scripture, that He always allows us to repent and come back into relationship with Him no matter how far we have fallen.

"The God of Abraham, and of Isaac, and of Jacob, the God of our fathers, hath glorified His Son Jesus; whom ye delivered up, and denied Him in the presence of Pilate, when he was determined to let Him go. But ye denied the Holy One and the Just [righteous, virtuous, keeping the commandments of God, innocent, faultless, guiltless, only Christ truly]*, and desired a murderer to be granted unto you; And killed the Prince of life, whom God hath raised from the dead; whereof we are witnesses. And His name through faith in His name hath made this man strong, whom ye see and know: yea, the faith which is by Him hath given him this perfect soundness* [unimpaired condition of the body, in which all its members are healthy and fir for use, good health] *in the presence of you all. And now, brethren, I wot* [discern, perceive, know] *that through ignorance ye did it, as did also your rulers. But those things, which God before had shewed by the mouth of all His prophets, that Christ should suffer, He hath so fulfilled. Repent ye therefore, and be converted, that your sins may be blotted out, when the times of refreshing* [revival] *shall come from the presence of the Lord; And he shall send Jesus Christ, which before was preached unto you: Whom the heaven must receive until the times of restitution of all things, which God hath spoken by the mouth of all His holy prophets since the world began."*
Acts 3:13-21

In the above verses, Peter also understood that the people did what they did during the crucifixion out of ignorance, and that they were influenced poorly by their leaders. He helped them to see that they still were not out of reach of God's forgiveness if they only repented of their sins and the sins of their fathers. God does not want any of us to perish (*spiritually*) and fall into destruction. He wants us to live (*spiritually*) with Him forever in heaven as His chosen.

> *"But God commendeth* [by way of presenting, show, prove, establish, exhibit] *His love toward us, in that, while we were yet sinners, Christ died for us."* Romans 5:8

> *"Cast away from you all your transgressions, whereby ye have transgressed; and make you a new heart and a new spirit: for why will ye die, O house of Israel? For I have no pleasure in the death of him that dieth, saith the Lord GOD: wherefore turn yourselves, and live ye."* Ezekiel 18:31-32

We will see more evidence of Jane coming to a place of forgiveness over past hurts as we venture deeper into her story. Her childlike understanding of love, forgiveness, and what both should look and feel like, develops into a beautiful form of spiritual discernment as she gets older, begins to understand the scriptures better, and is influenced by good, godly people.

Throughout this chapter, we see how utterly despairing she is. Her depression over her life seems to have come to a head and we can almost feel how broken she is. She has an opportunity to relieve some of her woes to Mr. Lloyd, but his sympathies seem to mirror those of other adults in her life. He does, however, grant her some comfort in the prospect of escaping the home of Mrs. Reed.

This is the beginning of Jane's journey to school.

"'I should indeed like to go to school,' was the audible conclusion of my musings.

'Well, well! Who knows what may happen?' said Mr. Lloyd, as he got up. 'The child ought to have change of air and scene,' he added, speaking to himself; 'nerves not in a good state.'"

<u>How Can You Apply This to Your Own Life?</u>

It is very easy for us to fall into the temptation to give into envy, jealousy, bitterness, unforgiveness, etc. However, if Jesus could forgive the people who plotted against Him and ultimately killed Him, then we have the power to do the same.

God has given us all the power in Jesus' name to refuse these temptations and to even rid ourselves of these evil spirits who want us to be divided. If you have allowed one or more of these things into your heart and mind, you now have the tools you need to rid yourself of them.

In chapter one, you will remember that we discussed the 8 Rs to Freedom. This is a biblical way for us to restore our relationship with our heavenly Father and beat the devil.

Now remember, just because you have removed them from your life, does not mean that they will not try and get back in. Patterns of thinking and behaving need to be changed over time. Be patient as you continue to choose God's way of thinking and behaving. Continue to arm yourself with

God's word and the Fruits of the Spirit. Resist the devil and he will flee from you.

"Submit yourselves therefore to God. Resist the devil, and he will flee from you." James 4:7

"Wherefore take unto you the whole armour of God, that ye may be able to withstand in the evil day, and having done all, to stand [to make firm, fix establish, continue safe and sound, stand unharmed, to stand ready or prepared]. *Stand therefore, having your loins girt about with truth, and having on the breastplate of righteousness; and your feet shod with the preparation of the gospel of peace* [the glad tidings of salvation through Christ, the proclamation of the grace of God manifest and pledged in Christ]; *above all, taking the shield of faith, wherewith ye shall be able to quench all the fiery darts of the wicked. And take the helmet of salvation, and the sword of the Spirit, which is the word of God. Praying always with all prayer and supplication* [seeking, asking, entreating] *in the Spirit, and watching thereunto with all perseverance and supplication for all saints;"* Ephesians 6:13-18

Chapter IV

"…a change seemed near — I desired and waited it in silence."

The talk Jane had with Mr. Lloyd about the possibility of Mrs. Reed sending her to school, gives Jane a glimmer of hope that she could be rid of the cruel household in which she lives.

As she waits for a sign of this expected change, Jane is further subjected to isolation by Mrs. Reed who now seems to be very suspicious of whether Jane is possessed. She cuts off all communication between her children and Jane. John seems to be afraid of Jane after her outburst toward him and runs from her whenever she looks at him in a challenging way.

We have already discussed how ineffective Mr. Reed is in correcting or disciplining her children. There is further evidence of this in the paragraph that explains John's reaction to Jane challenging him. The coddling has made him weak and pouty.

Correction is love, so do you think that maybe he felt unloved in a way? John runs from challenges and only enjoys conflict when he is at the antagonistic end. This shows the beginnings of why John never truly became a man emotionally or spiritually, but in body only.

This feeling of being unloved can easily turn into rebellious, antagonistic, and unruly behavior to gain attention. Because

John has been raised in this way, it has become habit and he continues to grow worse and worse in his attitude and actions.

Unfortunately, the bible tells us how these types of people are to be received by God if they are unrepentant of their actions. Mrs. Reed has certainly done an injustice in her son's life, but how could we blame her completely when she has her own baggage that she carries? He must, at some point, take authority over his own actions.

John constantly disobeys his mother and certainly does not bring blessings upon her. Up until the end of his life, John continues down this path of unrepentant and destructive behavior.

"There is a generation that curseth [to make despicable, to treat with contempt, bring contempt or dishonour] *their father; and doth not bless* [blaspheme, curse] *their mother."* Proverbs 30:11

"The eye that mocketh [ridicule, deride] *at his father; and despiseth* [hold as insignificant, hold in contempt] *to obey his mother, the ravens of the valley shall pick it out, and the young eagles shall eat it."* Proverbs 30:17

"A foolish [stupid fellow, simpleton, arrogant one] *son is a grief* [vexation, anger, frustration] *to his father, and bitterness* [sorrow] *to her that bare him."* Proverbs 17:25

If we remember the story of the prodigal son in Luke, we get a better picture of how deeply God loves us and how He desires that we repent and run back into His arms again.

"Likewise, I say unto you, there is joy in the presence of the angels of God over one sinner that repenteth. And He said, A certain man had two sons: and the younger of them said to his father, Father, give me the portion of goods that falleth to me. And he divided unto them his living. And not many days after the younger son gathered all together, and took his journey into a far country, and there wasted his substance [what one has, i.e. property, possessions, estate] *with riotous* [dissolutely, profligately] *living. And when he had spent all, there arose a mighty famine in that land; and he began to be in want. And he went and joined himself to a citizen of that country; and he sent him into his fields to feed swine. And he would fain* [covet, lust, to have the desire for, long for] *have filled his belly with the husks that the swine did eat: and no man gave unto him. And when he came to himself, he said, How many hired servants of my father's have bread enough and to spare, and I perish with hunger! I will arise and go to my father, and will say unto him, Father, I have sinned against heaven, and before thee, and am no more worthy to be called thy son: make me as one of thy hired servants. And he arose, and came to his father. But when he was yet a great way off, his father saw him and had compassion*[1]*, and ran and fell on his neck* [to seize, take possession of, to fall into one's embrace] *and kissed him. And the son said unto him, Father, I have sinned against heaven, and in thy sight, and am no more worthy to be called thy son. But the father said to his servants, Bring forth the best robe, and put it on him; and put a ring on his hand, and shoes on his feet: And bring hither the fatted calf, and kill it; and let us eat, and be merry: For this my son was dead* [spiritually dead, destitute of life that recognizes and is

devoted to God, because given up to trespasses and sins], *and is alive again* [regain strength, to be restored to a correct life]; *he was lost, and is found. And they began to be merry.*"
Luke 15:10-24

You see, even though we want desperately to hate the character of John, we cannot. He is so lost. And the fact that (*pardon my jumping forward into the story – please skip if you would like to avoid spoiling parts*) we know that John died in debt and unloved, often hated by many, because of his scheming ways, makes him even more piteous.

If only there were someone in his life to share God's Fatherly love for him and help him understand what it feels like to be truly loved and cared for, John could have been a very different person.

"'What would Uncle Reed say to you, if he were alive?' was my scarcely voluntary demand. I say scarcely voluntary, for it seemed as if my tongue pronounced words without my will consenting to their utterance: something spoke out of me over which I had no control.

'What?' said Mrs. Reed under her breath: her usually cold, composed grey eye became troubled with a look like fear; she took her hand from my arm, and gazed at me as if she really did not know whether I were child or fiend. I was now in for it.

'My Uncle Reed is in heaven, and can see all you do and think; and so can papa and mama: they know how you shut me up all day long, and how you wish me dead.'"

In this chapter, we notice that Mrs. Reed is recognizing her faults in the way she has treated Jane. Jane is literally holding her accountable for her actions through her words. This frightens Mrs. Reed because she has never really been called to discernment over or challenged in her own character before.

Continuing in the waiting process, Jane watches as everyone in the family, including the servants, celebrate the holidays without her. She is shunned and feels "only bad feelings surging in [her] breast." And yet, she also finds comfort in her solace because being alone was better than being ignored within a group of people. This is what would happen every time she was included in the festivities and parties of the house in the past.

What is interesting is that we see a glimpse of how desperately Jane wants to love others. Being as abused as she is, and child that she is, she is not finding it possible to show love to her aunt, cousins, or even to the maids. Instead, she showers her love on a beloved doll.

"To this crib I always took my doll; human beings must love something, and, in the dearth of worthier objects of affection, I contrived to find a pleasure in loving and cherishing a faded graven image, shabby as a miniature scarecrow. It puzzles me now to remember with what absurd sincerity I doted on this little toy, half fancying it alive and capable of sensation. I could not sleep unless it was folded in my night-gown; and when it lay there safe and warm, I was comparatively happy, believing it to be happy likewise."

Moving forward in the story, Jane has now reached the climax of her waiting period. She is now preparing for the change that she had hoped would come. Unfortunately, the change is not as sweet and pure as she dreamed it would be, as we will see in a moment. Bessie helps her prepare for a visitor, who has come specifically to meet Jane.

"I now stood in the empty hall; before me was the breakfast-room door, and I stopped, intimidated and trembling. What a miserable little poltroon had fear, engendered of unjust punishment, made of me in those days! I feared to return to the nursery, and feared to go forward to the parlour; ten minutes I stood in agitated hesitation; the vehement ringing of the breakfast-room bell decided me; I must enter."

Here we meet Mr. Brocklehurst for the first time. "…face…like a carved mask." This is also where we begin the decent into the legalistic, Calvinistic, and often cruel and blunt form of Christianity that was popular at the time of Jane Eyre. As the book progresses, we will dig a little deeper into why Mr. Brocklehurst's beliefs are so destructive.

"'No sight so sad as that of a naughty child,' he began, 'especially a naughty little girl. Do you know where the wicked go after death?'

'They go to hell,' was my ready and orthodox answer.

'And what is hell? Can you tell me that?'

'A pit full of fire.'

'And should you like to fall into that pit, and to be burning there for ever?'

'No, sir.'

'What must you do to avoid it?'

I deliberated a moment: my answer, when it did come, was objectionable: 'I must keep in good health, and not die.'"

As funny and cheeky as this answer may be to us as readers, Jane was very serious. She had clearly not been taught about the realities of heaven. The only thing that seems to have been taught at this time, was that if you did not follow the scriptures or perform good works, you would go to hell. And hell was a horrible place, so of course no child would want to go there.

The problem with this type of teaching is that so much focus was laid on how bad hell was and that we should not want to be suffering for all eternity, that they lost focus on all the beautiful parts of scripture. They missed the whole point of eternity and what is required of God's people in order to be with Him forever in paradise. They focus more on hell than on heaven, scaring children especially, into belief.

"For God so loved the world, that He gave His only begotten [single of its kind, only born] *Son, that whosoever believeth in Him should not perish, but have everlasting life. For God sent not His Son into the world to condemn the world; but that the world through Him might be saved."* John 3:16-17

"That if thou shalt confess [to agree with, assent, to praise] *with thy mouth the Lord Jesus, and shalt believe in thine*

heart that God hath raised Him from the dead, thou shalt be saved. For with the heart[2] man believeth unto righteousness; and with the mouth confession is made unto salvation. For the scripture saith, Whosoever believeth on Him shall not be ashamed [disgraced, to dishonor]. *For there is no difference between the Jew and the Greek: for the same Lord over all is rich* [to have abundance, is affluent in resources so that he can give blessings of salvation to all] *unto all that call upon Him. For whosoever shall call upon the name of the Lord shall be saved.*" Romans 10:9-13

Mr. Brocklehurst's answer brought more fear with it, and a weaker child than Jane would have lived in extreme fear of dying from that point on in their life. He points out that children die every day and that when she should die, she would not go to heaven.

That is quite the curse to be stating over a child!

"Let no corrupt [rotten, putrefied, no longer fit for use, worthless] *communication proceed out of your mouth, but that which is good to the use of edifying* [the act of one who promotes another's growth in Christian wisdom, piety, happiness, holiness], *that it may minister* [grant, give] *grace* [that which affords joy, pleasure, delight, sweetness, charm, loveliness] *unto the hearers. And grieve not the Holy Spirit of God, whereby ye are sealed* [for security or preservation] *unto the day of redemption* [deliverance]. *Let all bitterness* [extreme wickedness, bitter hatred], *and wrath, and anger, and clamour* [outcry], *and evil speaking* [slander, speech injurious to another's good name], *be put away from you, with all malice* [ill-will]: *And be ye kind one to another,*

tenderhearted [compassionate], *forgiving one another, even as God for Christ's sake hath forgiven you."* Ephesians 4:29-32

Do you think that anything of what we observe Mr. Brocklehurst saying is edifying or tenderhearted? Absolutely not. In fact, everything he says encourages fear, despair, and bitterness. This goes against the scriptures he claims to know by heart and love completely. Mr. Brocklehurst makes his debut into our story as a hypocrite and shines a very ill light on Christianity itself.

It is also interesting to point out that Jane enjoyed reading the challenging scriptures, especially Job, Samuel, and Exodus. She did not care for only reading the good and lovely Psalms. Though all of scripture is meant for edification and bringing us closer to God, I have a feeling that Jane appreciated being challenged in her beliefs. She has a strong sense of discernment in her, which is a gift, and something that we will continue to see flourish as the story progresses.

Upon hearing that Jane does not like the Psalms because they are not interesting, Mr. Brocklehurst calls her a wicked child and compares her to a more "angelic" child who adores them. She is constantly being compared to those "greater" than herself. This feeds bitterness and envy. Both of which come from Satan's kingdom and not God's.

"Now the works of the flesh are manifest, which are these; adultery, fornication, uncleanness, lasciviousness [lust, shamelessness]*, idolatry, witchcraft, hatred, variance* [contention, debate]*, emulations* [jealousy, indignation,

rivalry], *wrath, strife, seditions* [dissension, division], *heresies, envyings, murders, drunkenness, revellings* [drunken parties, rioting], *and such like: of the which I tell you before, as I have also told you in time past, that they which do such things shall not inherit the kingdom of God. But the fruit of the Spirit is love, joy, peace, longsuffering* [patience, steadfastness, constancy], *gentleness* [integrity, kindness], *goodness* [uprightness in heart and life], *faith, meekness, temperance* [self-control]: *against such there is no law. And they that are Christ's have crucified the flesh with the affections and lusts. If we live in the Spirit, let us also walk in the Spirit. Let us not be desirous of vain glory* [glorying without reason, conceited, eager for empty glory], *provoking one another, envying one another."* Galatians 5:19-26

"'…I should be glad if the superintendent and teachers were requested to keep a strict eye on her, and, above all, to guard against her worst fault, a tendency to deceit…'

Well might I dread, well might I dislike Mrs. Reed; for it was her nature to wound me cruelly; never was I happy in her presence; however carefully I obeyed, however strenuously I strove to please her, my efforts were still repulsed and repaid by such sentences as the above. Now, uttered before a stranger, the accusation cut me to the heart; I dimly perceived that she was already obliterating hope from the new phase of existence which she destined me to enter. I felt, though I could not have expressed the feeling, that she was sowing aversion and unkindness along my future path; I saw myself transformed, under Mr. Brocklehurst's eye, into an artful, noxious child, and what could I do to remedy the injury?"

The conversation between these adults hits Jane hard. She begins to feel discouraged that nothing would ever get better for her in life, even were she to attend school. At ten years old, this is a heavy burden to bear.

As his personality seems to already show us, Mr. Brocklehurst continues to make matters worse and worse by intimating, in the very presence of Jane, that she will never be good or achieve heaven. Then, the final nail in the coffin of Jane's hope, he hands her a story about a girl who died suddenly from, what he claims, an addiction to lying and deceitfulness.

What a way to strike fear into the life of a child! God does not rule through fear, guilt, or shame. God will never make us feel fearful but wants us to come to Him *with* our fears so that He can help us through them. Pastors are meant to be representations of Christ's love. When have we ever seen Christ use fear, guilt, or shame to bring His followers to the Father?

Ruling through fear is not what God intended for His church. But He did hold people accountable for their actions.

"And we have known and believed the love that God hath to us. God is love; and he that dwelleth [to abide, to continue to be present, to remain as one] *in love dwelleth in God, and God in him. Herein is our love made perfect* [complete, fulfill], *that we may have boldness* [freedom in speaking, frank, free and fearless confidence, cheerful courage,

assurance] *in the day of judgement: because as He is, so are we in this world. There is no fear in love; but perfect love casteth out* [the throw or let go of a thing without caring where it falls] *fear: because fear hath torment. He that feareth is not made perfect in love. We love Him, because He first loved us. If a man say, I love God, and hateth his brother, he is a liar: for he that loveth not his brother whom he hath seen, how can he love God whom he hath not seen? And this commandment have we from Him, That he who loveth God love his brother also."* 1 John 4:16-21

Once Mr. Brocklehurst leaves, Jane has reached her limit of reserve. She uses this final audience with her aunt to defend her honor which was cruelly destroyed in his presence, the presence of a stranger, and retaliate against how she has been treated.

"Speak I must: I had been trodden on severely, and must turn: but how? What strength had I to dart retaliation at my antagonist? I gathered my energies and launched them in this blunt sentence —

'I am not deceitful: if I were, I should say I loved you; but I declare I do not love you: I dislike you the worst of anybody in the world except John Reed; and this book about the Liar you may give to your girl, Georgiana, for it is she who tells lies, and not I.'

…'I am glad you are no relation of mine. I will never call you aunt again as long as I live. I will never come to see you when I am grown up; and if anyone asks me how I liked you, and how you treated me, I will say the very thought of you

makes me sick, and that you treated me with miserable cruelty.'

'How dare you affirm than, Jane Eyre?'

'How dare I, Mrs. Reed? How dare I? Because it is the truth. You think I have no feelings, and that I can do without one bit of love or kindness; but I cannot live so: and you have no pity…People think you a good woman, but you are bad, hard-hearted. You are deceitful.'"

At this sudden outburst from Jane, Mrs. Reed seems to be fearful of the discernment that Jane expresses. People like Mrs. Reed, who are continually dealing with their own torments, know that they are treating others ill but do not have control over their emotions or actions.

I believe that Mrs. Reed is fully aware of her deceitfulness and her envious thoughts toward Jane, but she has not been shown how to choose differently. She is fully aware of everything that Jane has accused her of, and it frightens her that Jane is completely aware of it as a child. And this brings us to a glimpse of remorse in Mrs. Reed, a glimpse of a repentant spirit. But only a glimpse.

Jane has "won the field." Yet, in the glory of winning, Jane finds that vengeance does not always taste sweet. She feels that she should ask forgiveness for her behavior. This is the first time we see the prodding of the Holy Spirit in Jane. She knows now that revenge is not going to solve her problems and it certainly will not repair her relationship with her aunt.

We close the chapter with a conversation between Jane and Bessie.

"'Bessie, you must promise not to scold me any more till I go.'

'Well, I will; but mind you are a very good girl, and don't be afraid of me. Don't start when I chance to speak rather sharply: it's so provoking.'

'I don't think I shall ever be afraid of you again, Bessie, because I have got used to you, and I shall soon have another set of people to dread.'

'If you dread them, they'll dislike you.'

'As you do, Bessie?'

'I don't dislike you, Miss; I believe I am fonder of you than of all the others.'"

This conversation is curious because it gives us some insight into Jane's weaknesses. Granted, she is a child who has not been nurtured or loved well, so fearfulness is bound to take its hold. Bessie is provoked by Jane's fear but does not give her guidance on how to be rid of the fear of the people around her and how they will treat her. Jane has had no guidance on how to form a strong identity in who she was created to be as a daughter of God. This opens her up to fears and insecurities.

As Jane matures, she meets people who will help her in this. People who will help her understand what God's love is and how He feels about her.

<u>How Can You Apply This to Your Own Life?</u>

Feeling unloved by those around you can be an excruciating thing to bear. God has created us to desire to love others and to be loved in return because we were created out of the love our heavenly Father.

If you feel that you are unloved by those around you, just know that you have a Father who loves you so deeply that He calls you His child. He adopted you from the very beginning into His family.

In addition, you should also know that I love you. Even though you are only reading my words and thoughts, know that I wrote them because I love you. I pray that you find someone who can be God's love to you here on earth. A friend, family member, or even just a stranger.

As you go about your day, remember that there are people out in the world who do not feel loved. They are miserable in their spirit. With this in mind, be the love of Christ to them.

Smile, genuinely ask about their day, help them out if they are struggling, and just be there. Simply having someone present who is oozing love, will rub off on and positively affect that person who is not in such a good place. This is a beautiful way to be a disciple of Christ in your everyday.

"There is no fear in love; but perfect love casteth out fear: because fear hath torment. He that feareth is not made perfect in love. We love him, because he first loved us." 1 John 4:18-19

"Who shall separate us from the love of Christ? Shall tribulation, or distress [dire calamity, extreme affliction], *or persecution, or famine, or nakedness, or peril, or sword? As it is written, for thy sake we are killed* [literally or figuratively; destroy, render extinct, mortify] *all the day long; we are accounted as sheep for the slaughter. Nay, in all these things we are more than conquerors through him that loved us. For I am persuaded, that neither death, nor life, nor angels, nor principalities, nor powers* [armies, forces], *nor things present, nor things to come, nor height, nor depth, nor any other creature, shall be able to separate us from the love of God, which is in Christ Jesus our Lord."*
Romans 8:35-39

Footnotes

[1] Compassion based on the interlinear, Greek text (G4697 – splagchnizomai σπλαγχνίζομαι) – to be moved as to one's bowels, hence to be moved with compassion, have compassion (for the bowels were thought to be the seat of love and pity)

[2] With the Heart based on the interlinear, Greek text (G2588 – καρδία) – denotes the centre of all physical and spiritual life; the vigour and sense of life; the soul or mind, as it is the fountain and seat of the thoughts, passions, desires, appetites, affections, purposes, endeavours; of the understanding, the faculty and seat of the intelligence.

Chapter V

As we begin this chapter, we follow Jane through the halls of Gateshead one last time as a young girl. We feel her sense of relief that she is leaving a place that has brought her so much unhappiness. Unfortunately, as hopeful as Jane is now, once she arrives at Lowood school, she sees that hard times are not quite behind her.

"Thus was I severed from Bessie and Gateshead; thus whirled away to unknown, and, as I then deemed, remote and mysterious regions."

How many of us, at the age of ten, would be as strong and courageous as Jane seems to be at this moment? Her courage fails her a little as she is left alone at the inn, her imagination running away with her a little. Though she does show some fear, as any child would, her constitution remains strong. This is one of Jane's greatest qualities that carries on into her adulthood.

Her first reception at Lowood school was a positive one as she is able to warm herself by the fire and is spoken to kindly. However, things change quickly as Jane realizes that the food portions during supper are small, heating is scarce, and sleep is limited. The students were subjected to burnt porridge in the morning and are constantly hungry and cold throughout the day.

"I heard the name of Mr. Brocklehurst pronounced by some lips, at which Miss Miller shook her head disapprovingly;

but she made no great effort to check the general wrath; doubtless she shared in it."

Clearly Mr. Brocklehurst has built a very poor reputation for himself among the fellow students and the teachers at the school. This will become even clearer in future chapters.

Miss Temple, the superintendent of Lowood enters, beautiful, refined, and carrying herself "with a stately air and carriage." Throughout Jane's time at the school, Miss Temple will represent the true love of Christ through her actions and the way she treats the students. In this case, she hears of how the girls have not eaten breakfast due to the spoiling of their porridge and orders a lunch of bread and cheese, which we can imagine would have been such a treat for them.

"'Lowood Institution. – This portion was rebuilt A.D. –, by Naomi Brocklehurst, of Brocklehurst Hall, in this county.'

'Let your light so shine before men that they may see your good works, and glorify your Father which is in heaven.' – St. Matt. V. 16.

I read these words over and over again. I felt that an explanation belonged to them, and was unable fully to penetrate their import."

This is where we begin to understand how ignorant Jane was of the Scriptures and what it meant to be follower of Christ. True enough, she did not really have any role models to look up to in this regard. This process of being more exposed to the Bible and people outside of her small circle of family and servants at Gateshead, will ultimately help Jane grow spiritually and mentally into an intelligent and discerning woman.

A Brief History of the Church in the 1800s and Charlotte Brontë's Perspective on Religion and Faith

In order to fully understand why Lowood is run the way it is and why Mr. Brocklehurst is the way he is, you need to have a brief understanding of what was going on in the Church of England at the time of Jane Eyre.

At the time of the authorship, the Church of England was going through a divide between Roman Catholic and the Anglican Church. According to various historians, Patrick Brontë, Anne, Charlotte, and Emily Brontë's father, was highly influenced by Wesleyan Methodism and Evangelicalism. At the same time, Calvinism was a very prominent form of Christianity as well and was enveloped in Evangelicalism along with other popular sects.

Charlotte Brontë and her sisters were raised as Protestants/Evangelicals but were encouraged to discover what faith meant to them on their own and decide for themselves what sect they wanted to follow. Their father never pressured them into the same beliefs as himself but also did not seem to provide a whole lot of direction for them in their faith, especially when they were young.

This would place the Brontë's in the Anglican Church, considering there were only two distinct parts to the Church of England at the time. In the Anglican Church, Scripture was often quoted and both the Apostles' Creed and Nicene Creed were recited. However, the church did not stress a call to action in the form of belief or faith in what the congregation quoted and recited.

The problem with not calling people to accountability in their own faith is that they are not cultivating a true and lasting relationship with God. They are speaking the words and showing up for service every Sunday, but are they truly understanding what is in the Word or what it means to have a relationship with the Father? Or are they just going through the motions of faith?

"Wherefore the Lord said, Forasmuch as this people draw near Me with their mouth, and with their lips do honour Me, but have removed their heart far from Me, and their fear [reverence] *toward Me is taught by the precepts* [commandment] *of men:"* Isaiah 29:13

In fact—and this is the last thing I will say about the Anglican Church—the 39 Articles (*the doctrinal statement of the Protestant Church of England*) were "deliberately written to be so vague that they were open to various interpretations by Protestants and Catholics."[1]

"Knowing this first, that no prophecy[2] *of the scripture is of any private* [pertaining to one's self, one's own] *interpretation* [explanation, application]. *For the prophecy came not in old time* [times past] *by the will of man* [what one wishes or has determined shall be done, inclination, desire]*: but holy men of God spake as they were moved* [bear, bring forth] *by the Holy Ghost."* 2 Peter 1:20-21

"Study [give diligence, endeavour] *to shew thyself approved* [pleasing, acceptable] *unto God, a workman that needeth not to be ashamed, rightly dividing* [to make straight and smooth, to teach the truth directly and correctly] *the word of truth. But shun profane* [of men, ungodly] *and vain babblings* [empty discussion, discussion of vain and useless matters]: *for they will increase unto more ungodliness."* 2 Timothy 2:15-16

"Take heed [pay attention, observe] *unto thyself, and to the doctrine; continue in them: for in doing this thou shalt both save thyself, and them that hear thee."* 1 Timothy 4:16

"Ye worship ye know not what: we know what we worship: for salvation [deliverance] *is of the Jews* [belonging to Judea]. *But the hour cometh, and now is, when the true* [that which has not only the name and resemblance, but the real nature corresponding to the name, in every respect corresponding to the idea signified by the name, real, true genuine] *worshippers shall worship the Father in spirit and in truth: for the Father seeketh such to worship him. God is a Spirit: and they that worship Him must worship Him in spirit and in truth."* John 4:22-24

It is said, however, that Charlotte herself rejected Calvinism. She was very firmly set against the idea of religious teachers and leaders who would set themselves as being morally superior to their congregation and extol their actions above everyone else's. I believe this is why we see a lot of Calvinistic themes throughout Jane Eyre in the form of the more unlikable characters – Mr. Brocklehurst, Mrs. Reed, and even St. John (*who we will learn about later*).

Aside from Calvinism, there are other denominations of Christianity that adopt legalistic ways of worship and ways to gain salvation. Legalism requires strict and rigid rules, created under the Old Testament laws. What these leaders forget is that Christ died and was resurrected so that we could have direct relationship with the Father. He cancelled the laws of the Old Testament.

To balance out the legalism, some churches also go in the opposite direction. This is where we begin to see less call to action or accountability and more open acceptance of worldly behaviors. As worldly views gain a footing in Christianity, people become more and more confused.

The most effective churches are those that focus on teaching the Word in its entirety through the inspiration of the Holy Spirit. Everything we need is found in the bible. God is very clear as to how we are to evangelize, teach, grow, and obtain eternal life with Him. None of which require legalistic behaviors and accusation to gain acceptance.

The following conversation, later in the book between Jane and Helen, shows the perspectives of the two leaders of the school and how they differ.

"'Is he a good man?' [Jane]

'He is a clergyman, and is said to do a great deal of good.'"
[Helen]

VS.

"'But Miss Temple is the best — isn't she?' [Jane]

'Miss Temple is very good, and very clever; she is above the rest, because she knows far more than they do.'" [Helen] – *brackets added by me*

The idea of harsh punishment for children who misbehaved or showed an "evil" propensity in order to achieve godliness and wholeness in Christ, is largely Calvinistic and was believed by many Evangelicals at the time.

I cannot truthfully say what Charlotte believed or where she stood in her faith. I think that more study would have to accompany this to gain a better understanding. However, what I do know is that the history of the church shows itself in a large part in this novel. We can clearly see the influence that faith and religion (*because they are, in fact, not equal or the same*) played in the life of Charlotte through her writing.

"So then faith[3] cometh by hearing, and hearing by the word of God." Romans 10:17

"Now faith is the substance of things hoped for, the evidence of things not seen." Hebrews 11:1

"That your faith should not stand [be] *in the wisdom of men, but in the power of God."* 1 Corinthians 2:5

Religion is an organization of worship. It is more often than not, rules by the wisdom of man. It typically requires showy practices and regiments to feel spiritual and close to God. Religion does not necessarily always incorporate faith into its belief system. This is how religion and faith differ.[4]

Jane has grown into a very angry child, more of which we will see as her time at Lowood progresses. She is bitter and jaded and this creates rebellion in her heart and fuels her unforgiveness. This makes her a very bold, whining, unhappy child. She needs true representation of faith, forgiveness, and love. This is why Miss Temple is such an important character. Helen Burns, Jane's only friend at Lowood, also helps Jane understand more of what faith looks like and how it can be applied to everyday life.

"I hardly know where I found the hardihood thus to open a conversation with a stranger. The step was contrary to my nature and habits; but I think her occupation touched a chord of sympathy somewhere, for I, too, liked reading, though of a frivolous and childish kind. I could not digest or comprehend the serious or substantial."

Helen is going to play a very big part in Jane's spiritual development. She does adhere to the very legalistic ideals that are taught at Lowood, however, there is a depth in Helen that Jane finds very fascinating. Thus, the friendship grows into something quite beautiful.

In the chapters leading up to this one, we have seen a lot of discernment from Jane. This is a gift from God. Even as a young child, Jane can see things that a lot of adults cannot. In the following paragraph, we are able to see this on an even greater scale as she wonders about Helen and how she can put up with a punishment that, in Jane's eyes, is quite severe.

"...I saw the girl with whom I had conversed with in the verandah...sent to stand in the middle of the large schoolroom. The punishment seemed to me in a high degree

ignominious, especially for so great a girl – she looked thirteen or upwards. I expected she would show signs of great distress and shame; but to my surprise she neither wept nor blushed. Composed, though grave, she stood, the central mark of all eyes. 'How can she bear it so quietly – so firmly?' I asked of myself. 'Were I in her place, it seems to me I should wish the earth to open and swallow me up. She looks as if she were thinking of something beyond her punishment – beyond her situation: of something not round her nor before her. I have heard of day-dreams – is she in a day-dream now? Her eyes are fixed on the floor, but I am sure they do not see it – her sight seems turned in, gone down into her heart: she is looking at what she can remember, I believe; not at what is really present. I wonder what sort of a girls she is – whether good or naughty.'"

<u>How Can You Apply This to Your Own Life?</u>

Bitterness truly is a poison. It eats away at your heart and soul until you are in utter despair and torment. Bitterness feeds off unforgiveness and if we do not keep both in check, we will end up down a very dark path. Unforgiveness can feed off anger, envy, and resentment. It is a perpetual cycle that we need to learn how to shut down quickly.

God has called us to be at peace and to love one another as ourselves; the second greatest commandment.

"A new commandment I give unto you, That ye love one another; as I have loved you, that ye also love one another. By this shall all men know that ye are my disciples, if ye have love one to another." John 13:34-35

"These things I have spoken unto you, that in me ye might have peace. In the world ye shall have tribulation: but be of good cheer; I have overcome the world." John 16:33

Being at peace means that we must first choose forgiveness. Holding onto unforgiveness, not only physically and spiritually hurts yourself, but it also damages your relationship between others, yourself, and God. As I mentioned, it feeds off anger. So, if you are continually holding onto unforgiveness, you are likely holding onto anger and bitterness as well. This means that you are acting in direct disobedience to God's word.

"Be ye angry, and sin not: let not the sun go down upon your wrath: neither give place to the devil." Ephesians 4:26-27

"Forbearing [bear up, sustain, to hold up] *one another, and forgiving one another, if any man have a quarrel against any: even as Christ forgave you, so also do ye. And above all these things put on charity* [affection, good will, love, brotherly love], *which is the bond of perfectness."*
Colossians 3:13-14

You will feel emotions like anger and frustration. It is normal to experience them. But allowing yourself to wallow in them and let them fester in your heart is when an emotion becomes sin. If you are angry at your brother or sister, pray about it, talk to them about what is causing the anger, and resolve it quickly.

"Let all bitterness, and wrath, and anger, and clamour, and evil speaking [slander, speech injurious to another's good name], *be put away from you, with all malice: be ye kind one to another, tenderhearted* [compassionate], *forgiving one another, even as God for Christ's sake hath forgiven you."*
Ephesians 4:31-32

No one ever said that it was an easy thing to do. However, as believers, we are called to pattern our lives after Christ. If He could forgive the very people who accused Him and crucified Him, then certainly, we can humble ourselves and forgive one another. It is a process and sometimes it will not happen right away. This is why we must have mercy with ourselves as we work toward perfecting ourselves in Christ every day.

Footnotes

[1] 39 Articles: https://www.gotquestions.org/Anglicans.html

[2] Prophecy based on the interlinear, Greek text (G4394 – prophēteia προφητεία) – a discourse emanating from divine inspiration and declaring the purposes of God, whether by reproving and admonishing the wicked, or comforting the afflicted, or revealing things hidden; esp. by foretelling future events. Of the prediction of events relating to Christ's kingdom and its speedy triumph, together with the consolations and admonitions pertaining to it, the spirit of prophecy. Of the endowment and speech of the Christian teachers called prophets.

[3] Faith based on the interlinear, Greek text (G4102 – pistis πίστις) – conviction of the truth of anything, belief; in the NT of a conviction or belief respecting man's relationship to God and divine things, generally with the included idea of trust and holy fervour born of faith and joined with it. The conviction that God exists and is the creator and ruler of all things, the provider and bestower of eternal salvation through Christ. A strong and welcome conviction or belief that Jesus is the Messiah, through whom we obtain eternal salvation in the kingdom of God. Assurance, fidelity, moral conviction of truth.

[4] Religion:
http://catdir.loc.gov/catdir/samples/cam032/99010369.pdf#:~:text=The%20terms%20in%20which%20Hoxie%20Neal%20Fairchild%20describes,RadcliVe%20contended%20for%20mastery%2C%20was%20a%20Broad%20Churchwoman

Chapter VI

Jane is beginning to play a role in the daily goings-on at the school; learning, memorizing, reciting, sewing. As someone who loves to observe people, I love getting a small glimpse into what Jane is observing of the teachers and students; how they interact with each other and how the classes are run. Students are placed at the head of classes and upon incorrect pronunciation or failure to follow orders, brought back to the bottom.

"…there were sundry questions…which most of them [the students] appeared unable to answer; still, every little difficulty was solved instantly when it reached Burns: her memory seemed to have retained the substance of the whole lesson, and she was ready with answers on every point. I kept expecting that Miss Scatcherd would praise her attention; but, instead of that, she suddenly cried out –

'You dirty, disagreeable girl! You have never cleaned you nails this morning!'

Burns made no answer: I wondered at her silence.

'Why,' thought I, 'does she not explain that she could neither clean her nails nor wash her face, as the water was frozen?'"
– brackets added by me

As her observations continue, Jane's curiosity falls on Helen Burns. She is beginning to realize even more that there is something different about this girl. Helen seems to do everything right and yet the teachers lecture her and whip her. After observing Helen return from being whipped on the neck with sticks, Jane begins to make her way through the room toward Helen to speak to her.

"…I could distinguish from the gleeful tumult within, the disconsolate moan of the wind outside.

Probably, if I had lately left a good home and kind parents, this would have been the hour when I should most keenly have regretted the separation; that wind would then have saddened my heart; this obscure chaos would have disturbed my peace; as it was, I derived from both a strange excitement, and reckless and feverish, I wished the wind to bowl more wildly, the gloom to deepen to darkness, and the confusion to rise to clamour."

I believe that this brief paragraph gives us insight into how Jane is feeling within her spirit. She is in a tumult of anger, hatred, loneliness, confusion, rejection, and needing to be accepted. She needs to feel something. If she cannot feel loved or accepted, she would settle for tumultuous weather and chaotic excitement.

When she arrives by the side of Helen, Jane wants to know, if Helen has proved herself competent a student, why she is so abused by her teacher, Miss Scatcherd.

"'And if I were in your place I should disklike her; I should resist her, If she struck me with that rod, I should get it from her hand; I should break it under her nose.'

'Probably you would do nothing of the sort: but if you did,
Mr. Brocklehurst would expel you from the school; that
would be a great grief to your relations. It is far better to
endure patiently a smart which nobody feels but yourself,
than to commit a hasty reaction whose evil consequences will
extend to all connected with you; and besides, the Bible bids
us return good for evil.'

...I heard her with wonder: I could not comprehend this
doctrine of endurance; and still less could I understand or
sympathise with the forbearance she expressed for her
chastiser. Still I felt that Helen Burns considered things by a
light invisible to my eyes."

Here, Jane's discernment surfaces yet again. She does not
understand why Helen is so calm and peaceful. Inward peace
attracts people. Helen is living out patience, forbearance, and
love. This is the first time that this type of behavior has been
demonstrated to Jane. She has always seen people lash out
and return hate for hate. Now, here is this young girl, who
seems to do everything right but is treated poorly and
responds with grace. This is extremely foreign to Jane. I
believe this awakens a deep desire in Jane's heart to be at
peace like Helen.

"*But be ye doers* [one who obeys or fulfils the law,
performer] *of the word, and not hearers only, deceiving* [to
cheat by false reckoning or reasoning, delude] *your own
selves. For if any be a hearer of the word, and not a doer, he
is like unto a man beholding his natural face in a glass: For
he beholdeth himself, and goeth his way, and straightway
forgeteth what manner of man he was. But whoso looketh*

[inspect curiously, to look carefully into] *into the perfect law of liberty, and continueth therein, he being not a forgetful hearer, but a doer of the work, this man shall be blessed in his deed.*" James 1:22-25

Helen is actually living out the Word of God. She understands what it means to be a doer of the Word and not a hearer only. Helen demonstrates these verses very well throughout her time with us –

"With my whole [entirety] *heart* [inner man, soul] *have I sought thee: O let me not wander from* [be deceived, transgress, go astray] *thy commandments. Thy word have I hid* [treasure, store up, to protect] *in mine heart, that I might not sin against thee. Blessed art thou, O LORD: teach me thy statutes* [commandments]." Psalm 119:10-12

"Ye have heard that it hath been said, thou shalt love thy neighbor, and hate thine enemy. But I say unto you, Love your enemies, bless them that curse you, do good to them that hate you, and pray for them which despitefully use you [to treat abusively, revile, insult, to threaten]*, and persecute you; That ye may be the children of your Father which is in heaven: for He maketh His sun to rise on the evil and on the good, and sendeth rain on the just and on the unjust. For if ye love them which love you, what reward have ye? Do not even the publicans* [tax collector] *the same?"* Matthew 5:43-46

Helen begins to point out some of her faults. As we can see, she is prone to some laziness at times. It is honorable for Helen to continue to work out these issues continually and discern how she can do better. However, a lot of what she has learned in this legalistic environment has taught her to focus on the things she does poorly rather than all the wonderful things about herself. She dwells on what she cannot do and forgets the lovely things she is gifted at. Jane realizes this and I believe this is why she finds Helen's situation so intriguing.

It seems that Jane is working out who she can trust in Lowood. She already knows that there is something very trustworthy in Helen, but she is still unsure of Miss Temple. As readers, we can see that Jane really and truly wants to believe in her heart that Miss Temple is a good person who treats people, especially children, with kindness. Jane asks Helen if she is treated unkindly by Miss Temple.

"'Miss Temple is full of goodness; it pains her to be severe to anyone, even the worst in the school: she sees my errors, and tells me of them gently; and, if I do anything worthy of praise, she gives me my meed liberally. One strong proof of my wretchedly defective nature is, that even her expostulations, so mild, so rational, have not influence to cure me of my faults; and even her praise, though I value it most highly, cannot stimulate me to continued care and foresight.'

'That is curious,' said I; 'it is so easy to be careful.'

'For you I have no doubt it is. I observed you in your class this morning, and saw you were closely attentive: your thoughts never seemed to wander while Miss Miller explained the lesson and questioned you. Now, mine continually rove away; when I should be listening to Miss

Scatcherd, and collecting all she says with assiduity, often I lose the very sound of her voice; I fall into a sort of dream. Sometimes I think I am in Northumberland, and that the noises I hear round me are the bubbling of a little brook which runs through Deepden, near our house; —then, when it comes to my turn to reply, I have to be wakened; and, having heard nothing of what was read for listening to the visionary brook, I have no answer ready.'"

The conversation that progresses between Jane and Helen reveals even more of Jane's bitterness and anger. She talks about vengeance and retaliation against the people who abuse her. What she does not understand is that God says, vengeance is His, not ours. That we should be love to all those who cross our paths. To turn the other cheek and respond with grace. Bless those that persecute us that we may be called God's children. The question then is, are we willing to trust God to take care of that justice for us so that we are able to lay it down? We are His children, and He knows how to restore. His example of forgiveness is a gift to a weary soul.

"But I say unto you which hear, Love your enemies, do good to them which hate you. Bless them that curse you, and pray for them which despitefully use you. And unto him that smiteth thee [strike, wound] *on the one cheek offer also the other; and him that taketh away thy cloak forbid not to take thy coat also. Give to every man that asketh of thee; and of him that taketh away thy goods ask them not again. And as ye would* [to desire, to wish, intend] *that men should do to you, do ye also to them likewise. For if ye love them which love you, what thank[1] have ye? For sinners also love those*

You see, Jesus was preaching to the people to love all
people, not just the ones who will love you back or who have
loved you from the beginning. Love your enemies because
love casts out fear and torment. If you are love to even the
most ungodly and unkind person, they will notice and might
even begin to wonder why you are showing love to them.

If we continually go around hating and abusing people who
treat us poorly or hate us, there will be no end to the hate. It
would be a perpetual cycle of torment on both sides.

But if we break the cycle and be like Christ, showing love
and being love, the possibility of these ungodly people
turning away from their own hate and desiring to reach for
that same peace and love, could quite possibly inspire them
to learn about Christ.

"*And we have known and believed the love* [affection, good
will, benevolence, brotherly love] *that God hath to us. God
is love; and he that dwelleth* [remain, abide, not to depart,
continue] *in love dwelleth in God, and God in him. Herein is
our love made perfect* [complete, consecrate, fulfil]*, that we*

Jane will learn better, as time goes on and she matures and
grows. Helen begins this teaching process with her. She
points her toward the verses mentioned above and tries to
explain what Jesus meant when he told the people what love
looks like. Helen helps Jane understand how destructive it
can be to hold onto the wrongs of the past and grudges
against others.

As Jane continues to stew on her past, she becomes more
and more bitter and vengeful. She almost lives and breathes
the bitterness of how she was treated by Mrs. Reed.

Life is too short to be holding so tight to the past. Which is
why we are called to release it to God, that He may lift the
burden from us so that we may live in peace and rest. That is
the only way we can truly be there for others and lift others
up.

"'…Surely it will never, on the contrary, be suffered to
degenerate from man to fiend? No, I cannot believe that: I
hold another creed, which no one ever taught me, and which
I seldom mention, but in which I delight, and to which I

cling, for it extends hope to all; it makes Eternity a rest – a mighty home, not a terror and an abyss. Besides, with this creed, I can so clearly distinguish between the criminal and his crime, I can so sincerely forgive the first while I abhor the last; with this creed, revenge never worries my heart, degradation never too deeply disgusts me, injustice never crushes me too low; I live in calm, looking to the end.'"

The above paragraph is an example of the separation we must use with everyone. Separation between the person God created and the sin that dwells within them. Our battle is spiritual, not against people.

> *"For we wrestle not against flesh and blood, but against principalities* [of angels and demons], *against powers, against the rulers of the darkness of this world, against spiritual wickedness* [evil purposes and desires] *in high places. Wherefore take unto you the whole armor of God, that ye may be able to withstand* [stand against, resist, oppose, to set against] *in the evil day, and having done* [accomplish, achieve, to work fully] *all, to stand* [to make firm, fix establish, be kept intact, to uphold or sustain the authority or force of anything, continue safe and sound, stand unharmed, to stand ready or prepared, to be of steadfast mind, of quality, one who does not hesitate, does not waver]." Ephesians 6:12-13

You see, Helen was girded with the Word of God which was her sword in the spiritual battle. She had the great discernment to be able to separate the sin from the sinner. Thus, she was able to forgive easily and be a source of wisdom and love for others.

"And Jesus answered him, The first of all the commandments is, Hear, O Israel; The Lord our God is one [only] *Lord* [supreme authority]*: And thou shalt love the Lord thy God with all* [completely, whole] *thy heart, and with all thy soul, and with all thy mind* [thoughts, understanding]*, and with all thy strength: this is the first commandment. And the second is like* [similar]*, namely this, Thou shalt love thy neighbour as thyself. There is none other commandment greater than these."* Mark 12:29-31

This commandment is very clear that we are to hold loving ourselves and others in line with loving God. We cannot have love for one and not the other two. Love is all encompassing and never ending.

We are called to stand against the wickedness of the world and when having done all we can to fight off the devil, to stand firm and of a steadfast mind, not wavering in our faith or love for God the Father.

What is Separation? And How Can You Apply it to Your Own Life?

Jesus practiced separation throughout His time on earth. This was how He was able to teach and heal without being judgmental or unforgiving. He did not come to condemn the world but to save it.

As believers, it is tempting to give into the guilt and shame that comes from falling into sin. However, separation allows us to be able to understand how we can walk out our faith, even when we might be struggling with sin in our lives.

Even Paul struggled with sin. He admitted that the worldly lusts that draw people into sinning and going against God's word tempted him as well. Even though he desired above all else to be honorable to God, he still dealt with temptation.

Paul is not coming up against himself but recognizing his own struggle and sharing it with others that they may be able to come to a place of restoration.

"Now if I do that I would not, it is no more I that do it, but sin that dwelleth in me. I find then a law [regulation, or figuratively a principle], *that, when I would do good, evil is present* [to be near, at hand] *with me. For I delight in the law of God after the inward* [soul] *man: but I see another law in my members* [body], *warring* [oppose] *against the law of my mind* [judgement, reasoning, intellectual faculty, the power of considering and judging soberly, calmly and impartially], *and bringing me into captivity* [lead away] *to the law of sin which is in my members. O wretched* [enduring trial, afflicted] *man that I am! Who shall deliver me from the body* [figuratively – slave] *of this death* [miseries arising from sin, loss of a life consecrated to God and blessed in him on earth]*? I thank God through Jesus Christ our Lord. So then with the mind I myself serve the law of God; but with the flesh the law of sin."* Romans 7:20-25

We need to understand that the battle between the spiritual realm is real. That Satan has beings that fight on his playing field just as God has His angels. These spiritual beings speak to us at a spiritual level tempting us into sin just as the Holy Spirit speaks truth. This could be through fear, guilt, rejection, anxiety, depression, shame, lust, self-loathing, anger, bitterness, self-idolatry, hopelessness, doubt and unbelief, etc. We see a perfect example of this in Genesis –

"And He said, Who told thee that thou wast naked? Hast thou eaten of the tree, whereof I commanded thee that thou shouldest not eat?" Genesis 3:11

WHO told you?

This brings us back to Ephesians 6:12 – *"For we wrestle not against flesh and blood, but against principalities, against powers, against the rulers of the darkness of this world, against spiritual wickedness in high places."*

Who is this <u>who</u> God is referring to?

We are fighting a hidden battle of spirits – Satan and his kingdom – that want nothing more than to divide us from God and His love and acceptance for us. Recognizing the enemy for who he truly is, is the first step to overcoming.

Recognizing the reason why these thoughts come into our minds and the minds of others is going to help us know exactly where and how to do battle. We are not fighting against ourselves, and we are not fighting against other people; we are fighting against the sin that is in them and wants to overtake them.

"For we know that the law is spiritual: but I am carnal [flesh, temporal]*, sold under sin* [entirely under the control of the love of sinning, slavery – figuratively]*. For that which I do I allow not: for what I would, that do I not; but what I hate, that do I. If then I do that which I would not, I consent to the law that it is good. Now then it is no more I that do it,*

As believers, we are called to walk in the fruits of the spirit, but temptation interferes with that. Temptation wants to lead us into allowing that temptation to become sin. Temptation is not sin until you agree with it, as you will recall from chapter two.

Thoughts only come from intelligent beings. This means that these intelligent, spiritual beings from Satan's kingdom are behind the thoughts that Paul is wrestling with in the verse above. They are also the "who" in Genesis that told Adam and Eve they were naked.

Paul wants to do good and has good intentions, but he is constantly battling with the temptation to sin. When he begins to do good, sin drags him back down. As you read about Paul's life in the Bible, you can see that he did many good and wonderful things for the kingdom of heaven. But Satan does not want us to ever do good or succeed for God and heaven. He does not want us to live forever in everlasting peace with our Father. He wants to divide us from all blessings.

Remember, I mentioned in chapter two that evil exists for all people, including Christians. If this were not the case, temptation would not exist and there would not be a need for repentance.

Temptation is Satan's way of drawing us further and further away from God. We have a choice whether to give in to it or to resist. God does not want you in bondage to Satan and his will to destroy you. You have the power in Jesus' name to rebuke Satan and his minions.

Do not lose hope and do not get discouraged.

God will give you the strength you need, the discernment you need, and the tools you need to do battle. All you have to do is ask.

"Put on the whole armor of God, that ye may be able to stand against the wiles [cunning arts, deceit, craft, trickery, lie in wait] *of the devil."* Ephesians 6:11

"Stand therefore, having your loins girt about [to equip one's self with knowledge of the truth] *with truth, and having on the breastplate of righteousness* [the condition acceptable to God, integrity, virtue, purity of life, correctness of thinking feeling, and acting]*; and your feet shod with the preparation* [readiness] *of the gospel* [good tidings, the glad tidings of salvation] *of peace* [security, prosperity, safety, the tranquil state of a soul assured of its salvation through Christ, quietness]*; Above all, taking the shield of faith, wherewith ye shall be able to quench all the fiery darts of the*

wicked. And take the helmet of salvation, and the sword of the Spirit [Holy Spirit], *which is the word of God: praying always with all prayer* [worship, earnest] *and supplication* [a seeking, asking, entreating, entreaty to God, request] *in the Spirit, and watching* [to be circumspect, attentive, ready] *thereunto with all perseverance and supplication for all saints;"* Ephesians 6:14-18

God has our backs. We, after putting on the full armor of God, have protected our front so that we can effectively do battle head-on. We must then have faith that God will not forsake us even in the direst of circumstances.

Thinking positively and desiring to follow God is not going to defeat sin. Recognizing the enemy for who he is, knowing how we can achieve our freedom, and taking action toward it, is how we overcome our sin. Believers, no matter how good they are, still battle.

Separation between the enemy and God's good and perfect creation (*you*) helps you create a healthy identity that does not include fear, rejection, shame, and others. You cannot just blame Satan for bad behavior but take accountability for how you think and act. Recognize sin for what it is and shut it down. You have the power in the name of Jesus to refuse these thoughts.

Helen knows the difference between both kingdoms and is able to separate the person from the sin in them. This is truly a gift from God that she was able to understand the importance of this without having been taught. The Holy Spirit is working through Helen to bring Jane to a place of healing and forgiveness which will ultimately allow Jane to pass on this love to others in her life as an adult.

"That Christ may dwell in your hearts by faith; that ye, being rooted [to render firm, to fix, establish, cause a person or a thing to be thoroughly grounded, stable] *and grounded* [to lay the foundation, to make stable, to establish] *in love, may be able to comprehend* [lay hold of so as to make one's own, to obtain, to find, apprehend] *with all saints what is the breadth, and length, and depth, and height; and to know the love of Christ, which passeth* [to transcend, surpass, exceed, excel] *knowledge, that ye might be filled with all the fullness* [abundance] *of God. Now to Him that is able to do exceeding* [in behalf of, for the sake of, beyond] *abundantly* [beyond all measure, extraordinary] *above all that we ask or think, according to the power that worketh in us, unto Him be glory in the church by Christ Jesus throughout all ages, world without end* [an unbroken age, perpetuity of time, eternity]. *Amen* [so it is, so be it]." Ephesians 3:17-21

Footnotes

[1] Thank [what thank have ye] based on the interlinear, Greek text (G5485 – charis χάρις) – grace; that which affords joy, pleasure, delight, sweetness, charm, loveliness: grace of speech. Of the merciful kindness by which God, exerting his holy influence upon souls, turns them to Christ, keeps, strengthens, increases them in Christian faith, knowledge, affection, and kindles them to the exercise of the Christian virtues. The token or proof of grace benefit. Of manner or act or concrete; literal, figurative or spiritual; especially the divine influence upon the heart, and its reflection in the life; including gratitude.

Chapter VII

Chapter seven makes it hard for us to be forgiving of Mr. Brocklehurst and the way he runs his school. We find that the children are not eating enough to properly grow, they are not wearing enough to keep warm, they are not brought up in love but developing a fear of failure, and they are not being nurtured in their spiritual walk or in life in general.

"The fear of failure in these points harassed me worse than the physical hardships of my lot, though these were no trifles."

As Jane outlines her sufferings, I feel a lump rise in my throat as I imagine children, young girls, being treated as the worst type of creature. Their bodies suffering from earthly ills but their spirits suffering from a different type of malnourishment. The older students, acting out of starvation, steal from the younger students only to survive.

The teachers do not have it in them to encourage as they themselves are put in the position of freezing and hungering. And yet, Miss Temple continues in her positivity and encouraging attitude to try and fortify the students in any way she can, aside from literally feeding them more.

Upon Mr. Brocklehurst's arrival, we are given a glimpse into how he intends to run the school. He is fully aware of the meager clothing and the impossibly small portions of food given to the students.

"'Madam, allow me an instant. You are aware that my plan in bringing up these girls is, not to accustom them to habits of luxury and indulgence, but to render them hardy, patient, self-denying. Should any little accidental disappointment of the appetite occur, such as the spoiling of a meal, the under or the over dressing of a dish, the incident ought not to be neutralized by replacing with something more delicate the comfort lost, thus pampering the body and obviating the aim of this institution; it ought to be improved to the spiritual edification of the pupils, by encouraging them to evince fortitude under temporary privation. A brief address on those occasions would not be mistimed, wherein a judicious instructor would take the opportunity of referring to the sufferings of the primitive Christians; to the torments of martyrs; to the exhortations of our blessed Lord Himself, calling upon His disciples to take up their cross and follow Him; to His warnings that man shall not live by bread alone, but by every word that proceedeth out of the mouth of God; to His divine consolations, "If ye suffer hunger or thirst for My sake, happy are ye." Oh, madam, when you put bread and cheese, instead of burnt porridge, into these children's mouths, you may indeed feed their vile bodies, but you little think how you starve their immortal souls!'"

As I am writing and reading this chapter, my blood is boiling. This man, because we know that men like this did exist at the time of Jane Eyre's conception, represents everything that is corrupt in the church. He is so easy to hate. Even easier to hate than John Reed. We do not get a good picture of how this man was raised or what happened in his past to make him such a despicable human being. Because of this, we can be tempted, as readers, to justify hating him. The scriptures tell us that there are generational iniquities that are passed on to numerous generations. So, we could conclude that his lack of compassion and mercy is what he was shown as a young man, and he is passing this iniquity on to others.

I will be completely honest. I have had a very difficult time with this character and breaking down why he is like this. But above all, and after reading about what separation is, I want to bring only love into this devotional, not hate.

What have we learned so far? Hate upon hate brings nothing good. There will be a time when we will come across people like Mr. Brocklehurst. How will we respond? Will we respond in hate or in love?

This is why classic books such as Jane Eyre provide us with good practice in separation. Fictional characters are still based on human emotions, thoughts, and actions. If we cannot respond well to a fictional character and understand that separation must be applied, how are we expected to respond to a human being with similar traits?

Let me first begin by saying that Mr. Brocklehurst is demonstrating religion NOT faith. In fact, there is a spirit of religion that was and is present in a lot of legalistic Christians that does not represent faith appropriately. Religion is a belief system that is guided by creeds, denominations, doctrine, and theology. It does not always require faith in order for followers to claim religion. Faith on the other hand is a belief, conviction, hopefulness, trust, and dependence on something completely unseen. It does not require elaborate shows or public self-deprecation. Faith is understanding that there is something that we cannot see – God, a loving Father – that upholds us and fights for us.

In addition to this, Mr. Brocklehurst seems to be trying to get rid of the poor because they are useless to society. The weak are not needed. Only the strong can survive. Whether he is doing or thinking about this inadvertently or not, it was a very common thought at this time that the weak should be got rid of.

Second, Mr. Brocklehurst is misquoting Scripture entirely. The closest verses that I found during my studies to what he quoted above were the following:

> *"Blessed are they which do hunger* [to crave ardently, to seek with eager desire] *and thirst* [eagerly long for, those things by which the soul is refreshed, supported, strengthened] *after righteousness* [integrity, virtue, purity of life, rightness, correctness of thinking, feeling, and acting]*: for they shall be filled* [satisfied]." Matthew 5:6

> *"And Jesus said to them, I am the bread of life* [life real and genuine, a life active and vigorous, devoted to God, blessed, in the portion even in this world of those who put their trust in Christ]*: he that comes to Me shall never hunger* [suffer want, crave ardently, to seek with eager desire]*; and he that believes on Me shall never thirst* [figuratively, those who are said to thirst who painfully feel their want of, and eagerly long for, those things by which the soul is refreshed, supported, strengthened]." John 6:35

In these verses, Jesus himself is teaching the people that if they hunger after righteousness and follow Him, that they will be satisfied. He is using the analogy of hunger in both verses but not referring to literal hunger. Jesus is the way, the truth, and the life for all people. If we follow Him, we shall be satisfied for all eternity. However, this still does not justify self-deprecation, starvation, or bringing others down for Christ's sake.

What is actually happening, is Mr. Brocklehurst is opening doors to rejection (*both of self and from others*), fear of failure, religious spirits, loss of identity, shame, and guilt in the girls. All of these are evil spirits that speak lies to draw us away from God's love. Everything that comes out of Mr. Brocklehurst's mouth is hypocrisy and NOT love.

What is he teaching in the church if he is misquoting Scripture at this moment? What is his congregation learning and taking to heart? Many in the church believe that because you are a Christian, you cannot be influenced by the Enemy of our souls. This is simply not true. The scriptures tell us to;

"Be sober [be calm and collected], *be vigilant* [watchful]; *because your adversary the devil, as a roaring lion, walketh about, seeking whom he may devour* [swallow up, destroy]:"*
1 Peter 5:8

This was spoken to the Church. Keeping this in mind, we are to hold every thought captive to the obedience of Christ. This is for our protection and the protection of His children. Our pain can be used against another, by the enemy, to cause destruction in the body of believers.

To add more fuel to the fire of our dislike for this man, he sees a girl with naturally curly hair and demands that it be cut off. This is a snub in the face of God and how He created this girl. God created this young lady to have red, curly hair.

"'...but we are not to conform to nature.'"

Clearly the girls can hear the conversation going on between Mr. Brocklehurst and Miss Temple, so this young lady, Julia, must wonder if there is something wrong with her. It is possible that Mr. Brocklehurst could have just opened a door to self-rejection in Julia, thinking that God made a mistake creating her with curly hair that conformed to nature. That her hair, out of her control, is sinful.

"Leaning a little back on my bench, I could see the looks and grimaces with which they commented on this manoeuvre: it was a pity Mr. Brocklehurst could not see them too; he would perhaps have felt that, whatever he might do with the outside of the cup and platter, the inside was further beyond his interference than he imagined."

"'...I have a Master to serve whose kingdom is not of this world: my mission is to mortify in these girls the lusts of the flesh, to teach them to clothe themselves with shame-facedness and sobriety, not with braided hair and costly apparel; and each of the young persons before us has a string of hair twisted in plaits which vanity itself might have woven; these, I repeat, must be cut off; think of the time wasted...'"

Enter Mr. Brocklehurst's wife and daughters, elaborately dressed in furs, silks, and velvet.

"There is a generation that are pure [clean, fair, pure in a moral sense] *in their own eyes, and yet is not washed from their filthiness* [pollution, excrement, dung]. *There is a generation, O how lofty* [lifted up, exalted, to exalt oneself, magnify oneself] *are their eyes! And their eyelids are lifted up. There is a generation, whose teeth are as swords, and their jaw teeth* [incisors] *as knives, to devour* [consume – figuratively, slay, destroy] *the poor* [weak, humble] *from off the earth, and the needy* [in want, subject to oppression, destitute] *from among men."* Proverbs 30:12-14

Mr. Brocklehurst is building hypocrisy upon hypocrisy. He is constantly raising himself up as some sort of deity. We see that what he is teaching these students is definitely not what he teaches in his own home. What makes these girls different from his own? Is it that they are poor? Or that they are somehow not godly? How godly are his own daughters? Would they accept the "sufferings of Christ" as these students are forced to?

Jane, in her effort to not bring any attention to herself, unfortunately drops her slate, bringing *all* attention on her. Anger surges in her as well as fear of further rejection (*by Miss Temple in particular*) and fear of failure, as she is publicly shamed and punished by Mr. Brocklehurst.

"'You see she is yet young; you observe she possesses the ordinary form of childhood; God has graciously given her the shape that He has given to all of us; no signal deformity points her out as a marked character. Who would think that the Evil One had already found a servant and agent in her? Yet such, I grieve to say, is the case.'

*…'My dear children…this is a sad, a melancholy occasion;
for it becomes my duty to warn you that this girl, who might
be one of God's own lambs, is a little castaway — not a
member of the true flock, but evidently an interloper and an
alien. You must be on your guard against her; you must
shun her example — if necessary, avoid her company, exclude
her from your sports, and shut her out from your converse.
Teachers, you must watch her: keep your eyes on her
movements, weigh well her words, scrutinse her actions,
punish her body to save her soul — if, indeed, such salvation
be possible, for (my tongue falters while I tell it) this girl,
this child, the native of a Christian land, worse than many a
little heathen who says its prayers to Brahma and kneels
before Juggernaut — this girl is — a liar!'"*

Let's see…shun…avoid…exclude…shut out…punish…are
these words of love?

Would Jesus ever shun or exclude someone? No! In fact, He
healed, taught, and helped the worst of sinners when He was
here on earth. He did not just go to the healthy, good,
righteous people. He came to save the lost as a good
shepherd does.

"And when they were come, and had gathered the church [a
gathering of citizens] *together, they rehearsed* [to announce,
make known, to report, bring back tidings] *all that God had
done with them, and how He had opened the door of faith to
the Gentiles."* Acts 14:27

*"Even us, whom He has called, not of the Jews only, but also
of the Gentiles?"* Romans 9:24

"And Jesus said to him, This day is salvation come to this house, forsomuch as he also is a son of Abraham. For the Son of man is come to seek and to save that which was lost."
Luke 19:9-10

"Jesus cried and said, he that believeth on me, believeth not on me, but on Him that sent me. And he that seeth me seeth Him that sent me. I am come a light into the world that whoseoever believeth on me should not abide in darkness [ignorance, wickedness]. *And if any man hear my words, and believe not, I judge* [rule, govern] *him not: for I came not to judge the world, but to save* [deliver, protect, heal] *the world."* John 12:44-47

"Then said Jesus unto them again, Verily, verily, I say unto you, I am the door of the sheep. All that ever came before me are thieves and robbers: but the sheep did not hear [to attend to, consider what is or has been said] *them. I am the door* [entrance to the kingdom of heaven]: *by me if any man enter in, he shall be saved, and shall go in and out, and find pasture. The thief cometh not, but for to steal, and to kill, and to destroy: I am come that they might have life, and that they might have it more abundantly* [over and above, more than is necessary, supremely, extraordinary]. *I am the good shepherd: the good shepherd giveth his life for the sheep."*
John 10:7-11

Furthermore, Mr. Brocklehurst goes beyond this to say that salvation might not even be possible for Jane.

Who is he to tell anyone that they are beyond redemption and salvation? It says in the Scriptures previously quoted that Jesus came to save *all* people and bring His sheep to good pasture. He came for *all* unbelievers. It is not the call of Mr. Brocklehurst to say that anyone is beyond God's love and forgiveness.

Throughout this process of getting to know Mr. Brocklehurst, we have seen very un-Christ-like behavior. Christian = Christ-follower. If we are Christ followers, we are called to be Christ-minded which comes with the spiritual discernment from the Holy Spirit and the Word of God.

"Now we have received, not the spirit of the world, but the spirit which is of God; that we might know the things that are freely given [in kindness, gratuitously, benevolent] *to us of God. Which things also we speak, not in the words which man's wisdom* [worldly] *teacheth, but which the Holy Ghost teacheth; comparing* [combine spiritual ideas with appropriate expressions] *spiritual things with spiritual. But the natural* [sensual, passionate] *man receiveth not the things of the Spirit of God: for they are foolishness unto him: neither can he know* [understand] *them, because they are spiritually* [by the aid of the Holy Spirit] *discerned* [investigate, question, examine, search]. *But he that is spiritual judgeth all things, yet he himself is judged of no man. For who hath known the mind* [thought, feeling, will] *of the Lord, that he may instruct him? But we have the mind of Christ."* 1 Corinthians 2:12-16

"…now exposed to general view on a pedestal of infamy. What my sensations were, no language can describe; but, just as they all rose, stifling my breath and constricting my throat, a girl came up and passed me: in passing, she lifted

*her eyes. What a strange light inspired them! What an
extraordinary sensation that ray sent through me! How the
new feeling bore me up! It was as if a martyr, a hero, had
passed a slave or victim, and imparted strength in the
transit. I mastered the rising hysteria, lifted up my head, and
took a firm stand on the stool."*

As unnecessary and cruel as this punishment is for Jane, I
believe God gave her strength in this moment. Strength to
uphold the punishment, whether deserved or not. Throughout
this book, we can see evidence that God has not forsaken
Jane.

*"Such is the imperfect nature of man! Such spots are there
on the disc of the clearest planet; and eyes like Miss
Scatcherd's can only see those minute defects, and are blind
to the full brightness of the orb."*

The only way to treat the girls the way Mr. Brocklehurst did
was to demoralize, demean, and dehumanize them. Breaking
their spirits. This is satanic. He was in no way acting as
Christ. We can come in as a:

B-O-M-B or as a B-A-L-M.

And, unfortunately, because the teachers themselves are not
cared for as they should be, they have lost all drive to change
anything or stand up for their students. The motivation is
gone and teachers such as Miss Scatcherd begin to see only
the flaws and minor annoyances that each student possesses.

<u>How Can You Apply This to Your Own Life?</u>

Will you be a B-O-M-B or a B-A-L-M?

Will you return hate for hate? Or will you show love in the face of hate?

This is a huge challenge for all of us. I have already revealed my struggle with working through this chapter. It is so hard in the moment, to be loving to a hateful person or in the midst of a challenging situation. And yet, this is what we are called to do, as believers.

Being love to a hateful, abusive person does not necessarily mean that you are required to be in constant communion with them. This is where we begin to see toxic relationships flourish. The call to be love can keep a person in a toxic relationship because they feel they must stay with that abusive person. I do not believe that God would call us, or want us, to remain in a toxic, abusive relationship. Loving that person could be as simple as forgiving them for their behavior but remaining at a distance.

From what you have learned on this journey through Jane Eyre so far, you have most of the tools you need to be loving and forgiving. If you feel that you cannot possibly be love in the face of hate, that is when you call on God for supernatural strength. The Holy Spirit is our strength against the enemy. When we feel that we are weak or unable to continue, He is right there to gird us up. All we have to do is ask.

If you are struggling today, pray that God will give you the wisdom, discernment, and strength you need. Read the Word and really meditate on it. Take it to your heart as Paul did.

"And this is the confidence that we have in him, that, if we ask any thing according to his will, he heareth us: and if we know that he hear us, whatsoever we ask, we know that we have the petitions that we desire of him." 1 John 5:14-15

"Pray without ceasing." 1 Thessalonians 5:17

Chapter VIII

"…left to myself I abandoned myself, and my tears watered the boards. I had meant to be so good, and to do so much at Lowood: to make so many friends, to earn respect, and win affection. Already I had made visible progress: that very morning I had reached the head of my class; Miss Miller had praised me warmly; Miss Temple had smiled approbation; she had promised to teach me drawing, and to let me learn French, if I continued to make similar improvement two months longer: and then I was well received by my fellow pupils; treated as an equal by those of my own age, and not molested by any; now, here I lay again crushed and trodden on; and could I ever rise more?

'Never,' I thought; and ardently I wished to die."

Thus, we have reached the height of Jane's childhood struggles. She has been humiliated and broken down and her hope has been destroyed. Wishing to die is a serious thing. Once those thoughts have entered in, it is hard to regain any hope, peace, or feelings of love without miraculous intervention or people surrounding you who genuinely love you.

If only Mr. Brocklehurst truly understood the Scriptures. If only he had the wisdom and discernment of the Holy Spirit. If only he saw the damage that he was doing to these poor young girls, not only on the surface, but deep within their spirits as well. If he had possessed any of this knowledge or discernment from the Holy Spirit, or if he possessed a true and godly love for others, I believe Mr. Brocklehurst could have done many good things.

"Though I speak with the tongues of men and of angels, and have not charity [affection, good will, benevolence, brotherly love, a love feast, dear love], *I am become as sounding* [roaring, to make a loud noise] *brass, or a tinkling* [wail, lament, to ring loudly] *cymbal. And though I have the gift of prophecy, and understand all mysteries, and all knowledge; and though I have all faith, so that I could remove mountains, and have not charity, I am nothing. And though I bestow all my goods to feed the poor, and though I give my body to be burned, and have not charity, it profiteth* [to be useful, to benefit, assist, advantageous] *me nothing. Charity suffereth long* [to persevere patiently and bravely in enduring misfortunes and troubles, to be mild and slow in avenging, slow to anger], *and is kind; charity envieth not; charity vaunteth not itself* [to boast one's self, a self display, employing rhetorical embellishments in extolling one's self excessively], *is not puffed up, doth not behave itself unseemly, seeketh not her own, is not easily provoked, thinketh no evil; rejoiceth not in iniquity, but rejoiceth in the truth; beareth all things* [to protect or keep by covering, preserve, to hide, conceal of the errors and faults of others], *believeth all things, hopeth all things, endureth all things* [to persevere: under misfortunes and trials to hold fast to one's faith in Christ, to endure, bear bravely and calmly]. *Charity never faileth* [to fall powerless, to be without effect]: *but whether there be prophecies, they shall fail; whether there be tongues they shall cease* [no longer stirred by its incitements and seductions]; *whether there be knowledge*

[general intelligence, understanding], *it shall vanish away* [to cause a person or thing to have no further efficiency, to deprive of force, influence, power]." 1 Corinthians 13:1-8

Jane's hope of being loved and having friends is gone. The one thing she desires above all else is to love and be loved in return. We then return to major rejection. The rejection that she has been subjected to throughout her young life has now extended to those outside of her small sphere of family, which we can see is one of Jane's biggest fears. No one has ever shown her the true love that comes from Christ.

The rejection, unloving spirits, bitterness, agony, self-pity and hopelessness have made a home in Jane's heart. Who will be her friend? Who will love her now? Who will fight for her and stand up for her? Who will believe in her innocence? I believe instinctually we all know we have value and will endlessly be searching for validation regarding it.

"One man of you shall chase a thousand: for the LORD your God, he it is that fighteth for you, as he hath promised you."
Joshua 23:10

"The LORD is my shepherd [teacher, companion, keep company with, pastor, friend]*; I shall not want* [lack, be without, decrease, have need]. *He maketh me to lie down in green pastures: he leadeth me beside the still waters. He restoreth* [refresh, restore, reward] *my soul: he leadeth me in the paths of righteousness for his name's sake. Yea, though I walk through the valley of the shadow of death, I will fear no evil: for thou art with me; thy rod and thy staff* [figuratively - sustenance, support, literally - walking stick] *they comfort me. Thou preparest a table before me in the presence of*

mine enemies: thou anointest my head with oil; my cup [lot] *runneth* [satisfaction, wealthy] *over. Surely goodness and mercy shall follow me all the days of my life: and I will dwell in the house of the LORD for ever.*" Psalm 23

Because Mr. Brocklehurst is not revealing God's true love and acceptance through his actions or speech, I believe God placed Helen in Jane's life for this very purpose. To teach Jane of God's love and what it *really* looks like to be a believer and to trust that there is a Father who loves us more deeply than any human can. She reveals the love of 1 Corinthians 13 beautifully. God always provides a way out of our torment and the friendship that exists between these two girls is His gift to Jane.

Helen enters the picture, silent and supportive.

"'Helen, why do you stay with a girl whom everybody believes to be a liar?'

'Everybody, Jane? Why, there are only eighty people who have heard you called so, and the world contains hundreds of millions.'

'But what have I to do with millions? The eighty I know despise me.'

'Jane, you are mistaken: probably not one in the school either despises or dislikes you: many, I am sure, pity you much.'

'How can they pity me after what Mr. Brocklehurst has said?'

'Mr. Brocklehurst is not a god: nor is he even a great and admired man: he is little liked here; he never took steps to make himself liked. Had he treated you as an especial favourite, you would have found enemies, declared or covert, all around you; as it is, the greater number would offer you sympathy if they dared. Teachers and pupils may look coldly on you for a day or two, but friendly feelings will ere long appear so much the more evidently for their temporary suppression...'"

Helen comes in as a balm, calming Jane's soul and giving her some semblance of hope back. She assures Jane that she can and will be loved and accepted by society as long as Jane believes herself truly worthy of love. I do not believe that Jane knows how to love *herself.* How could she? She does not really know what real love looks or feels like. Let alone the fact that she has been surrounded by adults who do not really seem to love *themselves.* In the face of this, how could she understand the importance of loving herself?

She says she would rather die than live unloved, alone, and hated. It is her worst fear. This fear drives her and feeds the anger, bitterness, and resentment toward those who have wronged her. Jane would give her life and would "willingly submit to have the bone of my arm broken..." just to gain the affection of another person. The years of neglect have left her with nothing.

Or so it seems.

God never leaves His children to suffer unnecessarily. He desires them to be at peace. For this reason, Helen, and as we will soon see, Miss Temple, are a part of Jane's life to provide her with the guidance and love she so desperately yearns for and in turn, strengthens Jane's faith in a loving God.

"For the LORD God is a sun [as object of illicit worship, glittering or shining] *and shield: the LORD will give grace and glory* [honour, abundance, splendour, dignity]*: no good thing will he withhold from them that walk uprightly* [innocent, having integrity, what is complete or entirely is accord with truth and fact]*. O LORD of hosts, blessed is the man that trusteth in thee."* Psalm 84:11-12

And yet, humans are fallible and will disappoint us all throughout our lives. Depending on them for constant love and affection can become idolatry. As you read in chapter one, rejection sets our value on what other people think of us rather than what God thinks of us. Jane is lifting up others above God without even realizing it. She is setting human beings on a pedestal which is why she is so crushed when disappointment and rejection comes. And yet, we cannot fault her in this as she has never seen the true love that God has for His children. God is always our provider of constant, unadulterated love and acceptance. He will never fail us or forsake us. His love is everywhere.

"For all have sinned, and come short of the glory of God; being justified freely by his grace through the redemption that is in Christ Jesus:" Romans 3:23-24

"For there is not a just [lawful, righteous] *man upon earth, that doeth good, and sinneth not."* Ecclesiastes 7:20

All Jane seems to know of God is that He lives in heaven
judging unfairly, those on earth, and deciding who goes to
heaven to be with Him and who goes to hell. If she is good,
she will go to heaven. If she is bad, she will go to hell. The
church does not seem to be teaching her a whole lot besides
this concept. Helen bluntly but gently helps Jane realize that
she is placing too much of her identity in the pain she has
received.

*"Hush, Jane! You think too much of the love of human
beings; you are too impulsive, too vehement; the sovereign
Hand that created your frame, and put life into it, has
provided you with other resources than your feeble self, or
than creatures feeble as you. Besides this earth, and besides
the race of men, there is an invisible world and a kingdom of
spirits: that world is round us, for it is everywhere; and
those spirits watch us, for they are commissioned to guard
us; and if we were dying in pain and shame, if scorn smote
us on all sides, and hatred crushed us, angels see our
tortures, recognize our innocence (if innocent we be: as I
know you are of this charge which Mr. Brocklehurst has
weakly and pompously repeated at second-hand from Mrs.
Reed; for I read a sincere nature in your ardent eyes and on
your clear front), and God waits only the separation of spirit
from flesh to crown us with a full reward. Why, then, should
we ever sink overwhelmed with distress, when life is so soon
over, and death is so certain an entrance to happiness — to
glory?"*

Helen knows instinctively that her time on earth is short. As
readers, we only get a small glimpse of this as her cough

worsens. This speech of hers reveals her hope of everlasting life with her Father in heaven as well as a tinge of sorrow that her life on earth is to be cut short.

We are left to ponder what is going on in Helen's young mind under her hopefulness and faith. Is she sad that she might never make it home again? Is she disappointed she might never see her father again? Does she seem sad that she might die in a place so cold and damp and joy-less?

Charlotte Brontë does not give us any more insight into these questions, but we can imagine that Helen wishes she had more time to live even in the presence of the hope and peace she has of entering Heaven's pearly gates.

If Jane's hope seemed to be returning, she receives another boost from Miss Temple.

"'…Have you cried your grief away?' [Miss Temple]

'I am afraid I never shall do that.'

'Why?'

'Because I have been wrongly accused; and you, ma'am, and everybody else, will now think me wicked.'

'We shall think you what you prove yourself to be, my child. Continue to act as a good girl, and you will satisfy us.'" – brackets added by me

Jane is accepted! She is believed! Jane's heart must be soaring with the fact that she has been allowed to speak to the accusation and give her testimony. And then to be believed as being innocent! No one, except for Helen, has ever given Jane the benefit of the doubt, especially not an adult. From this moment on, Miss Temple lives as a friend and confidant to Jane. A true example of goodness and faith, not to mention the love found in 1 Corinthians 13.

Miss Temple treats the young girls to tea and a warm fire. This soothes Jane's soul and brings her to a place of trust and peace. A place she has not been before, especially in the presence of an adult. Helen blossoms into beauty under the love of Miss Temple and the filling of her stomach. We can see the difference now that cold and hunger make on the girls. It destroys all creativity, all beauty, and all energy from the students. How are they able to serve God and others if they themselves are not able to function well?

A burden of survival has been placed on the shoulders of each student, which is something no child should have to bear. Being under-fed, under-nourished spiritually, and under-clothed does not bring out the martyr in a child, it breeds fear, rejection, and discontentment. These are all doorways in which other spirits can enter such as anger, bitterness, and envy. Miss Temple is able to recognize this, and though she does what she can, which is often not much at all, she is able to have compassion for what the students go through on a regular basis. This compassion is represented as love and acceptance.

As promised, Miss Temple is able to corroborate Jane's story and openly absolves her of any wrongdoing in front of the whole school. Here, Miss Temple represents justice; true and pure.

"The teachers then shook hands with me and kissed me, and a murmur of pleasure ran through the ranks of my companions.

Thus relieved of a grievous load, I from that hour set to work afresh, resolved to pioneer my way through every difficulty."

"Who shall lay any thing (to come forward as accuser against, bring charge against) *to the charge of God's elect* (God's chosen/children, Christians)*? It is God that justifieth* (to render righteous or such he ought to be, to declare, pronounce, one to be just). *Who is he that condemneth* (to give judgement against, to condemn)*? It is Christ that died, yea rather, that is risen again, who is even at the right hand of God, who also maketh intercession for us."* Romans 8:33-34

"For by thy words thou shalt be justified, and by thy words thou shalt be condemned." Matthew 12:37

With the weight of failure lifted off Jane's shoulders, she is now able to pioneer through her work with a dedicated resolve and hopeful heart again. The fear and burden of being accused has been removed from off her shoulders and she is able to move forward in her studies quickly, her creativity flourishing. Life takes a positive turn and God gives Jane her hope back. Love will always move mountains.

"Now the God of hope fill you with all joy and peace in believing, that ye may abound in hope, through the power of the Holy Ghost." Romans 15:13

"And we know that all things work together for good to them that love God, to them who are the called according to his purpose." Romans 8:28

"For I will restore health unto thee, and I will heal thee of thy wounds, saith the LORD; because they called thee an Outcast (to impel, thrust away, drive away, banish, outcast), *saying, this is Zion* (parched place), *whom no man seeketh after."* Jeremiah 30:17

"Well has Solomon said, 'Better is a dinner of herbs where love is, than a stalled ox and hatred therewith.'[1]

I would not now have exchanged Lowood with all its privations for Gateshead and its daily luxuries."

<u>How Can You Apply This to Your Own Life?</u>

Satan is the accuser[2]. According to the exhaustive Strong's concordance, satan means accuse and acting as my accuser in Hebrew.[3] God gave him that name because that is the character Satan established for himself.

Every evil spirit such as bitterness, envy and jealousy, anger, and occultism all build onto accusation. The nature of an accuser or an accusing spirit is to search for their own identity at the expense of another. This opens the door to the spirits mentioned above. Evil spirits have no identity. They do not have firm foundations on which to build. With no identity comes torment and lack of peace. They are constantly searching.

Our identity, as believers, should be in God our Father and the fact that we were made in His image. Our Father's love is our identity. Satan had this before his fall. He had the kinship of God, but he chose his will over God's and thus was sent from heaven.

"Thou wast perfect [complete, wholesome, innocent, having integrity] *in thy ways from the day that thou wast created, till iniquity was found in thee."* Ezekiel 28:15

"Thy pomp [exaltation, majesty, pride, arrogance] *is brought down to the grave* [hell, pit]*, and the noise of thy viols* [lyre, harp, musical instrument]*: the worm* [worm as cause and sign of decay] *is spread under thee, and the worms* [maggots] *cover thee. How art thou fallen* [cast out] *from heaven, O Lucifer* [light-bearer, shining one, morning star]*, son of the morning! How art thou cut down* [cut off] *to the ground, which didst weaken* [overthrow, decay, waste away] *the nations* [people]*! For thou has said in thine heart* [soul, mind]*, I will ascend into heaven, I will exalt* [to rise up, be lofty, to magnify oneself] *my throne* [seat of honor, authority, power] *above the stars of God: I will sit also upon the mount of the congregation* [appointed place of meeting, synagogue]*, in the sides* [border] *of the north: I will ascend above the heights* [high places as places of worship] *of the clouds; I will be like* [resemble, compare, to make oneself like, devise] *the most High."* Isaiah 14:11-14

Satan wants us to give up our identity, rebelling against God, so that we can be like him. He does evil in the world and blames God for it, or he will blame God for not stopping it. This is where doubt enters. Is God really all good? Does He pay attention to what is happening? Is He working in the world at all or having a hand in it?

Remember, Satan is trying everything in his power to make you ineffective as a believer. He does not want you to have a deep and loving relationship with God the Father. He feeds you fears to dampen your faith by sending accusing spirits into your life, he trains you to accuse yourself, God and others.

"Wherefore now let the fear [reverence] *of the LORD be upon you; take heed and do it: for there is no iniquity* [wickedness, perverseness, violence] *with the LORD our God, nor respect* [partiality, lifting up] *of persons, nor taking* [accepting, receiving of a bribe] *of gifts* [bribe]*."* 2 Chronicles 19:7

"He is the Rock [mighty one, strong]*, his work is perfect: for all his ways are judgment* [justice, order, discretion]*: a God of truth* [firmness, fidelity, steadfastness, security] *and without* [to be nothing or not exist] *iniquity, just* [lawful, righteous] *and right* [upright, correct] *is he."* Deuteronomy 32:4

Accusation comes from many different avenues. All of us have dealt with accusation at some point in our lives. It could be a thought that comes in our minds about ourselves (*EX: "I'm not enough"*), others (*EX: "they are not enough"*), and even God (*EX: "God's not enough"*).

Or, accusation could come from others, accusing you, accusing others in front of you, or accusing God in your presence. Accusation comes in the form of gossip, strife, murmuring, and ultimately leads to bitterness. The fruit of accusation breaks relationships with God, ourselves, and others and welcomes other spirits in to bring us torment.

"The words of a talebearer [backbiter, slander, whisperer] *are as wounds, and they go down into the innermost parts of the belly."* Proverbs 18:8

The thoughts that enter in, accusing, are not your thoughts but the thoughts of a spiritual being that deeply hates you and God and your relationship with Him. You do not have to live with accusing spirits. This is why we must have the Holy Spirit to help us bear up against them every day. Taking your thoughts captive is a daily challenge and is crucial to growing in your relationship with the Father.

"Casting down [with the use of force: to throw down, demolish] *imaginations* [thoughts, a reasoning: such as is hostile to the Christian faith]*, and every high thing that exalteth itself against the knowledge* [intelligence, understanding, moral wisdom] *of God, and bringing into captivity every thought to the obedience* [submission] *of Christ;"* 2 Corinthians 10:5

Recognizing accusation for what it is, as well as who is behind it, will help allow for every good and perfect thing that God wants to bring into our lives. Do not allow the accuser to change your identity. Do not allow these evil spirits to become who you are.

Forgiveness is going to be your best ally. Working through the process of forgiveness, whether it is forgiveness directed toward yourself, others, or God, is crucial for repairing your right relationship with your Father in heaven. This can be difficult, depending on the depth of the hurt, but necessary. This can be done with the blueprint of the 8 Rs to freedom in chapter one.

Your identity in Christ is to be protected and cherished.

"For I am persuaded [have confidence, to trust], *that neither death, nor life, nor angels, nor principalities, nor powers, nor things present, nor things to come, nor height, nor depth, nor any other creature, shall be able to separate us from the love of God, which is in Christ Jesus our Lord."* Romans 8:38-39

"But now thus saith the LORD that created thee, O Jacob, and he that formed thee [to mould into a form; especially as a potter], *O Israel, Fear not: for I have redeemed* [avenged, ransomed] *thee, I have called thee by thy name; thou art mine."* Isaiah 43:1

"Having predestinated [foreordain] *us unto the adoption of children* [Christian sonship in respect to God, the nature and condition of the true disciples in Christ, who by receiving the Spirit of God into their souls become sons of God] *by Jesus Christ to himself, according to the good pleasure* [delight, benevolence] *of his will, to the praise of the glory* [splendour, magnificence, praise] *of his grace, wherein he hath made us accepted* [indue with special honor, make accepted, be highly favored] *in the beloved."* Ephesians 1:5-6

Footnotes

[1] Proverbs 15:17 KJV

[2] References to the Accusation teaching from Be in Health ®

[3] Satan/Accusers based on the interlinear, Hebrew text (H7853 – śāṭan שָׂטַן) – to be or act as an adversary, resist, oppose, to attack (figuratively) accuse.

Chapter IX

In chapter nine, Jane is going to experience both joy and sadness. Both of these emotions prepare her for the continued spiritual and emotional growth that will shape her adulthood.

"April advanced to May – a bright serene May it was; days of blue sky, placid sunshine, and soft western or southern gales filled up its duration. And now vegetation matured with vigour; Lowood shook loose its tresses; it became all green , all flowery; its great elm, ash, and oak skeletons were restored to majestic life; woodland plants sprang up profusely in its recesses; unnumbered varieties of moss filled its hollows, and it made a strange ground-sunshine out of the wealth of its wild primrose plants: I have seen their pale gold gleam in overshadowed spots like scatterings of the sweetest lustre. All this I enjoyed often and fully, free, unwatched, and almost alone: for this unwonted liberty and pleasure there was a cause, to which it now becomes my task to advert."

With Jane now being free from the burden of accusation as well as the approach of spring weather, Lowood school does not seem as much a place of despair. The girls are able to go outdoors without the winter wind cutting through their clothing and making their skin raw and sore. They are able to sleep at night and learn in the school rooms without shivering. There is a little comfort in their lives again.

But the genial weather brought more than warmth. It also brought with it a deadly fever that made its way through the school leaving devastation and sadness in its wake.

"Semi-starvation and neglected colds had predisposed most of the pupils to receive infection: forty-five out of the eighty girls lay ill at one time. Classes were broken up, rules relaxed. The few who continued well were allowed almost unlimited license; because the medical attendant insisted on the necessity of frequent exercise to keep them in health: and had it been otherwise, no one had leisure to watch or restrain them."

Due to sickness running rampant throughout the school, Mr. Brocklehurst, rather than helping the teachers and being a present support, was a coward and stayed far away. As the owner and overseer of the school, we would expect that his presence would be necessary, especially since he was the clergyman of the local church. Would you not think that it was his duty to be there as a minister of God's word at such a difficult time? What is the role of a minister or pastor according to the Word?

> *"Take heed therefore unto yourselves, and to all the flock* [group of believers], *over the which the Holy Ghost hath made you overseers* [elder, bishop, pastor], *to feed* [govern, supply the requisites for the soul's need] *the church of God, which he hath purchased* [to preserve for one's self, to keep safe] *with his own blood."* Acts 20:28

> *"The elders* [those who presided over the churches] *which are among you I exhort* [admonish, encourage, strengthen,

instruct], *who am also an elder, and a witness of the sufferings of Christ, and also a partaker* [a partner, associate, companion] *of the glory* [judgement, splendour, worship, the glorious condition of blessedness into which is appointed and promised that true Christians shall enter after their Saviour's return from heaven] *that shall be revealed: feed* [to rule or govern, nourish] *the flock of God which is among you, taking the oversight* [to oversee, look diligently, beware] *thereof, not by constraint* [by force or constrain], *but willingly* [voluntarily, of one's own accord]; *not for filthy lucre* [eagerness for base gain], *but of a ready mind* [willingly]; *neither as being lords* [to bring under one's power, hold in subjection] *over God's heritage* [inheritance], *but being ensamples* [an example, a model] *to the flock. And when the chief Shepherd shall appear, ye shall receive a crown* [symbol of honor, external blessedness given as a prize to the genuine servants of God and Christ, reward for righteousness] *of glory that fadeth not away* [fadeless, a symbol of perpetuity and immortality]." 1 Peter 5:1-4

"A good tree cannot bring forth [bear] *evil fruit* [literally or figuratively; work, act, deed], *neither can a corrupt tree* [putrefied, of poor quality, unfit for use] *bring forth good* [suitable, honest, valuable] *fruit. Every tree that bringeth not forth good fruit is hewn down* [cut down], *and cast* [to throw, thrust] *into the fire. Wherefore by their fruits* [that which originates or comes from something, an effect, result, work, act, deed] *ye shall know them."* Matthew 7:18-20

Jesus himself set an example by spending time with the sick and injured. He specifically went to them and healed them. Not only that, but he also called his disciples to do the same.

"Whosoever shall seek to save his life shall lose it; and whosoever shall lose [figuratively or literally] *his life shall preserve it."* Luke 17:33

Mr. Brocklehurst is probably living in fear of losing what he has come to enjoy in life. We already know that he is a hypocrite, considering how his wife and daughters were arrayed in fine clothes and jewelry while he starves and neglects the girls of Lowood school. By his fruit, we know him. This is not a good representation of how God calls pastors to maintain and teach His church.

Things changed quite dramatically during this time of sickness, and the girls are fed better and given more freedoms. The teachers are so preoccupied with tending to the sick and dying that they do not have the time to reign in the other students or even hold classes. Jane relishes her new-found freedoms and spends time with other students. Her new companion is drastically different than Helen.

"…Mary Ann Wilson; a shrewd, observant personage, whose society I took pleasure in, partly because she was witty and original, and partly because she had a manner which set me at my ease. Some years older than I, she knew more of the world, and could tell me many things I liked to hear: with her my curiosity found gratification: to my faults also she gave ample indulgence, never imposing curb or rein on anything I said. She had a turn for narrative, I for analysis; she liked to inform, I to question; so we got on swimmingly together, deriving much entertainment, if not much improvement, from our mutual intercourse."

Helen had always presented a special discernment that called Jane to reflect upon her actions and thoughts. This new acquaintance, Mary, did not challenge Jane in her beliefs nor did she keep her accountable. At this crucial time in Jane's life and process of growing into the woman she is to eventually become; she needs to be challenged and held accountable. This is a huge turning point for her, as we will see soon.

> *"As newborn babies, desire* [long for] *the sincere* [undeceitful, unadulterated] *milk* [for the less difficult Christian truths] *of the word, that ye may grow* [become greater, increase, grow up] *thereby: if so be ye have tasted* [make trial of, experience] *that the Lord is gracious* [benevolent, kind, virtuous]." 1 Peter 2:2-3

Jane even admits that the shallow conversations that she had with Mary were not equal to those she had with Helen. Helen helped Jane grow in her relationship with God. Their friendship was pure and did not tire.

"…she could only tell me amusing stories, and reciprocate any racy and pungent gossip I chose to indulge in; while, if I have spoken truth of Helen, she was qualified to give those who enjoyed the privilege of her converse, a taste of far higher things.

True, reader; and I knew and felt this: and though I am a defective being, with many faults and few redeeming points, yet I never tired of Helen Burns; nor ever ceased to cherish for her a sentiment of attachment, as strong, tender, and respectful as any that ever animated my heart. How could it be otherwise, when Helen, at all times and under all circumstances, evinced for me a quiet and faithful friendship, which ill-humour never soured, nor irritation never troubled?"

Helen is the type of friend that everyone truly desires. A friend who is faithful and true no matter what happens. In the short time that Jane is able to know Helen, she has learned so much about life and what it is to be at peace and to be a true friend. Helen gave Jane such a wonderful gift without either girl realizing it right away.

"Iron sharpeneth iron; so a man sharpeneth the countenance of his friend." Proverbs 27:17

"Two are better than one; because they have a good reward for their labour. For if they fall, the one will lift up his fellow: but woe to him that is alone when he falleth; for he hath not another to help him up. Again, if two lie together [take rest, sleep], *then they have heat* [to be warm]*: but how can one be warm alone? And if one prevail against him* [overpower]*, two shall withstand him* [endure, stand fast or still]*; and a threefold* [three parts] *cord is not quickly broken."* Ecclesiastes 4:9-12

"Wherefore comfort [call to your side, to encourage and strengthen, exhort] *yourselves together* [reciprocally, mutually]*, and edify* [to promote growth in Christian wisdom, affection, grace, virtue, holiness, blessedness] *one another, even as also ye do."* 1 Thessalonians 5:11

"Ointment and perfume rejoice the heart: so doth the sweetness [pleasantness] *of a man's friend by hearty* [soul, life, desire, emotion, passion] *counsel."* Proverbs 27:9

"And let us consider one another to provoke [incitement] *unto love and to good works: not forsaking* [desert, abandon] *the assembling of ourselves together, as the manner* [custom] *of some is; but exhorting* [entreat, admonish, encourage, strengthen] *one another: and so much the more* [more, to a greater degree], *as ye see the day* [of the last day of this present age, the day Christ will return from heaven, raise the dead, hold the final judgement, and perfect his kingdom] *approaching."* Hebrews 10:24-25

"Open rebuke [reproof, correction, chastened] *is better than secret* [conceal, hidden] *love. Faithful are the wounds of a friend; but the kisses of an enemy are deceitful."* Proverbs 27:5-6

As Jane makes her way back to the school one night, she pauses and begins, for the first time, to contemplate heaven and hell very seriously. With all the death happening right in front of her, she is beginning to understand how precious life is and to think about what occurs after death. Her naivety is changing. Jane is realizing that death is very real and tangible. Life is short and fleeting.

Upon discovering that Helen does not have long to live, Jane felt the strong desire to be with her and give her a final embrace. When Jane sees her, Helen appears to be at peace.

"I am very happy, Jane; and when you hear that I am dead, you must be sure and not grieve: there is nothing to grieve

about. We all must die one day, and the illness which is removing me is not painful; it is gentle and gradual: my mind is at rest. I leave no one to regret me much: I have only a father; and he is lately married, and will not miss me. By dying young, I shall escape great sufferings. I had not qualities or talents to make my way very well in the world: I should have been continually at fault."

While reading this part of Helen's story, it reminded me of Beth from Little Women by Louisa May Alcott. My analysis will contain a few spoilers, but, with the rising popularity of the story, you might already know most of what occurs in Beth's life.

Throughout the book, Beth was always a constant support and loving sister to all of her "more talented" sisters. She felt that she was useless at times and did not see the beautiful merit of her own life and abilities. Self-pity, just like with Helen, was constant with Beth. Their faith was great, but self-pity and self-accusation tempted them into not realizing their own special place in Christ's kingdom on earth.

To quote Little Women for a moment:

"…I only mean to say that I have a feeling that it never was intended I should live long. I'm not like the rest of you. I never made any plans about what I'd do when I grew up. I never thought of being married, as you all did. I couldn't seem to imagine myself anything but stupid little Beth, trotting about at home, of no use anywhere but there."

I am not sure if both Beth and Helen were truly "giving up" on their lives, but they certainly did not seem to have a lot to live for according to their personal observations. They both have such a negative view of themselves – Helen cannot do anything correctly and Beth calls herself stupid. This mental negativity can most certainly affect the physical health of a person. If we are constantly down on ourselves, our bodies have nothing to be healthy for, do they?

Helen says that there is none who will miss her. This brings us back to when Helen believed that she was not doing anything to improve and only focusing on the negatives of who she was. She does not realize how much she brings into the world. How much light and life. She does not realize how much she has taught Jane and helped shaped who she will be as a grown woman.

We saw a glimpse of how intelligent and full of passion Helen is when she and Jane had tea with Miss Temple in the last chapter. God created Helen for a purpose, but it seems that nobody has been able, not even Miss Temple, to cultivate and encourage Helen in a greater path for her life.

"For we are his workmanship [of the works of God as creator], *created in Christ Jesus unto good works, which God hath before ordained* [to prepare before, to make ready beforehand] *that we should walk* [to live, deport oneself, follow] *in them."* Ephesians 2:10

"For I know the thoughts [plan, purpose] *that I think* [plan, imagine, regard, purpose] *toward you, saith the LORD, thoughts of peace* [soundness, welfare, health, prosperity, contentment, friendship], *and not of evil, to give you an*

expected [ground of hope, things hoped for, expectancy] *end* [length, reward, future, latter time]." Jeremiah 29:11

"Being confident [persuade, to believe, to trust, have confidence] *of this very thing, that he which hath begun a good* [pleasant, agreeable, joyful, excellent, honourable] *work in you will perform* [to bring to an end, accomplish, perfect, execute, complete] *it until the day of Jesus Christ."* Philippians 1:6

"'Where is God? What is God?' [Jane]

'My Maker and yours, who will never destroy what He created. I rely implicitly on His power, and confide wholly in His goodness: I count the hours till that eventful one arrives which shall restore me to Him, reveal Him to me.'" [Helen] – brackets added by me

Helen goes on to say that God is her father and her friend. I do not believe that Jane has ever been taught to view God in this way. Helen knows that God loves her and wants her to be with Him is heaven forever. This makes her unafraid of death.

I do believe that Jane grieved the loss of her friend. She never forgot the lessons that Helen taught her and the friendship she gave so freely.

<u>How Can You Apply This to Your Own Life?</u>

Have you been thinking about life in the way that Helen and Beth did? Do you believe that your purpose is not significant enough?

Toss that thought out!

God created each and every person with a purpose in this life. He created you to be a voice for truth and love. We cannot allow self-pity to drag us down into believing that we are ineffective and useless to God's kingdom here on earth. That is a lie. Remember, Satan is the ultimate accuser, and he will use lie after lie to get you to believe that you are useless.

Self-pity is not a sin, but it can lead to sin. Self-pity can lead to spirits of self-bitterness, self-accusation, self-idolatry, self-hate, and self-rejection. All these spirits are evil and tempt you into sinning against yourself, which ultimately leads to sinning against God. Harboring a hateful spirit toward yourself or even a bitter spirit toward yourself is a slap in God's face. He has called you perfect and beautiful and loved. Who are you to say otherwise? God is not a liar.

"Behold, what manner [what quality] *of love the Father hath bestowed* [to give] *up on us, that we should be called* [to be called by name, to bear a title] *the sons* [children, offspring] *of God: therefore the world knoweth* [be aware, understand] *us not, because it knew him not."* 1 John 3:1

"I will praise thee; for I am fearfully and wonderfully made [to be distinct, marked out, be separated, be distinguished, set apart]: *marvellous* [to be marvellous, be wonderful, be

surpassing, be extraordinary, separate by distinguishing action] *are thy works; and that my soul knoweth right well* [exceedingly, greatly]." Psalm 139:14

"The LORD thy God in the midst of thee [inward part, as seat of thought and emotion] *is mighty* [strong, brave]*; he will save* [defend, deliver, preserve, rescue, give victory to], *he will rejoice* [cheerful, be glad, joy, make mirth] *over thee with joy; he will rest* [hold peace, be silent, be still] *in his love, he will joy* [be joyful, rejoice, exult] *over thee with singing* [proclamation, rejoicing, triumph, joy]." Zephaniah 3:17

"The LORD hath appeared of old [from a distance, time, long ago] *unto me, saying, Yea, I have loved thee with an everlasting* [long duration, for ever, ever, evermore, perpetual, always, indefinite] *love: therefore with lovingkindness* [favour, merciful, mercy, faithfulness] *have I drawn thee* [forbear, give, lead]." Jeremiah 31:3

You are loved, cherished, and created with a purpose!

That purpose can be found in God's word and begins with your desire to seek it out. Start with small steps forward and eventually they will lead to bigger steps. God put dreams and desires in your heart for a reason, so pursue them with joy. When you feel stuck, pray that God will guide you and give you wisdom. The fruit of your effort will come, along with the blessing that God has promised as long as you continue to have faith.

Chapter X

The typhus fever made its way through the school, leaving devastation in its path. However, Jane recounts how the deaths of so many gained public notice which ended up changing the school for the better.

"Mr. Brocklehurst, who, from his wealth and family connections, could not be overlooked, still retained the post of treasurer; but he was aided in the discharge of his duties by gentlemen of rather more enlarged and sympathizing minds: his office of inspector, too, was shared by those who knew how to combine reason with strictness, comfort with economy, compassion with uprightness. The school, thus improved, became in time a truly useful and noble institution."

It is a shame that something this terrible should shift things for the better and gain public notice. It is also a shame that, even though Mr. Brocklehurst was so horrible to the girls in Lowood, he was still allowed a position on the board just because of his prominence in the community. Wealth and connections were all that was important. However, we can be comforted in the fact that nobler men were positioned in a higher power than he to help the school succeed and improve.

Though this may not be such a great consolation, we know that at least he was kept in check and the students thrived under the new management. In many ways, Mr. Brocklehurst had lost his power. He misused it and now is being punished for it.

"But whoso hath this world's good [that by which life is sustained, resources, wealth, goods], *and seeth his brother* [fellow man] *have need* [destitution, want], *and shutteth up* [withhold, to be devoid of pity] *his bowels* [inward affection, a heart in which mercy resides] *of compassion from him, how* [in what way] *dwelleth the love of God in him? My little children, let us not love in word* [saying, teaching], *neither in tongue* [speech]; *but in deed* [act] *and in truth."* 1 John 3:17-18

"There is [there are, he, thou] *that scattereth* [disperse, to scatter whether in enmity or bounty], *and yet* [still more] *increaseth* [to add, get more]; *and there is that withholdeth* [to restrain, hinder, hold back, refrain] *more than is meet* [right, upright, what is due], *but* [surely, truly] *it tendeth* [leads to] *to poverty. The liberal* [blessing, by implication prosperity] *soul shall be made fat* [anointed, satisfy]: *and he that watereth* [fill, satiate, abundantly satisfy] *shall be watered* [teach, direct, instruct] *also himself."* Proverbs 11:24-25

"The merciful [kindly, loving, merciful, pity] *man doeth good* [deal bountifully, reward, serve] *to his own soul: but he that is cruel troubleth* [to disturb or afflict] *his own flesh* [body]." Proverbs 11:17

Jane truly began to enjoy her time at the school. She excelled in her education and became a good teacher once her time as a student was over. Her relationship with Miss Temple blossomed into friendship and mentorship.

"Miss Temple, through all changes, had thus far continued superintendent of the seminary: to her instruction I owed the best part of my acquirements; her friendship and society had been my continual solace; she had stood me in the stead of mother, governess, and, latterly, companion."

Miss Temple helped Jane to reign in her emotions and become a settled and more peaceful person. She acted as a safety net to Jane and when she married, Jane was left feeling lost again taking "with her the serene atmosphere [Jane] had been breathing in her vicinity."

"He that walketh [be conversant, follow, live] *with wise men* [intelligent, skillful, wise-hearted] *shall be wise: but a companion* [keep company with, use as a friend, make friendship with] *of fools* [stupid, silly, arrogant one] *shall be destroyed* [to make or be good for nothing, afflict, do harm, do mischief, punish]." Proverbs 13:20

"Iron sharpeneth [be alert, be keen] *iron; so a man sharpeneth the countenance* [favour, presence, sight] *of his friend* [neighbor, brother]." Proverbs 27:17

Thus begins a new chapter in Jane's life. Up to this point, Lowood was safe, serene, and sure. With Miss Temple gone, Jane begins to contemplate the prospect of going out into the world "to seek real knowledge of life amidst its perils."

Since she was young, Jane longed for adventure and freedom! As a grown woman, she has become tired of the same place, the same routine, the same people. She wants more out of life than just Lowood and its four walls.

"I desired liberty; for liberty I gasped; for liberty I uttered a prayer; it seemed scattered on the wind then faintly blowing. I abandoned it and framed a humbler supplication: for change, stimulus. That petition, too, seemed swept off into vague space. 'Then,' I cried, half desperate, 'grant me at least a new servitude!'"

There is some doubt expressed during her soliloquizing that she may never experience true liberty, excitement, or enjoyment in life; a theme that will carry further into the book. However, despite it, and despite the fear she felt, Jane still has the courage to advertise for a new position in life.

Upon the unofficial entrance of Mrs. Fairfax into our story, Jane begins imagining what she looks like and what it would be like to live closer to London and a town with more life and excitement. Mrs. Reed relinquishes all authority over Jane's life, and she has given her leave to accept the position of governess at Thornfield Hall.

Her whole life is set before her. Preparations were made and Jane was ready to enter this new chapter of her life with excitement.

"I had brushed my black stuff travelling-dress, prepared my bonnet, gloves, and muff; sought in all my drawers to see that no article was left behind; and now having nothing more to do, I sat down and tried to rest. I could not; though I had been on foot all day, I could not now repose an instant; I was too much excited. A phase of my life was closing to-night, a new one opening to-morrow: impossible to slumber

in the interval; I must watch feverishly while the change was being accomplished."

We find now that Bessie has been married and has two children, one of which is named Jane. Jane's cousin Georgiana has grown into quite a beauty, Eliza is envious, John is useless in his trade, and Mrs. Reed is mentally uneasy. Such unhappiness in the lives of the Reeds is quite sad. There is no love to be seen in the description of each family member that Bessie shares.

Jane, although not considered a beauty by Bessie, is praised for her academic achievements. Though beautiful, the Reed girls could never match Jane's gentleness of spirit and artistic abilities. Her beauty shines from within and that is ultimately what draws people toward Jane throughout the book.

How Can You Apply This to Your Own Life?

"As a jewel [ring] *of gold in a swine's snout, so is a fair* [beautiful] *woman which is without discretion* [intelligence, judgement, reason, taste, behavior]." Proverbs 11:22

Jane's cousins have shown themselves to be such poor examples of inner beauty. They are beautiful on the outside and their accomplishments seem to be many according to the current times, however, their beauty is only skin deep. Envy, deceitfulness, pride, vanity, and bitterness ooze out of these young women.

On the other hand, Jane is no beauty and yet people are drawn to her because of her inner beauty, mannerisms, and intelligence. She has been surrounded by good people and has been taught how to control her temper while at Lowood.

Surrounding yourself with people who will bring out the best in you is vital. Having friends and family who are genuine in their love, faith, and joy will ultimately rub off onto you. If you are constantly surrounded by bitter, envious people, do you not think that you might end up representing those same feelings? This is why it is important that we stay in God's word. Our minds and hearts need cultivation in the fruits of the Spirit both in what we read or watch and who we are around, so that we know how to be that kind of person for others as well.

I pray that you find friends who will help you in your journey of overcoming and growing into the beautiful person God created you to be. Even if you have just one friend who represents God's love to you, that is going to bring blessing into your life. I also encourage you to *be* that one friend to someone who needs you.

"For we are his workmanship, created in Christ Jesus unto good works, which God hath before ordained that we should walk in them." Ephesians 2:10

Chapter XI

"A new chapter in a novel is something like a new scene in a play; and when I draw up the curtain this time, reader, you must fancy you see a room in the George Inn at Millcote…"

I wanted to take a moment to appreciate the beautiful writing that Charlotte Brontë presents at the opening of this chapter. It gives you a sense that you are there with Jane, embarking on her new journey and experiencing it by her side. This is the reason I love classic literature. Jane is now our friend and as she grows, we grow as well.

"It is a very strange sensation to inexperienced youth to feel itself quite alone in the world, cut adrift from every connection, uncertain whether the port to which it is bound can be reached, and prevented by many impediments from returning to that it has quitted. The charm of adventure sweetens that sensation, the glow of pride warms it; but then the throb of fear disturbs it; and fear with me became predominant when half an hour elapsed and still I was alone."

How many times have you begun something, whether it was starting a new job or just putting a dream into action, that felt so fresh and exciting but also carried with it a little fear? I feel that many of us have felt this in some form or other during our lives.

For me, being an entrepreneur and skipping college to save money in certifications instead was exciting, but also a little scary. Taking that big leap into the unknown brings a lot of different emotions with it.

God had a plan for Jane. He opened the door to her new career and life at Thornfield. She had no idea what to expect or what the people were like or even how she would fair in the job, and yet she took that first step toward this new adventure. Sometimes, changes can be scary. Most of us do not enjoy change, especially drastic change. However, we will never know what good that change can bring or how it can shape us into something far better unless we take that leap of faith.

Fear tries to keep us in our comfort zones, but faith allows us to break free.

"Peace [prosperity, rest, security] *I leave* [send forth] *with you, my peace I give unto you: not as the world giveth, give I unto you. Let not your heart be troubled* [of uncertain affinity, agitate]*, neither let it be afraid."* John 14:27

"Have not I commanded thee? Be strong and of good courage [steadfastly minded, fortify, strengthen, prevail, alert]*; be not afraid, neither be thou dismayed* [break down either by violence or confusion and fear, discourage, scare]*: for the LORD thy God is with thee whithersoever* [all, the whole, every, totality] *thou goest."* Joshua 1:9

"For God hath not given us the spirit of fear; but of power [ability, abundance, strength]*, and of love* [benevolence, brotherly love, affection]*, and of a sound mind* [self-control, discipline]*."* 2 Timothy 1:7

"'…I wonder if she [Mrs. Fairfax] lives alone except this little girl; if so, and if she is in any degree amiable, I shall surely be able to get on with her; I will do my best; it is a pity that doing one's best does not always answer. At Lowood, indeed, I took that resolution, kept it, and succeeded in pleasing; but with Mrs. Reed, I remember my best was always spurned with scorn. I pray God Mrs. Fairfax may not turn out a second Mrs. Reed; but if she does, I am not bound to stay with her: let the worst come to the worst, I can advertise again…'" – brackets added by me

Immediately upon entering Thornfield, and meeting Mrs. Fairfax, Jane is ushered into a peaceful, home-y, and welcoming environment. Jane is surprised at the welcome she receives from someone who she sees as her superior. Mrs. Fairfax immediately has Jane warm herself, eat, and tends to all the details that would be administered to an invited guest or cherished visitor.

"I felt rather confused at being the object of more attention than I had ever before received, and, that too, shown by my employer and superior; but as she did not herself seem to consider she was doing anything out of her place, I thought it better to take her civilities quietly."

We can already see the benefits and blessings of Jane taking the leap of faith in coming to Thornfield. Mrs. Fairfax is as much in need of companionship as Jane. Jane is always talking of being useful in the world and to the people around her. As we continue through this story, we will see how a deep friendship begins to blossom between these two ladies and how much they truly needed one another.

"The impulse of gratitude swelled my heart, and I knelt down at the bedside, and offered up thanks where thanks were due; not forgetting, ere I rose, to implore aid on my farther path, and the power of meriting the kindness which seemed so frankly offered me before it was earned. My couch had no thorns in it that night; my solitary room no fears. At once weary and content, I slept soon and soundly: when I awoke it was broad day."

It is in times of great tribulation that we usually seek out God for answers and aid. However, we often forget that He is also the bearer of blessings and prosperity. Jane is aware of this and prays in gratitude.

"I thought that a fairer era of life was beginning for me, one that was to have its flowers and pleasures, as well as its thorns and toils."

Jane is now hopeful that she is on the precipice of positive change in her life. That this new life that she has entered into will bring her the pleasantness that she has always yearned for and possibly people who will love and accept her for who she is.

The only wish she may still have in her heart is that she was more beautiful. Like any young woman, Jane desires to be pretty and admired. However, she reconciles her plain looks and accepts that though she may not be conventionally beautiful, at least she can be useful, orderly, and kind.

One of Jane's greatest joys is the ability to read books. In Thornfield, Jane has access to more books than she has probably ever had access to in her life. Adèle, her student, is vain but loving and respectful, which Jane is pleased with. At least she will not be a naughty, disrespectful student.

Mrs. Fairfax takes Jane on a tour of her new, beautiful home, keeping the master of the house shrouded in mystery. She learns that he is never home, but in expectation of his unannounced arrivals, Mrs. Fairfax maintains a clean and tidy mansion. As Jane tries to ascertain what type of man this Mr. Rochester is, she learns that he is well-liked, a bit sarcastic but fair, adventurous, and very clever.

"Mr. Rochester was Mr. Rochester in her eyes; a gentleman, a landed proprietor – nothing more: she inquired and searched no further, and evidently wondered at my wish to gain a more definite notion of his identity."

Mr. Rochester's travels seem to display themselves in his home as furnishings, embroideries, vases, and other decorative pieces which leave Jane in awe of the splendor of this vast house.

As the mystery of this story deepens, I believe that Jane becomes more interested in the goings on of this great mansion. In just one chapter, we can see the bright and beautiful parts of Jane's new life emerging and yet, this shroud of mystery adds a deeper level of intrigue to our story.

How Can You Apply This to Your Own Life?

Jane took a huge leap of faith. Leaving a place she knew so well and that was comfortable for her. However, the routines became monotonous, and she desired to see what else lay before her in the world.

Change is a scary thing. Stepping outside of your comfort zone can be scary. But, if we do not take that first step outside of it, our growth can become hindered. Just as with bones and muscle, our spiritual health requires stimulation and conditioning to become strong and resilient. Experiencing life is so important. Being around others, getting involved in your community, or just searching out little experiences in your day-to-day can help with this growth.

"The LORD is on my side; I will not fear: what can man do unto me?" Psalm 118:6

"Fear thou not; for I am with thee: be not dismayed [bewildered, to look away, gaze about in anxiety]; *for I am thy God: I will strengthen thee* [steadfastly minded, courageous, fortify, increase]; *yea, I will help thee* [aid, uphold]; *yea, I will uphold thee* [follow close, to help, maintain, hold up] *with the right hand* [as the stronger and more dexterous] *of my righteousness* [prosperity, justice]." Isaiah 41:10

God is with you, every step you take. He helps guide and direct your path if you put your trust in Him. We are called to not fear because He goes before us to create a path for us.

"And the LORD, he it is that doth go before thee; he will be with thee, he will not fail thee, neither forsake thee: fear not, neither be dismayed." Deuteronomy 31:8

What does your comfort zone look like?

What are some small steps that you could take outside that comfort zone?

Write down a few, some small and some big, that will challenge your comfort level. The key is to take that first small step and then you can eventually begin taking bigger leaps as you fully rely on God's guidance. Fear will be at the door to try and convince you that it is a bad idea. But you know what to do with fear. Tell fear to go away in Jesus' name!

I have often struggled with taking steps outside of my comfort zone. It is a daily decision I have to make for myself. But the more I stay within my comfortable borders, the more discontented I feel. I, like Jane, require stimulation.

Staying in your comfort zone is safe but imagine all the adventures you could have if you just took that small step toward change. Fill your heart with the Word of God and He will give you direction and peace.

Chapter XII

Jane is settling into her comfortable new career with very comfortable people. Adèle becomes very fond of Jane right away and they share a special attachment to one another, though perhaps not a deep adoration or love toward each other.

I believe that Jane has become a little guarded and is unable to freely express love at this stage in her life. At the same time, Jane understands the professionalism that must exist between her and Adèle.

"This, par parenthèse, will be thought cool language by persons who entertain solemn doctrines about the angelic nature of children, and the duty of those charged with their education to conceive for them an idolatrous devotion. But I am not writing to flatter parental egotism, to echo cant, or to prop up humbug; I am merely telling the truth. I felt a conscientious solicitude for Adèle's welfare and progress, and a quiet liking for her little self; just as I cherished towards Mrs. Fairfax a thankfulness for her kindness, and a pleasure in her society proportionate to the tranquil regard she had for me, and the moderation of her mind and character."

Part of this detachment could be from past relationship experiences. Jane's relationships with people either never really lasted very long or they were very abusive. Nevertheless, she is there to teach Adèle, not be her best friend. This can best be done when there is a natural differentiation between them.

All the comfort now present in Jane's life has made her antsy for something new and exciting. She is not good at being still and quiet and serene. It has never really been her nature. Jane is grateful and is doing her job well and with efficiency, but there still seems to be something missing.

"I valued what was good in Mrs. Fairfax, and what was good in Adèle; but I believed in the existence of other and more vivid kinds of goodness, and what I believed in I wished to behold."

Jane has tasted adventure and has experienced stepping outside of her comfort zone and now craves more. She wants to see people of all types and experience the wide-open spaces she has only read about in books. Discontentment begins to set in, which is something she wishes was not so.

"It is in vain to say human beings ought to be satisfied with tranquillity: they must have action; and they will make it if they cannot find it. Millions are condemned to a stiller doom than mine, and millions are in silent revolt against their lot. Nobody knows how many rebellions besides political rebellions ferment in the masses of life which people earth. Women are supposed to be very calm generally: but women feel just as men feel; they need exercise for their faculties, and a field for the efforts, as much as their brothers do; they suffer from too rigid a restraint, too absolute a stagnation, precisely as men would suffer; and it is narrow-minded in their more privileged fellow-creatures to say that they ought

to confine themselves to making puddings and knitting stockings, to playing on the piano and embroidering bags. It is thoughtless to condemn them, or laugh at them, if they seek to do more or learn more than custom has pronounced necessary for their sex."

A Short Study of Feminism & God's Role for Men and Women

We get a hint of Charlotte Brontë's views on feminism in this short little paragraph. Before the feminist movement we know of today began, writers such as Charlotte and her sisters began writing novels with viewpoints that supported the feminist agenda and the suffering of women under the patriarchy. In fact, Jane Eyre is often touted as being a feminist novel through and through. In addition to this information, theorists have written papers and theses on the similarity between Jane Eyre and more blatantly feministic novels such as The Handmaid's Tale (*written in 1985*). Though I cannot disagree with the similarities, I do disagree that Jane Eyre is a purely feminist novel.

This is a debate I would rather not get into in great detail. However, I do believe a few points should be made on the subject before moving forward.

First of all, Jane requires stimulation of mind and body. She loves to learn, which is something we picked up on in her personality when she was very young. She loves being challenged. Rather than condemning the entirety of men, she simply states that women desire activity and stimulation of mind as much as they. This is not wholly feministic as it is simply stating fact. We are all human and were all created to desire to grow and learn and be something in this world.

Second, part of the feministic agenda itself causes division between women and men. It effectually tears men down in order to lift up women. What is Satan's greatest desire? To create division and hateful thoughts and feelings toward one another. It is never necessary to bring one down to draw attention to another's value.

> *"Now I beseech* [to call near, implore, desire, exhort] *you, brethren, mark* [regard, take heed] *them which cause* [band together, commit, perform] *divisions* [disunion, dissention] *and offences* [snare, stumbling block, cause of displeasure or sin] *contrary to the doctrine which ye have learned; and avoid them. For they that are such* [to denote character or individuality] *serve not our Lord Jesus Christ, but their own belly* [selves, heart]; *and by good words* [smooth and plausible address which simulates goodness] *and fair speeches* [fine discourse, polished language, language artfully adapted to captivate the hearer] *deceive* [to seduce wholly] *the hearts of the simple* [unsuspecting, harmless, free from guilt, innocent]." Romans 16:17-18

> *"For God is not the author of confusion* [instability, disorder, commotion, tumult], *but of peace* [prosperity, one, peace, quietness, set at one again], *as in all churches of the saints."*
> 1 Corinthians 14:33

Those who were against Christ and His teachings divided themselves against those who followed Him. Who takes an opposite stand against Christ and the Father? Satan. Which is why we cannot be divided in our own selves and our general beliefs, and therefore, fall into the enemy's hands. Communicating our differences is an opportunity for understanding and unity, not division.

"Now the works of the flesh [carnally minded] *are manifest, which are these; adultery, fornication* [homosexuality, lesbianism, intercourse with animals, intercourse with close relatives, eating sacrifices to idols], *uncleanness* [lustfulness, of impure motives], *lasciviousness* [unbridled lust, shamelessness, insolence, wantonness], *idolatry* [worship of false gods], *witchcraft* [poisoning, sorcery, use or the administering of drugs, magic], *hatred, variance* [contention, strife, debate, variance], *emulations* [envious and contentious rivalry, jealousy, indignation], *wrath* [anger, passion, heat, fierceness, indignation], *strife* [contention], *seditions* [dissension, division], *heresies* [disunion], *envyings, murders, drunkenness, revellings* [rioting], *and such like: of the which I tell you before, as I have also told you in time past, that they which do such things shall not inherit the kingdom of God."* Galatians 5:19-21*

The whole history behind the feminist agenda encourages many of the above; not readily apparent at first glance but upon digging deeper, you will fall down a rabbit hole. Often, women do not look to where the source of this agenda began and blindly embrace it as a movement to raise women up to where they belong in society. There is so much pain that women have endured over the centuries as a result of sinful men and so much bitterness can come out of that. But bitterness is unforgiveness and that unforgiveness can be a poison against men and women themselves. We are to forgive and be united to our brethren, using the tools of love and forgiveness that our Heavenly Father has provided for us. If we are forgiven, how much more then shall we forgive?

I highly encourage, if this is a topic that you are interested in, that you read the book, *The Way Home: Beyond Feminism, Back to Reality* by *Mary Pride*. It is a very interesting book that outlines exactly what feminism is and why is goes against the Bible. The idolatry in feminism says that women are to celebrate their inner goddess. This "inner goddess" blinds us and divides us from God and His love for us.

We are going to shift gears now.

What is godly order?

"But I would have you know, that the head [chief, prominent] *of every man is Christ; and the head of the woman is the man; and the head of Christ is God."* 1 Corinthians 11:3

"For the man is not of [from, out of] *the woman; but the woman of the man. Neither was the man created for the woman; but the woman for the man. For this cause* [reason] *ought the woman to have power* [competency, freedom, mastery, delegated influence, jurisdiction, strength, power] *on her head because of the angels. Nevertheless neither is the man without* [separate, apart] *the woman, neither the woman without the man, in the Lord. For as the woman is of the man, even so is the man also by* [because of] *the woman; but all things of God."* 1 Corinthians 11:8-12

"And the LORD God said, it is not good that the man should be alone; I will make him an help meet [aid, counterpart] *for him."* Genesis 2:18

Help meet here is defined as someone who is a helper to Adam (*man*) that is worthy and equal to him. A partner who is complimentary, supports, encourages, and communicates well with him. The other definition is counterpart. This shows that the woman not only makes the man complete but balances him out. Femininity balances masculinity and brings peace. Whether you are right-handed or left-handed, you are always going to have a dominant hand, however, both of your hands work together.

We can then respect what God has designed men to be. They are not meant to be women and vice versa. We balance each other out; men and women. When contentment in who we are and who we were created to be is embraced, we do not crave or desire to be like men. Men and women work hard individually but when their gifts and talents are combined, the benefits are many.

All these verses support a beautiful balance between man and woman and why both are so integral to the furthering of God's kingdom. We cannot have one without the other. Yes, man and woman can live well on their own, however, they are more powerful together.

"For as the body is one, and hath many members, and all the members of that one body, being many, are one body: so also is Christ. For by one Spirit are all baptized into one body, whether we be Jews or Gentiles, whether we be bond [slave, under subjection, subserviency] *or free; and have*

been all made to drink [to imbue] *into one Spirit.*" 1
Corinthians 12:12-13

*"And he answered and said unto them, Have ye not read,
that he which made them at the beginning made them male
and female, and said, For this cause* [because, by reason of]
shall a man leave father and mother, and shall cleave [to
glue to, figuratively to adhere, join oneself closely] *to his
wife: and they twain* [two] *shall be one flesh* [being, body]*?
Wherefore they are not more twain, but one flesh. What
therefore God hath joined together, let not man put asunder*
[to place room between, separate]*."* Matthew 19:4-6

But women are not just asked to submit to their husbands
without reward. Men are called to love their wives as Christ
loved the church and gave himself for it. *"...He that loveth
his wife loveth himself. For no man ever yet hated his own
flesh; but nourisheth it and cherisheth it, even as the Lord
the church..."* Women who are loved and cherished will give
love and cherishing in return. Again, there must be a
balance. You can read the whole verse in Ephesians 5:22-33.

With the godly order in place, women can now take on their
roles in the home and wherever they are called to serve.
They are not just to be there to look at and admire. Women
have a great and important role. Just look at Proverbs 31:10-
31. It these verses, we learn that this woman is more
valuable than rubies and she is trusted and loved by her
husband. She does not stir up strife or contention. She works
with her hands, creating clothing for her family, grows and
buys good food, rises early to supply her household with
food to start their day, strengthens her body with physical

labor and even has a business on the side. The Proverbs 31 woman provides her family with warm clothing that is not torn or tattered, serves her community, brings honor upon her husband, speaks wisdom and kindness, is never idle, and teaches her daughters the same. This is truly a woman of honor.

One thing that we need to understand about this woman, is that she did not have to strive. Women do not have to be everything all the time and that is something a lot of us struggle with. Even though there is a lot that the Proverbs 31 woman does daily, that does not mean that she never took time for herself to be at peace. We are also called to be at peace and to search the scriptures, so I guarantee that she had some down-time to spend with God. But we also have to remember that you cannot pour from an empty cup. We must take time to replenish what we have given away.

Feminists contend that godly women are weak and submissive to men. Far from it! God created women to be strong, capable, wise human beings. I highly recommend reading the stories of some of the greatest women of the Bible – Ruth (*the book of Ruth*), Mary Magdalene (*Matthew 27 & 28, Mark 15 & 16, Luke 8 & 24, John 19 & 20*), Hannah (*1 Samuel 1 & 2*), Deborah (*Judges 4 & 5*), Esther (*the book of Esther*), Miriam (*Exodus 15:20-21*), Elizabeth (*Luke 1*), Priscilla (*Acts 18*), Rahab (*Joshua 2:1-3, Joshua 6, Hebrews 11:31, James 2:25*), and many more.

Returning to our story, we are introduced to the mysterious Mr. Rochester.

"He had a dark face, with stern features and a heavy brow; his eyes and gathered eyebrows looked ireful and thwarted just now; he was past youth, but had not reached middle-age; perhaps he might be thirty-five. I felt no fear of him, and but little shyness."

We get a pretty good picture of what Mr. Rochester looks like and why he is such a perfect addition to the mystery that surrounds Thornfield. Had he been more handsome, younger, or perhaps more amiable, our story would probably end up being as monotonous as Jane's life seems to be at this moment. Little does Jane realize that her life is about to gain the spark of adventure she craves, that will change the serenity of her position and home.

"The incident had occurred and was gone for me: it was an incident of no moment, no romance, no interest in a sense; yet it marked with change one single hour of a monotonous life. My help had been needed and claimed; I had given it: I was pleased to have done something; trivial, transitory though the deed was, it was yet an active thing, and I was weary of an existence all passive."

Jane needs stimulation. She needs to be around a variety of people. I feel that most, if not all of us have been in this situation before. A certain place or situation feels lonely, stagnant, or empty. Mr. Rochester represents a change. Whether that change is for the better or not is for the reader to decide as the story progresses. I, personally, believe that this change is for the better. That through knowing Mr. Rochester, Jane grows even more depth to her character. But we will not jump ahead too much.

"I did not like re-entering Thornfield. To pass its threshold was to return to stagnation; to cross the silent hall, to ascend the darksome staircase, to seek my own lonely little room, and then to meet tranquil Mrs. Fairfax, and spend the long winter evening with her, and her only, was to quell wholly the faint excitement wakened by my walk – to slip again over my faculties the viewless fetters of an uniform and too still existence; of an existence whose very privileges of security and ease I was becoming incapable of appreciating."

How Can You Apply This to Your Own Life?

Have you felt, or do you currently feel stuck? Discontented with where your life is headed or where it is currently? There are some who feel perfectly and serenely happy with regular routines, the same types of people, and the same places. It gives them comfort and security. However, there are others, like Jane, who desire more in life than routine and a constant state of serenity. They desire adventure and stimulation, meeting new people, and learning new things. Both are valid.

Discontentment is a tricky thing. Like self-pity, discontentment can crop up in your life and feed envy and jealousy, bitterness, and anger. We have already seen what self-pity can lead to in Helen's example in chapter nine. More than that, discontentment is the enemy's way of drawing you further from God's promise that He can bring contentment.

How content we are in our lives and who we are depends on what we believe. Do you have faith that God is working in your life and that He knows exactly where you need to be in this moment?

As we will learn, Jane is exactly where she needs to be at this time of her life. And though discontentment looms before her, she will soon learn that adventure is right around the corner.

Being discontented, like self-pity, does not become a sin until you begin grumbling, envying, or even falling into unbelief. This is the reason why it must be checked and left at the door.

What are you discontented in today?

Is your discontentment coming from something that you can or cannot control?

If you are able to control the situation, change it. Why would you continue to live in a place of discontent and misery if you know exactly how you can make the change toward joy? Stop comparing yourself and your journey with that of others. Be in thanks for the blessings and provisions that God *has* brought into your life. Pray that God will help you and give you the wisdom you need to take that first step toward change.

"Comparison is the thief of joy" – Theodore Roosevelt

"For we dare not make ourselves of the number [count among], *or compare ourselves with some that commend* [to exhibit, approve, to show] *themselves: but they measuring*

[to judge according to any rule or standard] *themselves by themselves, and comparing* [to judge of one thing in connection with another] *themselves among themselves, are not wise."* 2 Corinthians 10:12

*Themselves in this context includes a special translation: [own conceits, own selves]

"But godliness [holiness, reverence] *with contentment* [sufficiency, competence] *is great* [exceedingly, mighty] *gain."* 1 Timothy 6:6

If you are unable to control your situation, trust God that He knows how you feel and where you need to be. Study the word and really search to understand God's desire for you and your identity in Him. Be in prayer, talking to your Father about everything that is weighing on your heart. Be honest with Him. And finally, release that control to Him, trusting in His sovereignty.

"Thou wilt keep [protect, to guard, maintain] *him in perfect peace* [complete, prosperity, great, rest, happy, safe], *whose mind is stayed* [establish, hold, stand fast, sustain] *on thee: because he trusteth in thee. Trust ye in the LORD for ever: for in the LORD JEHOVAH* [the proper name for the one true God] *is everlasting* [eternity, eternal, perpetual, world without end] *strength:"* Isaiah 26:3-4

"Humble yourselves therefore under the mighty hand of God, that he may exalt [raise up, lift up on high] *you in due time: casting all your care* [anxiety] *upon him; for he careth for you."* 1 Peter 5:6-7

Chapter XIII

"I discerned in the course of the morning that Thornfield Hall was a changed place: no longer silent as a church, it echoed every hour or two to a knock at the door, or a clang of the bell; steps, too, often traversed the hall, and new voices spoke in different keys below. A rill from the outer world was flowing through it. It had a master; for my part, I liked it better."

And just like that, the world in which Jane lives has undergone a significant change for the better. Her life is no longer quiet and plain but filled with noises and voices and intrigue. The master of the house carries quite a bit of mystery with him which I believe interests Jane greatly as well as us, the readers.

I remember the first time reading Jane Eyre, how exciting it was for me to experience everything along with Jane. So, if this is your first time, I hope you are as excited and intrigued as I was at this moment in the story.

In case you would appreciate a translation of Adèle's monologue:

"And this must mean that there will be a gift for me inside, and perhaps for you too, mademoiselle. Monsieur speaks of you: he asked me the name of my governess, and if she was not a small person, quite thin and a little pale. I said yes: for it is true, is it not, mademoiselle?"

I always try and make a point of keeping a translator of sorts by me when a different language is presented in a book I am reading. It provides more meaning to the story. If you do not understand French and decided not to translate this monologue, you would have missed a very funny representation of Adèle's prattling.

Returning to the story, Jane officially meets Mr. Rochester. She can now perceive more of his personality, being within his own home and surrounded by personal comforts.

"Half reclined on a couch appeared Mr. Rochester…The fire shone full on his face. I knew my traveler, with his broad and jetty eyebrows; his square forehead, made squarer by the horizontal sweep of his black hair. I recognized his decisive nose, more remarkable for character than beauty; his full nostrils, denoting, I thought, choler; his grim mouth, chin, and jaw — yes, all three were very grim, and no mistake. His shape, now divested of cloak, I perceived harmonized in squareness with his physiognomy: I suppose it was a good figure in the athletic sense of the term — broad-chested and thin-flanked, though neither tall nor graceful."

<u>Choler</u>: irascibility, anger, wrath, irritability. The description that Jane gives his nose gives us a perfect picture of what he might look like as well as what could be lying below the surface.

His rough manners are continually apparent, and he doesn't show any grace of character. This type of man would make most women of this time rather irritated and indifferent, but for Jane, his manners produced a small amount of comfort.

She has never truly been treated well by men in her past, so she is used to disgruntled behaviors and terseness. Though he is, by no means, treating her poorly.

"I sat down quite disembarrassed. A reception of finished politeness would probably have confused me: I could not have returned or repaid it by answering grace and elegance on my part; but harsh caprice laid me under no obligation; on the contrary, a decent quiescence, under the freak of manner, gave me the advantage. Besides, the eccentricity of the proceeding was piquant: I felt interested to see how he would go on."

<u>Piquant</u>: agreeably stimulating, interesting, attractive, of lively character.

Perhaps without fully realizing it, Mr. Rochester gives Jane one of the highest compliments toward her cultivation of Adèle. He is impressed by how she has tempered Adèle in certain ways and given her the beginnings of a well-rounded education.

The back and forth between Jane and Mr. Rochester is amusing and I believe is a test to see how well-matched Jane's wit is to his. He wants to discover her character for himself. Her replies are ready and intelligent.

As bored and intellectually unchallenged as Jane has felt the past few years of her life, I believe Mr. Rochester feels the same in his own life. He is surrounded by interesting people but likely none of them fully understand or are comfortable with his temper and personality. Now, finally, he is in the presence of a person who is intrigued by his lack of manners and is quite possibly as capable as he is at verbal and intellectual sparing.

This is also the first mention that Providence brought Jane to Thornfield Hall. From the beginning of this story, we have discussed how God is working in Jane's life. Despite all the hurt and the scars of the past, Jane is still strong in who she is and what she believes and that intrigues others. As we continue to read about her time at Thornfield, God will continue to work in the lives of those around her because she chooses to have faith and follow the path that led her here.

"'I disliked Mr. Brocklehurst; and I was not alone in the feeling. He is a harsh man; at once pompous and meddling; he cut off our hair; and for economy's sake bought us bad needles and thread, with which we could hardly sew…He starved us when he had the sole superintendence of the provision department, before the committee was appointed; and he bored us with long lectures once a week, and with evening readings from books of his own inditing, about sudden deaths and judgements, which made us afraid to go to bed.'"

Mr. Rochester learns more of Jane's past and now intrigue is on both sides. He is curious about Jane's depth of character. All of which is revealed a bit more through her curious pieces of art.

"'Not quite: you have secured the shadow of your thought; but no more, probably. You had not enough of the artist's skill and science to give it full being: yet the drawings are, for a schoolgirl, peculiar. As to the thoughts, they are elfish.

These eyes in the Evening Star you must have seen in a dream. How could you make them look so clear, and yet not at all brilliant? for the planet about quells their rays. And what meaning is that in their solemn depth? And who taught you to paint wind? There is a high gale in that sky, and on this hill-top. Where did you see Latmos? For that is Latmos. There — put the drawings away!'"

Abruptly, Jane is dismissed to take Adèle to bed.

"'You said Mr. Rochester was not strikingly peculiar, Mrs. Fairfax,' I observed, when I rejoined her in her room, after putting Adèle to bed.

'Well, is he?'

'I think so: he is very changeful and abrupt.'

'True: no doubt he may appear so to a stranger, but I am so accustomed to his manner, I never think of it; and then, if he has peculiarities of temper, allowance should be made.'

'Why?'

'Partly because it is his nature — and we can none of us help our nature; and partly because he has painful thoughts, no doubt, to harass him, and make his spirits unequal.'"

Here we receive a small glimpse into Mr. Rochester's family history. His father loved money and his brother conspired with his father to lead Rochester into a "painful position" to make his own fortune to protect the name of Rochester. His history fascinates Jane and produces a desire to know more about the man in whose house she now resides.

His history will continue to reveal itself as Jane breaks through the barrier of hurt and anger. Mr. Rochester plays such a crucial part in our story of forgiveness, humility, and love. Though Mrs. Fairfax says that none of us can change our nature, we will see how untrue this really is. Mr. Rochester chooses to change as Jane shows him what it is like to be loved. None of us are stuck in who we are as we are constantly being renewed in Christ.

How Can You Apply This to Your Own Life?

People are not always as they seem. This has been a constant theme throughout the book. We can see the surface of who they are based on how they act and how they treat others. However, there is often an underlying reason why they are acting the way they are. It is usually due to anger, bitterness, sadness, or hurt that leads to unforgiveness. As we will see with Mr. Rochester, there is a deep underlying need to be loved for who he is; to be understood, to be forgiven, and to *forgive*.

I do believe that he wants to come to a place of reconciliation and forgiveness over how he was treated by his father and brother. We may not see that in this moment or get a deeper picture of this need quite yet, but as we delve deeper into his history, we begin to see that Mr. Rochester wants, more than anything, to just be loved and to love others. When we hold onto unforgiveness and bitterness, it can eat away at us. He has been so for such a long time that love and understanding are the only things that can bring him back to a place of rest and peacefulness.

Jane is an excellent person to gently teach him how to receive love and acceptance from others. She is continually working through the forgiveness of Mrs. Reed and others that have hurt her in the past. However, because Jane had a mentor in both Helen and Miss Temple, who understood God's word and His love, she can move forward with more understanding.

This is why Jane is such a blessing in Mr. Rochester's life. Neither of them realizes this quite yet, but Mrs. Fairfax is firm in her opinion that Jane was brought to Thornfield by God and for a reason. Jane will begin to realize this as she continues to spend more time with Mr. Rochester and Mrs. Fairfax. For so long, Jane has wanted adventure and stimulation and yet here she is placed.

Jane's spiritual journey may not always be apparent to even herself, but we can see the effects that it has on those around her. Her quiet demeaner and desire to go deeper in life allow her to teach well and with kindness.

We, just as Jesus's disciples, are called to share the scriptures with others and to walk in the spirit of God, making us "fishers of men". Walking in the Spirit can be both intentional and unintentional. When we are so engrossed by God and His word and love, we cannot help but live it out every day.

"And he saith unto them, Follow me, and I will make you fishers of men." Matthew 4:19

"I am the vine [support], *ye are the branches: He that abideth* [continue, dwell, remain, stand fast] *in me, and I in*

him, the same bringeth forth much fruit: for without me ye can do nothing." John 15:5

"*If we live in the Spirit, let us also walk in the Spirit.*" Galatians 5:25

"*And he said unto them, Go ye into all the world, and preach* [proclaim, publish] *the gospel to every creature.*" Mark 16:15

We can also be prepared to be used as a catalyst for God's love in another's life and journey, just as He is using Jane in Mr. Rochester's. Knowing God's love and understanding it fully, allows us to be love to everyone, everywhere because it will shine from the inside out. Jane might not be preaching the scriptures, but she is setting aside any judgement of Mr. Rochester's character and simply *being* who she is; a humble, loving, quiet spirit.

"*Charity suffereth long* [patient]*, and is kind; charity envieth not; charity vaunteth not* [to boast] *itself, is not puffed up* [proud]*, doth not behave itself unseemly, seeketh not her own, is not easily provoked* [irritated]*, thinketh no evil; rejoiceth not in iniquity, but rejoiceth in the truth; beareth* [bear up against] *all things, believeth* [entrust, conviction] *all things, hopeth all things, endureth* [fortitude, persevere] *all things. Charity never faileth* [become inefficient]*: but whether there be prophecies, they shall fail; whether there be tongues* [languages]*, they shall cease; whether there be knowledge* [science]*, it shall vanish away* [made void]." 1 Corinthians 13:4-8

"I [Paul] *therefore, the prisoner of the Lord* [bound to the Lord]*, beseech* [exhort, intreat] *you that ye walk worthy of the vocation* [calling, of the divine invitation to embrace salvation of God] *wherewith ye are called, with all lowliness* [humility, modesty] *and meekness* [gentleness, humility]*, with longsuffering* [patience, endurance, fortitude]*, forbearing* [endure, bear with] *one another in love; endeavouring* [diligent, study, make effort] *to keep* [to guard, to maintain, hold fast] *the unity of the Spirit in the bond of peace* [prosperity, quietness, rest]*. There is one body, and one Spirit, even as ye are called in one hope* [expectation, confidence] *of your calling; one Lord, on faith, one baptism, one God and Father of all, who is above all, and through all, and in you all. But unto every one of us is given grace*[1] *according to the measure of the gift of Christ."* Ephesians 4:1-7

Always remember, that whenever doubt creeps in, know that God is by your side. Like with Moses, He will be there to inspire the right words for the people you speak to. All you have to do is be willing to be the vessel. You were created for "a good work" and He will continue to cultivate that work in you until the day of Jesus' return. Have hope in that for yourself.

"Now therefore go, and I will be with thy mouth [speech, mind, word]*, and teach thee* [instruct, direct] *what thou shalt say* [pronounce, utter, answer, declare]*."* Exodus 4:12

"Being confident of this very thing, that he which hath begun a good work in you will perform it until the day of Jesus Christ." Philippians 1:6

Footnotes

¹ Grace based on the interlinear, Greek text (G5485 – charis χάρις) – of the merciful kindness by which God, exerting his holy influence upon souls, turns them to Christ, keeps, strengthens, increases them in Christian faith, knowledge, affection, and kindles them to the exercise of the Christian virtues.

Chapter XIV

"...all my acquaintance with him [Mr. Rochester] was confined to an occasional rencontre in the hall, on the stairs, or in the gallery, when he would sometimes pass me haughtily and coldly, just acknowledging my presence by a distant nod or a cool glance, and sometimes bow and smile with gentlemanlike affability. His changes of mood did not offend me, because I saw that I had nothing to do with their alternation; the ebb and flow depended on causes quite disconnected with me." – brackets added by me

This is an excellent example of not taking things too personally. Other people's moods and irritability do not always have anything whatsoever to do with you. Mr. Rochester, we know, has a lot of past hurts as well as present business that both likely take a toll on his energy and patience. Jane knew she did not play any part in the moods with which Mr. Rochester greeted her.

The next few paragraphs from the book play such a crucial part in the story that I almost copied the entire chapter out. Jane and Mr. Rochester have their first real, deep conversation which opens yet another window into Mr. Rochester's life.

"'Don't draw that chair farther off, Miss Eyre; sit down exactly where I placed it – if you please, that is. Confound these civilities! I continually forget them. Nor do I particularly affect simple-minded old ladies. By-the-bye, I

must have mine in mind; it won't do to neglect her; she is a Fairfax, or wed to one; and blood is said to be thicker than water.'"

We can see that, like Jane, Mr. Rochester desires more social and mental stimulation in conversations. However, though he does not appreciate the conversation that Mrs. Fairfax can offer, he does not forget her. He is trying to be civil and respectful, which shows a somewhat teachable spirit, capable of growth under the tenderness of Jane's personality.

"Mr. Rochester, as he sat in his damask-covered chair, looked different to what I had seen him look before; not quite so stern — much less gloomy. There was a smile on his lips, and his eyes sparkled, whether with wine or not, I am not sure; but I think it very probable. He was, is short, in his after-dinner mood; more expanded and genial, and also more self-indulgent than the frigid and rigid temper of the morning; still he looked preciously grim, cushioning his massive head against the swelling back of chair, and receiving the light of the fire on his granite-hewn features, and in his great, dark eyes; for he had great, dark eyes, and very fine eyes, too — not without a certain change in their depths sometimes, which, if it was not softness, reminded you, at least, of that feeling."

The observations Jane makes throughout the book are probably my favorite parts. She notices details such as the fact that Mr. Rochester's eyes held a softness. This softness, which I believe he had kept hidden for a very long time but felt comfortable, in the presence of Jane, in letting down some of the barriers that kept that secret hidden. He notices her studying him and asks if she finds him handsome. Here, we can see that Mr. Rochester is a bit vain in asking Jane this direct question.

"I am sure most people would have thought him an ugly man; yet there was so much unconscious pride in his port; so much ease in his demeanour; such a look of complete indifference to his own external appearance; so haughty a reliance on the power of other qualities, intrinsic or adventitious, to atone for the lack of mere personal attractiveness, that, in looking at him, one inevitably shared the indifference, and, even in a blind, imperfect sense, put faith in the confidence."

As much as he puzzles Jane, Jane puzzles him. She intrigues him as well and he desires to learn more about who she is. She is a match for his wits and temper and does not give in to his whims but challenges them gently. This silent challenging calls him to accountability for his behavior and words. He does not wish to treat her as an inferior being but as an equal, as much as possible providing what the large age difference and life experience can allow.

"'I don't think, sir, that you have a right to command me, merely because you are older than I, or because you have seen more of the world than I have; your claim to superiority depends on the use you have made of your time and experience.'"

This is where women see the feministic influences. Jane understands her place in the Thornfield household. She accepts her place there, respects the position of Mr. Rochester, but does not allow him to bully her. He commands her to speak and entertain him. However, he said that he desired to treat her as an equal and she holds him to this.

"'I have plenty of faults of my own: I know it, and I don't wish to palliate them, I assure you. God wot I need not be too severe about others; I have a past existence, a series of deeds, a colour of life to contemplate within my own breast, which might well call my sneers and censures from my neighbours to myself. I started, or rather (for, like other defaulters, I like to lay half the blame on ill fortune and adverse circumstances) was thrust on to a wrong tack at the age of one-and-twenty, and have never recovered the right course since: but I might have been very different; I might have been as good as you – wiser – almost as stainless. I envy you your peace of mind, your clean conscience, your unpolluted memory. Little girl, a memory without blot or contamination must be an exquisite treasure – an inexhaustible source of pure refreshment: is it not?'"

Mr. Rochester's pain is showing through in his speech.

"'Do you wonder that I avow this to you? Know, that in the course of your future life you will often find yourself elected the involuntary confidant of your acquaintances' secrets: people will instinctively find out, as I have done, that it is not your forte to tell of yourself, but to listen while other talk of themselves; they will feel, too, that you listen with no malevolent scorn of their indiscretion, but with a kind of innate sympathy; not the less comforting and encouraging because it is very unobtrusive in its manifestations.'"

One of Jane's greatest gifts is to listen without malice. She desires to understand Mr. Rochester and his life, but she never judges him based on his past. She does, however, call him, whether with words or not, to a sense of discernment and accountability about how he acts in the present and the choices he makes now.

"'I wish I had stood firm – God knows I do! Dread remorse when you are tempted to err, Miss Eyre; remorse is the poison of life.'

'Repentance is said to be its cure, sir.'

'It is not its cure. Reformation may be its cure; and I could reform – I have strength yet for that – if – but where is the use of thinking of it, hampered, burdened, cursed as I am? Besides, since happiness is irrevocably denied me, I have a right to get pleasure out of life: and I will get it, cost what it may.'

'Then you will degenerate still more, sir.'

'Possibly: yet why should I, if I can get sweet, fresh pleasure? And I may get it as sweet and fresh as the wild honey the bee gatherers on the moor.'

'It will sting – it will taste bitter, sir.'

'How do you know? – you never tried it. How very serious – how very solemn you look: and you are as ignorant of the matter as this cameo head' (taking one from the mantelpiece). 'You have no right to preach to me, you

neophyte, that have not passed the porch of life, and are absolutely unacquainted with its mysteries.'

'I only remind you of your own words, sir: you said error brought remorse, and you pronounced remorse the poison of existence.'

'And who talks of error now? I scarcely think the notion that flittered across my brain was an error. I believe it was an inspiration rather than a temptation: it was very genial, very soothing – I know that. Here it comes again! It is no devil, I assure you; of it if be, it has put on the robes of an angel of light. I think I must admit so fair a guest when it asks entrance to my heart.'

'Distrust it, sir; it is not a true angel.'

'Once more, how do you know? By what instinct do you pretend to distinguish between a fallen seraph of the abyss and a messenger from the eternal throne – between a guide and a seducer?'

'I judged by your countenance, sir, which was troubled when you said the suggestion had returned upon you. I feel sure it will work you more misery if you listen to it.'"

This conversation brings up a very fascinating and complicated topic, and that is the fact that evil spirits do masquerade as angels of light. It is very interesting that Jane almost inherently knows this as she warns Mr. Rochester that the angel of light that he is referring to is a false angel calling him into temptation. But it is also interesting that he even mentions that it could not be a devil because it is so soothing and friendly.

Light and darkness are used consistently throughout the Bible to differentiate between good and evil. However, because Satan is the father of lies and deceitfulness, he and his army of evil spirits use light to trick us into believing that they are from God. He is a master of deception, which is why we are constantly warned to be vigilant.

"Be sober [collected], *be vigilant* [watchful]; *because your adversary* [archenemy] *the devil* [false accuser, slanderer], *as a roaring lion, walketh about, seeking whom he may devour* [to gulp entirely, literally or figuratively drown, devour, swallow up]:" 1 Peter 5:8

"For such are false apostles [one who falsely claims to be an ambassador of Christ], *deceitful workers* [teacher], *transforming themselves* [transfigure, disguise] *into the apostles* [messenger, he that is sent] *of Christ. And no marvel* [surprise]; *for Satan himself* [the same] *is transformed into an angel* [messenger, to bring tidings] *of light* [1]. *Therefore it is no great thing if his ministers* [attendant, servant] *also be transformed as the ministers of righteousness; whose end shall be according to their works."* 2 Corinthians 11:13-15

"Beloved, believe not every spirit [angel, demon, the disposition or influence which fills and governs the soul of any one], *but try* [discern, examine, test] *the spirits whether they are of God: because many false prophets* [a spurious prophet, pretended foreteller or religious imposter] *are gone out* [spread abroad] *into the world."* 1 John 4:1

Jesus Christ is the only light of the world. The only bearer of the light of truth and hope.

"Then spake Jesus again unto them, saying, I am the light of the world: he that followeth me shall not walk in darkness [obscurity, ignorance], *but shall have the light of life."* John 8:12

Satan, before being cast out of heaven, was known as the "light-bearer, shining one, and morning star."[2] He was also cast out of heaven with a third of all angels which serve him continually.

"And no marvel; for Satan himself is transformed into an angel of light." 1 Corinthians 11:14

"How art thou fallen from heaven, O Lucifer, son of the morning! How art thou cut down to the ground, which didst weaken the nations!" Isaiah 14:12

"And he said unto them, I beheld [to be a spectator, look on] *Satan as lightning fall from heaven. Behold, I give unto you power* [mastery, authority, strength] *to tread on serpents* [figuratively – as a type of sly cunning, an artful malicious person, especially Satan] *and scorpions, and over all the power of the enemy: and nothing shall by any means hurt you. Notwithstanding* [save that, nevertheless] *in this rejoice not, that the spirits are subject* [subdue unto] *unto you; but rather rejoice, because your names are written in heaven."* Luke 10:18-20

"And there was war in heaven: Michael [archangel] *and his angels fought against the dragon* [a great serpent, Satan]*; and the dragon fought and his angels, and prevailed* [be of

strength, have force] *not; neither was their place* [position] *found any more in heaven. And the great dragon was cast out* [to throw with violence or intensity], *that old* [original] *serpent, called the Devil, and Satan, which deceiveth the whole world: he was cast out into the earth, and his angels were cast out with him."* Revelation 12:7-9

You see, Satan's goal is for us to fall into temptation and then sin so that we can be separated from God and His desires for us. However, we know, if we read God's word and meditate on it, we then have the knowledge to discern between this false light and the true light of Christ. This discernment comes from the Holy Spirit.

"Thy word [commandment, provision, promise] *is a lamp* [light – figuratively or literally] *unto my feet* [a step, journey], *and a light* [luminary – in every sense, including lightning, happiness, clear] *unto my path. I have sworn* [take an oath], *and I will perform* [accomplish, continue, stand, uphold] *it, that I will keep* [guard, protect, preserve, regard] *thy righteous judgments. I am afflicted* [to oppress, humble, be bowed down] *very much: quicken me* [revive, preserve, nourish up, restore, repair], *O LORD, according unto thy word."* Psalm 119:105-107

When we despair or find ourselves frustrated with God, that is when Satan has the perfect opportunity to slither into our hearts and minds, disguising himself and offering a light that gives us false peace. Without discernment, we, like the Israelites in Isaiah, fall into darkness without even realizing it. The light will fade, and the truth of bondage will then be revealed for what it is because we have then searched for light and hope outside of God's word and promise.

"To the law [instruction, teaching] *and to the testimony: if they speak* [answer, challenge, charge, declare, talk] *not according to this word* [on these conditions, as follows], *it is because there is no light* [dawn – literally or figuratively or adverbial, morning] *in them. And they shall pass through it, hardly bestead* [to be dense, tough or severe, fiercer, be cruel, make grievous] *and hungry: and it shall come to pass* [accomplished], *that when they shall be hungry* [suffer to, famish], *they shall fret themselves* [burst out in rage, be angry, displease, provoke to wrath], *and curse* [bring into contempt, despise, revile] *their king and their God, and look* [turn – aside, away, back, face, self] *upward. And they shall look* [regard with pleasure, favor, or care, look intently, have respect] *unto the earth; and behold trouble* [adversity, anguish, distress, tribulation] *and darkness* [misery], *dimness of anguish* [distress, pressure]*; and they shall be driven* [literally and figuratively – to expel, mislead, strike, inflict; banish, draw away, withdraw] *to darkness* [misfortune, wickedness]*."* Isaiah 8:20-22

God is the author of peace and light in the world. He is the one who can bring us out of darkness and give us the knowledge and discernment we need to resist the devil and his spirits.

"Every good gift and every perfect gift is from above [of things which come from heaven or God], *and cometh down from the Father of lights, with whom is no variableness*

[transmutation, fickleness], *neither shadow of turning [variation]."* James 1:17

"This then is the message [promise] *which we have heard of him, and declare unto you, that God is light, and in him is no darkness at all. If we say that we have fellowship* [participation, social intercourse, communion] *with him, and walk* [to live, deport oneself, be occupied with] *in darkness, we lie, and do* [agree, bear, bring forth, fulfil] *not the truth: but if we walk in the light, as he is in the light, we have fellowship one with another, and the blood of Jesus Christ his Son cleanseth* [purify] *us from all sin."* 1 John 1:5-7

"But ye are a chosen [favorite, elect, select by implication] *generation* [nation, offspring], *a royal* [kingly] *priesthood, an holy* [sacred – physically, pure, morally blameless or religious, consecrated] *nation* [people], *a peculiar* [far exceeding, continual] *people; that ye should shew forth* [publish, celebrate] *the praises* [excellence] *of him who hath called you out of darkness into his marvelous light:"* 1 Peter 2:9

"For God, who commanded the light to shine out of darkness, hath shined [radiate brilliancy, give light] *in our hearts, to give the light* [illumination, enlightening] *of knowledge of the glory* [honor, praise, worship] *of God in the face* [countenance, appearance, presence] *of Jesus Christ."* 2 Corinthians 4:6

How Can You Apply This to Your Own Life?

We are called to keep each other accountable for our actions and words as disciples of Christ. This is why being in fellowship with believers is so important to our spiritual growth.

> *"For where two or three are gathered together in my name, there am I in the midst of them."* Matthew 18:20

Accountability among believers should be done in love, without scorn or gossiping. We are all on a journey of growth and being kindly held accountable for our actions, thoughts, and words is an act of love. When Christ returns, we will all be accountable for those actions, thoughts, and words.

There will be times when holding yourself accountable just is not enough and this is where the body of Christ is to be of benefit. If you are surrounding yourself with trustworthy believers, there should be no fear in accountability. Accountability should come from God's Word, so when correction comes, the source must come from God. You can be a part of a Bible study, a church, or just have one good friend in which there is true and faithful accountability taking place. It should feel safe and in continuity with how God thinks. He is your counselor and your Father, spurring you on toward growth and peace, so be teachable. We all have so much to learn, and we are each other's teachers as we work through the truths that are given to us in His Word.

> *"Brethren, if a man be overtaken in a fault* [offense, sin, error or willful transgression], *ye which are spiritual*

[spiritually minded, of God the Holy Spirit, filled with the
Spirit of God], *restore* [repair, mend, perfectly join together]
such an one in the spirit [vital principle, mental disposition]
of meekness [gentleness, humility]; *considering* [look on]
thyself, lest thou also be tempted. Bear ye [endure, declare,
sustain, carry] *one another's burdens, and so fulfil the law of
Christ."* Galatians 6:1-2

"Confess [acknowledge, profess] *your faults one to another,
and pray one for another, that ye may be healed* [made
whole]. *The effectual fervent* [be mighty in, put forth power,
show oneself operative] *prayer of a righteous man* [holy,
innocent, acceptable to God] *availeth* [can do, be good, be of
strength, be whole, prevail] *much* [abundant, be of a great
deal, plenteous]." James 5:16

"Brethren, if any of you do err [roam from safety, truth, or
virtue, go astray, deceive, seduce, wander] *from the truth,
and one convert* [turn about again] *him; let him know, that
he which converteth the sinner from the error of his way
shall save a soul from death, and shall hide a multitude of
sins."* James 5:19-20

"Put on therefore, as the elect [favorite, chosen] *of God, holy*
[consecrated, morally blameless, pure] *and beloved* [to love
dearly], *bowels* [pity or sympathy, inward affection, tender
mercy] *of mercies* [compassion], *kindness* [gentleness,
goodness, excellence in character or demeanor], *humbleness
of mind* [modesty, humility], *meekness* [gentleness,
humility], *longsuffering* [forbearance, fortitude, patience];
forbearing [to hold oneself up against, endure] *one another,
and forgiving* [gratuitously, in kindness, pardon or rescue,

freely give, deliver] *one another, if any man have a quarrel* [complaint] *against any: even as Christ forgave you, so also do ye. And above all these things put on charity* [love, affection or benevolence, dear love], *which is the bond of perfectness* [completeness]. *And let the peace* [quietness, prosperity, rest] *of God rule* [govern] *in your hearts, to the which also ye are called in one body; and be ye thankful. Let the word of Christ dwell* [inhabit] *in you richly* [abundantly] *in all wisdom; teaching and admonishing* [to caution or reprove gently, warn] *one another in psalms and hymns and spiritual songs, singing with grace* [the divine influence upon the heart and its reflection in the life, acceptable, gift, pleasure] *in your hearts to the Lord. And whatsoever ye do in word* [utterance, speech] *or deed* [an act, doing, labour, work], *do all in the name of the Lord Jesus, giving thanks to God and the Father by* [in, by reason of] *him."* Colossians 3:12-17

Others are sometimes better able to see parts of us that we might not. Weaknesses that we, ourselves, might not even perceive but a brother or sister in Christ might. Therefore, a close accountability partner is such a wonderful asset.

Though he might not like it, Mr. Rochester is receiving a call to accountability for his thoughts and words from Jane. We might not like being called out for things in the moment, but in the end, if it is done in love, it aids in our spiritual growth as believers. Even asking simple questions such as "Have you been spending time in God's word lately?" or "Have you read any good Bible verses today?" can be a call to accountability.

There should be no shame, no gossiping, and no malice in being held accountable. Proper accountability should make us want to spend *more* time in prayer and in God's word, not less. It should make us want to seek a godlier path for our lives.

Accountability also does not mean harsh judgement. God is the ultimate judge over our lives and the lives of others. However, we are called to judge[3] rightly (*Leviticus 19:15, Deuteronomy 1:16, 1 Kings 3:9, 2 Chronicles 19:6*) as a fellow believer, helping them to a place where they might come to repentance. It is encouragement to help them on their faith journey.

Judgement from humans feels like condemnation but accountability is a correction of direction. When condemnation is used between believers, it grows rejection, guilt, and shame rather than restoration and opens doors to what the enemy can use in that believer's life. Love your brethren and never use this path. We are all working toward sanctification (*the act of making something holy; the action or process of being freed from sin or purified; the action of causing something to be or seem morally right or acceptable*) and perfecting ourselves in Christ, and part of that is allowing space for others to make the decision to repent or not and move on in our own journey.

Be vigilant, always seeking God's word for the truth. Satan's ultimate goal for you (*and me*) is to bring you into eternal torment with him and his fallen angels. But God's ultimate goal for you is to bring you into a love of the truth, peacefulness, faith, and eternal life with Him.

Footnotes

[1] Light based on the interlinear, Greek text (G5457 – phōs φῶς) – luminousness (in the widest application, natural or artificial, abstract or concrete, literal or figurative).

[2] Lucifer based on the interlinear, Hebrew text (H1966 – hêlēl הֵילֵל) – in the sense of brightness, the morning-star; Lucifer, shining one, "light-bearer."

[3] Judge based on the interlinear Hebrew text (H8199 - šāpaṭ שָׁפַט) – to pronounce sentence (for or against); by implication, to vindicate or punish; by extension, to govern; passively, to litigate, avenge, that condemn, contend, defend, execute (judgement), plead, reason, rule. **There are a few different translations for the word "judge" and "judgement" that I encourage you to look at further in the Strong's Concordance and King James Bible.**

Chapter XV

Are you ready to get an even clearer picture as to who Mr. Rochester is?

I hope that through this book, so far, you have remained open-minded and open-hearted to him, allowing him to grow and learn right alongside us. Just as Jane has the opportunity to grow, we must also offer Mr. Rochester that same opportunity. Allowing fictional characters to do so helps us practice for when we come across people in our lives who require these same opportunities. Everyone deserves to show us who they really are rather than what we see on the surface.

We open this chapter with him detailing Adèle's entrance into his life. You can tell that Mr. Rochester is angry at himself for falling into the traps that he did as a younger man; falling for a woman that did not love him or care for him, out of lust.

"'You never felt jealousy, did you, Miss Eyre? Of course not; I need not ask you' because you never felt low. You have both sentiments yet to experience: your soul sleep; the shock is yet to be given which shall waken it. You think all existence lapses in as quiet a flow as that in which your youth has hitherto slid away. Floating on with closed eyes and muffled ears, you neither see the rocks bristling not fat off in the bed of the flood, nor hear the breakers boil at their base. But I tell you – and you may mark my words – you

will come some day to a craggy pass in the channel, where the whole of life's stream will be broken up into whirl and tumult, foam and noise: either you will be dashed to atoms on crag points, or lifted up and borne on by some master-wave into calmer current – as I am now.'"

"Envy and Jealousy will take your eyes God and put your eyes on others."[1] When contentment is not present, envy and jealousy can make their way into our hearts making us insecure, doubtful, and bitter about our futures. They draw the focus off ourselves and our own faith journeys and onto others'.

"But godliness with contentment [sufficiency] *is great gain."*
1 Timothy 6:6

Envy refers to the emotion that comes from wanting what someone else has, for yourself. "Envy and jealousy will make *others* your source of value and fulfillment when that source should be God."[2] It makes you feel inferior, spiteful, and often leads to hate. Comparison causes covetousness and bitterness that creates a divide between you and the person you are envious of.

Envy and jealousy can coexist, which is why they are often confused, and both are never satisfied.

In Mr. Rochester's case, he was afraid of losing the object of his affection to a better-looking, younger man.

Envy and jealousy also open the door to self-pity. Why am I not as successful? Why do I feel more stuck than so-and-so? Why am I not as strong spiritually as so-and-so when I have been doing the same things? Why are more people drawn to so-and-so than me?

It is a really sticky and sneaky trap that is so incredibly easy to fall into. Something as simple as working hard your whole life for a promotion but seeing it go to someone who just joined the company can open the door to envy and jealousy.

We all know that Satan is a master deceiver and that his one goal in life is to separate us from our Heavenly Father and the fellowship of others. These traps are easy to fall into, but it does not mean that we have to stay there or that we cannot resist when temptation comes. That is the beauty of God's grace and mercy, providing us a way out. We will talk about this some more at the end of this chapter.

"Some hated thought seemed to have him in its grip, and to hold him so tightly that he could not advance.

We were ascending the avenue when he thus paused; the hall was before us. Lifting his eye to its battlements, he cast over them a glare such as I never saw before or since. Pain, shame, ire, impatience, disgust, detestation, seemed momentarily to hold a quivering conflict in the large pupil dilating under his ebon eyebrow. Wild was the wrestle which should be paramount; but another feeling rose and triumphed: something hard and cynical: self-willed and resolute: it settled his passion and petrified his countenance: he went on — "

Mr. Rochester struggles with so many feelings of unhappiness and hopelessness. He seems to be disgusted with the choices he has made and the life he has so far led. I believe that Jane not only brings out the good in him that he wishes he could be more of, but she somehow also makes him realize that there is a possibility for change. She gives him hope.

> "*Hope deferred* [to remove, to prolong, to delay, forbear] *maketh the heart sick* [afflicted, infirmity, be grieved, become weak]*: but when the desire* [a longing, a delight, satisfaction] *cometh, it is a tree of life.*" Proverbs 13:12

"'...I will keep my word; I will break obstacles to happiness, to goodness – yes, goodness. I wish to be a better man than I have been, than I am; as Job's leviathan broke the spear, the dart, and the habergeon, hindrances which others count as iron and brass, I will esteem but straw and rotten wood.'"

He desires more than anything to be a better man. He desires that his hope in life return. This small glimpse into his past reveals only a small portion of his internal struggle against what he believes is his nature. He truly believes that it is in his nature to be all of these things that he abhors, and that goodness is too far away from his reach. But we know from previous study that our identity is founded on something much more precious and lasting; Jesus Christ and God the Father.

"'When I saw my charmer thus come in accompanied by a cavalier, I seemed to hear a hiss, and the green snake of jealousy, rising on undulating coils from the moonlit balcony, glided within my waistcoat, and ate its way in two minutes to my heart's core.'"

Is not this an interesting and very visual depiction of what envy and jealousy does to a person? It is always shown in artistic renderings and described by authors as being a green snake that wraps itself around you and hisses in your ear the thoughts it wants you to hear. This is how deceptive envy and jealousy can be.

Serpent in the Strong's Concordance is defined as a type of sly cunning, an artful malicious person, especially Satan.[3]

"'…you, with your gravity, considerateness, and caution were made to be the recipient of secrets. Besides, I know what sort of a mind I have placed in communication with my own: I know it is one not liable to take infection: it is a peculiar mind: it is a unique one. Happily I do not mean to harm it: but, if I did, it would not take harm from me. The more you and I converse, the better; for while I cannot blight you, you may refresh me.'"

Mr. Rochester feels comfortable and safe with Jane. He knows that she is strong and capable of listening to even the darkest parts of his past without judgement. Jane has proven herself trustworthy and full of mercy and understanding. This patience and kindness are much to be desired of many. Which is why Jane is the perfect confidant of Mr. Rochester's. In being able to share his past with her, he is better able to move forward and come to a place of forgiveness of himself.

Even though Jane knows the history behind why Adèle was left in the care of Mr. Rochester, she chooses to love and accept Adèle despite her lurid past. Jane chooses to be a friend to her as if she were an orphan, appreciating her positive merits while not dwelling on those that are superficial or stupid. She is sad that Adèle is not only rejected by her mother, but also by Mr. Rochester as well, just as Jane was rejected by her own family members. This is why I believe Jane and Adèle share a deeper kinship than teacher and student.

"The confidence he had thought fit to repose in me seemed as tribute to my discretion: I regarded and accepted it as such. His deportment had now for some weeks been more uniform towards me than at the first. Never seemed in his way; he did not take fits of chilling hauteur: when he met me unexpectedly, the encounter seemed welcome; he had always a word and sometimes a smile for me: when summoned by formal invitation to his presence, I was honoured by a cordiality of reception that made me feel I really possessed the power to amuse him, and that these evening conferences were sought as much for his pleasure as for my benefit."

Now Jane feels needed. We all want to be needed to bring pleasure, love, or companionship into people's lives. The recipients of this feel loved for who we are in spite of past faults. Not only did Mr. Rochester need Jane, but she also needed him. They mutually benefit from their regular conversations; Mr. Rochester in having a confidant and Jane in using her desire to love and be of use to others.

"I felt at times as if he were my relation rather than my master: yet he was imperious sometimes still, but I did not mind that; I saw it was his way. So happy, so gratified did I become with this new interest added to life, that I ceased to

pine after kindred: my thin-crescent destiny seemed to enlarge; the blanks of existence were filled up; my bodily health improved; I gathered flesh and strength.

And was Mr. Rochester now ugly in my eyes? No, reader: gratitude, and many associations, all pleasurable and genial, made his face the object I best liked to see; his presence in a room was more cheering than the brightest fire. Yet I had not forgotten his faults; indeed, I could not, for he brought them frequently before me. He was proud, sardonic, harsh to inferiority of every description: in my secret soul I knew that his great kindness to me was balanced by unjust severity to many others. He was moody, too; unaccountably so; I more than once, when sent for to read to him, found him sitting in his library alone, with his head bent on his folded arms; and, when he looked up, a morose, almost a malignant, scowl blackened his features. But I believed that his moodiness, his harshness, and his former faults of morality (I say former, for now he seemed corrected of them) had their source in some cruel cross of fate. I believed he was naturally a man of better tendencies, higher principles, and purer tastes than such as circumstances had developed, education instilled, or destiny encouraged. I thought there were excellent materials in him; though for the present they hung together somewhat spoiled and tangled. I cannot deny that I grieved for his grief, whatever that was, and would have given much to assuage it."

All Jane needed up to this point was a friend. She needed someone to accept her and love her the way she was without judgment. To be seen for who we are is a great gift we give to another. Jane patiently allows Mr. Rochester to reveal his personality and who he wants to be, separating that from his past actions. Mr. Rochester became her family. They were there for one another and understood each other. She saw the best in him, even though she knew his past was tainted. We can now see that both were, perhaps without knowing it themselves at present, beginning to love one another despite their errors, past hurts, and secrets.

As the chapter continues to develop, the mystery of Thornfield continues to unfold as Jane finds Mr. Rochester asleep amid a fire in his room and bed. There is something very dark and sinister at work in this large home. Something that desires to destroy Mr. Rochester and all he holds dear.

As the chapter closes, the first note of deep affection between Mr. Rochester and Jane surfaces briefly. This is our first real glimpse into the beginnings of their love story.

As we have been reading through their growing friendship, we can see that their relationship is purely based on mutual respect. No other person in their lives has ever tried to dig deeper to understand the depth of character that each possesses. Out of this mutual respect, the need to be loved for who they are, and fondness for education and adventure, they begin to realize a love that never existed in their lives before.

<u>How Can You Apply This to Your Own Life?</u>

Envy and jealousy can lead to bitterness when we continue to dwell on other's successes and attributes. When we focus too much on their successes, we are blinded to our own journey and then bitterness can come out of, "well, why do I not have that if I have worked just as hard?" Or "they do not deserve that because they have not been faithful enough to deserve it. I have seen their sinfulness come out. I have been faithful and yet I do not have that."

"Envy and Jealousy will not allow you to be content. Envy and Jealousy will not allow you to be at peace. Envy and Jealousy will prevent you from godliness, and without godliness you are not going to have any peace whatsoever."[4]

Can you see how sneaky Satan is? We allow something so simple, so small, to corrupt our thoughts slowly so as to go almost undetected at first. And then those small thoughts can grow, if not tended to, into something much bigger and more corrupt, which finally leads to division and strife.

This little serpent of envy and jealousy does, figuratively, as Mr. Rochester described it, eat away to your heart's core until it has taken over completely, and your thoughts are focused on nothing but the envy and jealousy you feel.

"A sound [deliverance, healing, wholesome, health] *heart is the life* [maintenance, merry, living] *of the flesh: but envy the rottenness* [decay] *of the bones."* Proverbs 14:30

This is why we see so much division in the church. This is why we have so many who do not have their own identity. They adopt the identity of another so that they can be as successful or have more perceived purpose in the world. "If I just follow exactly what this person does, I will have the same successes, be as rich, and be as happy."

For this reason, I have always seen books, blogs, and articles written on celebrities or successful business people's routines and how to make them *your* routine, as being harmful. Just because it works for someone else, does not mean that it will be what is right for *you*. You cannot force yourself to be something you are not. Take what you can from a practical standpoint but leave a large margin for your own unique creativity to shape your life and strategies.

It is all about identity! Where is your identity placed? Do you have to turn to TV shows, personality quizzes, star signs, or enneagrams to find your identity? Or are you finding your identity in who God created you to be; unique and beautiful on your own?

So much in our world can get in the way of us finding our true identity in God. There are so many who are watching too much television, adopting the personality traits of their favorite characters, living in a fictional world of fantasy and romance novels to the point of not being satisfied with reality, isolation, surrounding themselves with companions who inspire rebellion, discontent, and ungodly behaviors. These people do not understand what God's purpose for them is. They have lost the knowledge of who they are. This confusion in their identity causes a rejection of themselves; especially if they are not taught well by proper leadership and through godly examples.

Finding your identity in God and His word is key to recognizing when envy and jealousy come to tempt you.

God's word is constantly showing us that we have an identity in Christ that is so much better than anything we could ever imagine.

"Being confident [trust, assure] *of this very thing, that he which hath begun a good work in you will perform it until the day of Jesus Christ."* Philippians 1:6

"According as he hath chosen [choose out] *us in him before the foundation of the world, that we should be holy* [sacred, consecrated] *and without blame* [blemish, fault, spot] *before him in love: having predestinated us unto the adoption* [sonship in respect to God, children of God] *of children by Jesus Christ to himself, according to the good pleasure* [satisfaction, wish, delight, desire] *of his will, to the praise of the glory of his grace* [favour, gift, liberality, divine influence upon the heart], *wherein he hath made us accepted* [indue with special honor, be highly favored] *in the beloved."* Ephesians 1:4-6

Accepting yourself and not running to the next personality quiz or adhering to star signs and enneagrams for your identity can only come from a solid understanding of who you were created to be as God's son or daughter. Deeply beloved and chosen.

Even personality quizzes that are meant to be fun can create a toxic chain reaction of questioning, "but I thought I was more like this." Because even though they might be labelled as fun, they begin the process of questioning your identity, creating cracks in your foundation.

Discovering your identity must first start with a proper understanding of God's word. Having accountability or mentorship with people you trust and who are godly examples is also important for growth. If you ever have questions about who you are and why you are here on earth, the verses below should help you understand yourself and your purpose better, as well as God's deep and abiding love for you.

"So God created man in his own image, in the image of God created he him; male and female created he them." Genesis 1:27

"Before I formed thee [to mold into a form, especially as a potter] *in the belly* [womb] *I knew thee; and before thou camest forth out of the womb I sanctified* [make clean, appoint, dedicate, prepare] *thee, and I ordained* [used with greatest latitude of application, bestow, deliver up, direct, etc.] *thee a prophet* [inspired man] *unto the nations."* Jeremiah 1:5

A potter intentionally forms their creation with details and a purpose in which it will be used. Likewise, God has created us with a purpose and in His image.

"But now, O LORD, thou art our father; we are the clay, and thou our potter; and we all are the work of thy hand." Isaiah 64:8

"For I know the thoughts [purpose, intention] *that I think* [regard, value, consider, esteem] *toward you, saith the LORD, thoughts of peace* [prosperity, good health], *and not of evil* [affliction, adversity, calamity, grief, misery,

wretchedness], *to give you an expected* [hope, thing that I long for] *end* [the future, reward]." Jeremiah 29:11

"For we are his workmanship, created in Christ Jesus unto good works [deed], *which God hath before ordained* [to fit up in advance, prepare afore] *that we should walk* [deport oneself, be occupied with] *in them."* Ephesians 2:10

"Ye have not chosen me, but I have chosen you, and ordained you, that ye should go and bring forth fruit [that which originates or comes from something, an effect, result], *and that your fruit should remain* [dwell, endure, abide]: *that whatsoever ye shall ask of the Father in my name, he may give it you."* John 15:16

"Behold [to discern clearly] *he fowls of the air: for they sow* [spread seed] *not, neither do they reap* [harvest crop], *nor gather into barns; yet your heavenly Father feedeth them. Are ye not much better* [be of more value, excellent] *than they?"* Matthew 6:26

Footnotes

[1] Envy & Jealousy by Dr. Henry Wright page 1

[2] Envy & Jealousy by Dr. Henry Wright page 2

[3] Serpent based on the interlinear, Greek text (G3789 – ophis ὄφις) – serpent is through the idea of sharpness of vision, a snake, figuratively, as a type of sly cunning, an artful malicious person, especially Satan [can also be found in the Bible as Hebrew text (H5175 – nāḥāš נָחָשׁ) – serpent, snake]

[4] Envy & Jealousy by Dr. Henry Wright page 14

Chapter XVI

In the aftermath of such a frightening ordeal the night before, Jane is confused when she meets Grace Poole in Mr. Rochester's room, preparing new hangings for his bed. Why would the master of the house keep a woman on staff who presumably tried to murder him in his bed?

I suspect, if this is your first time reading Jane Eyre, that you did not expect such a dark and sinister mystery to surround this story. Especially since we are turning it into devotional material. But life is never perfect, and the mystery adds to our observation of Jane and Mr. Rochester, both their pasts and their present. It is also quite exciting to accompany Jane as she unravels the secrets that surround Thornfield Hall.

"…I occupied in puzzling my brains over the enigmatical character of Grace Poole, and still more in pondering the problem of her position at Thornfield and questioning why she had not been given into custody that morning, or, at the very least, dismissed from her master's service. He had almost as much as declared his conviction of her criminality last night: what mysterious cause withheld him from accusing her? Why had he enjoined me, too, to secrecy? It was strange: a bold, vindictive, and haughty gentleman seemed somehow in the power of one of meanest of his dependents; so much in her power, that even when she lifted her hand against his life, he dared not openly charge her with the attempt, much less punish her for it."

Our imaginations can run away with us sometimes; Jane's seems to be doing this right now as she imagines a story in which Grace Poole and Mr. Rochester had a past romance that she now uses to manipulate him into doing anything she desires. Of course, this is only effects of imagination and nothing else.

Translation of Adèle's observation:

"What have you got, mademoiselle? Your fingers tremble like the leaf, and your cheeks are red: but, red like cherries."

Jane's thoughts begin to wander to Mr. Rochester and this new-found discovery of the closeness in their relationship. Unfortunately, we see that Jane does not think very highly of herself. She believes that if Mr. Rochester, a great, wealthy man of the world could (*in her imagination, let us not forget*) fall for a woman so far under him and unattractive as Grace Poole, then it is possible that she, plain, unbeautiful Jane, could have a chance at winning Mr. Rochester's heart.

"I hastened to drive from my mind the hateful notion I had been conceiving respecting Grace Poole: it disgusted me. I compared myself with her, and found we were different. Bessie Leaven had said I was quite a lady; and she spoke truth — I was a lady. And now I looked much better than I did when Bessie saw me; I had more colour and more flesh, more life, more vivacity, because I had brighter hopes and keener enjoyments."

Little does Mr. Rochester know how much he is sorely missed. Jane wishes above all else to discuss the mysterious affair of the night before with him. To press him for details and gain a better understanding of the situation.

"It little mattered whether my curiosity irritated him; I knew the pleasure of vexing and soothing him by turns; it was one I chiefly delighted in, and a sure instinct always prevented me from going too far; beyond the verge of provocation I never ventured; on the extreme brink I liked well to try my skill. Retaining every minute form of respect, every propriety of my station, I could still meet him in argument without fear or uneasy restraint; this suited both him and me."

Much to Jane's disappointment, she finds that Mr. Rochester has gone and will not likely be back for some time. I believe that this is the first hint of envy and jealousy that Jane has ever experienced. When Mrs. Fairfax describes Blanche Ingram, the first pang hits Jane as deftly as it did Mr. Rochester.

> *"But I tell you — and you may mark my words — you will come some day to a craggy pass in the channel, where the whole of life's stream will be broken up into whirl and tumult, foam and noise: either you will be dashed to atoms on crag points, or lifted up and borne on by some master-wave into calmer current — as I am now." Chapter 15*

This speech made by Mr. Rochester in the previous chapter has much more meaning now. Jane looks envy and jealousy in the face. Does she respond by mastering it and moving on, or does she give in and allow the bite of envy and jealousy to eat away at her heart?

"'Tall, fine bust, sloping shoulders; long, graceful neck: olive complexion, dark and clear; noble features; eyes rather like Mr. Rochester's, large and black, and as brilliant as her jewels. And then she had such a fine head of hair, raven-black, and so becomingly arranged; a crown of thick plaits behind, and in front the longest, the glossiest curls I ever saw.'"

Not only is Blanche beautiful, but she is also very accomplished and supposedly held in high admiration by Mr. Rochester. The cherry on top is that she is yet unmarried. This opens the door of comparison. Envy has taken its hold.

"That a greater fool than Jane Eyre had never breathed the breath of life; that a more fantastic idiot had never surfeited herself on sweet lies, and swallowed poison as if it were nectar.

'You,' I said, 'a favourite with Mr. Rochester? You gifted with the power of pleasing him? You of importance to him in any way? Go! Your folly sickens me. And you have derived pleasure from occasional tokens of preference — equivocal tokens shown by a gentleman of family and a man of the world to a dependent and a novice. How dared you? Poor stupid dupe! — Could not even self-interest make you wiser? You repeated to yourself this morning the brief scene of last night? Cover your face and be ashamed! He said something in praise of your eyes, did he? Blind puppy! Open their bleared lids and look on your own accursed senselessness! It

does good to no woman to be flattered by her superior, who cannot possibly intend to marry her; and it is madness in all women to let a secret love kindle within them, which, if unreturned and unknown, must devour the life that feeds it; and, if discovered and responded to, must lead, ignis-fatuus-like, into miry wilds whence there is no extrication.'"

This whole passage reeks of self-loathing, self-pity, and such sadness. We know that all Jane desires in this world is to love and be loved. Mr. Rochester has given her the opportunity for both. And yet here Jane is, rejecting the truth and allowing envy and jealousy to take her into the depths of bitterness and questioning the beautiful identity that she has discovered for herself.

As further punishment to herself, she sits and draws herself with chalk, softening no line, giving no grace to her features. Her view of herself is so poor and belittling. She sees no beauty and no purpose. Then she draws Blanche, as imagined, with the highest quality materials and in the most beautiful respect that she can imagine.

Remember how disgusted she was at herself earlier on comparing herself to Grace Poole? And yet, here she is yet again, comparing herself to another. Yet this time, she is comparing herself to someone of accomplishment, famed beauty, and wealth. How is this comparison different?

Comparison in all forms is the same. We are not to compare ourselves to others because each one of us is created vastly different, with different purposes in life, and different struggles. Comparison just leads to more discontent and seeing ourselves as lesser than (*or more than in some cases*) what we truly are, belittling ourselves (*and others*).

How Can You Apply This to Your Own Life?

We all find ourselves, especially in this age of technology and social media, comparing ourselves to others. Their journeys, their bodies, their friends, their romances, their homes, their adventures, their money…the list goes on, and on, and on.

What do we end up getting in return?

Discontentment can open the door to many other unpleasant spirits including self-rejection, self-loathing, bitterness, envy and jealousy, and more.

Remember, Satan wants to divide us from others and God above all else. When we are divided, we are not able to stand against the Enemy and his kingdom well. We can more easily be defeated and quickly despair when we are fighting this battle alone. Not only that, but hopelessness can begin to set in as we do not see a future or purpose in ourselves.

When you begin to understand that this is a spiritual battle, we can better come to an understanding that we are not our own enemy. We can better love and accept ourselves when we realize that an evil spirit is whispering in our ears that we are unworthy. But we have the power to shut those evil thoughts and words down immediately.

"For we dare not make ourselves of the number [count ourselves among those], *or compare ourselves with some that commend* [introduce favorably, approve, band together] *themselves: but they measuring* [estimate, to judge according to any rule or standard] *themselves by* [against, with] *themselves, and comparing themselves among themselves, are not wise."* 2 Corinthians 10:12

"For I say, through the grace [joy, favor, gift, pleasure, divine influence upon the heart] *given unto me, to every man that is among you, not to think of himself more highly* [to esteem oneself overmuch, be vain or arrogant] *than he ought to think; but to think soberly* [abundantly, concerning, continual], *according as* [in that manner, to wit] *God hath dealt* [apportion, bestow, distribute] *to every man the measure* [portion] *of faith* [assurance, belief, fidelity, especially reliance upon Christ for salvation]. *For as we have many members* [parts of the body, limbs] *in one body, and all members have not the same office* [work, job]: *So we, being many, are one body in Christ, and every one members one of another."* Romans 12:3-5

"Examine [scrutinize, discipline, prove] *yourselves, whether ye be in the faith; prove* [by implication, discern] *your own selves. Know ye not your own selves, how that Jesus Christ is in you, except ye be reprobates* [rejected, worthless, castaway]*? But I trust that ye shall know that we are not reprobates."* 2 Corinthians 13:5-6

We were each created with a purpose and an identity in Christ. We were all created with a measure of faith in ourselves that we can call upon at any time. We are not rejected, worthless, or castaways! In Christ, we are new creations with beautiful, honorable purposes here on earth as well as in heaven.

"Judge [condemn, punish, conclude, decree, determine] *not, that ye be not judged. For with what judgement ye judge, ye shall be judged: and with what measure* [proverbially, the rule or standard of judgment] *ye mete* [measure]*, it shall be measured to you again* [return, repay]*. And why beholdest* [perceive, see] *thou the mote* [dry twig or straw] *that is in thy brother's eye, but considerest* [observe fully, perceive] *not the beam that is in thine own eye?"* Matthew 7:1-3

Judgement comes in the form of comparison. When comparing ourselves with others we are judging both ourselves and the person we are comparing ourselves to. Jesus said in Matthew to not judge either yourself or others as that is how you will be judged.

"And these things, brethren, I have in a figure transferred [to transfigure or disguise] *to myself and to Apollos* [a learned Jew from Alexandria and mighty in the scriptures who became a Christian and a teacher of Christianity] *for your sakes; that ye might learn in us not to think of men above* [higher than, beyond, superior] *that which is written, that no one of you be puffed up* [proud, haughty] *for one against* [accusative, over against, according to] *another. For who maketh thee to differ* [make a distinction] *from another? And what hast thou* [such as possession, ability, relation, necessity, reign] *that thou didst not receive it, why dost thou glory* [boast, rejoice]*, as if thou hadst not received it* [obtained, accepted]*?"* 1 Corinthians 4:6-7

Human beings were created in God's image, for his glory, and out of great love. We are his sons and daughters. As such, we must not raise ourselves higher than our Father. This is what Satan did which is why he was cast out of heaven. We are to be as Christ, revealing God's great love for the world and His people but we are not to be equal with God the Father. This brings us back to the godly order from chapter twelve.

Jesus always pointed to His Father in heaven. Through every miracle, every person brought to the faith, and every baptism, Jesus never took credit but pointed all the attention to the Father.

We have a great purpose that we have been called to following Jesus. He said that we would do greater things than He with the Holy Spirit, with the power of the Father, and in the name of Jesus. If we can understand this great calling and realize that each and every person is created differently, with unique purposes here on earth, then comparison ceases to be our first thought.

As the body of Christ, we work better together, each having our own role, rather than all doing the same thing. We are not all leaders just as not all are followers. There is always balance. A beautiful balance that works to glorify God in the end.

Chapter XVII

"Mrs. Fairfax said she should not be surprised if he were to go straight from the Leas to London, and thence to the Continent, and not show his face again at Thornfield for a year to come; he had not unfrequently quitted it in a manner quite as abrupt and unexpected. When I heard this, I was beginning to feel a strange chill and failing at the heart. I was actually permitting myself to experience a sickening sense of disappointment; but rallying my wits, and recollecting my principles, I at once called my sensations to order; and it was wonderful how I got over the temporary blunder — how I cleared up the mistake of supposing Mr. Rochester's movements a matter in which I had any cause to take a vital interest."

Jane continues to punish herself for having strong attachments to Mr. Rochester. Finally realizing that he might not return for quite some time, her heart drops for a moment in despair. In response to wanting to "rally her wits," Jane seriously considers advertising for a new position far away from Thornfield. She does not have a lot of time to consider this prospect, however, as a letter announcing Mr. Rochester's return arrives.

Even though she will not admit to the deep feelings she has toward Mr. Rochester to anyone, let alone herself, Jane cannot hide the involuntary nervousness and excitement she feels when she learns of his return. Immediately, the whole household is thrown into action, cleaning and preparing for their master and his guests.

"During the intervening period I had no time to nurse chimeras; and I believe I was as active and gay as anybody — Adèle excepted. Still, now and then, I received a damping check to my cheerfulness; and was, in spite of myself, thrown back on the region of doubts and portents, and dark conjectures."

<u>Chimeras</u>: a thing that is hoped or wished for but in fact is illusory or impossible to achieve[1].

Grace Poole continues to "haunt" the third floor mysteriously. Jane does not understand why others in the house do not see or recognize the fact that she lives in isolation and seems to do nothing to contribute to the household. She eats, smokes, remains silent, and lives secluded. Not only does she get paid more than any other at Thornfield, but she also has a mysterious business to take care of. Jane now realizes that she is not party to a very big secret of the household. A secret in which Grace Poole is the primary subject.

Translation of Adèle's conversation:

"'At Mom's,'" said she, "'when there were people, I followed them everywhere, in the living room and in their rooms; often I watched the maids do their hair and dress the ladies, and it was so much fun: that way you learn.'

'Don't you feel hungry, Adèle?'

'But yes, mademoiselle: we have not eaten for five or six hours.'"

As you all know by now, one of my favorite parts of this book, and any book really, are the observations made by the main character. Miss Brontë did such a beautiful job using Jane to describe different people and situations to allow us, as readers, to feel as if we were right there too.

In this chapter, we meet many new characters which will reveal quite a few new characteristics that we have not yet observed. They will also be shaping a few of the upcoming chapters, which is why it is so important that we observe their characters right along with Jane.

"Lady Lynn was a large and stout personage of about forty, very erect, very haughty-looking, richly dressed in a satin robe of changeful sheen: her dark hair shone glossily under the shade of an azure plume, and within the circlet of a band of gems.

Mrs. Colonel Dent was less showy; but, I thought, more ladylike. She had a slight figure, a pale, gentle face, and fair hair. Her black satin dress, her scarf of rich foreign lace, and her pearl ornaments, pleased me better than the rainbow radiance of the titled dame."

People who are showy with their looks and money are often more unpleasant, gaudy, and distasteful than those who wear their superiority with grace. Mrs. Colonel Dent wore her money simply and carried herself as a lady which was more pleasant to behold.

*"[In reference to the Dowager Lady Ingram] Most people
would have termed her a splendid woman of her age: and so
she was, no doubt, physically speaking; but then there was
an expression of almost insupportable haughtiness in her
bearing and countenance. She had Roman features and a
double chin, disappearing into a throat like a pillar: these
features appeared to me not only inflated and darkened, but
even furrowed with pride; and the chin was sustained by the
same principle, in a position of almost preternatural
erectness. She had, likewise, a fierce and a hard eye: it
reminded me of Mrs. Reed's; she mouthed her words in
speaking; her voice was deep, its inflections very pompous,
very dogmatical – very intolerable, in short." – brackets added
by me*

Jane's observation of Lady Ingram having similar
characteristics to Mrs. Reed is very important. It sets the
tone for the whole Ingram family. This woman rules with
pride and presents a very unimpressive figure to, not only
Jane, but us as well.

*"[In reference to Blanche Ingram] Her face was like her
mother's; a youthful unfurrowed likeness: the same low
brow, the same high features, the same pride. It was not,
however, so saturnine a pride: she laughed continually; her
laugh was satirical, and so was the habitual expression of her
arched and haughty lip.*

*Genius is said to be self-conscious. I cannot tell whether
Miss Ingram was a genius, but she was self-conscious –
remarkably self-conscious indeed. She entered into a*

discourse on botany with the gentle Mrs. Dent. It seemed Mrs. Dent had not studied that science: though, as she said, she liked flowers, 'especially wild ones'; Miss Ingram had, and she ran over its vocabulary with an air. I presently perceived she was (what is vernacularly termed) trailing Mrs. Dent; that is, playing on her ignorance — her trail might be clever, but it was decidedly not good-natured. She played: her execution was brilliant; she sang: her voice was fine; she talked French apart to her mamma; and she talked it well, with fluency and with good accent." – brackets added by me

It is no wonder, now that we know how her mother is described, why Blanche is the way she is. She has inherited her mother's pride and haughtiness as well as her desire to rule over others weaker than herself, not in strength but in knowledge. Blanche uses ignorance to her advantage and plays off other's weaknesses skillfully.

"Mary had a milder and more open countenance than Blanche; softer features too, and a skin some shades fairer (Miss Ingram was dark as a Spaniard) — but Mary was deficient in life: her face lacked expression, her eye lustre; she had nothing to say, and having once taken her seat, remained fixed like a statue in its niche."

Mary is such a sad creature. She, and the rest of her family I believe, exhibit the personification of fabricated personalities. We will discuss this in detail toward the end of this chapter.

"I try to concentrate my attention on those netting-needles, on the meshes of the purse I am forming — I wish to think only of the work I have in my hands, to see only the silver beads and silk threads that lie in my lap; whereas, I distinctly behold his figure, and I inevitably recall the moment when I last saw it; just after I had rendered him, what he deemed, an essential service, and he, holding my hand, and looking down on my face, surveyed me with eyes that revealed a heart full and eager to overflow; in whose emotions I had a part. How near had I approached him at this moment!"

Enter Mr. Rochester! Jane tries to force herself to ignore his presence. To avoid thinking of him or seeing him. But this is impossible. Eventually, she allows herself the pleasure of watching him.

"I looked, and had an acute pleasure in looking — a precious yet poignant pleasure; pure gold, with a steely point of agony: a pleasure like what the thirst-perishing man might feel who knows the well to which he has crept is poisoned, yet stoops and drinks divine draughts nevertheless."

She sees Mr. Rochester as beautiful even though he is not generally considered by worldly ideals as attractive. "He made me love him without looking at me." She finally puts into words her unmistakable love for him.

"'He is not to them what he is to me,' I thought: 'he is not of their kind. I believe he is of mine — I am sure he is — I feel akin to him — I understand the language of his countenance and movements: though rank and wealth sever us widely, I

have something in my brain and heart, in my blood and nerves, that assimilates me mentally to him.'"

Through all the conversations, deep and intimate, Jane knows Mr. Rochester better than anyone. She understands his thoughts, agonies, and hopes. They understand each other deeply. His guests, though beautiful and accomplished, do not offer the same depth of character or unflinching way of being honest with him. Jane and Mr. Rochester are tied to one another by a profound connection.

The conversation about governesses is targeted toward Jane, knowing she is in the presence of the guests. It is full of bitterness and disgust. These types of people are the ones that find joy in tearing others down to raise themselves higher. We can tell through conversation that Blanche is a bully, known for getting her own way, and nobody bothers standing up to her or telling her no. She is spoiled and relentless toward others, not allowing for faults.

Jane decides to leave and is caught off-guard in the hall by Mr. Rochester.

"'Good-night, my — ' He stopped, bit his lip, and abruptly left me."

<u>How Can You Apply This to Your Own Life?</u>

Throughout the observations of the guests of Thornfield as well as during their conversations, we get a good look at what fabricated personalities look like.

The Ingrams in particular, are perfect examples. We do not know anything of their past up to this point. We do not know what type of father figure Blanche, Mary, and their brother had growing up. I have a feeling that Lady Ingram ruled the household based on her personality and Jane's comparison to Mrs. Reed.

There may very well be past hurts that have allowed them to take on fabricated personalities in order to protect themselves from further hurt.

What Are Fabricated Personalities? Where Do They Come From?

Fabricated personalities come from accusing spirits. Remember, Satan is the ultimate accuser. He wants us to come to a place in which we are accusing God, ourselves, and others for all the problems we face.

Accusation tells us that we are somehow not good enough and that others are disapproving of our decisions. When we encourage self-accusation to speak to our hearts, self-rejection enters in. We will perceive disapproval as rejection which will lead to creating a new identity or personality that will please others more than our true personality.

This is especially dangerous when you have people in your life who have unreasonably high expectations, do not allow failure under any circumstances, or are constantly voicing their disapproval. This heaps coals on the rejection. This all comes back to self-accusation.

If someone disapproves, your personality changes. If someone else disapproves of that personality, it changes again. It then becomes an extreme lack of identity because you ultimately lose yourself and the beautiful person God created you to be. It all becomes a performance that changes based on the people you are around.

In Blanche's case, she strives to be accomplished in many areas so that she can reign superior over other people. She is probably living up to the high and unreachable standards of her own mother. She has very likely been "formed in the expectation of a parent…[led to] performance to meet the expectation of another…conforming to the image of success."[2] Everything is performance based. Everything is a show. Her lack of true identity drives her to become a shallow, prideful version of herself with false confidence to maintain her.

This is an obvious form of fabricated identity, but unfortunately, it can go the other way as well. It can come in the form of false piety in the church.

People in the church who have a lack of identity will strive to do everything they can to feel useful. They dedicate all their time to others and exhausting themselves all while saying it is all for Christ and to bring others to Him.

We are called, as believers, to honor Christ with our actions and to serve others, however, we are not useful to anybody if we are burnt out and sick. It is still a performance. It is still fabricated personality. It is still a lack of identity. It is also a fear of conflict.

A lot of churches push evangelism but not everyone is called to be an evangelist. Along the same vein, not everyone is called to be a pastor, or a leader, or a missionary. If we were all called to the same purpose, not a whole lot would change. That is why the body of believers is so varied and why there are multiple gifts of the Holy Spirit. We are all called to minister and share the gospel, but we are not all called to do it the same way.

There are some that will begin to feel guilty that they cannot, or do not feel the calling to, evangelize or minister in the way others are doing so. There is no "typical" or "normal" way that ministry should look. Sometimes the unconventional is what we are called to. Just look at the story of Hosea. Now, that was extremely unconventional, but it was what he was called by God to do. Only you know what God has called you to and how He is calling you.

"But as it is written, eye hath not seen, nor ear heard, neither have entered [arise, ascend, spring up] *into the heart of man, the things which God hath prepared for them that love him. But God hath revealed them unto us by his Spirit: for the Spirit searcheth all things, yea, the deep things* [mystery, depth] *of God."* 1 Corinthians 2:9-10

This is why so many in the church are sick. We are not taking care of the church by instilling a firm sense of identity and what that looks like. So many pastors and teachers are only scratching the surface of what this means and looks like. Which is why it is so important for us to be in fellowship with our Father, reading His word and being in prayer. THAT is where we find our identity.

We are now back at identity. We discussed identity in detail in both chapter eight and chapter fifteen. The personality quizzes, enneagrams, and star signs all promote fabricated personalities because they are boxing us into designated personality types. It is all astrology whether it is labeled as such or not. Astrology is idolatrous and occultic because it takes your focus off God and obscures His goodness.

"God forbid [absolute denial, never]*: yea, let God be true, but every man a liar; as it is written, that thou mightest be justified* [to render just or innocent, free, be righteous] *in thy sayings* [communication, doctrine, speech, talk, words]*, and mightest overcome* [to subdue, prevail, get the victory] *when thou art judged* [to try, punish, decree, determine, ordain, sentence]*."* Romans 3:4

God wants us to move past what the world says about what our personalities should be and seek out the true purpose of why we are here. Jesus said in John 14 that we would do greater things than he did. So, why is this not happening? It is because we are becoming distracted by all these worldly things that impede our progress in furthering God's kingdom on earth. This is exactly where Satan wants us.

"Verily [figuratively trustworthy, surely, so be it]*, verily, I say unto you, he that believeth on me, the works that I do shall he do also; and greater* [exceedingly, mighty] *works than these shall he do; because I go unto my Father."* John 14:12

"Let your light [luminousness, to shine or make manifest] *so shine* [radiate brilliancy] *before* [in the presence] *men, that*

they may see your good works, and glorify your Father which is in heaven." Matthew 5:16

"*And be not conformed* [fashioned alike] *to this world: but be ye transformed* [changed, metamorphose] *by the renewing of your mind, that ye may prove* [to approve, discern, examine, try] *what is that good, and acceptable* [well pleasing]*, and perfect* [completeness]*, will of God.*" Romans 12:2

What we fill our hearts and minds with is ultimately what comes out in our words and behaviors. If we are filled with the world, we will act like the world. On the other hand, if we are filled with God's word, then we will begin to think, speak, and act the Word.

"*O generation of vipers* [poisonous snake, malignant, wicked men]*, how can ye, being evil, speak good things? For out of the abundance of the heart the mouth speaketh. A good man out of the good treasure of the heart bringeth forth good things: and an evil man out of the evil treasure bringeth forth evil things.*" Matthew 12:34-35

To put this into perspective for you –

Have you ever been so engulfed in a television show or movie that you began to act like your favorite character, or the one you most identified with?

I have often binged a favorite series, identifying with a character, and finding myself acting like that character. Picking up accents and mannerisms and adopting them as my own. If the character was moody, I found that I was moody. If the character was particularly comical or goofy, I would act more comical or goofy.

This is just a small version of what it looks and feels like to adopt a fabricated personality that can come about just through outside influences. There are many reasons why people change their personality. For Blanche, she created a personality that allowed her to remain top tier in society. As for Mary, it seems she has lost sight of her personality altogether due to neglect or being brought into submission, or overshadowed, by her sister and mother.

As believers, we are to adopt the ways of Christ. To live and breathe His word as life and to embody the fruits of the Holy Spirit.

"But the fruit of the Spirit is love [benevolence, a love-feast, dear love], *joy* [gladness, calm delight, cheerfulness], *peace* [prosperity, quietness, rest, set at one again], *longsuffering* [forbearance or fortitude, patience], *gentleness* [usefulness, morally, excellence in character or demeanor, kindness], *goodness* [virtue, beneficence], *faith* [truth, trust, constancy, fidelity], *meekness* [humility], *temperance* [self-control]*: against such there is no law."* Galatians 5:22-23

"Nevertheless the foundation of God standeth [covenant, establish, hold up] *sure* [solid, stable, steadfast, strong], *having this seal* [a signet as fencing in or protecting from misappropriation, genuineness], *the Lord knoweth them that are his. And, let every one that nameth* [profess, utter, call] *the name of Christ depart* [desist, desert, withdraw self] *from iniquity."* 2 Timothy 2:19

Are you known of God? Is he a part of who you are and the breath you breathe?

"Therefore if any man be in [give self wholly to] *Christ, he is a new creature* [creation]*: old things are passed away; behold, all things are become* [come into being, fulfilled, be brought to pass] *new."* 2 Corinthians 5:17

"That ye put off [cast off] *concerning the former conversation* [behavior, manner of life] *the old man, which is corrupt* [defile, destroy] *according to the deceitful lusts* [desire, longing]*; and be renewed in the spirit of your mind; and that ye put on* [invest with clothing – literally or figuratively, array] *the new man, which after God is created in righteousness and true holiness."* Ephesians 4:22-24

"And have put on the new man, which is renewed in knowledge [discernment] *after the image of him that created him:"* Colossians 3:10

Footnotes

[1] Oxford Languages Online

[2] Dr. Henry Wright; Who Am I – Part 1 – Henry Wright – Be in Health Specialty Conference Soundbite | Be In Health YouTube Channel

Chapter XVIII

"Merry days were these at Thornfield Hall; and busy days too: how different from the first three months of stillness, monotony, and solitude I had passed beneath its roof! All sad feelings seemed now driven from the house, all gloomy associations forgotten: there was life everywhere, movement all day long."

Human nature observed is how we learn and what better way to do this than to have a keen observer watching those around her very carefully.

Jane uses separation and discernment to separate the person from whatever is driving their actions and words in the moment. Is it really them or is it a personality they have adopted? This chapter is truly amazing in its insight, so I hope that you take your time.

"One of the gentlemen, Mr. Eshton, observing me, seemed to propose that I should be asked to join them; but Lady Ingram instantly negatived the notion.

'No,' I heard her say: 'she looks too stupid for any game of the sort.'"

There have been quite a few characters in Jane Eyre that make us want to despise them. Lady Ingram is one of these. She is very similar to Mrs. Reed in many ways. Remember, she is only acting on what we can imagine are very deep spiritual hurts that could have come out of her childhood or even her marriage. We do not know her history and thus it makes us easier to dislike her. Do you know the history of every disagreeable person you encounter? Probably not. And this is where separation continues to come in. We cannot go around hating people because they represent a bitter outward appearance, but we can be love to them in spite of it.

> *"And he answering said, Thou shalt love the Lord thy God with all thy heart, and with all thy soul, and with all thy strength, and with all thy mind; and thy neighbour* [fellow man, countryman, friend] *as thyself."* Luke 10:27

That is such a hard thing to do. Especially in the case of Mrs. Reed and Lady Ingram. We all have people that come into our lives that are difficult to love. The only way to obey this commandment to love others, is by asking God to help us see who He created them to be despite the evil working through them. It takes enormous amounts of practice to do this. God is faithful in all things. He allows us to make mistakes and to get back up again. If we ask Him to help us in this area, He is faithful to do so.

On another note, the game of charades has definitely become very simplistic compared to the version we see in Jane Eyre. At best, we will act out scenes if we were to play it now, but in this case, so much thought, costuming, and incorporating of props went into elaborate displays for the guessing game. I think it would be fun to play this version of charades.

"I have told you, reader, that I had learnt to love Mr. Rochester: I could not unlove him now, merely because I found that he had ceased to notice me — because I might pass hours in his presence, and he would never once turn his eyes

in my direction — because I saw all his attentions appropriated by a great lady, who scorned to touch me with the hem of her robes as she passed; who, if ever her dark and imperious eye fell on me by chance, would withdraw it instantly as from an object too mean to merit observation. I could not unlove him, because I felt sure he would soon marry this very lady…

There was nothing to cool or banish love in these circumstances, though much to create despair, Much too, you will think, reader, to engender jealousy: if a woman, in my position, could presume to be jealous of a woman in Miss Ingram's. But I was not jealous: or very rarely — the nature of the pain I suffered could not be explained by that word. Miss Ingram was a mark beneath jealousy: she was too inferior to excite the feeling. Pardon the seeming paradox: I mean what I say. She was very showy, but she was not genuine: she had a fine person, many brilliant attainments; but her mind was poor, her heart barren by nature: nothing bloomed spontaneously on that soil; no unforced natural fruit delighted by its freshness. She was not good; she was not original: she used to repeat sounding phrases from books: she never offered, nor had, an opinion of her own. She advocated a high tone of sentiment; but she did not know the sensations of sympathy and pity; tenderness and truth were not in her. Too often she betrayed this, by the undue vent she gave to a spiteful antipathy she had conceived against little Adèle: pushing her away with some contumelious epithet if she happened to approach her; sometimes ordering her from the room, and always treating her with coldness and acrimony. Other eyes besides mine watched these manifestations of character — watched them closely, keenly, shrewdly. Yes; the future bridegroom, Mr. Rochester himself, exercised over his intended a ceaseless surveillance; and it was from this sagacity — this guardedness of his — this perfect, clear consciousness of his fair one's defects — this obvious absence of passion in his sentiments towards her, that my ever-torturing pain arose.

I saw he was going to marry her, for family, perhaps political reasons, because her rank and connections suited him; I felt he had not given her his love, and that her qualifications were ill-adapted to win from him that treasure. This was the point — this was where the nerve was touched and teased — this was where the fever was sustained and fed: she could not charm him. . . .

If Miss Ingram had been a good and noble woman, endowed with force, fervour, kindness, sense, I should have had one vital struggle with two tigers — jealousy and despair: then, my heart torn out and devoured, I should have admired her — acknowledged her excellence, and been quiet for the rest of my days: and the more absolute her superiority, the deeper would have been my admiration — the more truly tranquil my quiescence. But as matters really stood, to watch Miss Ingram's efforts at fascinating Mr. Rochester, to witness their repeated failure — herself unconscious that they did fail; vainly fancying that each shaft launched hit the mark and infatuatedly pluming herself on success, when her pride and self-complacency repelled further and further what she wished to allure – to witness this, was to be at once under ceaseless excitation and ruthless restraint.

Because, when she failed, I saw how she might have succeeded. Arrows that continually glanced off from Mr. Rochester's breast and fell harmless at his feet, might, I knew, if shot by a surer hand, have quivered keen in his proud heart – have called love into his stern eye, and softness into his sardonic face; or, better still, without weapons a silent conquest might have been won."

Wow!

This chapter is so good! People like Blanche never know how easily their facade can slip, and any keen observer can see right to their true person. Even those who have built a seemingly perfect fabrication of who they want others to see, their true identity never disappears. Blanche did not realize that Mr. Rochester was one of these observant people. He noticed all the disparaging remarks and empty kindnesses. None of which impressed him. How exhausting it must have been for her to uphold this fallacy of character while denying the potential identity that was given to her by her Creator.

In this way, we see how closely Mr. Rochester and Jane resemble each other in understanding the true character of a person and not allowing shallow vanity to impress them.

"Who can find a virtuous [valor, strength, able, might, substance, worthy] *woman? For her price* [value] *is far above rubies. The heart of her husband doth safely trust* [put confidence] *in her, so that he shall have no need of spoil. She will do him good and not evil* [misery, hurt, distress] *all*

the days of her life. Se seeketh wool, and flax [linen]*, and worketh willingly* [pleasure, desire, delight, purpose] *with her hands.*" Proverbs 31:10-13

"*Strength* [security, might, strength, boldness] *and honour* [magnificence, splendor, comeliness, beauty] *are her clothing; and she shall rejoice in time to come. She openeth her mouth with wisdom; and in her tongue is the law of kindness* [beauty, favor, merciful, pity]." Proverbs 31:25-26

When a woman is filled with the Holy Spirit, she exudes strength, honor, kindness, and wisdom. This is so attractive to the outside observer. It shows that this woman is secure in her identity, knows who she is as a daughter of God, is a hard worker, and is not afraid of the future.

Comparing the Proverbs 31 woman to Blanche gives us an even starker contrast between true beauty and feigned beauty. This is what Mr. Rochester and Jane have observed in her.

And yet, in everything she has observed, Jane holds no judgement over the decisions that Mr. Rochester and Blanche make regarding marrying for position. This is because she does not have the same perspective in life as they. She would marry for love, regardless of whether the man she loved were wealthy or poor. However, Mr. Rochester and Blanche have been raised by lines of wealthy and prominent people who drove into them the importance of marrying for wealth, position, and advantage.

Naturally, Blanche would seek out a man of character who held money and advantage in society in order to support her extravagant wants and needs. We cannot rightfully judge her for this as I believe most of us would like to live in comfort and security. However, few of us would sacrifice love for this end.

As we progress further into the story, a new stranger arrives at Thornfield that has Jane quite confused.

"For a handsome and not an unamiable-looking man, he repelled me exceedingly: there was no power in that smooth-skinned face of a full oval shape; no firmness in that aquiline nose and small cherry mouth; there was no thought on the low, even forehead; no command in that blank, brown eye."

This is another very interesting observation. Here we have a very handsome man with no depth of character. This seems to be a bit of a running theme in this book. I think that these beautiful people – Blanche and Mr. Mason – take their beauty for granted, attracting others through their outward appearance without cultivating their inner beauty or personality. There is no originality. Perhaps those with the advantage of beauty must work at their inner beauty even more so because it is so easy to rely on their outer beauty for attention and acceptance. It is in everyone's best interest to have depth of character to hold themselves fast when life's challenges come.

With the introduction of the gypsy woman who says that she will tell all the young, single women their fortunes, Blanche is thrown some sort of blow.

"I watched her for nearly half an hour…her face grew momently darker, more dissatisfied, and more sourly

expressive of disappointment. She had obviously not heard anything to her advantage: and it seemed to me, from her prolonged fit of gloom and taciturnity, that she herself, notwithstanding her professed indifference, attached undue importance to whatever revelations had been made her."

As the chapter closes, the gypsy woman refuses to leave until all the single, young ladies have seen her and thus, we leave Jane in her hands for now.

How Can You Apply This to Your Own Life?

You already have a good understanding of how important it is to maintain our own hearts and minds, representing the love of Christ and building our identity in Him. How do we then use this to minister to others?

Ministry is not a one-size-fits-all. You do not have to be a pastor or a missionary to minister to others. Ministry can be as simple as sitting with your neighbor on their porch and talking to them. Or writing a devotional book based on a book you love. When we look at Jesus' ministry, he preached in parables on hilltops and in boats, teaching anyone who wished to hear and making the Word accessible to all. He also made a point of building relationships with people.

Building relationships is one of the greatest ways to minister. When you begin building relationships, caring about people, showing them kindness, being present in their lives, they begin to trust you. Trust leads to conversations and questions. If they trust you with their hearts and that you will not judge them but have an open and loving heart for them, that is when they might begin to ask questions about your faith and your peace.

In order to be prepared for this kind of ministry, we must be in the Word. The Word arms us with how God thinks about us. He loves and He corrects. Loving and correcting are inseparable and honor the sacrifice of Jesus for our salvation and continued growth as believers. Knowledge of the Word allows the Holy Spirit to use this preparation for discernment and teaching.

We are called to love our neighbor, correct?

Love casts out fear.

"There is no fear in love; but perfect love casteth out fear: because fear hath torment. He that feareth is not made perfect in love." 1 John 4:18

There are so many people who are afraid. Afraid of judgement, afraid of their futures, afraid of failure…There are also so many people who have been hurt by the church and that causes fear as well. Young people especially are not as receptive of traditional ministry as they might have been a couple of decades ago.

These young people just need to be loved. They need to feel accepted and safe and the only way to do this is to create relationship with them and teach them the freedom that they can have in Christ Jesus.

I think that we get so caught up in avoiding legalism that we become too passive and vice versa. There is no middle ground anymore. Then, when we see believers choosing to forge that middle ground, they are looked at as crazy or heathenistic. What is the best way to reach people? That should be our first question. Are we all called to be pastors? Some are, but not all. Are we all called to be missionaries? Some are, but not all. Are we all called to use our faith as an inspiration to others and spread the word of God? Yes.

How you go about this is a personal decision between you and your Father. For me, personally, I have been called to be an author and teacher. That is how I share my faith and minister to people of all ages and backgrounds.

If you are willing, God can use you in any situation to bring others to Christ. You may never see the fruit, but as long as you are being love and building relationships, God can do great things in those people's lives and yours.

The key is to be ready!

"But sanctify [purify, holy] *the Lord God in your hearts: and be ready always to give an answer to every man that asketh you a reason of the hope that is in you with meekness* [humility] *and fear* [reverence]*: having a good conscience; that, whereas they speak evil of you, as of evildoers, they may be ashamed that falsely accuse your good conversation* [behavior, manner of life] *in Christ."* 1 Peter 3:15-16

"The preparations of the heart in man, and the answer of the tongue, is from the LORD. All the ways of a man are clean in his own eyes; but the LORD weigheth [estimate, ponder, test,

prove] *the spirits. Commit thy works unto the LORD, and they thoughts shall be established* [faithfulness, confirm, perfect, stable]." Proverbs 16:1-3

Chapter XIX

We left Jane, in the last chapter, heading into the room with a gypsy woman that has told the fortunes of all the single young ladies.

Throughout Jane Eyre, we have had glimpses into Jane's observations of others, but we have yet to hear a description of our main character herself.

"'The flame flickers in the eye; the eye shines like dew; it looks soft and full of feeling; it smiles at my jargon: it is susceptible; impression follows impression through its clear sphere; where it ceases to smile, it is sad; an unconscious lassitude weighs on the lid: that signifies melancholy resulting from loneliness. It turns from me; it will not suffer further scrutiny; it seems to deny, by a mocking glance, the truth of the discoveries I have already made — to disown the charge both of sensibility and chagrin: its pride and reserve only confirm me in my opinion. The eye is favourable.

As to the mouth, it delights at times in laughter; it is disposed to impart all that the brain conceives; though I daresay it would be silent on much the heart experiences. Mobile and flexible, it was never intended to be compressed in the eternal silence of solitude: it is a mouth which should speak much and smile often, and have human affection for its interlocutor. That feature too is propitious.

I see no enemy to a fortunate issue but in the brow; and that brow professes to say — "I can live alone, if self-respect, and circumstances require me so to do. I need not sell my soul to buy bliss. I have an inward treasure born with me, which can keep me alive if all extraneous delights should be withheld, or offered only at a price I cannot afford to give." The forehead declares, "reason sits firm and holds the reins, and she will not let the feelings burst away and hurry her to wild chasms. The passions may rage furiously, like true heathens, as they are; and the desires may imagine all sorts of vain things: but judgement shall still have the last word in every argument, and the casting vote in every decision. Strong wind, earthquake-shock, and fire may pass by: but I shall follow the guiding of that still small voice which interprets the dictates of conscience."

Well said, forehead; your declaration shall be respected.'"

As we see now, Mr. Rochester understands and knows Jane as he does his own self. He observes her just as often as she observes him. Jane has had good teachers in her life to help her have self-control and maintain self-respect. She is smart and strong and shows true character in everything she does.

All of this is to be admired in Jane. She has an inward peace and strength that is foreign to Mr. Rochester, who inwardly struggles with his past faults on a regular basis.

Some strange change comes over Mr. Rochester at the mention of Mr. Mason which leads him to some self-reflection. We do not know all the details of Mr. Rochester's past yet, but it is a mystery that seems to cause him pain.

"'If all these people came in a body and spat at me, what would you do, Jane?'

'Turn them out of the room, sir, if I could.'

He half smiled. 'But if I were to go to them, and they only looked at me coldly, and whispered sneeringly amongst each other, and then dropped off and left me one by one, what then? Would you go with them?'

'I rather think not, sir: I should have more pleasure in staying with you.'

'To comfort me?'

'Yes, sir, to comfort you, as well as I could.'

'And if they laid you under a ban for adhering to me?'

'I, probably, should know nothing about their ban; and if I did, I should care nothing about it.'

'Then, you could dare censure for my sake?'

'I could dare it for the sake of any friend who deserved my adherence; as you, I am sure, do.'"

<u>How Can You Apply This to Your Own Life?</u>

The thing about Jane is that she sees the good in Mr. Rochester. She discerns that he truly wants to be a good man and to be honorable with his life. Jane is loyal to him and would stick by him if all others would not.

If secrets from Mr. Rochester's past came out that shocked its hearers, what would we do in her place? Would we ridicule Mr. Rochester, spitting at him, and leave him to his misery without aid? Or would we stand by him, hearing him out and helping him, being a godly support to him in his time of need?

It is hard to say because we do not have the full picture.

The question then stands, how would we treat another in a position of defeat? Would we follow the crowd and ignore that person and tear them down further into despair?

Believers are called to be set apart. We are not to follow the crowd and their thinking and ways of living. We are called to raise up a generation of believers who recognize God's love in their lives and the lives of others. How can we do this if we are following a hateful and mocking crowd?

"And be ye not conformed [fashion oneself to] *to this world: but be ye transformed by the renewing of your mind, that ye may prove* [discern, allow] *what is that good, and acceptable, and perfect, will of God. For I say, through the grace given unto me, to every man this is among you, not to think of himself more highly than he ought to think; but to think soberly* [continual, for intent], *according as God hath dealt to every man the measure* [portion] *of faith."* Romans 12:2-3

"Recompense [reward, deliver, repay] *to no man evil for evil, provide things honest in the sight of all men."* Romans 12:17

"If the world hate you, ye know that it hated me before it hated you. If ye were of the world, the world would love his

Unfortunately, people like Mr. Rochester isolate themselves as a source of protection. Or they surround themselves with people with lower standards in life to help them feel better about themselves. The people that surround Mr. Rochester on a regular basis are not exactly the greatest influences of moral character. We are told in 1 Corinthians that we should be careful who we spend our time with as those who do not understand God's word or choose to rebel against it, will corrupt our own character.

"Be not deceived: evil communications [companionship] *corrupt* [destroy, defile] *good manners* [moral habits]." 1 Corinthians 15:33

Relationship is always the first step to restoring a brother or sister in Christ. Being love to others despite their past brings a sense of safety that they otherwise lack. The world is not safe, but God is safe. These types of people just need to be loved. Not romantic love, but the kind of love that is honest and uplifting. The type of love that Jesus had for every single person he came across during his ministry.

"Two are better than one; because they have a good reward for their labour. For if they fall, the one will lift up his fellow: but woe to him that is alone when he falleth; for he hath not another to help him up." Ecclesiastes 4:10

*"A man that hath friends must shew himself friendly: and
there is a friend that sticketh closer than a brother."*
Proverbs 18:24

Then, and only then, can these hurting people see what it is
like to walk with God. To be filled with serenity and
confidence in something much greater than themselves and
be restored to the wholeness He wants for them.

*"Let them now that fear the LORD say, that his mercy
endureth for ever. I called upon the LORD in destress: the
LORD answered me, and set me in a large place*
[figuratively – liberty]. *The LORD is on my side; I will no
fear: what can man do unto me? The LORD taketh my part
with them that help me* [succor, aid, surround, protect]:
*therefore shall I see my desire upon them that hate me. It is
better to trust in the LORD than to put confidence in man."*
Psalm 118:4-8

It should not matter what a person's past is. If they are
choosing a path toward righteousness but have no idea where
to begin, we should not just ignore them. And even when
terrible things come in to further divide them from God,
hope never diminishes. Nobody is exempt from repentance.
The key is relationship.

For further reading, I encourage you to look into Galatians 6.

Chapter XX

We now enter deep into the mystery at hand. If this is your first time reading Jane Eyre, I will not spoil anything for you. But, more than ever, it would be best for you to read chapter twenty *before* going through this devotional chapter.

A loud and frightening cry is uttered which wakes the entire household who gathers in the hall in a frenzy. Jane notices the severe irritability of Mr. Rochester as he works to calm his guests and get them to return to their rooms. However, Jane knows better and waits patiently to see if she will be needed.

"'You don't turn sick at the sight of blood?' [Mr. Rochester]

'I think I shall not: I have never been tried yet.' [Jane Eyre]

I felt a thrill while I answered him; but no coldness, and no faintness.

'Just give me your hand,' he said: 'it will not do to risk a fainting fit.'

I put my fingers into his. 'Warm and steady,' was his remark: he turned the key and opened the door." – brackets added by me

I am not sure about you, but I know that I would feel rather taken aback at Mr. Rochester's first question. What has happened? What will Jane see when she enters this locked room above her own?

Jane enters into a scene which she never questions. Mr. Mason has been injured and is threatened not to speak to her while Mr. Rochester is away.

"Here then I was in the third storey, fastened into one of its mystic cells; night around me; a pale and bloody spectacle under my eyes and hands; a murderess hardly separated from me by a single door: yes — that was appalling — the rest I could bear; but I shuddered at the thought of Grace Poole bursting out upon me."

"...all the night I heard but three sounds at three long intervals — a step creak, a momentary renewal of the snarling, canine noise, and a deep human groan.

Then my own thoughts worried me. What crime was this, that lived incarnate in this sequestered mansion, and could neither be expelled nor subdued by the owner? — what mystery, that broke out now in fire and now in blood, at the deadest hours of night? What creature was it, that, masked in an ordinary woman's face and shape, uttered the voice, now of a mocking demon, and anon of a carrion-seeking bird of prey?"

Jane questioned why Mr. Mason had been targeted and then hidden. Why had he endured this threat and attack so tamely without any true indignation toward his host or his attacker? It all seems very strange.

"...I saw Mr. Mason was submissive to Mr. Rochester; that the impetuous will of the latter held complete sway over the inertness of the former: the few words which had passed

between them assured me of this. It was evident that in their former intercourse, the passive disposition of the one had been habitually influenced by the active energy of the other: whence then had arisen Mr. Rochester's dismay when he heard of Mr. Mason's arrival? Why had the mere name of this unresisting individual – whom his word now sufficed to control like a child – fallen on him, a few hours since, as a thunderbolt might fall on an oak?"

As if things could not get any more confusing or sinister, the doctor comes and makes an alarming discovery as to Mr. Mason's wound.

"'…but how is this? The flesh on the shoulder is torn as well as cut. This wound was not done with a knife: there have been teeth here!'

'She bit me,' he [Mr. Mason] murmured. 'She worried me like a tigress, when Rochester got the knife from her.'" – brackets added by me

"I saw Mr. Rochester shudder: a singularly marked expression of disgust, horror, hatred, warped his countenance almost to distortion; but he only said –

'Come, be silent, Richard, and never mind her gibberish: don't repeat it.'

'I wish I could forget it,' was the answer.

'You will when you are out of the country: when you get back to Spanish Town, you may think of her as dead and buried – or rather, you need not think of her at all.'

'Impossible to forget this night!'"

Clearly Mr. Rochester is aware that there is a murderess sheltered in his home and is not making any move to remove her. He is hiding, and has been for some time, a secret which weighs heavily on him but which he wishes to keep concealed at all cost.

Once Mr. Mason is removed from Thornfield, Jane and Mr. Rochester are able to breathe a little more freely in the fresh air of the early morning.

"'Come where there is some freshness, for a few moments,' he said; 'that house is a mere dungeon: don't you feel it so?'

'It seems to me a splendid mansion, sir.'

'The glamour of inexperience is over your eyes,' he answered; 'and you see it through a charmed medium: you cannot discern that the gilding is slime and the silk draperies cobwebs; that the marble is sordid slate, and the polished woods mere refuse chips and scaly bark. Now here' (he pointed to the leafy enclosure we had entered) 'all is real, sweet, and pure.'"

"'…To live, for me, Jane, is to stand on a crater-crust which may crack and spue fire any day.'

'But Mr. Mason seems a man easily led. Your influence, sir, is evidently potent with him: he will never set you at defiance or willfully injure you.'

'Oh, no! Mason will not defy me; nor, knowing it, will he hurt me – but, unintentionally, he might in a moment, by

one careless word, deprive me, if not of life, yet for ever of happiness.'"

Mr. Rochester has an intense fear that his happiness is bound with this Mr. Mason and that with one word, that happiness and future will be ripped from him forever.

"'…You are my little friend, are you not?'

'I like to serve you, sir, and to obey you in all that is right.'

'Precisely: I see you do. I see genuine contentment in your gait and mien, your eye and face, when you are helping me and pleasing me – working for me, and with me, in, as you characteristically say, "all that is right": for if I bid you do what you thought wrong, there would be no light-footed running, no neat-handed alacrity, no lively glance and animated complexion. My friend would then turn to me, quiet and pale, and would say, "No, sir; that is impossible: I cannot do it, because it is wrong"; and would become immutable as a fixed star. Well, you too have power over me, and may injure me: yet I dare not show you where I am vulnerable, lest, faithful and friendly as you are, you should transfix me at once.'"

I believe, based on the above paragraph, that Mr. Rochester fears above all else that Jane will become privy to all his past faults and leave him utterly alone again. He has come to trust her, rely on her, and love her. If she were to be removed from his life, I believe he thinks he would dissolve into misery and greater torment.

In the following parable, we can decipher more of Mr. Rochester's past…

"'Well then, Jane, call to aid your fancy: suppose you were no longer a girl well reared and disciplined, but a wild boy indulged from childhood upwards; imagine yourself in a remote foreign land; conceive that you there commit a capital error, no matter of what nature or from what motives, but one whose consequences must follow you through life and taint all your existence. Mind, I don't say a crime; I am not speaking of shedding of blood or any other guilty act, which might make the perpetrator amenable to the law: my word is error. The results of what you have done become in time to you utterly insupportable; you take measures to obtain relief: unusual measure, but neither unlawful nor culpable. Still you are miserable; for hope has quitted you on the very confines of life: your sun at noon darkens in an eclipse, which you feel will not leave it till the time of setting. Bitter and base associations have become the sole food of your memory: you wander here and there, seeking rest in exile: happiness in pleasure — I mean in heartless, sensual pleasure — such as dulls intellect and blights feeling. Heart-weary and soul-withered, you come home after years of voluntary banishment: you make a new acquaintance — how or where not matter: you find in this stranger much of the good and bright qualities which you have sought for twenty years, and never before encountered; and they are all fresh, healthy, without soil and without taint. Such society revives, regenerates: you feel better days come back — higher wishes, purer feelings; you desire to recommence your life, and to

spend what remains to you of days in a way more worthy of an immortal being. To attain this end, are you justified in overleaping an obstacle of custom – a mere conventional impediment which neither your conscience sanctifies nor your judgement approves?

...Is the wandering and sinful, but now rest-seeking and repentant, man justified in daring the world's opinion, in order to attach to him for ever this gentle, gracious, genial stranger, thereby securing his own peace of mind and regeneration of life?'

'Sir,' I answered, 'a wanderer's repose or a sinner's reformation should never depend on a fellow-creature. Men and women die; philosophers falter in wisdom, and Christians in goodness: if anyone you know has suffered and erred, let him look higher than his equals for strength to amend and solace to heal.'

'But the instrument – the instrument! God, who does the work, ordains the instrument. I have myself – I tell it you without parable – been a worldly, dissipated, restless man; and I believe I have found the instrument for my cure in – '"

The chapter ends strangely with Mr. Rochester not quite completing his original thought but diverging onto another, changing his mood from introspective and serene to sardonic and bitter. We are seeing again this deep need that Mr. Rochester has to fill a hole in his life. He has fallen into worldly patterns of living that he deeply regrets. But he cannot find his way out because he simply does not know how.

The more he talks with Jane, and the more she continues to point him in the direction of searching for less worldly aids in repentance, Mr. Rochester becomes less severe on himself. He is softening. However, this dark and foreboding heaviness that weighs over him and the entirety of Thornfield Hall, keeps him from fully attaining that deliverance.

How Can You Apply This to Your Own Life?

This chapter reveals even more why fear, guilt, shame, and condemnation can keep us from attaining the freedom God has called us to. Condemnation, in this sense, is the agreement with the curse that came out of the decision made by Adam and Eve in the Garden, but which has been dealt with on the cross.

"Verily, verily, I say unto you, He that heareth my word, and believeth on him that sent me, hath everlasting life, and shall not come into condemnation [subjectively or objectively for or against, accusation, damnation, judgment]*; but is passed from death unto life."* John 5:24

"There is therefore now no condemnation [sentencing] *to them which are in Christ Jesus, who walk not after the flesh* [human nature with its frailties (physically or morally) and passions, carnally minded]*, but after the Spirit. For the law of the Spirit of life in Christ Jesus hath made me free from the law of sin and death."* Romans 8:1-2

A lot of people lose the crucial call to action at the end of Romans 8:1. We are only under no condemnation *if* we are walking after the Holy Spirit in repentance. There is always a call to action on our parts. We have to *choose* to follow God. This does not mean we will be perfect all the time, but that we are continually working toward perfecting ourselves in Christ through what we focus our hearts and minds on.

Guilt tells us that our pasts will become our futures. This type of thinking will keep us tied to our sins as we are being told that we are one with the sins we participated in and that we will never be free of them. Guilt can also start worrying you with "what if" questions. "What if I could have done better?" "What if I had said this instead of that?" "What if I had made a different decision?"

Do you see how that keeps you stuck in bondage?

You cannot change the past or go back and fix things that you did wrong. However, you *can* break free of the cycle of "what ifs" and leave those past fears, hurts, and sins in your past. Repentance breaks us free from these strongholds.

Guilt: the fact or state of having committed an offense, crime, violation, or wrong, especially against moral or penal law culpability: a feeling of responsibility or remorse for some offense, crime, wrong, etc., whether real or imagined.[1]

Guilt also opens the doors to unforgiveness toward yourself as well as self-hatred and self-rejection. And then, you can see the downward spiral.[2]

Shame occurs when we want to cover these sins that we are guilty about. We do not want to confess them but keep them hidden, fearful lest we get found out.[2]

"And the eyes of them both were opened, and they knew that they were naked; and they sewed fig leaves together, and made themselves aprons." Genesis 3:7

Adam and Eve hid themselves from God when they realized that they were naked. They felt shame for doing what God expressly told them not to. When we begin to allow guilt to enter in and then shame to cover it and then fear on top of that that someone would find us out, we are then living in bondage. When we are in this type of bondage, God's love is rejected because we do not feel worthy of that love that is freely given.

Then, the product of all of these lies is separation from God, ourselves, and others as we continue to hide away. Isolation is a huge part of fear, guilt, and shame.

What do you do with this now?

I will refer you back to the 8 Rs of Freedom back in chapter one first. You must remove these lies from your life. You are *not* your past. You are *not* your guilt. You are *not* your shame. You are *not* your fear. God's love and forgiveness is right in front of you, just waiting for you to reach out to grasp.

Repentance for participating with fear, guilt, and shame is your first step toward healing and restoring your relationship with yourself and with God. This is not just an, "I'm sorry God, please forgive me," but a decision to complete forsake and turn away from the participation completely.

<u>Repentance</u>: desistance (interlinear Hebrew H5164), compunction [for guilt, including reformation]; by

implication, reversal of another's/one's decisions (interlinear Greek G3341).

"If we confess our sins, he is faithful and just to forgive us our sins, and to cleanse us from all unrighteousness." 1 John 1:9

"Unto thee, O LORD, do I lift up my soul. O my God, I trust in thee: let me not be ashamed, let not mine enemies triumph over me. Yea, let none that wait on thee be ashamed: let them be ashamed which transgress without cause [emptily, ineffectually, in vain]. *Shew me thy ways, O LORD; teach me thy paths. Lead me in thy truth, and teach me: for thou art the God of my salvation; on thee do I wait all the day."* Psalm 25:1-5

David is called a man after God's own heart and yet he was involved in both murder and adultery. How is this possible? David chose to come to God with his guilt and shame and repent for the sins he committed. This repentance restored his relationship with himself and God. This does not mean that he did right by any means. However, the Bible says that when we repent for our sins and turn from our wicked ways and live a life pleasing and acceptable to God, he is faithful to forgive our sins and bring us into our salvation (*1 John 1:9*).

We can see clearly through the Psalms that David did turn away from his sins and chose to dedicate his life wholly to God in the end.

"For there is no respect of persons [partiality, favoritism] *with God. For as many as have sinned without law shall also*

perish without law: and as many as have sinned in the law shall be judged by the law [the Gospel, a principle]; *(for not the hearers of the law are just before God, but the doers of the law shall be justified* [to render (i.e., show or regard as) just or innocent, free, be righteous]." Romans 2:11-13

"Let us therefore come boldly unto the throne of grace, that we may obtain mercy, and find grace to help in time of need." Hebrews 4:16

"There is no fear in love; but perfect love casteth out fear: because fear hath torment. He that feareth is not made perfect in love." 1 John 4:18

You are already accepted and loved by a holy and merciful heavenly Father. If you are able to come to a place of understanding of how deeply you are loved, you will then be able to fully accept and receive the forgiveness God has for you.

What will you project into the future? Fear, guilt, shame, and condemnation? Or love, peace, joy, and forgiveness?

Footnotes

[1] Collins English Dictionary – Complete & Unabridged 2012 digital edition (dictionary.com)

[2] Be In Health © references on their various teachings on fear, shame, and guilt

Chapter XXI

Jane has, for the past week, had strange dreams in which a child is always a part. Superstition was built into her as a child which led her to believe that dreaming of children or infants meant that there was trouble ahead.

At this time in history, superstition and the occult were very prominent parts of everyday living. Society was (*and still is*) constantly looking for ways outside of God for answers. This brings us to a very interesting subject—occultism.

<u>What is Occultism?</u>

"Therefore my people are gone into captivity [to uncover, lay bare, to carry away into exile], *because they have no knowledge* [unaware]: *and their honorable men are famished, and their multitude dried up with thirst. Therefore hell hath enlarged* [to grow wide] *herself, and opened her mouth* [entry] *without measure* [an appointment of time, space, quantity, labor or usage, decree, due, ordinance, set time]: *and their glory, and their multitude* [tumult, abundance, rumbling], *and their pomp* [destruction, horrible, noise, tumultuous], *and he that rejoiceth, shall descend into it."* Isaiah 5:13-14

Many Christians do not fully understand what occultism is and why we need to be wary of it. Occultism has found its way into many churches through very sneaky avenues. Because the churches are not teaching discernment the way they should, Christians are not realizing that they are allowing spirits of occultism into their lives and homes through movies, books, music, etc. There is a snare before our feet and if we do not recognize it for what it is, we will ultimately fall into that snare. This is why God's word is power and knowledge. He gives us all the tools we need to recognize occultism for what it is.

"We think Occultism is like going to a fortune-teller, doing tea readings, playing with Ouija boards or having seances. No. Occultism is anything that offers itself as truth – in place of God – and is not."[1]

The way we define occultism is simple. It is a belief or act that does not line up with God's word or it overshadows who He is. God is very clear about who He is and what we are to believe.

God is described as –

"I am Alpha and Omega, the beginning and the ending, saith the Lord, which is, and which was, and which is to come, the Almighty." Revelation 1:8

"Wherefore thou art great, O LORD God: for there is none like thee, neither is there any God beside thee, according to all that we have heard with our ears." 2 Samuel 7:22

"For I am the LORD, I change not; therefore ye sons of Jacob are not consumed." Malachi 3:6

"Hast thou not known? Hast thou not heard, that the everlasting God, the LORD, the Creator of the ends of the

earth, fainteth not, neither is weary? There is no searching of his understanding." Isaiah 40:28

"This then is the message which we have heard of him, and declare unto you, that God is light, and in him is no darkness at all. If we say that we have fellowship with him, and walk in darkness, we lie, and do not the truth: but if we walk in the light, as he is in the light, we have fellowship one with another, and the blood of Jesus Christ his Son cleanseth us from all sin." 1 John 1:5-7

There is never hypocrisy in the Bible. God's word is infallible because it came directly from Him through the inspiration of the Holy Spirit. Thus, we must understand that anything that strays against everything that is pure, lovely, admirable, just, peaceful, joyful, patient, and kind is not of God. (*Galatians 5:19*)

"But the wisdom that is from above is first pure, then peaceable, gentle, and easy to be intreated, full of mercy and good fruits, without partiality, and without hypocrisy." James 3:17

"He hath shewed thee, O man, what is good; and what doth the LORD require of thee, but to do justly, and to love mercy, and to walk humbly with thy God?" Micah 6:8

"And when he putteth forth his own sheep, he goeth before them, and the sheep follow him: for they know his voice." John 10:4

In the Old Testament, we see that God's people were continually taken into captivity because they kept choosing to follow pagan religions, worshipping idols, and following the occultic practices of these nations. In response to this, God allowed them to be taken captive because that is what they chose. Remember, we have free will to choose. God loves us enough to give us right to choose who and what we follow or believe. But there is still judgement that comes from poor decisions just as there are blessings that come from good decisions. Whatever we sow, that is also what we shall reap (*Galatians 6:7*). It is all about personal choice.

Superstition falls under occultism because it is providing you with a thought process that does not align up what God said about putting our faith in Him. That we be not anxious about our futures. Superstition tells us that something bad could or would happen if… This feeds fear, discontent, and unbelief, all of which take our thoughts away from God and onto our own, fallible selves or physical objects. We are trusting worldly influences to predict our futures instead of trusting in an Almighty God who created us and our futures.

Superstition is founded in occultism because it uses lies to make you believe that it is the truth.

"Occultism must always produce something in the physical realm to make you believe it is of God. That is why you have to be careful of lying signs and wonders, words and things that are coming in the physical dimension when you should believe God without them."[2]

Superstition:[3]

- *A belief or notion, not based on reason or knowledge, in or of the ominous significance of a particular thing, circumstance, occurrence, proceeding, or the like.*

- *A system or collection of such beliefs.*

- *Irrational fear of what is unknown or mysterious, especially in connection with religion.*

- *Any blindly accepted belief or notion.*

This can then become idolatry because we are placing our trust in something other than God and raising it higher than Him. When we rely on numbers or words or even physical signs to tell us our future or give us hope or peace, that is another form of idolatry. We are essentially elevating what God created above the Creator.

"They are of the world: therefore speak they of the world, and the world heareth them. We are of God: he that knoweth God heareth us; he that is not of God heareth not us. Hereby know we the spirit of truth, and the spirit of error." 1 John 4:5-6

"And this I say, lest any man should beguile [delude, deceive] *you with enticing words* [speech adapted to persuade, specious discourse leading others into error]. *For though I be absent in the flesh, yet am I with you in the spirit, joying and beholding your order, and the stedfastness of your faith in Christ. As ye have therefore received Christ Jesus the Lord, so walk ye in him: rooted and built up in him, and stablished in the faith, as ye have been taught, abounding therein with thanksgiving. Beware lest any man spoil you through philosophy* [love of wisdom] *and vain*

[empty] *deceit* [delusion]*, after the tradition of men, after the rudiments* [principle, element] *of the world, and not after Christ.*" Colossians 2:4-8

"*Have ye not seen a vain* [false, deceptive, lying] *vision, and have ye not spoken a lying* [deceptive] *divination, whereas ye say, the LORD saith it; albeit I have not spoken?*" Ezekiel 13:7

"*This wisdom descendeth not from above, but is earthly, sensual, devilish. For where envying and strife is, there is confusion and every evil work. But the wisdom that is from above is first pure, then peaceable, gentle, and easy to be intreated, full of mercy and good fruits, without partiality* [uncertainty, ambiguity]*, and without hypocrisy.*" James 3:15-17

"*And when they shall say unto you, seek unto them that have familiar spirits* [necromancer, ghost, spirit of a dead one]*, and unto wizards* [a conjurer] *that peep* [chatter, whisper]*, and that mutter* [meditate, mourn, roar, utter]*: should not a people seek unto their God? For the living to the dead?*" Isaiah 8:19

"*And lest thou lift up thine eyes unto heaven, and when thou seest the sun, and the moon, and the stars, even all the host of heaven, shouldest be driven to worship them, and serve them, which the LORD thy God hath divided unto all nations under the whole heaven.*" Deuteronomy 4:19

The general rule is if the world loves it and gawks over it, it is likely that it is not of God and should be avoided or at least questioned. Occultism is such a complicated subject that needs to be addressed among believers more often.

God loves us so much that He wants us to recognize what is not of Him. But He also wants us to have the knowledge to know *how* to discern between good and evil. If you are ever unsure about something, God tells us to go to Him for wisdom and discernment. Pray about it. The Holy Spirit will give you discernment regarding the thing you are questioning as long as you are seeking truth, setting aside your own wisdom and desires.

I also recommend that if you have any questions regarding occultism, that you check out the book I have quoted and listed in the footnotes of this chapter. It will help provide you with excellent guidance on this very important topic.

"'Mr. John died yesterday was a week, at his chambers in London.' [Mr. Leaven]

'And how does his mother bear it?' [Jane]

'Why, you see, Miss Eyre, it is not a common mishap: his life has been very wild: these last three years he gave himself up to strange ways, and his death was shocking.'

'I heard from Bessie he was not doing well.'

'Doing well! He could not do worse: he ruined his health and his estate amongst the worst men and the worst women. He got into debt and into jail: his mother helped him out twice, but as soon as he was free he returned to his old companions and habits. His head was not strong: the knaves he lived

It is such a sad thing to see someone fall so far in life. If you
remember back when we discussed John's character more
fully, we recognized that he was pampered and coddled and
not punished for his wrongs. Because of this, his character
was spoilt. He became a lawless, drunken, desperate man.
Unfortunately, this also spread to his family and brought his
mother into desecration and illness.

*"On a dark, misty, raw morning in January, I had left a
hostile roof with a desperate and embittered heart – a sense of
outlawry and almost of reprobation – to seek the chilly
harbourage of Lowood: that bourne so far away and
unexplored. The same hostile roof now again rose before me:
my prospects were doubtful yet; and I had yet an aching
heart. I still felt as a wanderer on the face of the earth; but I
experienced firmer trust in myself and my own powers, and
less withering dread of oppression. The gaping wound of my
wrongs, too, was now quite healed; and the flame of
resentment extinguished."*

Healing is occurring in Jane's heart and has for a while. Her
resentment and anguish over her childhood has been
softened.

Jane sees her cousins for the first time in many years and they are almost unrecognizable from the last time we were acquainted with them.

"..sundry side-glances that measured me from head to foot – now traversing the folds of my drab merino pelisse, and now lingering on the plain trimming of my cottage bonnet. Young ladies have a remarkable way of letting you know that they think you a 'quiz' without actually saying the words. A certain superciliousness of look, coolness of manner, nonchalance of tone, express fully their sentiments on the point, without committing them by any positive rudeness in word or deed.

A sneer, however, whether covert or open, had now no longer that power over me it once possessed: as I sat between my cousins, I was surprised to find how easy I felt under the total neglect of the one and the semi-sarcastic attentions of the other – Eliza did not mortify, nor Georgiana ruffle me. The fact was, I had other things to think about; within the last few months feelings had been stirred in me so much more potent than any they could raise – pains and pleasures so much more acute and exquisite had been excited than any it was in their power to inflict or bestow – that their airs gave me no concern either for good or bad."

During this trip, Jane is reliving painful memories, perhaps without the former sting, but nonetheless, she is remembering her life at Gateshead with discomfort. It is truly amazing to see how far she has come since her childhood with her aunt and cousins. She has come to a place of peace regarding her past and forgiveness has released her from bitterness and resentment toward these people who should have loved her.

"It is a happy thing that time quells the longings of vengeance and hushes the promptings of rage and aversion. I had left this woman in bitterness and hate, and I came back to her now with no other emotion than a sort of ruth for her great sufferings, and a strong yearning to forget and forgive all injuries — to be reconciled and clasp hands in amity.

The well-known face was there: stern, relentless as ever — there was that peculiar eye which nothing could melt, and the somewhat raised, imperious, despotic eyebrow. How often had it lowered on me menace and hate! And how the recollection of childhood's terrors and sorrows revived as I traced its harsh line now! And yet I stooped down and kissed her: she looked at me."

"Again she regarded me so icily, I felt at once that her opinion of me — her feeling towards me — was unchanged and unchangeable. I knew by her stony eye — opaque to tenderness, indissoluble to tears — that she was resolved to consider me bad to the last; because to believe me good would give her no generous pleasure: only a sense of mortification.

I felt pain, and then I felt ire; and then I felt a determination to subdue her — to be her mistress in spite both of her nature and her will."

Here is where we get a better picture as to why Mrs. Reed acts with so much hostility toward Jane, which is important for helping us separate Mrs. Reed, the person God created, from her bitterness.

"'I had a dislike to her mother always; for she was my husband's only sister, and a great favourite with him: he opposed the family's disowning her when she made her low marriage; and when news came of her death, he wept like a simpleton. He would send for the baby; though I entreated him rather to put it out to nurse and pay for its maintenance. I hated it the first time I set my eyes on it – a sickly, whining, pining thing! It would wail in its cradle all night long – not screaming heartily like any other child, but whimpering and moaning. Reed pitied it; and he used to nurse it and notice it as if it had been his own: more, indeed, than he ever noticed his own at that age. He would try to make my children friendly to the little beggar: the darlings could not bear it, and he was angry with them when they showed their disklike. In his last illness, he had it brought continually to his bedside; and but an hour before he died, he bound me by vow to keep the creature. I would as soon have been charged with a pauper brat out of a workhouse: but he was weak, naturally weak.'"

Mrs. Reed saw her husband as weak. This is probably why she was resentful and felt she had to rule her household with an iron fist. As we have already seen, the bitterness of the mother has passed to the children. Eliza in particular is ripe with bitterness and lashes out at her sister in one final monologue.

"'Georgiana, a more vain and absurd animal than you was certainly never allowed to cumber the earth. You had no right to be born, for you make no use of life. Instead of living for, in, and with yourself, as a reasonable being ought, you seek only to fasten your feebleness on some other person's strength: if no one can be found willing to burden her or himself with such a fat, weak, puffy, useless thing, you cry out that you are ill-treated, neglected, miserable. Then, too, existence for you must be a scene of continual change and excitement, or else the world is a dungeon: you must be admired, you must be courted, you must be flattered — you must have music, dancing, and society — or you languish, you die away…Take this advice: the first and last I shall offer you; that you will not want me or anyone else, happen what may. Neglect it — go on as heretofore, craving, whining, and idling — and suffer the results of your idiocy, however bad and insufferable they may be. I tell you this plainly; and listen: for though I shall no more repeat what I am now about to say, I shall steadily act on it. After my mother's death, I wash my hands of you: from the day her coffin is carried to the vault in Gateshead Church, you and I will be as separate as if we had never known each other. You need not think that because we chanced to be born of the same parents, I shall suffer you to fasten me down by even the feeblest claim: I can tell you this — if the whole human race, ourselves excepted, were swept away, and we two stood alone on the earth, I would leave you in the old world, and betake myself to the new.'"

There is so much hurt going around in this home. Everyone is hurting each other through their words and actions. It is very sad to think that Eliza believes that this type of behavior would be accepted and rewarded by God. It is by no means humble or loving.

"True, generous feeling is made small account of by some, but here were two natures rendered, the one intolerably acrid, the other despicably savourless for the want of it. Feeling without judgment is a washy draught indeed; but judgment untampered by feeling is too bitter and husky a morsel for human deglutition."

To conclude, Jane allows peace and forgiveness to cover herself and her aunt.

"'Love me, then, or hate me, as you will.' I said at last. 'you have my full and free forgiveness: ask now for God's, and be at peace.'"

"A strange and solemn object was that corpse to me. I gazed on it with gloom and pain: nothing soft, nothing sweet, nothing pitying, or hopeful, or subduing did it inspire; only a grating anguish for her woes – not my loss – and a sombre, tearless dismay at the fearfulness of death in such a form."

Jane is sad for the loss of the woman Mrs. Reed could have been. She is sad that this woman died with such pain and torment in her spirit.

How Can You Apply This to Your Own Life?

This chapter contains so much! It is a lot to take in.

Throughout this book, we have seen how bitterness, envy, and other spiritual torments can be passed through the generations. Occultism can also be inherited from a generation that is so involved with these practices including massive amounts of fear.

The Victorian age in particular was obsessed with all kinds of occultism. Tarot cards, Ouija boards, and seances for example. Because of this, these practices were accepted and sought after. This opened doors to many other deceptions and spiritual discernment went to an all-time low.

The church is struggling to help congregants understand the meaning of discernment, or they simply overlook the subject entirely because it is a very difficult one. I strongly encourage you to dig deeper into occultism as you might find some things wrapped up in occultism that you never considered before. Like I said earlier in this chapter, occultism is a tricky thing. It can come in various forms to tempt and deceive us. Knowing just how slimy it is and in what avenues it takes a foothold is the first step to removing it from your life.

And, as I mentioned toward the beginning, Christians are constantly deceived because occultism can hide in some of our favorite books, movies, television shows, music, toys, and more.

Footnotes

[1] Introduction to Occultism by Henry W. Wright page 1

[2] Introduction to Occultism by Henry W. Wright page 48

[3] Collins English Dictionary – Complete & Unabridged 2012 digital edition (dictionary.com)

Chapter XXII

"Georgiana said she dreaded being left alone with Eliza; from her she got neither sympathy in her dejection, support in her fears, nor aid in her preparations; so I bore with her feeble-minded wailings and selfish lamentations as well as I could, and did my best in sewing for her and packing her dresses. It is true, that while I worked, she would idle; and I thought to myself, 'If you and I were destined to live always together, cousin, we would commence matters on a different footing. I should not settle tamely down into being the forbearing party; I should assign you your share of labour, and compel you to accomplish it, or else it should be left undone: I should insist, also, on your keeping some of those drawling, half-insincere complaints hushed in your own breast. It is only because our connection happens to be very transitory, and comes at a peculiarly mournful season, that I consent thus to render it so patient and compliant on my part.'"

All the Reed children have been coddled to the point of uselessness. Jane bears her cousin's ennui and ramblings well and patiently because she understands that Georgiana was raised in a way that did not require her to raise a hand to do anything for herself.

Eliza, on the other hand, though extremely bitter and resentful, shows more competency toward labor and rejects idleness.

"When we parted, she said: 'Good-bye, cousin Jane Eyre; I wish you well: you have some sense.'

I then returned: 'You are not without sense, cousin Eliza; but what you have, I suppose, in another year will be walled up alive in a French convent. However, it is not my business, and so it suits you, I don't much care.'"

Finally, after a month of being from her home, Jane is free to return! For the first time in her life, she is experiencing the joy of going back home without fear.

"I knew there would be pleasure in meeting my master again, even though broken by the fear that he was so soon to cease to be my master, and by the knowledge that I was nothing to him: but there was ever in Mr. Rochester (so at least I thought) such a wealth of the power of communicating happiness, that to taste but of the crumbs he scattered to stray and stranger birds like me, was to feast genially. His last words were balm: they seemed to imply that it imported something to him whether I forgot him or not. And he had spoken of Thornfield as my home – would that it were my home!"

"Mr. Rochester had sometimes read my unspoken thoughts with an acumen to me incomprehensible: in the present instance he took no notice of my abrupt vocal response; but he smiled at me with a certain smile he had of his own, and which he used but on rare occasions. He seemed to think it too good for common purposes: it was the real sunshine of feeling – he shed it over me now."

Peace resides over the whole Thornfield home. Jane is, at last, in a place where she is loved, admired, cared for, and wanted. It is everything she has ever wanted and prayed for.

"...there is no happiness like that of being loved by your fellow-creatures, and feeling that your presence is an addition to their comfort."

"If, in the moments I and my pupil spent with him, I lacked spirits and sank into inevitable dejection, he became even gay. Never had he called me more frequently to his presence; never been kinder to me when there – and, alas! Never had I loved him so well."

How Can You Apply This to Your Own Life?

It is a wonderful and glorious thing to be loved!

Not just romantically, but as a human being and a friend.

There is a reason why love is considered the greatest gift you can give a person. So many people wither away in their desires to be loved. Lack of love and even the inability to receive love can lead to addictions, self-hatred, rejection, and door points to other spiritual oppression.

What is an unloving spirit?

"It is an anti Christ spirit sent to steal, kill and destroy – you. It's a spirit that makes you feel unclean and unworthy. You feel like you don't measure up, you're no good. When you hear your voice talking it sounds like a piece of sandpaper on the side of an old piece of metal. When you look at yourself in the mirror, it says, 'you are not the fairest of them all, you old ugly thing.' When you look at someone else, you're sure they hate your guts. You think you can see it in their eyes. Yet, Psalm 139 says you are 'fearfully and wonderfully made.' When you understand the Unloving, you will have the discernment to resist the devil so he must flee from you."[1]

"But God, who is rich in mercy, for his great love wherewith he loved us, even when we were dead in sins, hath quickened us together [to make one alive together] *with Christ, (by grace ye are saved;) and hath raised us up together, and made us sit together in heavenly places in Christ Jesus:"*
Ephesians 2:4-6

"Though I speak with the tongues of men and of angels, and have not charity [affection or benevolence, love-feast, dear, love, brotherly love], *I am become as sounding brass* [money, coins], *or a tinkling cymbal. And though I have the gift of prophecy, and understand all mysteries, and all knowledge; and though I have all faith, so that I could remove mountains, and have not charity, I am nothing. And though I bestow all my goods to feed the poor, and though I give* [surrender, put in prison, cast] *my body to be burned, and have not charity, it profiteth me nothing. Charity suffereth long* [longsuffering, patient, patiently endure], *and is kind; charity envieth not; charity vaunteth* [boast, a self display] *not itself, is not puffed up* [make proud, haughty],

doth not behave itself unseemly, seeketh not her own [own conceits – selfish], *is not easily provoked, thinketh no evil; rejoiceth not in iniquity* [injustice, wrongfulness of character, unrighteousness, wrong], *but rejoiceth in the truth; beareth* [to cover with silence, endure patiently] *all things, believeth all things, hopeth all things, endureth* [have fortitude, persevere, abide] *all things. Charity never faileth: but whether there be prophecies, they shall fail; whether there be tongues, they shall cease; whether there be knowledge, it shall vanish away. For we know in part, and we prophesy in part. But when that which is perfect is come, then that which is in part shall be done away. When I was a child, I spake as a child, I understood as a child, I thought as a child: but when I became a man, I put away childish things. For now we see through* [behold, perceive, take heed] *a glass* [mirror] *darkly; but then face to face: now I know in part; but then shall I know even as also I am known. And now abideth faith, hope, charity, these three; but the greatest of these is charity."* 1 Corinthians 13

Love is the greatest gift God gave us and thus should be shared with others. If you are feeling unloved today, know that you have a Father in heaven who loves you so deeply that He gave His one and only Son to die for you. You are more precious to Him than anything else in Creation. You were designed so beautifully in His image. He knew you before you were born and will continue to love you no matter how far you fall in life.

For further reading, I urge you to search these scriptures. They are filled with the love that our Father feels toward us; the love that you should have for yourself and others. There are so many verses that express His love that it would take up many more pages. The following verses are an excellent place to begin.

- Psalm 46:1
- Zephaniah 3:17
- Lamentations 3:22-24
- Jeremiah 31:3
- John 15:9
- Isaiah 43:1
- 1 John 3:1
- Matthew 11:28
- Exodus 14:14
- Ephesians 2:10
- John 10:10

Footnotes

[1] Unloving by Henry W. Wright (For My Life ™ © 2012 Be In Health workbook page 119)

Chapter XXIII

"A splendid midsummer shone over England: skies so pure, suns so radiant as were then seen in long succession, seldom favour even singly, our wave-girt land. It was as if a band of Italian days had come from the South, like a flock of glorious passenger birds, and lighted to rest them on the cliffs of Albion."

This paragraph starts a beautiful chapter in the life of Jane and Mr. Rochester. We're opening with the hope that there are better days ahead for them both. And then, Jane receives a crushing blow as Mr. Rochester begins to discuss the probability of her moving away from Thornfield to seek a new position when he is married.

"'…You'll like Ireland, I think: they're such warm-hearted people there, they say.'

'It is a long way off, sir.'

'No matter — a girl of your sense will not object to the voyage or the distance.'

'Not the voyage, but the distance: and then the sea is a barrier —'

'From what, Jane?'

'From England and from Thornfield: and —'

'Well?'

'From you, sir.'

I said this almost involuntarily, and, with as little sanction of free will, my tears gushed out. I did not cry so as to be heard, however; I avoided sobbing. The thought of Mrs. O'Gall and Bitternutt Lodge struck cold to my heart; and colder the thought of all the brine and foam, destined, as it seemed, to rush between me and the master at whose side I now walked, and coldest the remembrance of the wider ocean — wealth, caste, custom intervened between me and what I naturally and inevitably loved."

This is the first time that Jane has openly told Mr. Rochester how she feels. She has always been more reserved when conversation veered toward emotions and how she was feeling in certain moments. In this moment, Jane is openly grieving the fact that she is being sent away…far away from the people she has begun to love dearly.

Not only is Jane revealing her true feelings about Mr. Rochester, but he is also finding that he is able to do the same in regard to his feelings toward Jane.

"'Because,' he said, 'I sometimes have queer feeling with regard to you — especially when you are near me, as now: it is as if I had a string somewhere under my left ribs, tightly and inextricably knotted to a similar string situated in the corresponding quarter of your little frame. And if that boisterous Channel, and two hundred miles or so of land come broad between us, I am afraid that cord of communion will be snapped; and then I've a nervous notion I should take to bleeding inwardly. As for you — you'd forget me.'"

This paragraph is one of my favorite explanations of how distance between two people who love one another can feel. It reveals how deeply Mr. Rochester has begun to regard Jane and how reliant he is on her for balance in his life. He loves her…more than he is admitting and more than she is aware.

"The vehemence of emotion, stirred by grief and love within me, was claiming mastery, and struggling for full sway, and asserting a right to predominate, to overcome, to live, rise, and reign at last: yes — and to speak.

'I grieve to leave Thornfield: I love Thornfield — I love it, because I have lived in it a full and delightful life — momentarily at least. I have not been trampled on. I have not been petrified. I have not been buried with inferior minds, and excluded from every glimpse of communion with what is bright and energetic and high. I have talked, face to face, with what I reverence, with what I delight in — with an original, a vigorous, an expanded mind. I have known you, Mr. Rochester; and it strikes me with terror and anguish to feel I absolutely must be torn from you for ever. I see the necessity of departure; and it is like looking on the necessity of death.'"

Because Jane Eyre is written from the perspective of Jane, giving us as readers the windows through her own eyes, we do not get a better idea of what is going on in the heads of others. We know that Jane deeply loves Mr. Rochester for who he is. She does not set him up on a pedestal of idolatry, thinking he is a perfect, heroic, completely moral man. Even though she does not yet understand the gravity of his past, she receives the fact that he is actively trying and choosing to be a better man.

For years, he has tried so hard to escape his past, searching for anything to redeem him. But through all that searching, he did not really have something to be better for. The moment Jane, with the innocent, depths to her character, entered his life, he found that he wanted to be a better man *for her*. To live up to a standard that would deserve her companionship and admiration; and eventually, her love.

"'My bride is here,' he said, again drawing me to him, 'because my equal is here, and my likeness. Jane, will you marry me?'"

Now that we know that Mr. Rochester has no intention of marrying Blanche Ingram, it seems cruel to us that he would string Jane along like this. Why torture her with the idea of sending her away when he had no desire to do so in the first place?

Perhaps Mr. Rochester needed to know where Jane stood as far as her affection toward him. She had never communicated anything of love toward him. Why risk his heart if she was indifferent?

On the other hand, perhaps Mr. Rochester is battling with a bigger fear that we have yet to discover. His desire to be with Jane and not lose her could quite possibly put him in a moral dilemma (*of which we will learn of soon*). And with his additional desire to be worthy of her love and be a better man, does he allow his morality to be compromised? There are so many factors that lead to why Mr. Rochester is acting the way he is and until we get the bigger picture in the next few chapters, we cannot fully grasp his reasoning.

"But what had befallen the night? The moon was not yet set, and we were all in shadow: I could scarcely see my master's face near as I was. And what ailed the chestnut tree? It writhed and groaned; while wind roared in the laurel walk, and came sweeping over us."

"Before I left my bed in the morning, little Adèle came running in to tell me that the great horse-chestnut at the bottom of the orchard had been struck by lightning in the night, and half of it split away."

Charlotte Brontë uses these "signs" to tell of a greater turmoil going on beneath the surface of the story we are reading. The splitting of the chestnut tree under which Jane and Mr. Rochester were sitting the night before, confessing their love, is very symbolic at this moment in the story. In fact, this symbolism will return in the second-to-last chapter of the book.

There is something lurking in the background that has yet to be revealed. We cannot forget the mystery that surrounds Thornfield and keeps Mr. Rochester tethered to his past. Once that mystery is revealed, we can delve further into the battle going on in Mr. Rochester's heart and mind, dividing him between the man he desperately wants to be and the man he is trying to leave in the past.

How Can You Apply This to Your Own Life?

One of the elements I hope my writing and analysis of literary works highlights is how different people are. This may seem an obvious conclusion to anyone even if they are not readers. However, the beauty of books, Jane Eyre specifically, is that they offer us such a realistic interpretation of human nature and how to approach differing personalities, backgrounds, and perspectives in the real world.

Though these characters that we have grown to love (*or not care too much about*) are fictional, they offer up a realistic version of a person that we might meet in our own everyday lives. How do we approach them? How do we respond to their differing views? How can we practice separation with particularly difficult personalities?

I love Jane Eyre because Charlotte Brontë has written it in such a way that we are able to look at people for who they were created to be from the perspective of an outside observer. We can practice, right along Jane, what it is like to separate the other characters from their sin and poor decisions. Not only that, but we are also able to learn how to use our skills of observation to help understand people and why they act out in certain ways. It often has nothing to do with us, but something stirring deep within them.

One of my goals when doing literature analysis is to help open a world of possibilities to generations of believers and non-believers to aid them in understanding the complexity of our world and the people in it. Even with books that were not meant to be direct influences of faith such as those written by Alexandre Dumas (*The Three Musketeers, The Count of Monte Cristo, etc.*) or Anthony Trollope (*Doctor Thorne, Barchester Towers, etc.*) can be used as ways to teach us honor, nobility, the price of poor decisions and the blessings of good, and how relationship and love can be a cornerstone to growth.

Whether they meant to or not, most classic authors have some element of faith attached to their works. Most were raised in a culture that respected faith and God's word, while current generations have lost sight of scripture and its importance. We are all were created by a wonderful and loving Father and He has given every one of us a measure of faith (*Romans 12:3*). In a lot of classic literature, we see that measure of faith either in big ways, such as here in Jane Eyre, or in small veins of thought, such as in Doctor Thorne.

While I love analyzing literature, the Bible is the ultimate source of wisdom. It is the best book in the world to teach us about who we are, why we were created and for what purpose, as well as how to treat others. It is the perfect blueprint for life. As wonderful as these classic novels are, they could never hold a candle to the perfection and holiness that is the Bible. This is because it came from the most perfect being of all; God the Word inspired by the Holy Spirit.

"All scripture is given by inspiration of God, and is profitable for doctrine, for reproof, for correction, for instruction in righteousness; that the man of God may be perfect, thoroughly furnished unto all good works." 2 Timothy 3:16-17

"Thy word is a lamp unto my feet, and a light unto my path."
Psalm 119:105

I hope that through these devotionals, you have learned something about yourself, others, and God. One of the biggest themes we have been discussing in the past couple of chapters is allowing people to show you who they are before making a decision on their character. This is such a difficult thing to do, especially when we meet someone who rubs us the wrong way. It is easy to write them off and not give them a chance. But often times, the harder path is the one that brings the most beautiful results. Sometimes the hardest people to get to know can become the dearest of friends.

Our calling, as believers, is to spread the Gospel and share the love of Christ with everyone. How can we do this if we are being held up by uncomfortable personalities? There will be times when the Holy Spirit will release us from a person who has made up their mind in a certain way. However, we must always be open to be a loving and shining example of God's love regardless of whether we are called to minister to the people we are around. Be a light on the hill!

"Ye are the light of the world. A city that is set on a hill cannot be hid. Neither do men light a candle, and put it under a bushel, but on a candlestick; and it giveth light unto all that are in the house. Let our light so shine before men, that they may see your good works, and glorify your Father which is in heaven." Matthew 5:15-16

Chapter XXIV

"While arranging my hair, I looked at my face in the glass, and felt it was no longer plain: there was hope in its aspect and life in its colour; and my eyes seemed as if they had beheld the fount of fruition, and borrowed beams from the lustrous ripple. I had often been unwilling to look at my master, because I feared he could not be pleased at my look; but I was sure I might lift my face to his now, and not cool his affection by its expression. I took a plain but clean and light summer dress from my drawer and put it on: it seemed no attire had ever so well become me, because none had I ever worn in so blissful a mood."

Jane is so happy that she wants everyone else to be happy too. Even the birds could not hold a candle to the musical sound of her rejoicing heart. Love has altered her perspective on her outward appearance as well, finding herself attractive and pleasing. All this sudden change to her life, however, seems too good to be true and Jane refers to it as being a fairytale.

"'Jane, you look blooming, and smiling, and pretty,' said he: 'truly pretty this morning. Is this my pale little elf? Is this my mustard-seed? This little sunny-faced girl with the dimpled cheek and rosy lips; the satin-smooth hazel hair, and the radiant hazel eyes?' (I had green eyes, reader; but you must excuse the mistake for him they were new-dyed, I suppose)"

This is the first time anyone has ever referred to Jane as being pretty. With all her descriptions of others, we have been left in the dark as to what Jane looks like, and now we have a better idea. Mr. Rochester is seeing Jane in a new and beautiful light.

"'You are a beauty in my eyes, and a beauty just after the desire of my heart – delicate and aerial.'

'Puny and insignificant, you mean. You are dreaming, sir – or you are sneering. For God's sake don't be ironical!'"

Jane might sound self-deprecating at this moment, but I believe that she is also trying to keep Mr. Rochester from seeing her as more than human. She wants him to see who she is and not be raised on a pedestal of perfection just because he loves her. Flattery does not appeal to Jane.

The conversation then changes as Jane desires to know why Mr. Rochester took such pains for her to believe that he wished to marry Blanche Ingram.

"'Well, I feigned courtship of Miss Ingram, because I wished to render you as madly in love with me as I was with you; and I knew jealousy would be the best ally I could call in for the furtherance of that end.'

'Excellent! Now you are small – not one whit bigger than the end of my little finger. It was a burning shame and a scandalous disgrace to act in that way. Did you think nothing of Miss Ingram's feelings, sir?'

'Her feelings are concentrated in one – pride; and that needs humbling. Were you jealous, Jane?'

'Never mind, Mr. Rochester: it is in no way interesting to you to know that...'"

He is always teasing and provoking a response from Jane in some form or other. We have discussed in the previous chapter how it is very probable that Mr. Rochester pulled Jane along a little because he wanted to be sure of her feelings toward him. Though we might not agree with the way in which he did this, it seems fair in this case. Remember, he is the master of the house with good standing in the community and Jane is simply a governess working for him. Jane could risk him sending her away if she were to share her love and have him not reciprocate it. Likewise, if he were to approach Jane and she not feel the same, she would be forced to leave her place for another reason.

On top of the culture at the time and the difficulties presented by their respective places in the Thornfield household, Mr. Rochester and Jane are not the type to openly express their emotions. Naturally then, special devices to determine mutual affection might seem necessary. Besides, both seemed to enjoy teasing and testing one another.

Switching gears, Jane continues to be honorable in her concern for others rather than focusing on her own life and happiness. She expresses that she cannot fully enjoy her love and happiness as long as she knows that another was suffering at the expense of losing theirs. In this case, and though she does not particularly like Blanche, she hopes that she does not feel thrown aside or rejected.

"He was quite peremptory, both in look and voice. The chill of Mrs. Fairfax's warnings, and the damp of her doubts were upon me: something of unsubstantiality and uncertainty had beset my hopes. I half lost the sense of power over him. I was about mechanically to obey him, without further remonstrance; but as he helped me into the carriage, he looked at my face.

'What is the matter?' he asked; 'all the sunshine is gone. Do you really wish the bairn to go? Will it annoy you if she is left behind?'

'I would far rather she went, sir.'

'Then off for your bonnet, and back like a flash of lightning!' cried he to Adèle."

Not having the approval of Mrs. Fairfax does hurt Jane. Jane has developed a very close kinship with her, and she is sad and irritated that there is now misunderstanding between them.

"'It would, indeed, be a relief,' I thought, 'if I had ever so small an independency; I never can bear being dressed like a doll by Mr. Rochester, or sitting like a second Danae with the golden shower falling daily round me.'"

Not having grown up in wealth or grandeur, Jane does not require or desire frivolity. She has simple needs and desires and does not like to be spoiled, petted, or fussed over. Above all, Jane abhors pampering another's vanity and setting them up as greater than they are.

"…I ventured once more to meet my master's and lover's eye, which most pertinaciously sought mine, though I averted both face and gaze. He smiled; and I thought his smile was such as a sultan might, in a blissful and fond moment, bestow on a slave his gold and gems had enriched: I crushed his hand, which was ever hunting mine, vigorously, and thrust it back to him red with the passionate pressure."

Romance is something that is very new to Jane. It seems to frighten her a little. After being sung to so sweetly by Mr. Rochester, she almost pushes him away instead of showering him with loving caresses. She will learn in time the ways in which Mr. Rochester shows his affection just as he will learn hers.

"I assured him I was naturally hard – very flinty, and that he would often find me so; and that, moreover, I was determined to show him divers rugged points in my character before the ensuing four weeks elapsed: he should know fully what sort of a bargain he had made, while there was yet time to rescind it."

Again, we see that she is avoiding the sappiness of romance by keeping Mr. Rochester at arm's length during their courtship phase. She even mentions that she does not want to "sink into a bathos of sentiment." This also shows that as much as Mr. Rochester teases her, she gives it right back to him.

"He was kept, to be sure, rather cross and crusty; but on the whole I could see he was excellently entertained, and that a lamb-like submission and turtle-dove sensibility, while

fostering his despotism more, would have pleased his judgement, satisfied his common-sense, and even suited his taste less."

"Yet after all my task was not an easy one; often I would rather have pleased than teased him. My future husband was becoming to me my whole world; and more than the world: almost my hope of heaven. He stood between me and every thought of religion, as an eclipse intervenes between man and the broad sun. I could not, in those days, see God for His creature: of whom I had made an idol."

In the end, Jane recognizes that she is beginning to hold Mr. Rochester in greater esteem than she ought to. She is losing sight of the fact that he is an imperfect person and not one to be idolized. God did not matter as much in her life as her dear Mr. Rochester did. This is a very dangerous place to be.

<u>How Can You Apply This to Your Own Life?</u>

We already know that love is a wonderful gift.

"Owe [be indebted, debt] *no man any thing, but to love one another: for he that loveth another hath fulfilled the law."*
Romans 13:8

"A new commandment I give unto you, that ye love one another; as I have loved you, that ye also love one another."
John 13:34

"Beloved, let us love one another: for love is of God; and every one that loveth is born of God, and knoweth God. He

that loveth not knoweth not God; for God is love." 1 John 4:7-8

"And above all things have fervent charity among yourselves: for charity shall cover the multitude of sins." 1 Peter 4:8

But when we start to raise that love for another up higher than the Creator, we have then entered into the territory of idolatry. Idolatry is expressly mentioned in one of the ten commandments.

"For thou shalt worship no other god: for the LORD, whose name is Jealous, is a jealous God:" Exodus 34:14

"Thou shalt have no other gods before me." Exodus 20:3

Setting up gods in our lives does not always come in the form of worshiping a statue, graven image, or mythical deity. A god can be anything that we raise higher than the one, true God and this is why idolatry goes hand-in-hand with occultism. Idolatry could come in the form of raising up a family member, a job, a friend or mentor, books, movies, music, anger, pride, money and wealth, envy, yourself, success, approval, health, food, knowledge or wisdom, or even creation itself above God and His holiness.

"The idols of the heathens are silver and gold, the work of men's hands. They have mouths, but they speak not; eyes have they, but they see not; they have ears, but they hear not; neither is there any breath in their mouths. They that make them are like unto them: so is every one that trusteth in them." Psalm 135:15-17

"They that observe [regard, give heed] *lying* [in the sense of desolating, evil, ruin, guile, uselessness, false] *vanities* [emptiness, something unsatisfactory] *forsake their own mercy* [beauty, favor, goodness, kindness]." Jonah 2:8

"Wherefore, my dearly beloved, flee from idolatry." 1 Corinthians 10:14

If you remember from our discussion about occultism, you already know that anything that eclipses (*just as Jane said*) God and His word, is occultism. Idolatry falls into this category because, being raised up in worship, it overshadows God. What we ultimately treasure above all else in our hearts is what we worship.

What do you treasure in your life? Are you treasuring another person, object, or achievement more than God?

"Lay not up for yourselves treasures upon earth , where moth and rust doth corrupt, and where thieves break through and steal: But lay up for yourselves treasures in heaven, where neither moth nor rust doth corrupt, and where thieves do not break through nor steal: for where your treasure is, there will your heart be also." Matthew 6:19-21

"For where your treasure is, there will your heart be also." Luke 12:34

"No servant can serve two masters: for either he will hate the one, and love the other; or else he will hold to the one, and despise the other. Ye cannot serve God and mammon [treasure, wealth, riches]." Luke 16:13

Jane is raising Mr. Rochester higher than her own faith. If you think back a couple chapters, we discussed her ability to see Mr. Rochester for his flaws as well as his virtues. She did not raise him above the fallibility of humankind. In this chapter, and as she fell more in love with Mr. Rochester, she puts so much faith in him and his fallibility instead of an infallible heavenly Father. Eventually, people will disappoint us. That is why loving your neighbor and forgiveness are so often spoken of in the Bible. It is because God knows that we are not perfect, and we will be at odds with our neighbors at some point in our lives.

What we think about, talk about, and participate in constantly, will become a part of us. Immersing ourselves in God's word helps us store up our treasures in heaven. Peacefulness, joy, love, kindness, forgiveness, gentleness, self-control, and truth will be your treasures.

Take your thoughts captive and mind where you are placing your trust and identity. Love the people around you as Christ loved, but do not raise one another higher than the God who created them. It is all about balance. And, if you ever feel that you are not sure about something, pray about it. The Holy Spirit will give you discernment and wisdom.

Chapter XXV

"The cards of address alone remained to nail on: they lay, four little squares, in the drawer. Mr. Rochester had himself written the direction, 'Mrs. Rochester – Hotel, London,' on each: I could not persuade myself to affix them, or to have them affixed. Mrs. Rochester! She did not exist: she would not be born till to-morrow, some time after eight o'clock A.M.; and I would wait to be assured she had come into the world alive before I assigned to her all that property."

Everything is all prepared for Jane and Mr. Rochester's wedding, which is to take place the following day. However, there is still some hesitancy in her preparations and thoughts as she finishes up the final details. Jane is experiencing some fears about this new phase of life she is about to embark on. Though she faces change head-on in most cases, Jane is not one who faces it without some amount of trepidation.

"I had at heart a strange and anxious thought. Something had happened which I could not comprehend; no one knew of or had seen the event but myself: it had taken place the preceding night. Mr. Rochester that night was absent from home; nor was he yet returned…I waited now his return; eager to disburthen my mind, and to seek of him the solution of the enigma that perplexed me. Stay till he comes, reader; and, when I disclose my secret to him, you shall share the confidence."

Though I do not believe that signs show us our futures or that nature mirrors our lives, authors will sometimes use this type of descriptive writing to express deeper meaning to their characters and storyline. The following paragraph struck me as a very interesting parallel for what we will see in the next chapter between Jane and Mr. Rochester and is something to remember.

"Descending the laurel walk, I faced the wreck of the chestnut tree; it stood up black and riven: the trunk, split down the centre, gasped ghastly. The cloven halves were not broken from each other, for the firm base and strong roots kept them unsundered below; though community of vitality was destroyed – the sap could flow no more: their great boughs on each side were dead, and next winter's tempests would be sure to fell one or both to earth: as yet, however, they might be said to form on tree – a ruin, but an entire ruin.

'You did right to hold fast to each other,' I said: as if the monster-splinters were living things, and could hear me. 'I think, scathed as you look, and charred and scorched, there must be a little sense of life in you yet, rising out of that adhesion at the faithful, honest roots: you will never have green leaves more – never more see birds making nests and singing idylls in your boughs; the time of pleasure and love is over with you: but you are not desolate: each of you has a comrade to sympathise with him in his decay.'"

Jane and Mr. Rochester have strong foundations of understanding and love built. They are so much alike, and they accept one another for who they are individually.

However, there is something that is keeping them apart…something, like I mentioned in an earlier chapter, lurking beneath the surface. These two characters have yet to experience a life-altering turn of events that will not leave them unscathed. Nor will it leave them wholly able to return to their former selves. They will always be bound together by a bond that no one can break, but these upcoming events will change the future they intended for themselves.

Here we have now reached an event that Jane takes as a foreboding sign. Remember, superstition is very common at this time and Jane was raised to believe that there are signs everywhere that can predict either future happiness or a future of sorrow.

This thought process brings us to a very common idea which is represented in many movies, television shows, and even in real life. Things cannot possibly stay happy all the time, and if life is too peaceful, too happy, and too content, there must be something disastrous around the corner. It is the anticipation of the "other shoe" dropping eventually.

How many movies and shows can you count that will lead you up to a joyful and happy reconciliation in which all the characters are content and peaceful, then out of the blue disaster strikes? Unfortunately, we have been trained to believe that this is an everyday life occurrence. We begin to believe that if happiness and joy surrounds us then surely something bad is just around the corner. Living in that fear takes away from the present enjoyment of life. Once in this realm of belief, we are then casting our fears into the future and fear of the future is torment.

We find out, later in this chapter, that Jane's secret is that she has had dreams that Mr. Rochester is abandoning her with a child without a parting word. Upon waking, she finds a strange woman, of which she has never seen, trying on her veil. This woman then tears the veil in two and mysteriously leaves in darkness while Jane faints away in fright.

Mr. Rochester tries to explain this experience away by intimating that Jane, half dreaming and half awake, saw Grace Poole in her room. Though this does not satisfy Jane, she accepts it since there is no other possible explanation available.

On closing the chapter, Jane, after a sleepless night, is eagerly if not a little anxiously beginning preparations for her wedding to Mr. Rochester. With all this information and the "signs" you have read, how do you think the wedding day will commence?

How Can You Apply This to Your Own Life?

One of the biggest subjects that comes up, not only in this chapter, but in a couple others as well, is fear of the future. Fear is a form of bondage and is not uncommon. Everyone deals with fear in some form or other in their lives.

God created us with a response system that helps us remove ourselves from dangerous situations. This system is called our "fight-or-flight" response.

However, the difference between this version of fear and living with constant anxiety and fear, is that the first is a naturally occurring part of our hormonal response, and the other is spiritual oppression. When fear oppresses you, you are barely able to function. Think of someone who has panic attacks. When they are in the midst of a panic attack, their lungs tighten restricting oxygen flow, their heart pounds, they get sweaty, dizzy, shaky, sometimes nauseous, and some even feel like they are dying.

Do you think that response is natural? Absolutely not.

Fear is torment. Torment is bondage. Bondage is slavery.

> *"For ye have not received the spirit* [demon, being] *of bondage* [slavery] *again to fear; but ye have received the Spirit* [being, of the divine God, Holy Spirit] *of adoption, whereby we cry, Abba, Father."* Romans 8:15

Many do not even realize that fear is working in them. One type of fear that gets overlooked is fear of the future. Fearing the future projects unbelief that God will not take care of your future. The questions of "what will happen tomorrow...what about the next day...what about five years down the road?" will begin to flood your thoughts.

> *"Be careful* [be anxious, have a care, take thought] *for nothing; but in every thing by prayer and supplication* [request, petition] *with thanksgiving let your requests be made known unto God."* Philippians 4:6

"Hebrews 11:6 says, 'Without faith, it is impossible to please God,' because faith represents your future. Fear represents the *destruction* of your future. Faith and Fear are equal in this dimension: both demand fulfillment.

Faith will always defeat Fear, because faith is a work of the Holy Spirit. Fear is a work of the created being named Lucifer, who fell and became Satan. He now rules a kingdom determined to destroy mankind…Fear is from that kingdom [the kingdom of principalities]. Fear is Satan's attempt to overthrow God's plan in the earth, using you to do it. Feelings cannot be trusted."[1]

> *"Now faith is the substance* [assurance, confidence, foundation] *of things hoped* [trust] *for, the evidence* [conviction] *of things not seen."* Hebrews 11:1

> *"Then touched he their eyes, saying, according to your faith be it unto you."* Matthew 9:29

"Fear can be the constant projection of danger. But a radar is not designed to *project* danger. Radar is set in a place to discern things that are dangerous in your pathway. If you are not careful, you will come up with a faulty radar that is not looking for danger, but projecting it. When you have the projection of danger in the future, you have torment. Discernment is a type of radar that gives you the ability to know good and evil."[2]

> *"For the thing which I greatly* [object feared, dread(ful), great fear, terror] *feared* [startled, sudden alarm, dread] *is come upon me, and that which I was afraid of is come unto me."* Job 3:25

When you begin to project fears into your future, the only thing that can recover those thoughts is faith. Choosing to have faith that God will provide for your needs, and already knows your future, helps to ground you. The only way to do this is by immersing yourself in God's word and truly applying what you learn. Know that God is for you, and if God is for you, who can be against you. (*Romans 8:31*)

Your future might contain some hardships and your life might not always look joyful and happy all the time. Sin has prevented perfect contentment all the time. However, if you choose to lay down your fears, giving them to Christ and pray for the Holy Spirit's discernment, wisdom, and strength to sustain you, you will prosper despite hardships.

God never promises a perfect life without sorrow. But He does promise that He will never leave you.

"Be strong and of good courage [steadfastly minded, firm, established, fortified], *fear not, nor be afraid of them: for the LORD thy God, he it is that doth go with thee; he will not fail* [leave, slack, cease] *thee, nor forsake* [fail, refuse, destitute] *thee."* Deuteronomy 31:6

Footnotes

[1] Fear by Henry W. Wright pages 4-5

[2] Fear by Henry W. Wright page 163

Chapter XXVI

Are you ready for the wedding between our two beloved characters? It may not all be smooth sailing.

"He took me into the dining-room, surveyed me keenly all over, pronounced me 'fair as a lily, and not only the pride of his life, but the desire of his eyes,' and then telling me he would give me but ten minutes to eat some breakfast, he rang the bell."

Mr. Rochester is in quite a hurry over getting this wedding under way.

"…my hand was held in a grip of iron: I was hurried along by a stride I could hardly follow; and to look at Mr. Rochester's face was to feel that not a second of delay would be tolerated for any purpose. I wonder what other bridegroom ever looked as he did – so bent up to a purpose, so grimly resolute: or who, under such steadfast brows, ever revealed such flaming and flashing eyes."

After the clergyman pronounces the call that if there be any impediment to the marriage about to take place, they must speak, Mr. Rochester's past comes up to haunt him one last time in our story.

"He paused, as the custom is. When is the pause after that sentence ever broken by reply? Not, perhaps, once in a hundred years. And the clergyman, who had not lifted his eyes from his book, and had held his breath but for a moment,

was proceeding: his hand was already stretched towards Mr. Rochester, as his lips unclosed to ask, 'Wilt thou have this woman for thy wedded wife?' –when a distinct and near voice said –

'The marriage cannot go on: I declare the existence of an impediment.'

The clergyman looked up at the speaker and stood mute; the clerk did the same; Mr. Rochester moved slightly, as if an earthquake had rolled under his feet: taking a firmer footing, and not turning his head or eyes, he said, 'Proceed.'"

"'It simply consists in the existence of a previous marriage. Mr. Rochester has a wife now living.'

My nerves vibrated to those low-spoken words as they had never vibrated to thunder – my blood felt their subtle violence as it had never felt frost or fire; but I was collected, and in no danger of swooning. I looked at Mr. Rochester: I made him look at me. His whole face was colourless rock: his eye was both spark and flint. He disavowed nothing: he seemed as if he would defy all things. Without speaking, without smiling, without seeming to recognize in me a human being, he only twined my waist with his arm and riveted me to his side."

So, the wedding is called off. The pieces of intrigue surrounding Mr. Rochester and his home are beginning to fall into place. Jane observes silently and Mr. Rochester instinctually clings to Jane, feeling that if he does not, she will disappear, and he will lose her forever.

"Mr. Rochester continued, hardily and recklessly: 'Bigamy is an ugly word! — I meant, however, to be a bigamist; but fate has out-manoeuvred me, or Providence has checked me — perhaps the last. I am little better than a devil at this moment; and, as my pastor there would tell me, deserve no doubt the sternest judgments of God, even to the quenchless fire and deathless worm. Gentlemen, my plan is broken up! — what this lawyer and his client say is true: I have been married, and the woman to whom I was married lives! You say you never heard of a Mrs. Rochester at the house up yonder, Wood; but I dare say you have many a time inclined you ear to gossip about the mysterious lunatic kept there under watch and ward. Some have whispered to you that she is my bastard half-sister: some, my cast-off mistress. I now inform you that she is my wife, whom I married fifteen years ago — Bertha Mason by name; sister of this resolute personage, who is now, with his quivering limbs and white cheeks, showing you what a stout heart men may bear…Bertha Mason is mad; and she came of a mad family; idiots and maniacs through three generations! Her mother, the Creole, was both a madwoman and a drunkard! — as I found out after I had wed the daughter: for they were silent on family secrets before. Betha, like a dutiful child, copied her parent in both points. I had a charming partner — pure, wise, modest: you can fancy I was a happy man. I went through rich scenes! Oh! My experience has been heavenly, if you only knew it!…You shall see what sort of a being I was cheated into espousing, and judge whether or not I had a right to break the compact, and seek sympathy with something at least human. This girl,' he continued, looking

*at me, 'knew no more than you, Wood, of the disgusting
secret: she thought all was fair and legal and never dreamt
she was going to be entrapped into a feigned union with a
defrauded wretch, already bound to a bad, mad, and
embruted partner!'"*

This is a lot to take in. At this moment in our story, Mr.
Rochester looks to be very deceitful. In fact, this is what
feminists focus on the most. How could Jane have fallen into
his trap? How could he be so selfish as to ruin the reputation
of a woman he claims to love and adore? He is a liar! He is
horrible! He is manipulative!

Taking a step back, what have we learned about Mr.
Rochester? We have learned that he is a very tortured man
with a tortured and secretive past who has not been loved
properly. Does this excuse his behavior? Absolutely not.
However, there is always more to the story than what we see
on the surface. I hope to help break this down for you.

There are four questions that come to mind as Mr. Rochester
begins to reveal his past completely, that we will break down
over the course of this and the next chapter:

1. Why did Mr. Rochester not divorce Bertha once he
    found her to be insane?
2. Why did Mr. Rochester not place her in an asylum
    where she could be kept out of his way?
3. Why did Mr. Rochester marry Bertha in the first
    place?
4. Was Jane tempted to stay because of manipulation or
    because of true feeling?

In this chapter, we will address the first two questions. Let us begin with the first. Why did Mr. Rochester not obtain, or try to obtain, a divorce from Bertha once he found her to be insane? To answer, we will briefly look at some divorce parameters laid out in the 19th century to get a better understanding of his inability.

Divorce in the 19th Century[1]

Divorce was extremely rare up until the 20th century. It was also considered taboo during this time in history and was very expensive and time consuming. Wealthy people were likely the only people able to afford a lengthy divorce, however, the tradeoff was that their personal life was now on display for all to see. Early on in the 1800s, the only legal grounds for a divorce in England was through providing proof of adultery. Even then, it was still not a guarantee that the courts would accept this proof. Unfortunately, as common as adultery was at this time, it was still hushed up. Should a divorce be called for, the act was then broadcast during public trial, showing the underbelly of the people involved.

Abuse, desertion, imprisonment, and insanity were not legal reasons to dissolve a marriage. The court would simply dismiss them altogether. Insanity was not considered mainly because a person of unsound mind did not have the ability to defend themselves. There had to be equal defense on both sides in order to prevent misuse of power to destroy another human being. This is probably why Mr. Rochester could not obtain a divorce.

This brings us to Mr. Rochester's other "viable" option. Why did he not place her in an asylum?

<u>19th Century Mental Asylums[2]</u>

It is no secret that people who were admitted to insane asylums were treated cruelly. They have been portrayed in many television shows and movies as being places of horror. Conditions improved during the 19th century, however, and patients were cared for better than in previous years but not by much.

Even though there were changes taking place, there was no guarantee that all asylums were administering the same treatment protocols or that the staff were treating patients with equal respect. Restraints were not used as liberally, and rooms became more spacious with proper airflow, but, unfortunately, these institutions were still cages for these people.

Bars and fences kept them in and once they were in, it was difficult to get them out again. They became wards of the state and staff forever saw patients as insane and could not be convinced otherwise. Even if patients were recovering, they were not trusted. And though treatments were less severe, staff still abused the patients. Even if patients complained of the beatings, teasing, having their hair ripped out, and torture, doctors regularly ignored their pleas.

It was a demeaning, destructive way to live. Many who were admitted for depressive conditions only got worse.

Though Bertha has been kept in a "prison" of sorts, she is treated respectfully and not with violence. Her living situation is less severe as we will see in the next few paragraphs.

"…a figure ran backwards and forwards. What it was, whether beast or human being, one could not, at first sight, tell: it grovelled, seemingly, on all fours; it snatched and growled like some strange wild animal: but it was covered with clothing, and a quantity of dark, grizzled hair, wild as a mane, hid its head and face."

Jane instantly recognizes Bertha as the woman who entered her room just a few nights ago and tore her veil in half. She was not imagining things after all. And here was Grace Poole, the woman blamed for all the horrible things that happened at Thornfield during Jane's residency. She was in fact caretaker, and not criminal mastermind.

Mr. Rochester, though he could easily subdue this fierce and vile woman with violent force, does not strike her as she attacks him, bites him, and scratches at him. In the next chapter we find that he refuses to treat her with the same brutality he receives and expects Grace Poole to respond in the same way. This is far better treatment than Bertha would receive in an asylum.

"'That is my wife,' said he. 'Such is the sole conjugal embrace I am every to know – such are the endearments which are to solace my leisure hours! And this is what I wished to have' (laying his hand on my shoulder): 'this young girl, who stands so grave and quiet at the mouth of

*hell, looking collectedly at the gambols of a demon. I wanted
her just as a change after that fierce ragout. Wood and
Briggs, look at the difference! Compare these clear eyes with
the red balls yonder – this face with that mask – this form
with that bulk; then judge me, priest of the gospel and man
of the law, and remember with what judgment ye judge ye
shall be judged! Off with you now. I must shut up my
prize.'"*

Can we truly blame Mr. Rochester for wanting a pure and
lovely, sound-minded, intelligent, thoughtful woman after
years of hateful words, beatings, screaming, scratching, and
snarling from this…wife?

Though we cannot overlook the deception that Mr.
Rochester has led Jane into, we must understand *why* he did
it in the first place. For fifteen years, Mr. Rochester,
manipulated into a marriage for money, has been tormented
by a woman that did not love him and who could not love
him. He was betrayed by people he thought he could trust
and now lives in torment.

I want to encourage you, as I have done since Mr. Rochester
first entered this story, not to judge him too harshly yet. I ask
that you allow Mr. Rochester to reveal himself further to you
before making claims on his character. He still has some
growing to do, of which Jane will play an important role. But
this will be done further in the next chapter.

Jane discovers that, not only is her uncle involved in
stopping this marriage, but he is close to death. What a sad
and desperate turn of events! Jane is in shock, moving

mechanically and reflecting on the morning and its strangely calm scenes. Not only has she now lost the love she relied so heavily upon, but she is also losing an uncle whom she has never met.

"Jane Eyre, who had been an ardent, expectant woman – almost a bride, was a cold, solitary girl again: her life was pale; her prospects were desolate. A Christmas frost had come at midsummer; a white December storm had whirled over June' ice glazed the ripe apples, drifts crushed the blowing roses; on hayfield and cornfield lay a frozen shroud: lanes which last night blushed full of lowers, to-day were pathless with untrodden snow; and the woods, which twelve hours since waved leafy and flagrant as groves between the tropics, now spread, waste, wild, and white as pine-forests in wintry Norway. My hopes were all dead – struck with a subtle doom, such as, in one night, fell on all the first-born in the land of Egypt. I looked on my cherished wishes, yesterday so blooming and glowing; they lay stark, chill, livid corpses that could never revive. I looked at my love: that feeling which was my master's – which he had created; it shivered in my heart, like a suffering child in a cold cradle; sickness and anguish had seized it; it could not seek Mr. Rochester's arms – it could not derive warmth from his breast. Oh, never more could it turn to him; for faith was blighted – confidence destroyed! Mr. Rochester was not to me what he had been; for he was not what I had thought him. I would not ascribe vice to him; I would not say he had betrayed me; but the attribute of stainless truth was gone from his idea, and from his presence I must go: that I perceived well…

I had no will, to flee I had no strength. I lay faint, longing to be dead. One idea only still throbbed life-like within me — a remembrance of God: it begot an unuttered prayer: these words went wandering up and down in my rayless mind, as something that should be whispered, but no energy was found to express them —

'Be not far from me, for trouble is near: there is none to help.'"

Jane describes herself as returning to the hurt little girl who was treated with contempt by her kin and forced to a horrid school where she felt isolated and alone. Hope has dissipated. Despair has entered in. A couple of chapters ago, we discussed Jane's realization that she was beginning to idolize Mr. Rochester. Her faith was beginning to waver and take a back seat to the worldly loves and pleasures in her life. This made her faith in Mr. Rochester too strong. She saw him as doing no wrong and now that his greatest wrong is revealed, she is crashing into utter despair.

In the end, she begins to understand that her faith is now the one thing that will give her the strength to endure this great shock and loss; that God is the only one strong enough to rely on.

<u>How Can You Apply This to Your Own Life?</u>

Our decisions and actions in life always have a trickle-down effect for either good or bad.

How we act when we are around others is vastly more important than we think. Our current culture tells us to ignore what others think of us and just be who we are. Live your truth! That phrase makes me want to wretch. We are not each given a separate truth to live by. There is <u>one</u> universal truth, period. If we decide to live according to the truth of the Word, we will be fruitful and blessed. If we decide to live according to the sins of the world, we will find ourselves in bondage.

"Look not every man on his own things, but every man also on the things of others." Philippians 2:4

Not taking any thought for how we are perceived or how we are possibly influencing those around us is the world's way of encouraging selfishness. The plain truth is that we *are* influencing others whether we know it or not. If we are living as salt and light to the world, the world will see Christ in us. Because we are, as believers, called to a higher purpose, our influence matters.

Consider how parents influence how their children think and behave. If parents are constantly complaining or lying, their children will grow up thinking this is normal behavior and will adopt it as their own. However, if parents are working hard to be positive and truthful, instructing their children in the word of God, their children will grow up to be positive, truthful people with a foundation of faith. They still have free will to decide how they will live and be perceived; however, the foundations are there and cannot be easily forgotten (*remember the story of the prodigal son in Luke 15*).

"So then every one of us shall give account of himself to God. Let us not therefore judge [condemn, punish, avenge] *one another any more: but judge* [decree, determine, esteem, ordain] *this rather, that no man put a stumblingblock* [occasion of apostasy] *or an occasion to fall* [snare] *in his brother's way."* Romans 14:12-13

This is why we have Jesus' example of how we are to live and share our faith. Because he was obedient to his Father, we were able to benefit from his great sacrifice for our lives. Jesus was not the only example of how decisions and influence affect others. David is another excellent example.

David lusted after his friend Uriah's wife and because he gave in to the temptation to have her, he slept with her, and she conceived a baby. To cover his first sin, David sent her husband to be killed in battle and after the mourning period, took Uriah's wife to be his. This displeased God and punishment came upon David which affected his son by Uriah's wife. When his son died, David grieved. In the end, David repented for his sins and his relationship with God was restored, but because of that first decision, much grief came upon all that were involved. (*2 Samuel 11-12*)

"For if by one man's offence [error or wilful transgression, fault] *death reigned by one; much more they which receive abundance of grace and of the gift of righteousness shall reign in life by one, Jesus Christ. Therefore as by the offence of one judgment came upon all men to condemnation; even so by the righteousness of one the free gift came upon all men unto justification of life. For as by one man's*

disobedience many were made sinners, so by the obedience of one shall many be made righteous." Romans 5:17-19

How are you choosing to live? Are you choosing to be an example of faith and integrity?

It is okay to slip up sometimes, we all do it. God will honor the desires of your heart. David is called a man after God's own heart because he recognized his sin and repented for it. He came into forgiveness and restored his relationship with his Father. We will not make good decisions or be good examples all the time. What we can do is try our very best.

And if you are having an off day, be honest with yourself and God and take time away from others to resolve things. If you need wisdom on how to deal with difficult people, ask for it. If you need strength to get you through the day, ask for it. God will sustain you if you come to Him with your requests.

Footnotes

[1] https://history.stackexchange.com/questions/26448/were-life-imprisonment-and-mental-insanity-the-only-reasons-a-divorce-couldnt-b

https://www.parliament.uk/about/living-heritage/transformingsociety/private-lives/relationships/overview/divorce/

[2] https://www.ranker.com/list/life-in-19th-century-mental-institutions-and-insane-asylums/christopher-myers

Chapter XXVII

"…the answer my mind gave – 'Leave Thornfield at once' – was so prompt, so dread, that I stopped my ears. I said I could not bear such words now. 'That I am not Edward Rochester's bride is the least part of my woe,' I alleged: 'that I have wakened out of most glorious dreams, and found them all void and vain, is a horror I could bear and master; but that I must leave him decidedly, instantly, entirely, is intolerable. I cannot do it.'

But, then, a voice within me averred that I could do it and foretold that I should do it. I wrestled with my own resolution: I wanted to be weak that I might avoid the awful passage of further suffering I saw laid out for me; and Conscience, turned tyrant, held Passion by the throat, told her tauntingly, she had yet but dipped her dainty foot in the slough, and swore that with that arm of iron he would thrust her down to unsounded depths of agony!"

It is possible to believe that Conscience here is the Holy Spirit, strengthening Jane and giving her wisdom in this moment of grief and despair. In her shock and despair, she wanted to ignore the voice and give in to the desire to stay. She wanted to give in to temptation.

Throughout this time, Mr. Rochester has been waiting outside her door for hours.

"'Jane, I never meant to wound you thus. If the man who had but one little ewe lamb that was dear to him as a

daughter, that ate of his bread and drank of his cup, and lay in his bosom, had by some mistake slaughtered it at the shambles, he would not have rued his bloody blunder more than I now rue mine. Will you ever forgive me?'

Reader, I forgave him at the moment and on the spot. There was such deep remorse in his eye, such true pity in his tone, such manly energy in his manner; and besides, there was such unchanged love in his whole look and mien — I forgave him all: yet not in words, not outwardly; only at my heart's core."

Is it wrong for Jane to have forgiven so easily? She has been deeply hurt by the man she loves. Why is she forgiving him so readily?

We have seen many examples of Jane's use of separation and how forgiveness comes easily as a result of this. Many women have looked at this scene as Mr. Rochester manipulating her into forgiving him and her turning a blind eye. On the contrary! As we continue to read further, we know that Jane is fully aware of the wrong done and how she must respond. She does not allow him to talk her into something that would compromise her morals. And yet, she forgives him because she sees how genuine he is in his repentance.

He wanted to tell her. He wanted to reveal everything and be honest with her. But he knew that she would not have stayed at Thornfield had he done so. His selfish desire to keep her with him, and his deep-seated fear of losing her, led him into making a very poor decision, ultimately hurting them both.

Mr. Rochester's heart is breaking as much as Jane's is at this moment. He knows that Jane, in her stubborn sense of morality, cannot now accept him in the same way as she had before. Their relationship cannot be what it once was.

She refuses his kisses and caresses, and rightly so. She will not allow the same liberties of love that he was allowed before her discovery of his marriage. In this, she is holding him accountable.

I said in the last chapter that Jane would play a large role in Mr. Rochester's continued growth. Part of that growth is that he has never really been held accountable for his actions. Because he had been so hurt as a young man, he lived his life to please himself in order to run away from loneliness and despair.

In past chapters, we have seen this same pattern of accountability between Jane and Mr. Rochester. This time, she is not only holding him accountable as a married man, but she is also holding herself accountable by not giving into temptation to be his comforter. Jane knows that there is a fine line between those who love each other as they do, and crossing those boundaries of propriety is unwise.

"'...and my plans would not permit me to remove the maniac elsewhere – though I possess an old house, Ferndean Manor, even more retired and hidden than this, where I could have lodged her safely enough, had not a scruple about the unhealthiness of the situation, in the heart of a wood, made my conscience recoil from the arrangement. Probably those damp walls would soon have eased me of her charge:

but to each villain his own vice; and mine is not a tendency to indirect assassination, even of what I most hate.'"

This is another example of how Mr. Rochester cared for Bertha despite his desire to be rid of her. He treated her as a human being, not an animal or something to be thrown away.

"'…did you ever hear that my father was an avaricious, grasping man?...

Well, Jane, being so, it was his resolution to keep the property together; he could not bear the idea of dividing his estate and leaving me a fair portion: all, he resolved, should go to my brother, Rowland. Yet as little could he endure that a son of his should be a poor man. I must be provided for by a wealthy marriage. He sought me a partner betimes. Mr. Mason, a West India planter and merchant, was his old acquaintance. He was certain his possessions were real and vast: he made inquiries. Mr. Mason, he found, had a son and daughter; and he learned from him that he could and would give the latter a fortune of thirty thousand pounds: that sufficed. When I left college, I was sent out to Jamaica, to espouse a bride already courted for me. My father said nothing about her money; but he told me Miss Mason was the boast of Spanish Town for her beauty: and this was no lie. I found her a fine woman, in the style of Blanche Ingram: tall, dark, and majestic. Her family wished to secure me because I was of a good race; and so did she. They showed her to me in parties, splendidly dressed. I seldom saw her alone, and had very little private conversation with her. She flattered me, and lavishly displayed for my pleasure her charms and accomplishments. All the men in her circle seemed to admire her and envy me. I was dazzled, stimulated: my senses were excited; and being ignorant, raw, and inexperienced, I thought I loved her. There is no folly so besotted that the idiotic rivalries of society, the prurience, the rashness, the blindness of youth, will not hurry a man to its commission. Her relatives encouraged me; competitors piqued me; she allured me: a marriage was achieved almost before I knew where I was. Oh, I have no respect for myself when I think of that act! – an agony of inward contempt masters me. I never loved, I never esteemed, I did not even know her. I was not sure of the existence of one virtue in her nature: I had marked neither modesty, nor benevolence, nor candour, nor refinement in her mind or manners – and, I married her: gross, grovelling, mole-eyed blockhead that I was!...

My bride's mother I had never seen: I understood she was dead. The honeymoon over, I learned my mistake; she was only mad, and shut up in a lunatic asylum. There was a younger brother, too – a complete dumb idiot…My father and my brother Rowland knew all this; but they thought only of the thirty thousand pounds, and joined in the plot against me.

…her character ripened and developed with frightful rapidity; her vices sprang up fast and rank: they were so strong, only cruelty could check them, and I would not use cruelty…

My brother in the interval was dead, and at the end of the four years my father died too. I was rich enough now — yet poor to hideous indigence: a nature the most gross, impure, depraved I ever saw, was associated with mine, and called by the law and by society a part of me. And I could not rid myself of it by any legal proceedings: for the doctors now discovered that my wife was mad — her excesses had prematurely developed the germs of insanity.'"

At twenty-six years old, Mr. Rochester was a trapped and miserable man. He contemplated shooting himself to have it over with but then thought better of it and decided to return to England and hide Bertha away, safe and cared for. He then travelled the world in search of love and comfort. To run away from his past and the woman he left behind in her madness.

Even his father wanted to hide the fact that his family was associated with the Masons. Those who knew about Bertha were limited and not even Mrs. Fairfax knew of her existence.

Mr. Rochester never intended to deceive anyone or manipulate a woman into marrying him without all the details of his past. He believed that his situation did not qualify as a true marriage and thus he felt that he deserved real love.

"'Disappointment made me reckless. I tried dissipation — never debauchery: that I hated, and hate. That was my Indian Messalina's attribute: rooted disgust at it and her restrained me much, even in pleasure. Any enjoyment that

bordered on riot seemed to approach me to her and her vices, and I eschewed it.'"

<u>Dissipation</u>: mental distraction, amusement, diversion, excessive drinking of liquor, to spend wastefully or extravagantly, squander[1]

<u>Debauchery</u>: excessive indulgence in sensual pleasures[1]

"'I don't like you so well as I have done sometimes, indeed, sir. Did it not seem to you in the least wrong to live in that way, first with one mistress and then another? You talk of it as a mere matter of course.'

'I was with me; and I did not like it. It was a grovelling fashion of existence: I should never like to return to it. Hiring a mistress is the next worse thing to buying a slave: both are often by nature, and always by position, inferior: and to live familiarly with inferiors is degrading. I now hate the recollection of the time I passed with Celine, Giacinta, and Clara.'

I felt the truth of these words; and I drew from them the certain inference, that if I were so far to forget myself and all the teaching that had ever been instilled into me, as — under any pretext — with any justification — through any temptation — to become the successor of these poor girls, he would one day regard me with the same feeling which now in his mind desecrated their memory. I did not give utterance to this conviction: it was enough to feel it. I

*impressed it on my heart, that it might remain there to serve
me as aid in the time of trial."*

Jane knows that she would be debasing herself and her own
character if she were to follow the course of temptation.
Perhaps not in the eyes of Mr. Rochester, but in her own
eyes, which was far more important. God's word is very
clear about sexual immorality and Jane is determined to hold
fast in this knowledge.

As Mr. Rochester continues to share everything with Jane,
he recognizes his fault in deceiving Jane the way he did. He
knows that he destroyed her trust and faith in him and takes
accountability for his actions, asking for forgiveness.

*"Terrible moment: full of struggle, blackness, burning! Not
a human being that ever lived could wish to be loved better
than I was loved; and him who thus loved me I absolutely
worshipped: and I must renounce love and idol. One drear
word comprised my intolerable duty – 'Depart!'"*

In his despair, Mr. Rochester blames Jane for being unkind
to him by taking away his happiness. He knows full well that
the type of happiness he seeks is now not in her power to
give. But he is existing in denial that he can keep her love
and companionship. Grief is muddling his reasoning. Despite
her own pain, she is able to separate his words from what his
heart is really feeling. Jane is continually tempted to stay,
especially when he says that she has no family to meddle
with a marriage or living situation between them. But she is
strong to resist.

Jane is able to maintain her fortitude because she has faith and knowledge that God will take care of her. Mr. Rochester does not even have this to fall back on. If she leaves him, hope will become nonexistent, and he will have nothing to rely on or believe in. She does fear for his future.

"…while he spoke my very conscience and reason turned traitors against me, and charged me with crime in resisting him. They spoke almost as loud as Feeling: and that clamoured wildly. 'Oh, comply!' it said. 'Think of his misery; think of his danger – look at his state when left along; remember his headlong nature; consider the recklessness following on despair – soothe him; save him; love him; tell him you love him and will be his. Who in the world cares for you? Or who will be injured by what you do?'

Still indomitable was the reply – 'I care for myself. The more solitary, the more friendless, the more unsustained I am, the more I will respect myself. I will keep the law given by God; sanctioned by man. I will hold to the principles received by me when I was sane, and not mad – as I am now. Laws and principles are not for the times when there is no temptation: they are for such moments as this, when body and soul rise in mutiny against their rigour; stringent are they; inviolate they shall be. If at my individual convenience I might break them, what would be their worth? They have a worth – so I have always believed; and if I cannot believe it now, it is because I am insane – quite insane, with my veins running fire, and my heart beating faster than I can count its throbs.

Preconceived opinions, foregone determinations, are all I have at this hour to stand by: there I plant my foot.'"

This is one of the greatest battles that Jane has ever had to undertake in her spirit. She must decide to leave the only person who has ever truly loved her. She must decide to leave him in his grief and brokenness. Or stay and listen to her emotions over wisdom, giving into sexual immorality and love.

We have to understand that both of these characters have lived lives in which they have not been loved well. Neither one of them has been properly loved by their family members. Jane was blessed to have Helen Burns as a confidant for a short time in her childhood, but Mr. Rochester has never had anyone to keep him accountable or truly care about him. With this in mind, we can see the struggle on both sides. Both want to be loved wholly. Both want to be accepted. Both found that in each other. Nonetheless, Jane leaves and says her final goodbye.

"'God bless you, my dear master!' I said. 'God keep you from harm and wrong — direct you, solace you — reward you well for your past kindness to me.'"

"I could go back and be his comforter — his pride; his redeemer from misery, perhaps from ruin. Oh, that fear of his self-abandonment — far worse than my abandonment — how it goaded me! It was a barbed arrow-head in my breast; it tore me when I tried to extract it; it sickened me when remembrance thrust it farther in."

You can feel the pain in her words…

*"Gentle reader, may you never feel what I then felt! May
your eyes never shed such stormy, scalding, heart-wrung
tears as poured from mine. May you never appeal to Heaven
in prayers so hopeless and so agonized as in that hour left
my lips; for never may you, like me, dread to be the
instrument of evil to what you wholly love."*

Jane fought against temptation every step of the way. She
tore herself from Mr. Rochester. In a way, what he said in
chapter twenty-three has become a very real feeling:

> *"'Because,' he said, 'I sometimes have queer feeling
> with regard to you – especially when you are near
> me, as now: it is as if I had a string somewhere
> under my left ribs, tightly and inextricably knotted
> to a similar string situated in the corresponding
> quarter of your little frame. And if that boisterous
> Channel, and two hundred miles or so of land come
> broad between us, I am afraid that cord of
> communion will be snapped; and then I've a nervous
> notion I should take to bleeding inwardly. As for
> you – you'd forget me.'"*

A cord of love and attachment has been severed and though
they will not bleed inwardly in a literal sense, we have a
feeling that there will be extreme heartache for a very long
time on both sides. And this heartache will be as painful as a
physical break.

<u>How Can You Apply This to Your Own Life?</u>

We have talked many times in previous chapters about rejection, bitterness, and familial love in contrast to romantic love. All these themes resurface in this chapter. We know that Mr. Rochester's father is selfish, but we can hope that part of his reasoning for providing a livelihood for his younger son is because he cared for him a little. Through this betrayal, however, doors opened for Mr. Rochester to harbor a lot of bitterness toward, and possibly rejection from, his father.

Since all these themes have been discussed in previous chapters very thoroughly, I want to take a different approach.

One of the biggest deciding factors for Jane was the knowledge that she would be participating in sexual immorality had she stayed with Mr. Rochester. She knew that there would be no way for them to live together without wanting to be together fully.

Purity is something to cherish but there has been a great push, even in the Christian church, to accept sex outside of marriage. Within Christian communities, I have seen the argument that we were created to be sexual beings and thus it is okay to act on that because that is how God created us.

However, the bible clearly warns us to be wary of sexual sin. Sex was designed for a purpose and that purpose is meant to be experienced only within the context of marriage.

Unfortunately, the temptations to sexual sin are more readily available to us now than ever before. Because of this, the dilemma of Jane's might seem trivial compared to most others she has had to deal with throughout this story. Why should she not stay with Mr. Rochester if they truly love each other and there is no one around to meddle with them? They can be married in spirit.

"Now the works of the flesh are manifest [made known, openly, publicly, apparent], *which are these; adultery, fornication, uncleanness* [in a moral sense: the impurity of lustful, luxurious, profligate living], *lasciviousness* [unbridled lust, shamelessness, wantonness]," Galatians 5:19

We could try and justify them staying together all we like. But the bottom line is that it is still a sin. Jane would forever feel shame for being in a position of mistress to a married man. It does not matter whether his wife is insane or not. He is still married. Thus, they would both be committing adultery. So, not only would Jane be giving up her purity as an unmarried woman, but she would also be participating in the sin of adultery.

"For this is the will of God, even your sanctification [purification, holiness], *that ye should abstain from fornication* [adultery, incest, idolatry, harlotry, illicit sexual intercourse]: *that every one of you should know how to possess his vessel* [body] *in sanctification and honour; not in the lust of concupiscence* [a longing (especially for what is forbidden), desire, lust after], *even as the Gentiles which know not God: that no man go beyond and defraud his brother in any matter: because that the Lord is the avenger of all such, as we also have forewarned you and testified. For God hath not called us unto uncleanness, but unto holiness."* 1 Thessalonians 4:3-7

"All things are lawful unto me, but all things are not expedient [be better for, be good, be profitable]*: all things are lawful for me, but I will not be brought under the power of any. Meats for the belly, and the belly for meats: but God shall destroy both it and them. Now the body is not for fornication, but for the Lord; and the Lord for the body. And God hath both raised up* [rouse from death, sleep, (figuratively) from obscurity, ruins, nonexistence] *the Lord, and will also raise up us by his own power. Know ye not that your bodies are the members of Christ? Shall I then take the members of Christ, and make them the members of an harlot* [any woman indulging in unlawful sexual intercourse, whether for gain or for lust]*? God forbid* [express an absolute denial]. *What? Know ye not that he which is joined to an harlot is one body? For two, saith he, shall be one flesh. But he that is joined unto the Lord is one spirit. Flee fornication. Every sin that a man doeth is without the body* [the body of Christ]*; but he that committeth fornication sinneth against his own body. What? Know ye not that your body is the temple of the Holy Ghost which is in you, which ye have of God, and ye are not your own? For ye are bought* [redeem] *with a price* [esteem, especially of the highest degree, precious]*: therefore glorify God in your body, and in your spirit, which are God's."* 1 Corinthians 6:12-19

Also read Romans 1:24-27.

When put in this context, we can then fully understand why she chose not to give in to temptation. Jane and Mr. Rochester both knew how easy it would be to live in sin together. After all, they loved each other deeply. But giving up morality for the love of another was not a worthy tradeoff for the acceptance of her heavenly Father, and acceptance of herself.

We are called to be set apart, remember? To be salt and light to the world (*Matthew 5:13-16*). If we are engaging in worldly lusts and adopting the way the world thinks, speaks, and acts, how are we to be set apart for the Kingdom of Heaven?

I have found that many Christians who are vocally supportive of sex outside of marriage, experimentation in the bedroom, or even lusting after famous actors, are justifying their own decisions of adopting worldly lusts into their homes. Temptation begins slowly and builds over time. It is not sin until that temptation is agreed with and acted upon. Additionally, temptation is not always easy or painless to step away from. Most of the time, the path of temptation is much easier than taking the path of God. Jane found this out for herself.

> *"But every man is tempted, when he is drawn away of his own lust* [desire, craving, longing], *and enticed* [beguile, allure, delude, entrap]. *Then when lust hath conceived* [to clasp, seize, arrest, capture], *it bringeth forth sin: and sin, when it is finished* [complete, consummate], *bringeth forth death[2]. Do not err, my beloved brethren."* James 1:14-16

God always provides a way out, but He also provides for reconciliation through repentance. Paul, one of the greatest followers of Christ's teachings, was once a wicked man who repented and was restored in his relationship with God.

"But we know that the law is good, if a man use it lawfully; knowing this, that the law is not made for a righteous man, but for the lawless and disobedient, for the ungodly and for sinners, for unholy and profane, for murderers of fathers [patricide] *and murderers of mothers* [matricide], *for manslayers* [murderer], *for whoremongers* [male prostitute, fornicator, a man who indulges in unlawful sexual intercourse], *for them that defile themselves with mankind* [sodomite, one who lies with a male as with a female, homosexual], *for menstealers* [enslaver, kidnapper], *for liars, for perjured persons* [a false swearer], *and if there be any other thing that is contrary to sound doctrine; according to the glorious gospel of the blessed God, which was committed to my trust. And I thank Christ Jesus our Lord, who hath enabled me, for that he counted me faithful, putting me into the ministry; who was before a blasphemer, and a persecutor, and injurious* [maltreater, insulter, spiteful]*: but I obtained mercy, because I did it ignorantly in unbelief."* 1 Timothy 1:8-13

Marriage is sacred. God created marriage to be a representation of Christ and His church. The two become one as Christ and His church become one. Because of this, marriage is to be protected and honored.

"For the husband is the head of the wife, even as Christ is the head of the church: and he is the saviour of the body." Ephesians 5:23

"Marriage is honourable in all, and the bed undefiled [unsoiled, pure]*: but whoremongers and adulterers God will judge."* Hebrews 13:4

Finally, because sexual sin in all forms (*i.e., pornography, adultery, general lusting after another, homosexuality, sex outside of marriage, etc.*) is so prominent in our world, it is considered a form of idolatry. Remember, we discussed in a previous chapter that idolatry is anything that takes the place of God in our lives.

If we are allowing ourselves to indulge regularly, it then becomes a focal point of our lives. But if you fill your mind and heart with the word of God and meditate on it day and night, then your main focus in life will be your relationship with your heavenly Father.

> *"Mortify* [put to death] *therefore your members* [in this sense, bodily/worldly desires] *which are upon the earth; fornication, uncleanness, inordinate affection* [vile passion, lust], *evil concupiscence, and covetousness* [greed, extortion, avarice], *which is idolatry: for which things' sake the wrath of God cometh on the children of disobedience:"* Colossians 3:5-6 (also read Ephesians 5:3-5)

> *"And he said, that which cometh out of the man, that defileth* [pollute, profane, make unclean] *the man. For from within, out of the heart of men, proceed evil thoughts, adulteries, fornications, murders, thefts, covetousness, wickedness* [malice, plots, iniquity], *deceit* [guile], *lasciviousness, an evil eye* [derelict, vicious, mischief, guilt, lewd], *blasphemy, pride, foolishness: all these evil things come from within, and defile the man."* Mark 7:20-23

> *"Finally, brethren, whatsoever things are true, whatsoever things are honest, whatsoever things are just, whatsoever things are pure, whatsoever things are lovely, whatsoever*

things are of good report; if there be any virtue, and if there be any praise, think on these things." Philippians 4:8

Remember, there is always reconciliation through repentance. God wants you to be restored in your relationship with Him. If you have been involved in sexual sin and you would have the desire to repent and be restored, I encourage you to revisit chapter one for the 8 Rs.

"If we confess our sins, he is faithful and just to forgive us our sins, and to cleanse us from all unrighteousness." 1 John 1:9

Footnotes

[1] Collins English Dictionary – Complete & Unabridged 2012 digital edition (dictionary.com)

[2] Death based on the interlinear, Greek text (G2288 – thanatos θάνατος) – the misery of the soul arising from sin, which begins on earth but lasts and increases after the death of the body in hell; in the widest sense, death comprising all the miseries arising from sin, as well as physical death as the loss of a life consecrated to God and blessed in him on earth, to be followed by wretchedness in hell.

Chapter XXVIII

Jane is lost in the world. She has no direction, no hope, and no one to help guide her.

"What was I to do? Where to go? Oh, intolerable questions, when I could do nothing and go nowhere! – when a long way must yet be measured by my weary, trembling limbs before I could reach human habitation – when cold charity must be entreated before I could get a lodging: reluctant sympathy importuned, almost certain repulse incurred, before my tale could be listened to, or one of my wants relieved."

Faith in human beings has been shattered. It is almost as if Jane expected rejection from her own kind as she did when she was a child.

"Nature seemed to me benign and good; I thought she loved me, outcast as I was; and I, who from man could anticipate only mistrust, rejection, insult, clung to her with filial fondness. To-night, at least, I would be her guest, as I was her child: my other would lodge me without money and without price."

And yet, her faith in God grew stronger and more secure.

"My rest might have been blissful enough, only a sad heart broke it. It plained of its gaping wounds, its inward bleeding, its riven chords. It trembled for Mr. Rochester and his doom; it bemoaned him with bitter pity; it demanded him with ceaseless longing; and, impotent as a bird with both wings

broken, it still quivered its shattered pinions in vain attempts to seek him.

Worn out with this torture of thought, I rose to my knees. Night was come, and her planets were risen: a safe, still night: too serene for the companionship of fear. We know that God is everywhere; but certainly we feel His presence most when His works are on the grandest scale spread before us; and it is in the unclouded night-sky, where His worlds wheel their silent course, that we read clearest His infinitude, His omnipotence, His omnipresence. I had risen to my knees to pray for Mr. Rochester. Looking up, I, with tear-dimmed eyes, saw the mighty Milky Way. Remembering what it was — what countless systems there swept space like a soft trace of light — I felt the might and strength of God. Sure was I of His efficiency to save what He had made: convinced I grew that neither earth should perish, nor one of the souls it treasured. I turned my prayer to thanksgiving: the Source of Life was also the Saviour of spirits. Mr. Rochester was safe; he was God's and by God would he be guarded. I again nestled to the breast of the hill; and ere long in sleep forgot sorrow."

Jane appreciated the sleep she was given and the life she was living but it seemed emptier now. Though she knew her soul was in God's keeping, her physical and mental suffering still endured. Through her pain, she still knew that both herself and Mr. Rochester were in God's hands, safe and loved. This shows Jane's courage. She is brave enough to allow her future to be placed in God's hands even though she is suffering acutely in this moment.

Upon waking, Jane realizes the need to find food quickly. Her endurance is failing, and she is ultimately led to beg for a bite of food which brings her shame that she has been brought so low. No help is found.

"Reader, it is not pleasant to dwell on these details. Some say there is enjoyment in looking back to painful experience past; but at this day I can scarcely bear to review the times to which I allude: the moral degradation, blent with the physical suffering, form too distressing a recollection ever to be willingly dwelt on. I blamed none of those who repulsed me. I felt it was what was to be expected, and what could not be helped: an ordinary beggar is frequently the object of suspicion; a well-dressed beggar inevitably so. To be sure, what I begged was employment; but whose business was it to provide me with employment? Not, certainly, that of persons who saw me then for the first time, and who knew nothing about my character. And as to the woman who would not take my handkerchief in exchange for her bread, why, she was right, if the offer appeared to her sinister or the exchange unprofitable."

Why is Jane not giving in to the death that she feels would be a relief?

"'…While the rain descends so, must I lay my head on the cold, drenched ground?…In all likelihood, though, I should die before morning. And why cannot I reconcile myself to the prospect of death? Why do I struggle to retain a valueless life? Because I know, or believe, Mr. Rochester is living: and then, to die of want and cold is a fate to which nature cannot

submit passively. Oh, Providence! Sustain me a little longer! Aid! – direct me!'"

Mr. Rochester is still alive. Jane lives because she knows that he is alive and thus she wants to live too.

Finally, Jane finds a glimmer of hope. She stumbles upon a homey little scene where two young sisters read while an older woman knits by the fire. These two sisters are a stark contrast to the two sisters we have already analyzed – Eliza and Georgiana. While Jane watches through the window, she comes to find that their father has recently passed away and that their brother is yet to return home.

"Till this moment, I had been so intent on watching them, their appearance and conversation had excited in me so keen an interest, I had half-forgotten my own wretched position: now it recurred to me. More desolate, more desperate than ever, it seemed from contrast. And how impossible did I appear to touch the inmates of this house with concern on my behalf; to make them believe in the truth of my wants and woes – to induce them to vouchsafe a rest for my wanderings!"

Mustering up courage, Jane knocks on their door and is turned away. But God provides for Jane. The brother, St. John, arrives in time to bring her in and care for her. Jane finds that these people are kind and generous. She assumes an alias for fear of anyone finding out about her and the place she has just come from.

As we will soon discover, she is now entering a new life as Miss Jane Elliott.

<u>How Can You Apply This to Your Own Life?</u>

Even through all the pain that Jane is going through, she is reminded to rely on God's strength. She trusts that He will take care of Mr. Rochester in these dark moments because that is all she can do. Jane cannot be there to console him and be his comforter, but God can.

When we know or see someone we love struggling, our first instinct is to step in and help. To be their sounding board, their comfort, and their strength. But there are times when we cannot be everything they need; only the Holy Spirit can speak directly to their hearts and give them what they truly need.

We are called to bear one another's burdens, but not to the point of self-destruction.

"Brethren, if a man be overtaken in a fault, ye which are spiritual, restore such an one in the spirit of meekness; considering thyself, lest thou also be tempted. Bear ye one another's burdens, and so fulfil the law of Christ." Galatians 6:1-2

"Put on therefore, as the elect of God, holy and beloved, bowels of mercies, kindness, humbleness of mind, meekness, longsuffering; forbearing [endure, bear with, sustain] *one*

another, and forgiving one another, if any man have a quarrel against any: even as Christ forgave you, so also do ye. And above all these things put on charity, which is the bond of perfectness. And let the peace of God rule in your hearts, to the which also ye are called in one body; and be ye thankful." Colossians 3:12-15

Every person has a right to choose their own path in life. Some may fall away from God and His teachings, while others will remain steadfast. As believers, we are to be there to support our fellow man but not take their sin, their fears, their insecurities, their shame, their guilt, their rejection, their anger, their bitterness, or their grief as our own.

The first part of Galatians 6 tells us to be careful not to fall into the same temptation that our neighbor has fallen into. We must guard our own hearts as we support those who are struggling.

What does it mean to bear one another's burdens?

The body of Christ is meant to support one another in their journeys of faith. We are instructed to love one another, keep one another accountable, and bear one another's burdens. To bear, in the Greek (*G941 in the Strong's Concordance*), means to carry, take up, sustain, or uphold.

If we go by this translation, we can come to understand that bearing each other's burdens means that we are standing alongside one another in times of hardship. To help carry the load of their sorrow without taking it fully on ourselves. We all have our own individual burdens to carry. We have obligations and responsibilities that God has given each of us.

Knowing this, God never intended that we assume the responsibility of another's burdens in addition to our own. We are not meant to take their sins or their behavior and place them on our shoulders.

However, we can join our neighbor who is struggling and help them shoulder the weight of the burdens that they carry through prayer, being available to them, and sharing God's word through exhortation.

Having two oxen pulling a heavily laden cart as opposed to only one will help lighten the load and make transportation that much easier.

We were never meant to be alone. That is why believers are called the body of Christ. As a body, we are better able to stand up and be strong against the wiles of the devil.

There will be times when we have done all we can and must step back and allow God to take over. One of the best examples of this is in Job.

Job was fearful that his children, in their partying and drinking that they would sin and curse God in their hearts. His fear was so strong that his children would ruin their relationship with God that he would fast, pray, and sacrifice to cover those sins. Ultimately, Job ended up losing his children and said—

"For the thing which I greatly feared is come upon me, and that which I was afraid of is come unto me." Job 3:25

When we are constantly in a state of dread over the people we love that fear will ultimately begin to have a rule over our lives and become an idol. It could turn into a fear of losing that relationship, a fear of them not going to heaven, or a fear of them turning away from God. Fear can also push away the people we are trying to hold close, thus bringing to fruition what we feared the most to begin with. Who wants to be around a constantly fearful person?

Job was not trusting that God had his children in His hands. He decided to control the situation for himself rather than place his faith in God for the future of his children.

Many churches have taught fear, shame, and guilt to "ensure" their congregation do not turn away from God and His love. However, in most circumstances, this type of preaching does the exact opposite. It pushes people away and gives them a poor representation of what Christianity is supposed to look like. This is not an example of placing your faith in God for your future. God has never and will never use fear, shame, or guilt to bring you closer to Him. A healthy way to address the Church is to teach God's Word as knowledge and with it, comes accountability and redemption. There is a journey we are all on in this process.

"Trust in the LORD with all thine heart; and lean not unto thine own understanding. In all thy ways acknowledge him, and he shall direct thy paths." Proverbs 3:5-6

When we begin to read the Word and be in regular conversation with God, faith begins to overshadow fear. Our futures, and the futures of those we love, begin to be less terrifying because we know that the Holy Spirit will guide us down the path of righteousness.

"He shall not be afraid of evil tidings: his heart is fixed, trusting in the LORD. His heart is established, he shall not be afraid, until he see his desire upon his enemies." Psalm 112:7-8

If our hearts are established in God and the Holy Spirit's guidance over our lives and the lives of others, we can place our complete trust in Him.

"It is of the LORD's mercies that we are not consumed [cease, end, fail, be wasted], *because his compassions* [tender love] *fail not. They are new every morning: great is thy faithfulness. The LORD is my portion* [inheritance, allotment], *saith my soul; therefore will I hope in him. The LORD is good unto them that wait for him* [expect, look for, patiently, hope], *to the soul that seeketh him."* Lamentations 3:22-25

The best we can do, and what is ultimately in our control, is to love others. By loving others, they will begin to see God in us.

"Beloved, if God so loved us, we ought also to love one another. No man hath seen God at any time. If we love one another, God dwelleth in us, and his love is perfected in us. Hereby know we that we dwell in him, and he in us, because he hath given us of his Spirit." 1 John 4:11-13

"Owe no man any thing, but to love one another: for he that loveth another hath fulfilled the law. For this, thou shalt not commit adultery, thou shalt not kill, thou shalt not steal, thou

shalt not bear false witness, thou shalt not covet; and if there be any other commandment, it is briefly comprehended in this saying, namely, thou shalt love thy neighbour as thyself. Love worketh no ill to his neighbour: therefore love is fulfilling of the law." Romans 13:8-10

If there is someone in your life who is struggling in faith or in life, pray for them. Be a sounding board if they need it, support them as a brother or sister in Christ. But stay strong against the temptation to take their grievances, frustrations, and fears on as your own. Take what they have to say and lay it down at the feet of Christ. Do not let it ferment in your heart but release it right away.

Pray that they will hear the Holy Spirit's voice in their hearts. Encourage them with the Word and just love them the way Christ loves them. Ultimately, whatever happens in their life is up to them and God, but your love for them could make the difference.

Chapter XXIX

It has been about four or five days since Jane left Thornfield and Mr. Rochester. She is now mentally and physically burnt out and exhausted but in the care of very generous and kind people, she quickly recovers. Even though she had deigned to be a beggar, Jane felt that she was not unwelcome and that gave her comfort.

I have always had a difficult time with St. John. Every time I read this book, I cannot seem to find myself liking him, even a little. Like all the characters we have analyzed, St. John will be given a fair shot to show us who he is.

St. John is a very blunt person, and he speaks his mind without considering how the person to which he is referring will receive his words. He bluntly observes that Jane is not a very attractive woman right in front of her.

A man who is supposed to be of the church should take more care in how his words are received. St. John is a very prideful man, and that pride often comes with a prejudice about how people should behave. This is something we will continue to unpack as we get to know him a little better.

"Prejudices, it is well known, are most difficult to eradicate from the heart whose soil has never been loosened or fertilised by education: they grow there, firm as weeds among stones. Hannah had been cold and stiff, indeed, at the first: latterly she had begun to relent a little; and when she saw me come in tidy and well-dressed, she even smiled."

Jane is always giving others the benefit of the doubt. She is seeing them at a greater depth than most would. In this case, she gives Hannah so much grace. Jane knows that she is an intruder in this quiet home and understands that Hannah is only seeing that part of her.

"'You munnut think too hardly of me,' she again remarked.

'But I do think hardly of you,' I said; 'and I'll tell you why —not so much because you refused to give me shelter, or regarded me as an impostor, as because you just now made it a species of reproach that I had no "brass" and no house. Some of the best people that ever lived have been as destitute as I am; and if you are a Christian, you ought not to consider poverty a crime.'

'No more I ought,' said she: 'Mr. St. John tells me so too; and I see I wor wrang — but I've clear a different notion on you now to what I had. You look a raight down dacent little crater.'

'That will do — I forgive you now. Shake hands.'

She put her floury and horny hand into mine; another and heartier smile illumined her rough face, and from that moment we were friends."

The description of this family is so different from that of the Reeds. Those children fought and disliked one another whereas this family never fights, and they love each other. They love to learn and had stable parents to raise them. They were "united." This is a little foreign to Jane.

"Diana had a voice toned, to my ear, like a cooing of a dove. She possessed eyes whose gaze I delighted to encounter. Her whole face seemed to me full of charm. Mary's countenance was equally intelligent – her features equally pretty; but her expression was more reserved, and her manners, though gentle, more distant. Diana looked and spoke with a certain authority: she had a will, evidently. It was my nature to feel pleasure in yielding to an authority supported like hers, and to bend, where my conscience and self-respect permitted, to an active will."

What lovely ladies to be surrounded by! Jane will be well-cared for and loved by them.

"Mr. St. John…was young – perhaps from twenty-eight to thirty – tall, slender; his face riveted the eye; it was like a Greek face, very pure in outline: quite a straight, classic nose; quite an Athenian mouth and chin. It is seldom, indeed, an English face comes so near the antique models as did his. He might well be a little shocked at the irregularity of my lineaments, his own being so harmonious. His eyes were large and blue, with brown lashes; his high forehead, colourless as ivory, was partially streaked over by careless locks of fair hair.

This is a gentle delineation, is it not, reader? Yet he whom it describes scarcely impressed one with the idea of a gentle, a yielding, an impressible, or even of a placid nature. Quiescent as he now sat, there was something about his nostril, his mouth, his brow, which, to my perceptions, indicated elements within either restless, or hard, or eager.

He did not speak to me one word, nor even direct to me one glance, till his sisters returned."

"St. John's eyes, though clear enough in a literal sense, in a figurative one were difficult to fathom. He seemed to use them rather as instruments to search other people's thoughts, than as agents to reveal his own: the which combination of keenness and reserve was considerably more calculated to embarrass than to encourage."

As always, Jane's observations of human behavior and how people interact with others is spectacular. At first glance, St. John seems a very cold, indifferent person who is aware of his good looks and education. Though this is not exactly untrue, Jane also observes something deeper. She sees that there is feeling within him and that he is not as cold and hard as he appears.

Although we will not get a better picture of the Rivers' past, I do believe that there has been some generational bitterness that has been passed from father to son. We will continue to break down St. John's character in the next chapter, but this is an important thing to remember as you move forward.

St. John tries to obtain some information into Jane's past and present condition. She gives him as many details as she can without revealing anything about Thornfield, Mr. Rochester, or her failed marriage. Jane explains that all she desires is to seek honest work and make her own living. She does not want to trespass on the hospitality of her benefactors for longer than she must.

"'My sisters, you see, have a pleasure in keeping you,' said Mr. St. John, 'as they would have a pleasure in keeping and cherishing a half-frozen bird, some wintry wind might have driven through their casement. I feel more inclination to put you in the way of keeping yourself, and shall endeavour to do so; but observe, my sphere is narrow. I am but the incumbent of a poor country parish: my aid must be of the humblest sort. And if you are inclined to despise the day of small things, seek some more efficient succour than such as I can offer.'

'She has already said that she is willing to do anything honest she can do,' answered Diana for me; 'and you know, St. John, she has no choice of helpers: she is forced to put up with such crusty people as you.'"

How Can You Apply This to Your Own Life?

One of the impressions I received when reading about St. John, and how he reacts to Jane, is that he is harboring some prejudice against her. She was dressed in clothing that showed she was a lady who was well-cared for, and she spoke intelligently. Perhaps he thought she was a wealthy woman who had run away and expected to be doted on by these kind people. We just do not know.

We are all subject to prejudice at some point in our lives. Has there ever been a time in your life where you made up your mind about someone without knowing anything about them?

"My brethren, have not the faith of our Lord Jesus Christ, the Lord of glory, with respect [favoritism, partiality] *of persons. For if there come unto your assembly a man with a gold ring, in goodly apparel, and there come in also a poor man in vile raiment; and ye have respect to him that weareth the gay clothing, and say unto him, sit thou here in a good place; and say to the poor, stand thou there, or sit here under my footstool: are ye not then partial* [discrimination, be partial] *in yourselves, and are become judges of evil thoughts* [discussion, dispute, imagination, reasoning]*?"*
James 2:1-4

"For I say, through the grace given unto me, to every man that is among you, not to think of himself more highly than he ought to think; but to think soberly [continually, abundantly, far more exceeding, to the intent that]*, according as God hath dealt to every man the measure of faith. For as we have many members in one body, and all members have not the same office: so we, being many, are one body in Christ, and every one members one of another."*
Romans 12:3-5

There is a reason why pride goes along with prejudice. Pride puffs a person up in haughty superiority, making them think higher of themselves than they ought. That pride in themselves then leads them to make up prejudicial thoughts and stories about others to make them feel better about themselves.

"An high [haughty] *look, and a proud heart, and the plowing* [fallow (uncultivated) ground] *of the wicked, is sin."*
Proverbs 21:4

I do hope that through this book, you have begun to realize how important it is for us to get to know people. Or at least to allow them to make decisions and mistakes without judgement. I will be the first to admit that I have had prejudices against both people I read about (*fictional or real*) and those I have met in person. We all do it!

It does make it more difficult when we come across characters like Mrs. Reed, John Reed, Mr. Brocklehurst, and even St. John. But this is the beauty of why separation is so important. There is always a reason why someone is acting the way they are. We can keep other believers accountable for their actions and teach those who do not know any better.

We are ultimately, to be examples of Christ. But we cannot be good examples of Christ if we are going into a situation with a prideful spirit. If pride is allowed in our hearts, God is not in our thoughts or actions. Instead, we are acting on our own will and discernment.

"The wicked, through the pride of his countenance, will not seek [worship, care for, diligently, inquire, search] *after God: God is not in all his thoughts."* Psalm 10:4

God is very clear about his thoughts and feelings toward prideful people.

"The LORD of hosts hath purposed it [to advise, consult, determine, guide], *to stain* [to wound, to dissolve, to profane, pollute, slay] *the pride* [arrogancy, excellency, pomp, swelling] *of all glory* [splendor, pleasant], *and to bring into contempt* [curse, despise, afflict, vile] *all the honourable*

[abounding with, more grievously afflict, boast, harden, self-honor, make self many] *of the earth."* Isaiah 23:9

"Pride goeth before destruction, and an haughty spirit before a fall. Better is it to be of an humble spirit with the lowly, than to divide the spoil with the proud." Proverbs 16:18-19

"Seest thou a man wise in his own conceit? There is more hope of a fool [stupid, silly] *than of him."* Proverbs 26:12

"But he giveth more grace [acceptable, benefit, favour, gift, joy, liberality, pleasure]. *Wherefore he saith, God resisteth* [to range oneself against, oppose themselves] *the proud, but giveth grace[1] unto the humble. Submit yourselves* [be under obedience] *therefore to God. Resist* [stand against, oppose, withstand] *the devil, and he will flee* [run away, to shun, to vanish, escape] *from you."* James 4:6-7

"The fear [reverence] *of the LORD is to hate evil: pride, and arrogancy, and the evil way, and the froward* [perverse] *mouth, do I hate."* Proverbs 8:13

"When pride cometh, then cometh shame [confusion, dishonor]: *but with the lowly is wisdom."* Proverbs 11:2

Pride is just as sticky as envy and jealousy, bitterness, and anger. It hangs on and makes us feel good about ourselves. Unfortunately, it is also not a very attractive thing to see in someone. St. John might seem okay now, but in the next couple chapters, we will see his pride come out full force. It is going to be a very unattractive trait.

If you feel that you have been struggling with pridefulness, I encourage you to revisit chapter one where we discuss the 8 Rs to Freedom ©. God wants you to be free from pride. He wants you to be humble in spirit and to be able to love and accept others without any barriers to stop you.

Releasing yourself from prideful thinking will help you be able to accept yourself as well. Many with prideful spirits have an inner torment going on toward themselves. A lot of the time self-rejection can accompany pride, which is what we will see represented in St. John.

I encourage you to go to God in prayer today for wisdom and discernment in this area. He wants you to be in good relationship with yourself as much as with Him and others. You are so precious to Him!

Footnotes

[1] Grace based on the interlinear, Greek text (G5485 – charis χάρις) – of the merciful kindness by which God, exerting his holy influence upon souls, turns them to Christ, keeps, strengthens, increases them in Christian faith, knowledge, affection, and kindles them to the exercise of the Christian virtues. That which affords joy, pleasure, delight, sweetness, charm, loveliness: grace of speech.

Chapter XXX

"The more I knew of the inmates of Moor House, the better I liked them. In a few days I had so far recovered my health that I could sit up all day, and walk out sometimes. I could join with Diana and Mary in all their occupations; converse with them as much as they wished, and aid them when and where they would allow me. There was a reviving pleasure in this intercourse, of a kind now tasted by me for the first time – the pleasure arising from perfect congeniality of tastes, sentiments, and principles."

Jane found many things in common with these ladies and found joy in sharing life's pleasures with them. She began to find joy in life again and be happy in being surrounded by like-minded people.

"They were both more accomplished and better read than I was; but with eagerness I followed in the path of knowledge they had trodden before me. I devoured the books they lent me: then it was full satisfaction to discuss with them in the evening what I had perused during the day. Thought fitted thought; opinion met opinion: we coincided, in short, perfectly."

Diana and Mary are very accomplished young women and take to teaching Jane what they can while Jane teaches Mary to draw. Diana and Jane in particular, grew to be very good friends as their personalities were so well matched. The former being very vigorous and loved to teach, and the later passionate and loved to learn.

"As to Mr. St. John, the intimacy which had arisen so naturally and rapidly between me and his sisters did not extend to him. One reason of the distance yet observed between us was, that he was comparatively seldom at home: a large proportion of his time appeared devoted to visiting the sick and poor among the scattered population of his parish.

No weather seemed to hinder him in these pastoral excursions: rain or fair, he would…go out on his mission of love or duty — I scarcely know in which light he regarded it. Sometimes, when the day was very unfavourable, his sisters would expostulate. He would then say, with a peculiar smile, more solemn than cheerful —

'And if I let a gust of wind or a sprinkling of rain turn me aside from these easy tasks, what preparation would such sloth be for the future I propose to myself?'"

When one cannot tell whether a believer's devotion is due to genuine love of serving others or the duty he or she feels to get into heaven, it is very confusing to non-believers. It does not represent a good example of Christianity and what it should look like to serve. St. John boarders on obligation with his works as we will find out further in the story.

This also encourages the idea that he is a very prideful person. His works supersede his desire to be a loving example of Christ.

Jane notices that St. John is not of a peaceful nature. His mind is always on alert, and he does not delight in the small things of life. He finds solace and joy in God's creation, frivolity.

I do find it interesting that she points out that there is an inward serenity (*peace*) that comes with being a follower of God. When we strive excessively for success in any aspect of life, it can overshadow the peace that God would have for us. St. John stives for perfection and expects the same from other believers. Again, his works become his main focus. This is something we will discuss in the devotional section of this chapter.

In regard to the first sermon that Jane heard him preach, we can see much of this observation coming through:

reference to these points sounded like a sentence pronounced for doom. When he had done, instead of feeling better, calmer, more enlightened by his discourse, I experienced an inexpressible sadness; for it seemed to me – I know not whether equally so to others – that the eloquence to which I had been listening had sprung from a depth where lay turbid dregs of disappointment, where moved troubling impulses of insatiate yearnings and disquieting aspirations. I was sure St. John Rivers – pure-lived, conscientious, zealous as he was – had not yet found that peace of God which passeth all understanding: he had no more found it, I thought, than had I with my concealed and racking regrets for my broken idol and lost Elysium – regrets to which I have latterly avoided referring, but which possessed me and tyrannized over me ruthlessly."

We have discussed in previous chapters the church and how it was often a source of fear, shame, and guilt to "encourage" congregants to live a pure life for God. St. John seems to have adopted these principles. More than this, however, Jane recognizes some bitterness, disappointment, and disquiet in his words.

There is always a greater depth of character to each individual and in the case of St. John, our observations might tell us that he has experienced quite a few disappointments in his life. Since St. John is not a very open individual, we can only speculate at where this bitterness and disappointment are coming from. What we do know is that when someone is self-accusing, bitter against themselves, and/or feeling guilty, they can turn it on others in an attempt to relieve the torment in their own soul. Thus, is born, misery loves company.

In my personal view, I believe that he never desired the calling of a clergyman. It feels to me that he inherited the position because his father was a clergyman and that is how he raised St. John. I feel that there is more that St. John would have wanted out of life and because of that, he holds on to some bitterness that he is now "trapped" in this position and field.

His heart is in turmoil and everything going on in the depths of his soul is oozing out into the words that he preaches. Instead of being encouraged, uplifted, and exhorted by the words of God, St. John's congregants are brought low, saddened, and feel doomed. There is no peace, no joy, no love. And though this is all speculation, we can agree that there is extreme discontent within the heart of St. John.

"And the peace of God, which passeth all understanding, shall keep your hearts and minds through Christ Jesus."
Philippians 4:7

"He put the question rather hurriedly; he seemed half to expect an indignant, or at least a disdainful rejection of the offer: not knowing all my thoughts and feelings, though guessing some, he could not tell in what light the lot would appear to me. In truth it was humble – but then it was sheltered, and I wanted a safe asylum: it was plodding – but then, compared with that of a governess in a rich house, it was independent; and the fear of servitude with strangers

*entered my soul like iron: it was not ignoble – not
unworthy – not mentally degrading, I made my decision."*

This entire conversation between Jane and St. John is just a
long-winded way of showing his piety. It also reveals, again,
his prejudice toward Jane. His mind is still made up about
her character. He believes she requires balancing out with
good, hard work.

However, Jane readily agrees to his proposal of her teaching
in a small school for poor girls in the village, which confuses
St. John at first. Jane has always surprised others with her
capacity to be more than what they see on the surface. St.
John asks her what she will do with all her accomplishments.
Jane answers simply,

"'Save them till they are wanted. They will keep.'"

It is at the end of this chapter that St. John admits to a feeling
of discontent, recognizing the hypocrisy of his teachings. He
feels stifled but he refuses to bend in the plan he has laid out
for his life.

His sisters love him and want what is best for him, but they
are afraid that he will not survive his missionary calling. St.
John is not a hearty man but one that is prone to anxious
wasting away, the evidence of which we will see in
following chapters. Keep in mind that the need to control
brings anxiety. They both stem from fear. Fear is very vocal
when bitterness is present. When we are in this trap, we are
unable to release our shackles and trust God for our future.
Satan pressures us but God walks with us and directs us. The
need for control is trying to make things right inside of us. It

makes ourselves the idol. It circumvents God's plans for our own. This can make the spirit hardened and angry. At this point, we can see it on full display in St. John.

How Can You Apply This to Your Own Life?

Striving is mentioned throughout scripture in both a positive and negative light. Often people get confused with the difference because it is not properly explained to them.

When we look at St. John, we can see that he is striving for a path that he feels is what is going to bring him worth, not only in the eyes of God, but also in the Kingdom of Heaven. This type of striving is mingled with straining and vanity.

Strive, according to the Greek translation (*G75 in the Strong's Concordance*) means to endeavor to accomplish something or labor fervently.

When Christians are taught about striving, it is most often within the context of being more like Christ. Unfortunately, many think that if they fail in this area, they are not striving hard enough.

Vanity joins in when too much introspection overtakes their thoughts. Too much introspection will eventually lead to self-idolatry because all your energy is focused solely on yourself. When you are too focused on yourself, your energy will be spent, and none will be left for others or even God. This is when striving becomes a need for perfection.

"I have seen all the works that are done under the sun; and, behold, all is vanity [unsatisfactory, vain, vapour] *and vexation* [longing, grasping after, striving] *of spirit."*
Ecclesiastes 1:14

"Better is an handful [palm] *with quietness* [quietness, restfulness], *than both the hands* [fists] *full with travail* [worry whether of body or mind, grievance, sorrow, toil, wearisome] *and vexation* [striving] *of spirit."* Ecclesiastes
4:6

Godly striving reveals that we cannot achieve our own sanctification simply through works and denying ourselves and our humanness daily. On the contrary, sanctification comes through being vigilant and standing firm against the Enemy.

"And he said to them all, if any man will come after me, let him deny [abstain] *himself, and take up* [bear, expiate sin] *his cross* [self-denial] *daily, and follow me. For whosoever will save his life shall lose* [perish, die] *it: but whosoever will lose his life for my sake, the same shall save it. For what is a man advantaged* [prevail, profit, benefit], *if he gain the whole world, and lose himself, or be cast away? For whosoever shall be ashamed of me and of my words, of him shall the Son of man be ashamed, when he shall come in his own glory, and in his Father's, and of the holy angels."* Luke
9:23-26

These verses are continually misused in the Church, especially in the nineteenth century. Denying yourself in this sense refers to the sin that entered the world at the time of

Adam. This humanness of giving into the lusts of the flesh is to be denied while the fruits of the spirit are to be accepted.

Turning away from God's word and Christ's teachings, being ashamed of them when tribulation comes, will lead to separation from our Father in heaven. Gaining all that the world offers will amount to nothing if we have not stored our treasures up in heaven.

The way this denying of oneself is taught is that we must go against ourselves in everything. But this is not loving ourselves, which is what God calls us to do. This goes back to introspection. Too much of which can lead to self-loathing if we are seeing so much fallibility in our character.

God says that He will fight for us and with us if we only have faith that He will do so. He loved us from the very beginning and will continue to love us to the end of time, despite our fallibility.

"Wherefore, my beloved, as ye have always obeyed, not as in my presence only, but now much more in my absence, work out [accomplish, perform] *your own salvation* [safety, deliver, save] *with fear* [reverence] *and trembling*[1]. *For it is God which worketh* [to be active, effectual, be mighty in, shew forth self] *in you both to will* [to determine, to choose or prefer, to delight in, to wish, love, please] *and to do* [to be active, effectual, shew forth self] *of* [regarding, exceeding, behalf of, concerning, for sake of] *his good pleasure* [satisfaction, delight, kindness, desire, good will, purpose]."
Philippians 2:12-13

God already loves us and proved how much by sending His only begotten Son to die for all our sins. All He asks of us is to have faith and obey His Word. The more we seek Him and His holiness, the more we become like Christ, and the more we become like Christ, the more we see His love for us.

Constantly working and striving to gain God's approval, as we would an earthly father, is never going to bring anything but stress, fear, and anxiety. We put burdens on ourselves to be more than we are or to be something God did not create us to be. This is ripe for the enemy of our souls to encourage us to turn against ourselves (*oppose ourselves*), destroying our potential freedom in Christ Jesus. God calls us to treat others the way He would treat others and this includes ourselves. You already have His approval. You already have His love. You will never lose that no matter what.

"And the servant of the Lord must not strive [fight, dispute]*; but be gentle unto all men, apt to teach, patient, in meekness* [humility] *instructing* [discipline, teach, train up a child] *those that oppose themselves* [to place one's self in opposition]*; if God peradventure* [whether or not, perhaps] *will give them repentance to the acknowledging* [full discernment, recognition] *of the truth; and that they may recover themselves* [become sober again, regain senses] *out of the snare* [stratagem, temptation, trick, trap] *of the devil, who are taken captive* [make a prisoner of war, catch] *by him at his will* [pleasure, desire, determination]*."* 2 Timothy 2:24-26

While we work hard, we are also called to be at peace and rest.

"Come [follow] *unto me, all ye that labour* [to feel fatigue, work hard, toil (with burdens or grief), be wearied] *and are heavy laden* [to load up, overburden with ceremony (or spiritual anxiety)], *and I will give you rest* [to refresh, take ease]. *Take my yoke* [used of any burden, pair of balances, (Christ's commands to be submitted to, though easier to be kept than the Pharisees' yoke)] *upon you, and learn* [understand] *of* [because of, from] *me; for I am meek* [gentle, humble] *and lowly* [humble] *in heart: and ye shall find rest unto your souls. For my yoke is easy* [gracious, kind], *and my burden* [load] *is light."* Matthew 11:28-30

Christ gives us rest from our striving. He gives us rest in His finished work that we might sanctified and united with Him in heaven one day. Through this, we are also restored to our relationship with our heavenly Father.

"For he that is entered into his rest, he also hath ceased from his own works, as God did from his. Let us labour [diligence, be earnest, endeavour] *therefore to enter into that rest², lest any man fall after the same example of unbelief* [obstinate and rebellious, disobedience]." Hebrews 4:10-11

"Be still [cease, let alone, relax, be quiet], *and know that I am God: I will be exalted among the heathen, I will be exalted in the earth."* Psalm 46:10

"Finally, brethren, farewell. Be perfect [fit, mend, make perfectly join together, prepare, restore], *be of good comfort, be of one mind* [of the same, agreed together], *live in peace;*

and the God of love and peace shall be with you." 2
Corinthians 13:11

Take your rest and be at peace in God's love and acceptance.
Give yourself grace as God gives you grace. He gives us a
chance to repent and restore our relationship with Him,
which is one of the most gracious and loving acts. Continue
working toward a right relationship with Him and trust that
He will be there to support you when you fall.

Footnotes

[1] Trembling based on the interlinear, Greek text (G5156 – tromos
τρόμος) – with fear and trembling, used to describe the anxiety of
one who distrusts the anxiety of one who distrusts his ability
completely to meet all requirements, but religiously does his
utmost to fulfil his duty.

[2] Rest based on the interlinear, Greek text (G2663 – katapausis
κατάπαυσις) – a resting place; the heavenly blessedness in which
God dwells, and of which he has promised to make persevering
believers in Christ partakers after the toils and trials of life on earth
are ended.

Chapter XXXI

"Some of them [students] are unmannered, rough, intractable, as well as ignorant; but others are docile, have a wish to learn, and evince a disposition that please me. I must not forget that these coarsely-clad little peasants are of flesh and blood as good as the scions of gentlest genealogy; and that the germs of native excellence, refinement, intelligence, kind feeling, are as likely to exist in their hearts as in those of the best-born. My duty will be to develop these germs: surely I shall find some happiness in discharging that office. Much enjoyment I do not expect in the life opening before me: yet it will, doubtless, if I regulate my mind, and exert my powers as I ought, yield me enough to live on from day to day." – brackets added by me

Jane is feeling lonely and desolate again with Mary and Diana gone. She has lost so much of what she loves so it is not surprising that she is not bouncing back immediately to her prior joyful state. There is still a grieving process that is going on in her heart.

She also feels that her status in life has fallen lower than what is considered socially acceptable. Her role as a governess was at least respectable, though she may have been treated as an additional servant. Now she lives in a hovel and educates girls who have never had the opportunity to be educated properly. She knew that these thoughts and feelings were uncharitable and unfair but had hope that things would get better as she continued to apply herself diligently.

"Meantime, let me ask myself one question — Which is better? — To have surrendered to temptation; listened to passion; made no painful effort — no struggle; — but to have sunk down in the silken snare; fallen asleep on the flowers covering it; wakened in a southern clime, amongst the luxuries of a pleasure villa: to have been now living in France, Mr. Rochester's mistress; delirious with his love half my time — for he would — oh, yes, he would have loved me well for a while. He did love me — no one will ever love me so again. I shall never more know the sweet homage given to beauty, youth, and grace — for never to anyone else shall I seem to possess these charms. He was fond and proud of me — it is what no man besides will ever be. But where am I wandering, and what am I saying, and above all, feeling? Whether is it better, I ask, to be a slave in a fool's paradise at Marseilles — fevered with delusive bliss one hour — suffocating with the bitterest tears of remorse and shame the next — or to be a village-schoolmistress, free and honest, in a breezy mountain nook in the healthy heart of England?

Yes; I feel now that I was right when I adhered to principle and law, and scorned and crushed the insane promptings of a frenzied moment. God directed me to a correct choice: I thank His providence for the guidance!"

God has never left Jane's side. He continues to guide and direct her down a path that is honorable. I believe that this time away from Mr. Rochester is good for her to re-establish her faith and how important it is. In this active time of grieving, she has her mind determined to keep setting her emotions into a place that does not overcome her desire to honor God in her actions. Her choices are being made daily, even moment by moment to keep fixed on her purpose at that time. She does not know what tomorrow will bring but today, she will utilize her gifts and talents to keep moving forward instead of giving into despair.

Moving from Jane, we will now have some insight into St. John's thoughts which will help us understand his cynicism and bitterness a little better.

"'A year ago I was myself intensely miserable, because I thought I had made a mistake in entering the ministry: its uniform duties wearied me to death. I burnt for the more active life of the world — for the more exciting toils of a literary career — for the destiny of an artist, author, orator; anything rather than that of a priest: yes, the heart of a politician, of a soldier, of a votary of glory, a lover of renown, a luster after power, beat under my curate's surplice. I considered; my life was so wretched, it much be changed, or I must die. After a season of darkness and struggling, light broke and relief fell: my cramped existence all at once spread out to a plain without bounds; my powers heard a call from heaven to rise, gather their full strength, spread their wings, and mount beyond ken. God had an errand for me; to bear which afar, to deliver it well, skill and strength, courage and eloquence, the best qualifications of soldier, statesman, and orator, were all needed: for these all centre in the good missionary.

A missionary I resolved to be. From that moment my state of mind changed; the fetters dissolved and dropped from every faculty, leaving nothing of bondage but its galling soreness — which time only can heal. My father, indeed, imposed the determination, but since his death, I have not a legitimate obstacle to contend with…an entanglement or two of the feelings broken through or cut asunder — a last conflict with human weakness, in which I know I shall overcome…'"

There are two important points in the above paragraph. One, is that St. John's father imposed (*forced*) the decision to become a minister and now that he is gone, St. John can choose his path. And two, he believes that feelings in general are a human weakness in his mind. He wants to overcome this "human weakness" so that he can better serve Christ.

God gave us human feelings. It is not a sin to feel things. We cannot be ruled by our emotions because they can lead to sin if we are not careful. The perfect example of this is Ephesians 4:26-27 – *"Be ye angry, and sin not: let not the sun go down upon your wrath: neither give place to the devil."* We can feel these feelings but not give place for the devil to enter.

Entering our story is Miss Oliver. Jane describes her as being the image of grace and beauty, being overly blessed in this as well as wealth. St. John is clearly in love with her.

"As she patted the dog's head, bending with native grace before his young and austere master, I saw a glow rise to that master's face. I saw his solemn eye melt with sudden fire, and flicker with resistless emotion. Flushed and kindled thus,

he looked nearly as beautiful for a man as she for a woman. His chest heaved once, as if his large heart, weary of despotic constriction, had expanded, despite the will, and made a vigorous bound for the attainment of liberty. But he curbed it, I think, as a resolute rider would curb a rearing steed. He responded neither by word nor movement to the gentle advances made him."

Master of his emotions, St. John cannot hide his inner feelings from such a keen observer as Jane. As much as he wants to master these human emotions, it is impossible.

"This spectacle of another's suffering and sacrifice rapt my thoughts from exclusive meditation on my own. Diana Rivers had designated her brother 'inexorable as death.' She had not exaggerated."

<u>Inexorable</u>: unyielding, unalterable, not to be persuaded, moved, or affected by prayers or entreaties.

<u>How Can You Apply This to Your Own Life?</u>

"For I know the thoughts that I think [imagine, esteem, purpose] *toward you* [concerning], *saith the LORD, thoughts of peace* [health, prosperity, rest, safety, welfare], *and not of evil* [affliction, distress, grief, harm, heaviness, wretchedness, misery], *to give you an expected* [hope, live, expectation] *end* [future, reward]." Jeremiah 29:11

Direction and purpose are two aspects of life that everyone searches for far and wide. Both have a lot to do with identity and expectations that are placed on us, by ourselves or by others.

False expectations are constantly being placed on us. The world's expectations for us and our futures, and even our own expectations for ourselves, do not often align with our true purpose in life. God's only expectation of us is that we live in obedience to His word and follow Christ's example; in this, God can accomplish His plans for us.

In addition, only God knows our futures. We all have different paths in life and ways in which God calls us to share the gospel. Comparisons and striving can fuel the burden of expectation.

We already know that St. John was pushed into his career by his father. He does not seem to enjoy his career or find peace, contentment, or joy in it. Even the thought of missionary work does not seem to give him any peace. The huge expectation on him to follow in his father's footsteps made St. John a bitter, self-pitying man. His life did not seem to fit him and so he became a fussy child wriggling in a tight suit.

We can see that God created St. John to be a very active and passionate person who desires to be something in the world. As readers with no background, we can only speculate whether St. John was truly called to be a pastor and missionary. We do not know if he chose to be a missionary for himself because he felt it the most honorable. Overall, St. John has an extreme lack of identity.

When expectations are placed on a person, that person begins to take on that expectation as their own (*lack of identity*). Part of this is because guilt might set in that we are not following the expectations of others, disappointing those we admire and love. Guilt keeps us trapped in trying to meet expectations outside of ourselves. This is a fear of rejection. It is an opportunistic fear that comes in when we lack a firm identity.

St. John appears to be going through the motions of piety but not really owning it as a true identity. Bitterness moves in when we are not our true selves. So, is it fair to give into fear of rejection, sacrificing the identity that God desires for us from the beginning of Creation? His thoughts toward us are so much more valuable than something to attain from another person.

> *"My soul, wait thou* [hold peace, be silent, rest] *only upon God; for my expectation* [hope, thing that I long for] *is from him. He only is my rock* [strength, refuge] *and my salvation* [deliverance, victory, health, prosperity]*: he is my defence* [refuge]*; I shall not be moved."* Psalm 62:5-6

At some point, we must make a choice. Are we going to follow along in the expectations of the world? Or are we going to forge our own path according to where the Holy Spirit is guiding us?

I am not telling you to be rebellious but to be courageous in your faith. To stand up against what the world is telling you is right and stand firm in where God is calling you.

Carving out your own path in life can be scary. But it can also be one of the greatest choices you will ever make. Trusting in the Holy Spirit's guidance is the best way to figure out which path is right for *you*. He will never steer you wrong and His ways will always be superior to any human plan.

Our ultimate purpose in life is to be the light of Christ and share His love with others. How we do that is between us and God. It could be through mission work, through opening a small business that serves your community, through going to college and getting a degree, or even through being a mentor to a young woman or man who is struggling to figure out their own purpose and direction. God will use you in any situation He places you if you allow Him.

What expectations are placed on you? Who places those expectations on you?

What would happen if you went against those expectations?

Have courage and claim your identity in Christ!

> *"What shall we then say to these things? If God be for* [exceeding, abundantly, on behalf of, more than, for sake of] *us, who can be against us?"* Romans 8:31

Chapter XXXII

Jane is adjusting to her teaching position and getting to know her students better. Those that were dull are now learning how to care for themselves and appreciate education. This is a testament to Jane's patience and dedication. Her students like her, and she starts spending time getting to know their parents.

"There was an enjoyment in accepting their simple kindness, and in repaying it by a consideration – a scrupulous regard to their feelings – to which they were not, perhaps, at all times accustomed, and which both charmed and benefited them; because, while it elevated them in their own eyes, it made them emulous to merit the deferential treatment they received.

I felt I became a favourite in the neighbourhood. Whenever I went out, I heard on all sides cordial salutations, and was welcomed with friendly smiles. To live amidst general regard, though it be but the regard of working people, is like 'sitting in sunshine, calm and sweet;' serene inward feelings bud and bloom under the ray. At this period of my life, my heart far oftener swelled with thankfulness than sank with dejection: and yet, reader, to tell you all, in the midst of this calm, this useful existence – after a day passed in honourable exertion amongst my scholars, an evening spent in drawing or reading contentedly alone – I used to rush into strange dreams at night...I still again and again met Mr. Rochester, always at some exciting crisis; and then the sense of being in his arms, hearing his voice, meeting his eye, touching his hand and cheek, loving him, being loved by him – the hope of passing a lifetime at his side, would be renewed, with all its first force and fire."

Contentment has found Jane again. She is finding joy in her life and is accepted by the people around her. And yet she still dreams and longs for Mr. Rochester and his love.

Speaking of love, St. John is madly in love with Rosamond Oliver.

"St. John, no doubt, would have given the world to follow, recall, retain her, when she thus left him; but he would not give one chance of heaven, nor relinquish, for the Elysium of her love, one hope of the true, eternal Paradise. Besides, he could not bind all that he had in his nature – the rover, the aspirant, the poet, the priest – in the limits of a single passion. He could not – he would not – renounce his wild field of mission warfare for the parlours and the peace of Vale Hall. I learnt so much from himself in an inroad I once, despite his reserve, had the daring to make on his confidence."

Rosamond has a lot in common with Adèle. She is pampered but not overly spoiled, has a heart for others but is a little vain, can deeply love but is a little flighty. She is the opposite of St. John in every possible way. At this point in the story, it might seem that they would be a good match, balancing one another out. However, we will soon find, in the next chapter, that St. John would not make a good husband or partner. His viewpoint on life is so heavily pessimistic that it would crush her delicate personality.

Jane is excellent at helping people talk and open up about themselves. She resolves to have St. John talk about how he feels about Rosamond. Holding onto all his emotions and not allowing them to have an outlet makes his whole demeaner like that of a trapped bird wishing to be free.

Jane is advocating their union firmly with the thought that St. John could do much more with the fortunes of Mr. Oliver than by neglecting his genius and allowing his body to wither up in the harsh climates of the East. He is relieved to be able to talk about the woman he loves…or at least to hear her talked of.

"Reserved people often really need the frank discussion of their sentiments and griefs more than the expansive. The sternest-seeming stoic is human after all; and to 'burst' with boldness and good-will into 'the silent sea' of their souls is often to confer on them the first of obligations."

For all his intelligence, St. John is extremely dense. He is so narrow-minded that anything outside of his immediate scope does not hold any importance. We can see that St. John does have a heart and deep feelings of love and admiration but he chooses to hide these feelings beneath a hard shell of piety. The common theme with St. John is finding nobility in self-sacrifice.

"'It is strange,' pursued he, 'that while I love Rosamond Oliver so wildly – with all the intensity, indeed, of a first passion, the object of which is exquisitely beautiful, graceful,

fascinating — I experienced at the same time a calm, unwarped consciousness that she would not make me a good wife; that she is not the partner suited to me; that I should discover this within a year after marriage; and that to twelve months' rapture would succeed a lifetime of regret. This I know.'"

St. John is not convinced that Rosamond would make a good missionary's wife. This assumption, without even giving her a chance, shows his prejudice. He truly does not allow anyone to be anything different than what he sees on the surface. No one will ever, it seems, live up to his lofty expectations. When Jane suggests that he consider another career so that he might have Rosamond as a wife, he is appalled and flatly refuses to consider it.

"'Relinquish! What! My vocation? My great work? My foundation laid on earth for a mansion in heaven? My hopes of being numbered in the band who have merged all ambitions in the glorious one of bettering their race — of carrying knowledge into the realms of ignorance — of substituting peace for war — freedom for bondage, religion for superstition, the hope of heaven for the fear of hell? Must I relinquish that? It is dearer than the blood in my veins. It is what I have to look forward to, and to live for.'"

He is stressed, anxious, and living in self-pity. Jane, and St. John's sisters, have expressed that they are concerned for his health. St. John is already getting thinner and paler and despises the weakness of love in himself because it has nothing to do with the soul.

I think that part of St. John believes that he would be much more effective for the Kingdom if natural affection were not to play a part. He is purposefully self-debasing, which is often taught in legalistic circles of religion, believing that his only goal is to claim a space in heaven.

God said that we are to love our neighbor *as ourselves*. This must mean that we are to love ourselves, right? How is St. John missing this vastly important part of God's word?

The issue with this type of thinking is that when the heart is heavy and when spiritual torment takes refuge, the physical body of a person begins to break down.

"A merry [joyful, glad, rejoicing] *heart doeth good* [make well, beautiful, happy, successful, benefit, make cheerful, be comely, be content, diligent, make sweet] *like a medicine* [a cure, healing]*: but a broken* [stricken, afflicted, wounded] *spirit drieth* [wither] *the bones."* Proverbs 17:22

"Be not wise in thine own eyes: fear the LORD, and depart from evil. It shall be health to thy navel [specifically the umbilical cord (figuratively, the center of strength)]*, and marrow* [refreshment] *to thy bones* [the body, life, strength]*."* Proverbs 3:7-8

St. John is not joyful. He is not able to fully enjoy life for the great blessings it provides. In this, he is always anxious to do good, to be perfect, to maintain his position in the Kingdom of Heaven. Note, I said anxious and not eager. But what he is missing is that God does not call us simply to doing good and keeping our eyes on heaven, but to delight in the lives He has blessed us with.

He created such a wonderful and glorious world to live in. I am in awe every time I walk outside my door and breathe in the fresh air, smell the grass, hear the birds in the trees, and feel the sun on my face. Life is such a beautiful gift!

For some very sad reason, St. John was not taught this, or even worse, he rejects it.

How Can You Apply This to Your Own Life?

In the Bible, we are told that faith without works is dead. But the reverse is also true. Works without faith or love is not going to profit anyone.

"What doth it profit, my brethren, though a man say he hath faith, and have not works? Can faith save him? If a brother or sister be naked, and destitute of daily food, and one of you say unto them, depart in peace, be ye warmed and filled; notwithstanding ye give them not those things which are needful to the body; what doth it profit? Even so, faith, if it hath not works, is dead, being alone." James 2:14-17

Whenever the Bible talks about circumcision, (*G4061 in the Greek, Strong's Concordance*) it is referring the heart. Believers who have been circumcised in the faith are set apart and consecrated to God.

The law of the Old Testament was made null by the death and resurrection of Jesus Christ. He became our intercessor so that we could come boldly unto the Father in heaven. Circumcision then took on a whole new meaning in the New Testament and spoke of an inward working of the heart.

"And you, being dead in your sins and the uncircumcision [by implication a condition in which the corrupt desires rooted in the flesh were not yet extinct] *of your flesh* [human nature, carnal], *hath he quickened together* [to make one alive together; of Christians] *with* [union, companionship, completeness] *him, having forgiven* [pardon] *you all trespasses; blotting out* [obliterating, wipe away] *the handwriting* [legal bond] *of ordinances* [a law; civil, ceremonial, or ecclesiastical decree] *that was against us, which was contrary* [opposed, adversary] *to us, and took it out of* [vehemently, heartily] *the way, nailing it to his cross* [the atonement of Christ]; *and having spoiled* [wholly to strip off] *principalities* [evil spirits] *and powers* [token of control], *he made a shew* [to exhibit] *of them openly, triumphing over* [to conquer, to give victory] *them in it. Let no man therefore judge* [condemn, punish, decree, call in question] *you in meat* [eating, food], *or in drink, or in respect* [behalf] *of an holyday* [feast, festival], *or of the new moon* [festival of the moon], *or of the sabbath days* [day of weekly repose from secular avocations]: *which are a shadow of things to come; but the body is of Christ* [anointed]. *Let no man beguile you of your reward* [to defraud or deprive (of salvation)] *in a voluntary* [passive acquiescence, resolved, determined] *humility and worshipping of angels* [by implication, a pastor], *intruding into* [go into details in narrating, scrutinize minutely] *those things which he hath not seen, vainly* [without reason or effect, without a cause] *puffed up* [make proud, haughty] *by his fleshly* [carnal, human nature with its frailties and passions] *mind* [understanding, feeling, thought], *and not holding the Head* [Christ, the Lord of the husband and of the Church, the

corner stone], *from which all the body by joints and bands* [ligament, uniting principle] *having nourishment ministered* [fully supply, minister], *and knit together* [unite, assuredly gather], *increaseth* [cause to grow] *with the increase of God. Wherefore if ye be dead* [literal or figurative death] *with Christ from the rudiments* [fundamental, principle] *of the world, why, as though living in the world, are ye subject to ordinances, (touch* [attach oneself to, carnal intercourse] *not; taste not; handle* [to injure] *not; which all are to perish* [ruin, decay, destroy, corrupt] *with the using* [abuse, misuse]*;) after the commandments* [religious precepts] *and doctrines* [teachings] *of men? Which things have indeed a shew of wisdom in will worship* [piety, sanctimony, will worship], *and humility* [humiliation of mind, modesty, loneliness of mind], *and neglecting* [austerity, unsparing severity] *of the body; not in any honour* [dignity, precious, price] *to the satisfying* [gratification] *of the flesh."*
Colossians 2:13-23

The rituals and piety are not what counts as much as the state of the heart and whether the love of God reigns there. This is where St. John goes wrong in believing that love is a human weakness.

Fundamentalism is a movement that enforces rigid adherence to faith and religion. It is inherently strict, often incorporating the traditional teachings of the Old Testament laws and making them even more regimented to create the "perfect" Christian. This can include no smoking, no drinking alcohol, no dancing, and no watching movies or plays. There are strict guidelines on what to wear, what to teach, how to learn, and how to act.

Unfortunately, this type of Christianity has given the whole of the faith a bad reputation and has contributed to the mass exodus of young people leaving the church.

Tell me, where in the Bible was dancing said to be a sin?

Where in the Bible was drinking of alcohol said to be a sin?

David danced before the Lord and praised him with songs. Jesus turned water into wine and in the Old Testament, the people were warned not to drink in excess, but it never mentions to abstain completely.

This type of teaching also encourages works to gain access to heaven. Foreign missions, evangelism, and giving all of oneself to others are highly encouraged.

Selfishness is condemned. But what constitutes selfishness varies. If there is too much downtime in your day, if you do not feel called to foreign missions, if you are not physically or emotionally capable to be always available to others, these could be seen as selfishness and an unwillingness to serve God.

This brings us back to the chapter on striving. It is all about placing false expectations on the congregation of believers to become something they never can – perfect, infallible human beings. This is different from holiness which is a constant working toward being like Christ. And where does that lead back to? Lack of identity.

Everything keeps circling back to identity. Those who have a lack of identity strive to be useful, to meet expectations, and they tend to exhaust themselves for others, all in the name of Christ.

I am not saying that works and evangelizing and missionary work are bad in any way. They are all honorable but not all are called in the same way. Remember, we are to honor Christ with our actions and to serve others, but only the Holy Spirit knows what you will be best at and where you will thrive. No one can tell you where or how you are meant to serve but Him.

"Except the LORD build the house, they labour in vain that build it: except the LORD keep the city, the watchman waketh but in vain." Psalm 127:1

If we were all called the same way, life and the church would lack variety. We all have different strengths and weaknesses that God can use in unique ways to bring glory to His kingdom.

God does not rule through fear, shame, guilt, or religious legalism. Christ died and was resurrected so that we could have direct relationship with the Father through Him as well as to save us from our sins.

God does call us to purity, selflessness, peace, and humility. However, when that calling is turned into self-debasement, forced humility, false burden bearing, and fear of failing God, it becomes a hindrance and torment, not to mention a fabricated personality.

So many have turned away from the church because they have felt suffocated in the rigorous practices being taught. At that point, faith becomes religion (*refer back to chapter five for more details on the difference*). Religion tends to draw people into too much introspection which can lead to self-idolatry (*see chapter thirty*).

"And the peace of God, which passeth all understanding, shall keep your hearts and minds through Christ Jesus. Finally, brethren, whatsoever things are honest, whatsoever things are just, whatsoever things are pure, whatsoever things are lovely, whatsoever things are of good report; if there be any virtue, and if there be any praise, think on these things. Those things, which ye have both learned, and received, and heard, and seen in me, do: and the God of peace shall be with you." Philippians 4:7-9

If we know and understand God's word, we will have a foundation of strength for our faith. Be wary of teachings that do not utilize whole scripture verses or that teach self-debasement in order to fully honor God. Be Berean and search the scriptures for yourself with a readiness of mind.

"And the brethren immediately sent away Paul and Silas by night unto Berea: who coming thither went into the synagogue of the Jews. These were more noble that those in Thessalonica, in that they received the word with all readiness of mind, and searched the scriptures daily, whether those things were so." Acts 17:10-11

Chapter XXXIII

St. John is very good at inviting himself over unannounced which does not quite please Jane.

"…he put aside his snow-wet hair from his forehead and let the firelight shine free on his pale brow and cheek as pale, where it grieved me to discover the hollow trace of care or sorrow now so plainly graved…his hand was now at his chin, his finger on his lip: he was thinking. It struck me that his hand looked wasted like his face. A perhaps uncalled-for gush of pity came over my heart: I was moved to say —

'I wish Diana or Mary would come and live with you: it is too bad that you should be quite alone; and you are recklessly rash about your own health.'"

In response to Jane's concern, St. John is a little testy, saying that he takes care of himself just fine when he needs to. When he does not explain the reasons for his coming on such a stormy evening, and just sits in silence, Jane tries to make further conversation despite her irritation.

"'There has not been any change made about your own arrangements? You will not be summoned to leave England sooner than you expected?' [Jane]

'I fear not, indeed: such a chance is too good to befall me.'" –
brackets added by me

His cynicism about life, his own life, and self-pity is depressing. Pastor Henry Wright (*Hope of the Generations church & Be In Health* ®) used to say that self-pity is "the superglue of hell, binding you to your past" and this is such a true statement for St. John. It is almost as if he does not believe that any good can come to his life. But does that not go against his faith? Would he not have faith that good things can and will come to him if he continues to follow God's leading?

It is truly sad to see him dissolve into such hypocritical thinking and hopelessness. His false piety has become his whole personality.

Finally, through the course of his awkward stay, St. John finally gets to the point of why he is there. He shares his knowledge of Jane's past which comes as a great shock to her. Once she knows the extent of his knowledge, Jane asks after Mr. Rochester, afraid that he has been reckless in his desolation.

Automatically, St. John forms an opinion of the man based on the little he knows.

"'He must have been a bad man.,' observed Mr. Rivers.

'You don't know him – don't pronounce an opinion upon him,' I said with warmth."

Jane holds St. John accountable for his prejudices.

Do you remember Jane receiving news that she had an uncle that was dying? Do you remember when Diana, Mary, and St. John received news that they had an uncle recently pass away?

"'Merely to tell you that your uncle, Mr. Eyre of Madeira, is dead; that he has left you all his property, and that you are now rich — merely that — nothing more.'

'I! — rich?'

'Yes, you, rich — quite an heiress.'"

"It is a fine thing, reader, to be lifted in a moment from indigence to wealth — a very fine thing; but not a matter one can comprehend, or consequently enjoy, all at once…

My uncle I had heard was dead — my only relative; ever since being made aware of his existence, I had cherished the hope of one day seeing him: now, I never should. And then this money came only to me: not to me and a rejoicing family, but to my isolated self. It was a grand boon doubtless; and independence would be glorious — yes, I felt that — that thought swelled my heart."

Jane finds that she is now the owner of a small fortune of twenty thousand pounds. This sum is equal to roughly three million pounds today. St. John thinks she is too worked up for the rest of what he had to say but she insists on knowing the rest of the story he came to tell.

"'But I apprised you that I was a hard man,' said he, 'difficult to persuade.'

'And I am a hard woman — impossible to put off.'"

"I stopped: I could not trust myself to entertain, much less to express, the thought that rushed upon me — that embodied itself — that, in a second, stood out a strong, solid probability.

Circumstances knit themselves, fitted themselves, shot into order: the chain that had been lying hitherto a formless lump of links was drawn out straight — every ring was perfect, the connection complete. I knew, by instinct, how the matter stood, before St. John had said another word; but I cannot expect the reader to have the same intuitive perception, so I must repeat his explanation.

'My mother's name was Eyre; she had two brothers; one a clergyman, who married Miss Jane Reed, of Gateshead; the other John Eyre, Esq., merchant, late of Funchal, Madeira. Mr. Briggs, being Mr. Eyre's solicitor, wrote to us last August to inform us of our uncle's death, and to say that he had left his property to his brother the clergyman's orphan daughter, overlooking us, in consequence of a quarrel, never forgiven, between him and my father…'"

"'You three, then, are my cousins; half our blood on each side flows from the same source?'

'We are cousins; yes.'

I surveyed him. It seemed I had found a brother: one I could be proud of — one I could love; and two sisters, whose qualities were such, that, when I knew them but as mere strangers, they had inspired me with genuine affection and admiration. The two girls, on whom, kneeling down on the wet ground, and looking through the low, latticed window of Moor House kitchen, I had gazed with so bitter a mixture of interest and despair, were my near kinswomen; and the young and stately gentleman who had found me almost dying at his threshold was my blood relation. Glorious

*discovery to a lonely wretch! This was wealth indeed! –
wealth to the heart! – a mine of pure, genial affections. This
was a blessing, bright, vivid, and exhilarating; not like the
ponderous gift of gold: rich and welcome enough in its way,
but sobering from its weight. I now clapped my hands in
sudden joy – my pulse bounded, my veins thrilled."*

Almost immediately, she decides to divide up her inheritance
with her new-found cousins. Jane has found a true treasure in
the relationship she has with them and shows her gratitude
by sharing her wealth. She wants to bring them all together
again and provide them with a comfortable living that she
could share in.

Jane knows that she would feel oppressed to have twenty
thousand pounds all to herself, knowing that her cousins had
no part in the inheritance. We already know that Jane is not a
vain or self-seeking person. She does not desire to live in
wealth and grandeur. Sharing this wealth with those she
loves most is the best way she can think of using this money.

St. John is utterly confused with her reaction to his news and
acquiesces to her request to fetch Diana and Mary home and
allow her to share her inheritance. He says that he will find
no trouble making room in his heart for another sister and
they part on friendly terms.

How Can You Apply This to Your Own Life?

For so long, Jane has hoped for relationship with others.
Lasting, loving, and true relationships. She found that in Mr.

Rochester, and it bonded them for life. Now she finds that she has blood relatives whom she loved far before realizing their kinship.

She is receiving blessings in abundance for her faith and trust in God! She trusted in Him and His guidance, even though that meant leaving the person she loved the most. He brought blessing out of hardship through her faith.

Though life will never be easy or peaceful all the time, God says that He will bless those who are faithful and obedient to His word and teachings.

God blessed Job tenfold after all the hardship that befell him because Job never gave up his faith in God.

"The LORD bless thee, and keep thee: the LORD make his face shine upon thee, and be gracious [merciful, favor] *unto thee: The LORD lift up his countenance upon thee, and give thee peace."* Numbers 6:24-26

"And God is able to make all grace [favor, joy, pleasure] *abound toward you* [be in excess]; *that ye, always having all sufficiency* [contentedness] *in all things, may abound to every good work:"* 2 Corinthians 9:8

"Blessed be the God and Father of our Lord Jesus Christ, who hath blessed us with all spiritual blessings in heavenly places in Christ:" Ephesians 1:3

"Blessed is the man that trusteth in the LORD, and whose hope the LORD is." Jeremiah 17:7

"And ye shall serve the LORD your God, and he shall bless thy bread [food]*, and thy water; and I will take sickness away from the midst of thee."* Exodus 23:25

"O taste and see that the LORD is good: blessed is the man that trusteth in him." Psalm 34:8

"But he said, yea rather, blessed are they that hear [understand, to hear] *the word of God, and keep* [obey, preserve, keep] *it."* Luke 11:28

Even if life is a little rocky right now, know that God is by your side and will listen when you call out to him. He wants to bring blessing and peace into your life. All you have to do is ask for His wisdom and guidance with an earnest and ready heart.

If you would like to refresh your memory on why bad things happen in our world, you should go back to chapter two. God knows our heart's greatest desire. The Holy Spirit is there to bring comfort when you need it the most. The wonderful thing is that even in the midst of suffering, God is still there waiting for you to return to Him. He will take you back with open arms!

Chapter XXXIV

This chapter is very long! Because it is so long, you can divide it up into two parts or go straight through, but I encourage you to take your time. There is so much depth to this chapter that I had to break it down very carefully.

We will be revisiting quite a few of the subjects we have already discussed in previous chapters such as self-pity, self-hatred, bitterness, manipulation, expectation, pride, and I am sure many others.

"It was near Christmas by the time all was settled: the season of general holiday approached. I now closed Morton school, taking care that the parting should not be barren on my side. Good fortune opens the hand as well as the heart wonderfully; and to give somewhat when we have largely received, is but to afford a vent to the unusual ebullition of the sensations. I had long felt with pleasure that many of my rustic scholars liked me, and when we parted, that consciousness was confirmed: they manifested their affection plainly and strongly."

Jane is so proud of her students and how far they have come since her first day teaching. She promises to come each week for an hour to teach them as she "…had really a place in their unsophisticated hearts…"

"'Does not the consciousness of having done some real good in your day and generation give pleasure?' [St. John]

'Doubtless' [Jane]

'And you have only toiled a few months! Would not a life devoted to the task of regenerating your race be well spent?'

'Yes,' I said; 'but I could not go on for ever so: I want to enjoy my own faculties as well as to cultivate those of other people. I must enjoy them now; don't recall either my mind or body to the school; I am out of it and disposed for full holiday.'" – brackets added by me

This is just one of many conversations between Jane and St. John where he tries to compel Jane to choose a life of servitude and constant work. What he does not understand is that Jane, though willing to work hard and serve others, requires freedom to care for her own mind and body as well. She cannot always be giving *of* herself without providing for her own needs.

The perfect example of this is by using an analogy of two cups. One represents Jane and the other represents the people she is serving. If her cup is constantly pouring into the other without filling her own cup as she goes, eventually her own will become empty. You cannot pour from an empty cup. If we do not care for ourselves by finding peaceful moments and taking rest, our cup will become empty and will be of no use to others.

It is not a selfish thing to care for ourselves physically, spiritually, and mentally. God specifically tells us that we are to love our neighbor *as ourselves*. The act of loving ourselves means that we take care of our health physically and our health spiritually. When our spiritual health suffers by allowing principalities such as bitterness, envy, guilt, self-loathing, and fear into our hearts, our physical health begins to suffer due to unnatural physiological function (*i.e., stress causes excess cortisol release which can begin to break down tissues in the body.*).

Remember that in chapter thirty-two we discussed this very thing in regard to St. John? If you do not remember, I recommend going back and reading those verses.

God values our health, otherwise, He would not call His disciples to heal the sick or raise the dead to life.

> *"Beloved, I wish above all things that thou mayest prosper* [succeed] *and be in health* [have sound health, be uncorrupt, be whole], *even as thy soul prospereth."* 3 John 1:2

> *"For I will restore health unto thee, and I will heal thee of thy wounds* [pestilence, plague, sore], *saith the LORD; because they called thee an Outcast, saying, this is Zion, whom no man seeketh after."* Jeremiah 30:17

"'No, Jane, no: this world is not the scene of fruition; do not attempt to make it so: nor of rest; do not turn slothful.'"

"I looked at him with surprise. 'St. John,' I said, 'I think you are almost wicked to talk so. I am disposed to be as content as a queen, and you try to stir me up to restlessness! To what end?'

'To the end of turning to profit the talents which God has committed to your keeping; and of which He will surely one day demand a strict account. Jane, I shall watch you closely and anxiously — I warn you of that. And try to restrain the

disproportionate fervour with which you throw yourself into commonplace home pleasures. Don't cling so tenaciously to ties of the flesh; save your constancy and ardour for the adequate cause; forbear to waste them on trite transient objects. Do you hear, Jane?'

'Yes; just as if you were speaking Greek. I feel I have adequate cause to be happy, and I will be happy. Good-bye!'"

Anyone struggling with self-pity is going to try and get others to participate in it with them. For St. John, he is showing a complete lack of love for himself over and over again and the self-pity feeds this self-loathing. When someone is struggling with self-loathing, they are discontented with themselves and their lives. Discontentment breeds bitterness. All these spiritual influences tend to drag others down with them to make themselves feel more effective or superior.

It could also be assumed that St. John is envious of Jane and her ability to be at peace and to be content in her life. There is an innate desire in each of us to be content and peaceful. For many reasons, St. John has never, and sadly, will never find this.

Jane does not allow St. John to drag her down into self-pity or discontentment. She chooses to have joy and be at peace with her life. Her preparations to restore the old Moor house for the arrival of Diana and Mary bring her excitement and a change of activity.

"With some difficulty, I got him to make the tour of the house. He just looked in at the doors I opened; and when he

had wandered upstairs and downstairs, he said I must have gone through a great deal of fatigue and trouble to have effected such considerable changes in so short a time: but not a syllable did he utter indicating pleasure in the improved aspect of his abode.

This silence damped me. I thought perhaps the alterations had disturbed some old associations he valued. I inquired whether this was the case, no doubt in a somewhat crest-fallen tone.

'not at all; he had, on the contrary, remarked that I had scrupulously respected every association: he feared, indeed, I must have bestowed more thought on the matter than it was worth. How many minutes, for instance, had I devoted to studying the arrangement of this very room?...'"

St. John's whole attitude, in a sense, poisons the very air around him. He dampens any joy, any peace, any excitement.

"St. John was a good man; but I began to feel he had spoken truth of himself when he said he was hard and cold. The humanities and amenities of life had no attraction for him — its peaceful enjoyments no charm. Literally, he lived only to aspire — after what was good and great, certainly; but still he would never rest, nor approve of others resting around him. As I looked at his lofty forehead, still and pale as a white stone…I comprehended all at once that he would hardly make a good husband: that it would be a trying thing to be his wife."

The way St. John is acting shows Jane how very wrong it would be for him to marry Miss Oliver…or anyone for that matter. His wife would be constantly scrutinized and brought under a false sense of piety. She understands now how appropriate his calling to the mission field is. It would be an ever-active career, especially in the most dangerous parts of the world, that would keep him busy. He would never be bored or feel idle.

But this constant activity allows no time to be at rest in God. It does not allow for peaceful prayer and communion with the Father. How does he expect to hear the Holy Spirit if his mind is always focused on something or other?

When his sisters arrive, St. John is glad to see them and greets them calmly, but he is irritated by their cries of joy and glee at being home again and seeing all the lovely changes Jane has made.

During the course of the evening, a young man with an ailing mother comes to the door and St. John immediately takes his leave. He is glad to escape into the bitter cold and rough terrain in the dark to perform a duty far better, in his eyes, than sitting by the fire.

Throughout the Christmas holiday week, Jane, Diana, and Mary are refreshed by each other. They find delight in conversation and companionship. Whereas St. John escaped whenever he could to serve and "deny himself" to avoid the gaiety of the household.

Joy irritates him. Someone with as much spiritual junk as St. John find those that are happier than themselves an annoyance. This is because they want what they have but cannot seem to attain it. It starts to drive envy and jealousy and possible thinking along the lines of, "if I cannot have it, no one else should."

"He had not kept his promise of treating me like his sisters; he continually made little chilling differences between us, which did not at all tend to the development of cordiality: in short, now that I was acknowledged his kinswoman, and lived under the same roof with him, I felt the distance between us to be far greater than when he had known me only as the village schoolmistress. When I remembered how far I had once been admitted to his confidence, I could hardly comprehend his present frigidity."

St. John is testing Jane. He said he would watch her, and he is most certainly keeping his promise to do so. She kept up her weekly visits to the school and was always encouraged by him to go even when the weather was formidable.

"And when I returned, sometimes a good deal tired, and not a little weather-beaten, I never dared complain, because I saw that to murmur would be to vex him: on all occasions fortitude pleased him; the reverse was a special annoyance."

I want to point something out to you. Remember when we discussed the fact that there are a lot of women who claim that Mr. Rochester is extremely manipulative? Well, we established that he most certainly was not. Mr. Rochester allowed Jane to be her own person. He accepted and loved her for who she was and did not try to change her into something she was not.

On the flip side, we have St. John. He recognizes his influence over Jane and the fact that she is unable to say no to him. Because of this, he uses this knowledge to his advantage to mold her into who he believes she needs to be to be an effective Christian.

Why is it that we overlook this character altogether in most conversations? This type of person is extremely destructive within the Christian church. When we look at the leaders of fundamentalist Christians, this pattern turns up time and time again. They expect perfection and thus will punish in very specific ways, usually emotionally, to gain adherence from their followers.

<u>Manipulate:</u> to manage or influence skillfully, especially in an unfair manner.[1]

As we will see in the next couple paragraphs, St. John is an expert at manipulating the feelings of others with his attitude toward them.

"St. John was not a man to be lightly refused: you felt that every impression made on him, either for pain or pleasure, was deep-graved and permanent."

I want to refer you back to chapter twenty-nine when I presented the topic of pride and prejudice and how they typically go together. St. John is the type of person that will make up his mind about a person and will likely not change it. He remembers past faults and silently holds them against that person. This we will see more of later.

"By degrees, he acquired a certain influence over me that took away my liberty of mind: his praise and notice were more restraining than his indifference. I could no longer talk or laugh freely when he was by, because a tiresomely importunate instinct reminded me that vivacity (at least in me) was distasteful to him. I was so fully aware that only serious moods and occupations were acceptable, that in his presence every effort to sustain or follow any other became vain: I fell under a freezing spell. When he said 'go,' I went; 'come,' I came; 'do this,' I did it. But I did not love my servitude: I wished, many a time, he had continued to neglect me."

"…I daily wished more to please him; but to do so, I felt daily more and more that I must disown half my nature, stifle half my faculties, wrest my tastes from their original bent…"

Jane is losing herself in this constant censure and scrutiny. St. John is raising her up to impossible standards of perfection that are stifling the way God made her. This brings us back to our subject of having burdens of false expectations placed on us and the guilt of not following through on them. St. John is ruling through fear, shame, and guilt. If Jane were to divert from his path, she would feel that she had failed him and, consequently, God.

Who is St. John that he should tell her how to act and who she should be?

This thinking is *not* of God.

Despite all the changes that are occurring in Jane's life, she has never once forgotten Mr. Rochester. She desperately wants to know what has become of him and her anxieties increase over his current condition when she does not hear any news in response to letters sent.

When Diana realizes that Jane is looking sad and despondent, she suggests a day by the sea to bring her solace. St. John responds with…

"…he said I did not want dissipation, I wanted employment; my present life was too purposeless, I required an aim…I, like a fool, never thought of resisting him – I could not resist him."

He is, again, speaking for Jane. It looks as if St. John only wants a servant who follows his demands blindly. Instead of this character becoming more likeable as the story progresses, St. John is only growing more insufferable.

Jane acquiesces as he demands that they go on a walk after their studies.

"I know no medium: I never in my life have known any medium in my dealings with positive, hard characters, antagonistic to my own, between absolute submission and determined revolt. I have always faithfully observed the one, up to the very moment of bursting, sometimes with volcanic vehemence, into the other; and as neither present circumstances warranted, nor any present mood inclined me to mutiny, I observed careful obedience to St. John's directions…"

Another teaching of the churches is that we are all worms. Usually referring to the fact that we are so menial, vile, and low, being sinners who do not deserve the forgiveness of God but receive it anyway. Does that sound familiar? I have been blessed enough to never be surrounded by this type of teaching, however, I have known others who have been raised up in this.

This is another misinterpretation of scripture. Interestingly, if you search the Hebrew text, worm or tôlă (*H8438*) can mean maggot. But it is used very differently.

"But I am a worm, and no man; a reproach of men, and despised of the people." Psalm 22:6

The whole of Psalm 22 is a prophetic chapter of the crucifixion of Jesus Christ. The verse above reveals what Jesus himself said about being despised and rejected of men.

So, the translation of tôlă is the following:

The crimson-grub but used only of the color from it. "When the female of the scarlet worm species was ready to give birth to her young, she would attach her body to the trunk of a tree, fixing herself so firmly and permanently that she would never leave again. The eggs deposited beneath her body were thus protected until the larvae were hatched and able to enter their own life cycle. As the mother died, the crimson fluid stained her body and the surrounding wood. From the dead bodies of such female scarlet worms, the commercial scarlet dyes of antiquity were extracted.

What a picture this gives of Christ, dying on the tree, shedding his precious blood that he might 'bring many sons unto glory' (*Hebrews 2:10*)! He died for us, that we might live through him! This verse describes such a worm and gives us this picture of Christ."[2]

There are many other theologians that have also referenced this definition as well. I have provided another resource in the footnotes for you to look at if you would like to dig deeper into this subject.[3]

The reason I am bringing this up is because St. John refers to humankind as his "...feeble fellow-worms..." And yet, the way he talks, he seems to believe that he can somehow take the place of the Holy Spirit in the lives of others. That somehow, he can predict who they should be and how they should serve, regardless of their true desires. In his eyes, everyone should be missionaries and those who are not, are slothful and not heeding God.

"'If they are really qualified for the task, will not their own hearts be the first to inform them of it?'"

Here Jane realizes this and tries to call his attention to his need to control. She can feel where he is leading her in this conversation, and it makes her nervous. St. John "must speak for" her heart's calling himself.

"'Oh, St. John!' I cried, 'have some mercy!'

I appealed to one who, in the discharge of what he believed his duty, knew neither mercy nor remorse. He continued —

'God and nature intended you for a missionary's wife. It is not personal, but mental endowments they have given you: you are formed for labour, not for love. A missionary's wife you must – shall be. You shall be mine: I claim you – not for my pleasure, but for my Sovereign's service.'"

This is a lot to unpack…first of all, Jane recognizes that he has no mercy or remorse regarding his words or how he treats others. He has a plan in mind, and no one is going to dissuade him from it. This is a sign of an unteachable spirit.

> *"Seest thou a man wise in his own conceit* [in his own eye, favour]*? There is more hope of a fool* [stupid, silly] *than of him."* Proverbs 26:12

> *"Poverty and shame shall be to him that refuseth instruction: but he that regardeth reproof shall be honored."* Proverbs 13:18

We have to acknowledge that our entire lives are meant for us to continue learning, growing, and changing as people and experiences come into it. We cannot know everything. Life is a series of lessons and corrections. Being afraid of this process diminishes God's ability to work in us the masterpiece we were meant to be. Telling God who we are and what we are going to do is not allowing Him to be God but rather become our own god.

Second, would you like to be proposed to like this? It is genuinely one of the worst proposals I have ever read. How come feminists are not picking apart this entire conversation? St. John is telling, not suggesting but telling, Jane that she is meant for the mission field and that she is not meant for love, which in effect includes not being meant to be loved. Not only that, but he *claims her*. Excuse me?

Mr. Rochester, who encouraged Jane to be her own person, who never decided for her who she was meant to be, who gave her room to grow, who did not try to change her into something he thought was better, is now even more of a stark contrast to St. John. His proposal was not controlling or demanding but full of love and admiration.

"I claim you…" No woman ever wants to hear this, especially when what follows is that the man does not love her or insinuates that she is not meant for love. It is like a dagger to the heart.

He again refers to himself as dust and ashes, the chiefest sinner, and a vile person. He wants Jane to be like him and think like him and to have faith like him. I do not know about you, but this is wholly unattractive.

This brings us back to Mr. Brocklehurst telling Jane that she would always be a liar and that she might not even see heaven. Why do these men feel the need to dictate to Jane who she is? It all comes back to pride and self-loathing.

"'But my powers – where are they for this undertaking? I do not feel them. Nothing speaks or stirs in me while you talk. I am sensible of no light kindling – no life quickening – no voice counselling or cheering. Oh, I wish I could make you see how much my mind is at this moment like a rayless dungeon, with one shrinking fear fettered in its depths – the fear of being persuaded by you to attempt what I cannot accomplish!'"

All the qualities that Jane possesses were given her by God. How she utilizes these gifts and talents should not be dictated by anyone but the Holy Spirit. Not everyone who possesses these qualities is called to be a missionary. They could be called to something completely unique and wonderful – perfect for them. No one can dictate to you what you were meant for. That is a decision between you and the God.

"'...I feel mine is not the existence to be long protracted under an Indian sun. What then? He does not care for that: when my time came to die, he would resign me, in all serenity and sanctity, to the God who gave me...If I join St. John, I abandon half myself: If I go to India, I go to premature death. And how will the interval between leaving England for India, and India for the grave, be filled? Oh, I know well! That, too, is very clear to my vision. By straining to satisfy St. John till my sinews ache, I shall satisfy him – to the finest central point and farthest outward circle of his expectations...

Consent, then, to his demand is possible: but for one item – one dreadful item. It is – that he asks me to be his wife, and has no more of a husband's heart for me than that frowning giant of a rock, down which the stream is foaming in yonder gorge...Can I receive from him the bridal ring, endure all the forms of love (which I doubt not he would scrupulously observe) and know that the spirit was quite absent? Can I bear the consciousness that every endearment he bestows is a sacrifice made on principle? No: such a martyrdom would be monstrous.'"

Jane begins to stand up for herself. This is also a very important thing to remember as St. John will continue to bring it up as her making a promise to go. Jane says that she will go *if* she can go free. There is a caveat. There was no promise made that she *would* go to India. She suggests going as brother and sister, which he staunchly refuses.

"'I, too, do not want a sister: a sister might any day be taken from me. I want a wife: the sole helpmeet I can influence efficiently in life, and retain absolutely till death.'"

This picture of the life he wants with Jane is extremely authoritarian and more than a little selfish on his part. He points out that Jane has already said she would go with him, and he tries to make her bend in her feelings by saying that she cannot go back on her word. She never promised him anything.

One thing I also find interesting is that he admires her strength of character, and yet he tries to crush it into submission. You either admire and encourage strength of character in a person, or you do not. He wants to retain his influence over her forever, which shows his controlling nature. Be someone who builds someone up rather than tearing them down.

"Wherefore comfort yourselves together, and edify [build, embolden] *one another, even as also ye do."* 1 Thessalonians 5:11

However, now that she is standing up for herself and her future, Jane insists that she will not give her heart or her body to him as he has no use or desire for either of them. She will not go unless it is as brother and sister.

"'You cannot — you ought not. Do you think God will be satisfied with half an oblation? Will He accept a mutilated sacrifice? It is the cause of God I advocate: it is under His standard I enlist you. I cannot accept on His behalf a divided allegiance: it must be entire.'

'Oh! I will give my heart to God,' I said. 'You do not want it.'

"I will not swear, reader, that there was not something of repressed sarcasm both in the tone in which I uttered this sentence, and in the feeling that accompanied it. I had silently feared St. John till now, because I had not understood him. He had held me in awe, because he had held me in doubt. How much of him was saint, how much mortal, I could not heretofore tell: but revelations were being made in this conference: the analysis of his nature was proceeding before my eyes. I saw his fallibilities: I comprehended them. I understood that, sitting there where I did, on the back of heath, and with that handsome form before me, I sat at the feet of a man, erring as I. The veil fell from his hardness and despotism. Having felt in him the presence of these qualities, I felt his imperfection, and took courage. I was with an equal — one with whom I might argue — one whom, if I saw good, I might resist."

A wife to St. John would have no freedom of thought or action. He would control every aspect of her demeanor, not through physical control but emotional control. Her nature would be molded to his specifications, and he would essentially cage what is joyful, optimistic, and free.

This is how a harsh spirit in one person can damage another. St. John's spiritual filth is trying to poison another because Satan will stop at nothing to bring God's people into bondage. St. John has the capability of being a great man. But it seems his understanding of God and His love is so warped that he is not able to get free from his own bondage. When we are in bondage like this, we need others to do the same in order to affirm where we are. Anything else magnifies our own internal torture.

Jane could see the potential in him, just as she had seen the potential in many others in her life. But his need to control is making him unattractive in her eyes. She is not the type to be controlled, manipulated, or kept.

St. John is surprised at Jane's obstinance and cannot believe that she is actually standing up to him. He was so sure about getting his way that now he is surprised that he is not getting what he wanted. He thought her soft and yielding to his whims and desires and yet he finds that she is passionate and steadfast.

Jane, in speaking her mind and holding him accountable, hurts him without realizing it. He cannot take constructive criticism (*or any kind of criticism*) well. She simply states that his view of love is counterfeit and not real love. He does not know what real love is and she sees this in him.

"'Forgive me the words, St. John; but it is your own fault that I have been roused to speak so unguardedly.'"

Like a child throwing a tantrum, St. John responds
maliciously:

*"'…do not forget that if you reject it [his proposal], it is not
me you deny, but God. Through my means, He opens to you
a noble career; as my wife only can you enter upon it. Refuse
to be my wife, and you limit yourself for ever to a track of
selfish ease and barren obscurity. Tremble lest in that case
you should be numbered with those who have denied the
faith, and are worse than infidels!'" – brackets added by me*

This is just petty and mean. His control stems from the spirit
of fear and she has challenged its presence. Again, we cannot
decide the future of anyone. Only God knows their futures
and their purpose. God will bless Jane in this decision to
follow *His* path over St. John's.

Though St. John claims not to hold a grudge toward Jane, he
does not say his customary goodnight to her but walks away,
leaving her very hurt. This is the end of any friendship that
was ever between them. I have mentioned that St. John has a
fear that is being challenged. This is the fear of rejection.

Confrontation is often avoided because there is a fear of
losing connection with people. This is why it took so long
for Jane to stand up against St. John's behavior. However, in
the current case, St. John is feeling rejected by Jane and her
refusal. The most loving thing we can do for others and for
ourselves is to know who we are and not be afraid of
confronting people and standing up for what is right.

Jane's choice to follow God's path for her is not going to
separate her from the love of God. St. John is again speaking

things over her. He is telling her that she will live in barren obscurity because she will not marry him and follow him to India. Words have great power so be careful what you speak over others. The verse below tells us that nothing will separate us from the love of God.

> *"For I am persuaded* [convinced, assured, confident], *that neither death, nor life, nor angels, nor principalities, nor powers, nor things present, nor things to come, nor height, nor depth, nor any other creature, shall be able to separate us from the love of God, which is in Christ Jesus our Lord."*
> Romans 8:38-39

<u>How Can You Apply This to You Own Life?</u>

As I read through this chapter, I grew increasingly upset that people like St. John are influencing others every day in the church. Many are not being held accountable but are blindly followed. And yet, there are many who are standing up against this destructive version of Christianity.

Throughout this book, I have tried not to hasten toward judgement on the characters, but St. John has always been a hard one for me to accept and make accommodation for.

Even Jane has a difficult time being around him and living with him. This is the first time we have seen this from her.

The truth is that these types of people still exist, just as those like Mr. Brocklehurst, Mrs. Reed, and John Reed exist. We need to learn how to respond in situations where we are placed in the company of these types of people.

We have to understand that people like St. John are struggling with deep-seated spiritual issues. They probably hate themselves, are holding onto a lot of bitterness, and they are most likely deep in self-pity. All of this does not make them very delightful to be around. But they, too, need our love and acceptance.

This is one of the hardest callings. It takes a lot of practice and patience. But remember, God will grant you the strength and patience you need to be around these people as well as the wisdom on how to draw them out of the torment they are in.

"But they that wait [look, patiently, expect] *upon the LORD shall renew* [grow up, sprout, to hasten] *their strength; they shall mount up* [ascend up, exalt, excel, recover, restore] *with wings as eagles; they shall run, and not be weary; and they shall walk, and not faint."* Isaiah 40:31

Footnotes

[1] Collins English Dictionary – Complete & Unabridged 2012 Digital Edition

[2] Henry Morris; Biblical Basis for Modern Science, Baker Book House, 1985, page 73

[3] Additional reference: https://thebiblemadeplain.com/what-did-jesus-mean-i-am-a-worm/

Chapter XXXV

St. John continues to single Jane out for refusing him during the entire week before his departure.

"…he made me feel what severe punishment a good yet stern, a conscientious yet implacable man can inflict on one who has offended him. Without one overt act of hostility, one upbraiding word, he contrived to impress me momently with the conviction that I was put beyond the pale of his favor."

Jane is always giving others the benefit of the doubt. I would not be as gracious and accepting of this behavior from someone who claims to be a godly man. This is not how a pastor should act. His pettiness and emotional manipulation of Jane reveals that he has not quite forgiven her completely. The words she said to him were not forgotten.

This brings us to our devotional subject for this chapter, forgiveness. We will discuss this in detail at the end. Ultimately, true forgiveness would not hold on to a grudge.

"To me, he was in reality become no longer flesh, but marble; his eye was a cold, bright, blue gem; his tongue a speaking instrument – nothing more.

All this was torture to me – refined, lingering torture. It kept up a slow fire of indignation and a trembling trouble of grief, which harassed and crushed me altogether. I felt how, if I were his wife, this good man, pure as the deep sunless source, could soon kill me, without drawing from my veins a

*single drop of blood, or receiving on his own crystal
conscience the faintest stain of crime."*

There is a marked difference between how St. John treats his
sisters and how he treats Jane. He treats his sisters with more
love and affection than before while Jane is treated with
coldness.

More than anything, Jane desires to be loved by those she
loves and admires. She greatly desires his friendship. I
believe that this does blind her a little to his failings as she
still views him as a good man of God.

Though I will not argue against the fact that he has the
potential to be good, I do not believe he is acting in a way
that is godly. The fact that he does not take her refusal
seriously shows that he has very little respect for Jane.

*"Had I attended to the suggestions of pride and ire, I should
immediately have left him; but something worked within me
more strongly than those feelings could. I deeply venerated
my cousin's talent and principle. His friendship was of value
to me: to lose it tried me severely."*

Jane has always listened to the Holy Spirit and that choice
has never failed her. In this moment, she knows that it is
more important to be on good terms with her cousin than to
break their relationship altogether because of pride and
obstinacy. I believe that this working within her is the Holy
Spirit to restore her relationship with St. John.

*"'And you will not marry me! You adhere to that
resolution?'*

Reader, do you know, as I do, what terror those cold people can put into the ice of their questions? How much of the fall of the avalanche is in their anger? Of the breaking up of the frozen sea in their displeasure?

'No. St. John, I will not marry you. I adhere to my resolution.'"

Jane calls St. John to accountability for pressuring her into a decision that *he* wants. Though she is calling him to accountability for his actions and cold indifference, she does accuse him of something very serious. She accuses him of killing her, which hits straight to the core of his heart.

"'Now you will indeed hate me,' I said. 'It is useless to attempt to conciliate you: I see I have made an eternal enemy of you.'

A fresh wrong did these words inflict: the worse, because they touched on the truth. That bloodless lip quivered to a temporary spasm. I knew the steely ire I had whetted. I was heart-wrung.

'You utterly misinterpret my words,' I said, at once seizing his hand: 'I have no intention to grieve you or pain you – indeed, I have not.'

Most bitterly he smiled – most decidedly he withdrew his hand from mine."

In this brief moment, it seems he has begun to realize how merciless he has been to her. However, he again asks if she will give up her promise and not go to India with him. Jane reminds him that she will only go if it be as brother and sister, to which his reasoning claims it as utterly absurd and impossible. Jane is getting frustrated with his inflexibility and inability to comprehend her words.

"'Keep to common sense, St. John: you are verging on nonsense. You pretend to be shocked by what I have said. You are not really shocked: for, with your superior mind, you cannot be either so dull or so conceited as to misunderstand my meaning. I say again, I will be your curate, if you like, but never your wife.'"

Finally, he gets it! He finally acquiesces and offers to find a married missionary's wife that would take Jane under her wing so that she could keep her word of going to India with him.

"Now I never had, as the reader knows, either given any formal promise or entered into any engagement; and this language was all much too hard and much too despotic for the occasion. I replied —

'There is no dishonour, no breach of promise, no desertion in the case. I am not under the slightest obligation to go to India, especially with strangers. With you I would have ventured much, because I admire, confide in, and, as a sister, I love you; but I am convinced that, go when and with whom I would, I should not live long in that climate.'

'Ah! You are afraid of yourself,' he said, curling his lip.

'I am. God did not give me my life to throw away; and to do as you wish me would, I begin to think, be almost equivalent

to committing suicide. Moreover, before I definitely resolve on quitting England, I will know for certain whether I cannot be of greater use by remaining in it than by leaving it.'"

Again, St. John is losing in his aim to have his own way. Jane shares a point of view that he does not understand. She does not feel called to the mission field in India in the same way he does. The thought of serving his own countrymen as a missionary does not seem to have ever occurred to him as an option.

Ultimately, Jane knows that she must search for Mr. Rochester and what has become of him before she can think of doing anything else.

Diana and Mary had hoped that St. John would marry Jane, believing that it would keep him in England with them. Their anxieties for their brother are understandable. They do not want to see him wither away in a hot, foreign country. However, Diana notices how St. John pushes Jane to perform perfectly and urges Jane not to go to India.

"'St. John – you know him – would urge you to impossibilities: with him there would be no permission to rest during the hot hours; and unfortunately, I have noticed, whatever he exacts, you force yourself to perform.'"

The conversation between Diana and Jane must have been painful for Diana to hear. It must have been difficult for Diana to hear these things about her brother, regardless of the fact that she most likely knew them all to be true statements.

"'What makes you say he does not love you, Jane?'

'You should hear himself on the subject. He has again and again explained that it is not himself, but his office he wishes to mate. He had told me I am formed for labour — not for love: which is true, no doubt. But, in my opinion, if I am not formed for love, it follows that I am not formed for marriage. Would it not be strange, Die, to be chained for life to a man who regarded one but as a useful tool?'

'Insupportable — unnatural — out of the question!'"

Jane observes something very interesting. If she were to eventually come to a point of loving him a little. She would have to repress that affection as St. John looks at love and affection as superfluity and unbecoming in a person.

When it comes to St. John's path toward greatness, she believes that it would be better for the lesser, insignificant people to keep out of his way lest they be trampled on. Human weakness should never exist in St. John's world which places an impeccable burden on anyone who crosses his path.

That evening, as is their custom, St. John is reading the bible aloud. He focuses on specific verses in Revelations.

"The succeeding words thrilled me strangely as he spoke them: especially as I felt, by the slight, indescribable alteration in sound, that in uttering them, his eye had turned on me.

'He that overcometh shall inherit all things; and I will be his God, and he shall be my son. But,' was slowly, distinctly read, 'the fearful, the unbelieving…shall have their part in the lake which burneth with fire and brimstone, which is the second death.'

Henceforward, I knew what fate St. John feared for me."

This brings up a very important question. If he believes this for Jane, what fate does he believe his sisters are headed for? Are they less important in the kingdom, or are they already promised a place in heaven? What makes Jane especially important?

"The reader believed his name was already written in the Lamb's book of life, and he yearned after the hour which should admit him to the city to which the kings of the earth bring their glory and honour; which has no need of sun or moon to shine in it, because the glory of God lightens it, and the Lamb is the light thereof."

This is yet another example of St. John's pride. Being prideful in your faith is still a stumbling block. Though it is implied that he does not even realize he is being prideful.

I have faith that I will end up in heaven with my Father, but there is a fine line between having faith in that end and having pride that you are somehow better than others. St. John crosses this line into religious pride.

When St. John and Jane are alone, he speaks earnestly and mildly to try and convince Jane that she can be a missionary's wife…his wife. He is manipulating her emotions with the tone of his words and the setting.

I believe that he truly cares for her spiritual welfare, but it is not his job to make sure that she is in right relationship with God. That is between her and God. We keep coming back to this same subject.

It is he that would not make a suitable husband, as a husband is to love his wife like Christ loved the Church and gave His life for it. If we are not loving others, we are not obeying the call to walk after Christ. To love like Christ is to sacrifice for the love of others.

His prior attitude toward her has now transformed into gentleness which he knows is much more effective on her over force and sternness.

"'I could decide if I were but certain,' I answered: 'were I but convinced that it is God's will I should marry you, I could vow to marry you here and now — come afterwards what would!'

'My prayers are heard!' ejaculated St. John. He pressed his hand firmer on my head, as if he claimed me: he surrounded me with his arm, almost as if he loved me (I say almost — I knew the difference — for I had felt what it was to be loved; but, like him, I had now put love out of the question, and thought only of duty.)…I sincerely, deeply, fervently longed to do what was right; and only that. 'Show me, show me the path!' I entreated of Heaven."

Before Jane can say anything more to St. John, a voice calls out to her from within her own heart. She recognizes it as Mr. Rochester's voice and calls out in response to it and even runs to the door after it. This forms her greater resolve to find Mr. Rochester. She cannot and *will not* marry St. John.

How Can You Apply This to Your Own Life?

What does true forgiveness look like?

We have talked a lot about how important forgiveness is throughout Jane Eyre. It is the first step toward reconciliation with God, ourselves, and others. But what does real forgiveness look like?

 First of all, love and forgiveness are synonymous. One of the issues I have with St. John is that he does not balance love with works. He despises how love feels and thinks it useless. This is expressed through, not only his romantic feelings toward Rosamond, but also when he tells Jane that he does not love her.

We have already established that St. John is dealing with a lot of bitterness which shows up as self-pity and self-loathing. When someone is self-loathing, they cannot properly express or show love to others or to themselves.

Though he said he forgives Jane, she can tell that he is constantly replaying her words in his mind and dwelling on them.

Unforgiveness hurts *us* more than it hurts those we are holding grudges against. St. John is in extreme bondage to his bitterness, and it is destroying a potentially great man of God.

The Enemy wants you to dwell on the words spoken to you. He wants you to remember them because that is how he can keep you trapped by them. Then when he has us in bondage, we become less affective for the kingdom of God. That breach of relationship is then created between you and God.

"For ye have not received the spirit of bondage [figuratively slavery] *again to fear; but ye have received the Spirit of adoption* [figuratively, Christian sonship in respect to God], *whereby we cry, Abba, Father."* Romans 8:15

We are called into the spirit of adoption as God's chosen people. We are His children through the Holy Spirit.

"Put on therefore, as the elect [favorite, chosen] *of God, holy and beloved, bowels* [inward affection, tender mercy] *of mercies, kindness, humbleness of mind, meekness, longsuffering; forbearing one another, and forgiving* [pardon or rescue, deliver, freely give, grant] *one another, if any man have a quarrel against any: even as Christ forgave you, so also do ye. And above all these things put on charity* [affection, dear, brotherly love, love feast], *which is the bond of perfectness* [completeness (mentally or morally)]."
Colossians 3:13

As God's children, we are called to love others freely and with that, comes the free gift of forgiveness. The above verse solidifies how we are to behave toward ourselves and others and so be in obedience to the Word. Do not let the enemy of our souls convince you to take on poison. It is never contained by our souls and will always find a way out to affect others.

"Let all bitterness [acridity, hatred]*, and wrath* [fierceness, indignation, passion]*, and anger* [excitement of the mind, violent passion, vengeance]*, and clamour* [tumult, grief, outcry]*, and evil speaking* [slander, injurious speech]*, be put away from you, with all malice* [wickedness, depravity]*: and be ye kind one to another, tenderhearted, forgiving one another, even as God for Christ's sake hath forgiven you."*
Ephesians 4:31-32

When we withhold forgiveness, we are not loving each other well but holding a record of wrongs against them. This stifles their growth and desire to do and be better.

"Thou shalt not hate thy brother in thine heart: thou shalt in any wise [correct, chasten, correction, plead, reason] *rebuke* [dispute, argue] *thy neighbor, and not suffer* [raise up, advance, swear, desire] *sin upon him. Thou shalt not avenge, nor bear any grudge* [cherish] *against the children of thy people, but thou shalt love thy neighbor as thyself: I am the LORD."* Leviticus 19: 17-18

There is also a call to forgive that you might also be forgiven of God. In Matthew, Jesus says that if we do not forgive our neighbors, our Father in heaven will not forgive us. Leviticus clearly shows us not to hold grudges and offences against one another. When we hold onto unforgiveness, we are breaking one of the most important commandments – love one another as Christ loves you.

"Be ye therefore merciful, as your Father also is merciful. Judge not, and ye shall not be judged: condemn not, and ye shall not be condemned: forgive, and ye shall be forgiven:" Luke 6:37

"For if ye forgive men their trespasses, your heavenly Father will also forgive you: but if ye forgive not men their trespasses [error or willful transgression, fault, offense, sin], *neither will your Father forgive your trespasses."* Matthew 6:14-15

The forgiveness we show here on earth is meant to represent the forgiveness of the Father in heaven.

"And they shall teach no more every man his neighbor, and every man his brother, saying, know the LORD: for they shall all know me, from the least of them unto the greatest of them, saith the LORD: for I will forgive their iniquity, and I will remember their sin no more." Jeremiah 31:34

"…and I will remember their sin no more." That is a very powerful statement! Satan's goal is to keep us in bondage, not only to our sin, but also the words and actions of others toward us. But God says that when we come to him in repentance for our sins, He will forget our sin completely.

In order to break free from this bondage, we must practice forgiving others. We might not forget as God does, but we can learn to train our minds and hearts to release spiritual gunk. Eventually, those hurts will disappear into the past and they will not be as painful as they were when they first happened.

It takes a lot of practice. It also takes a reliance on God's strength and love to keep us grounded as we learn.

As we continue to learn and practice loving others, forgiveness will become much easier to incorporate into our daily lives. As with all things that God commands, it for our growth and freedom, ultimately leading to communion and peace with our Father in heaven.

Chapter XXXVI

St. John leaves early in the morning before anyone else has woken up. Jane watches as he walks to meet the coach that will take him to Cambridge. Before leaving, he slips a note under Jane's door.

"'My spirit,' I answered mentally, 'is willing to do what is right; and my flesh, I hope, is strong enough to accomplish the will of Heaven, when once that will is distinctly known to me, At any rate, it shall be strong enough to search — inquire — to grope an outlet from this cloud of doubt, and find the open day of certainty.'"

"I recalled the voice I had heard; again I questioned whence it came, as vainly as before: it seemed in me — not in the external world."

Jane announces to Mary and Diana that she will be going on a journey, and they support her decision kindly. They know enough not to press the matter too hard, which gives Jane peace of mind and allows her to prepare for her trip quickly and efficiently.

Later that evening, Jane boards the same coach that, a year ago, took her *away* from Thornfield. It is a surreal feeling for her, but full of excitement and just a touch of anxiety.

When she arrives at an inn on Mr. Rochester's land, Jane knows that it would be best to inquire after him instead of blindly searching. She also needed to know if Mr. Rochester was indeed at Thornfield and not outside of the country.

"The suggestion was sensible, and yet I could not force myself to act on it. I so dreaded a reply that would crush me with despair. To prolong doubt was to prolong hope."

While she thinks about approaching the man at the inn, Jane ultimately decides to go on to Thornfield on her own. Her excitement overpowers her, and she runs to get there.

"'My first view of it shall be in front,' I determined, 'where its bold battlements will strike the eye nobly at once, and where I can single out my master's very window: perhaps he will be standing at it — he rises early: perhaps he is now walking in the orchard, or on the pavement in front. Could I but see him! — but a moment! Surely, in that case, I should not be so mad as to run to him? I cannot tell — I am not certain. And if I did — what then? God bless him! What then? Who would be hurt by my once more tasting the life his glance can give me? I rave: perhaps at this moment he is watching the sun rise over the Pyrenees, or on the tideless sea of the south.'"

"Hear an illustration, reader.

A lover finds his mistress asleep on a mossy bank; he wishes to catch a glimpse of her fair face without waking her. He steals softly over the grass, careful to make no sound; he pauses — fancying she has stirred: he withdraws: not for worlds would he be seen. All is still: he again advances: he bends above her; a light veil rests on her features: he lifts it,

*bends lower; now his eyes anticipate the vision of beauty —
warm, and blooming, and lovely, in rest. How hurried was
their first glance! But how they fix! How he starts! How he
suddenly and vehemently clasps in both arms the form he
dared not, a moment since, touch with his finger! How he
calls aloud a name, and drops his burden, and gazes on it
wildly! He thus grasps and cries, and gazes, because he no
longer fears to waken by any sound he can utter — by any
movement he can make. He thought his love slept sweetly: he
finds she is stone dead.*

*I looked with timorous joy towards a stately house; I saw a
blackened ruin."*

Jane approaches the horror before her, finding Thornfield a
burned and desolate place. Where is Mr. Rochester? Is he
alive?

Now Jane hopes that Mr. Rochester has left England. Unable
to find any answers in the desolation, she decides to return to
the inn to inquire after what happened to Thornfield and its
owner. The inn owner reveals that, to the best of his
knowledge, Mr. Rochester is still alive. This makes her
breathe more freely and makes her blood flow easier.

*"'Is Mr. Rochester living at Thornfield Hall now?' I asked,
knowing, of course, what the answer would be, but yet
desirous of deferring the direct question as to where he really
was.*

*'No, ma'am — oh no! No one is living there. I suppose you
are a stranger in these parts, or you would have heard what*

happened last autumn – Thornfield Hall is quite a ruin: it was burnt down just about harvest-time. A dreadful calamity!...The fire broke out at dead of night, and before the engines arrived from Millcote, the building was one mass of flame. It was a terrible spectacle: I witnessed it myself.'

'At dead of night!' I muttered. Yes, that was ever the hour of fatality at Thornfield. 'Was it known how it originated?' I demanded."

The inn owner begins to tell Jane the story of how Thornfield burned down. Mr. Rochester had a lunatic woman living in his house, who happened to be his wife. News went around that he fell in love with a governess about a year ago now.

"'…Mr. Edward fell in love…The servants say they never saw anybody so much in love as he was: he was after her continually. They used to watch him – servants will, you know, ma'am – and he set store on her past everything: for all, nobody but him thought her so very handsome. She was a little small thing, they say, almost like a child. I never saw her myself; but I've heard Leah, the house-maid, tell of her. Leah liked her well enough. Mr. Rochester was about forty, and this governess not twenty; and you see, when gentlemen of his age fall in love with girls, they are often like as if they were bewitched.'"

Finally, Jane is able to bring the man to the point of which she is most interested. He tells her that Mrs. Rochester (*Bertha*) was suspected of being the one who started the fire.

*"'…when Mrs. Poole was fast asleep after the gin and water,
the mad lady, who was as cunning as a witch, would take the
keys out of her pocket, let herself out of her chamber, and go
roaming about the house, doing any wild mischief that came
into her head…on this night, she set fire first to the hangings
of the room next her own, and then she got down to a lower
storey, and made her way to the chamber that had been the
governess's — (she was like as if she knew somehow how
matters had gone on, and had a spite at her) — and she
kindled the bed there; but there was nobody sleeping in it,
fortunately. The governess had run away two months before;
and for all Mr. Rochester sought her as if she had been the
most precious thing he had in the world, he never could hear
a word of her; and he grew savage — quite savage on his
disappointment: he never was a wild man, but he got
dangerous after he lost her. He would be alone, too. He sent
Mrs. Fairfax, the housekeeper, away to her friends at a
distance; but he did it handsomely, for he settled an annuity
on her for life:…Miss Adèle, a ward he had, was put to
school. He broke off acquaintance with all the gentry, and
shut himself up like a hermit at the Hall.'"*

Mr. Rochester had become a recluse. He ventured out only
during the night. As the fire grew, Mr. Rochester saved all
his servants and tried to save Bertha too, before she jumped
to her death off the roof.

Some claim that what happened next was a judgement for
keeping his marriage a secret and trying to wed another.

"'It was all his own courage, and a body may say, his kindness, in a way, ma'am: he wouldn't leave the house till every one else was out before him. As he came down the great staircase at last, after Mrs. Rochester had flung herself from the battlements, there was a great crash – all fell. He was taken out from under the ruins, alive, but sadly hurt: a beam had fallen in such a way as to protect him partly; but one eye was knocked out, and one hand so crushed that Mr. Carter, the surgeon, had to amputate it directly. The other eye inflamed: he lost the sight of that also. He is now helpless, indeed – blind, and a cripple.'"

This news is both painful and hopeful for Jane. Mr. Rochester, her Mr. Rochester, is alive! She immediately requests a chaise to take her to the isolated farmhouse in which Mr. Rochester is living.

How Can You Apply This to Your Own Life?

I want to remind you of a very important topic that we have discussed in chapter two and thirty-three. We discussed God's justice and judgement.

The reason I want to revisit this subject now is because it will be important in the next chapter. It was also briefly mentioned by the well-meaning innkeeper that Jane spoke to in reference to judgement upon Mr. Rochester.

God does not cause bad things to happen in the lives of the people He created. He is love and mercy always. But unfortunately, disobedience brings injustices and pain of the world. God wants us to be in agreement and fellowship with Him.

Jane chose to follow God's leading in her life and received blessing. The pain that came before did not come from a sin that she committed herself, but a poor choice made on the part of Mr. Rochester's. Remember, sometimes other people's sins do fall on us.

Mr. Rochester was a broken and hurting man who simply wanted to have joy and love in his life. In his mind, this could only be achieved by marrying Jane. However, God had other plans for these two. He knew that they both needed to come to a place that would help them return to Him and their foundations of faith.

Had Jane given in to the temptation to stay with Mr. Rochester, their growth might not have been the same. So, pain came from a poor decision, but God will reconcile that pain and bring joy back into the lives of these dear characters.

Jane never blamed God for the fact that she had to leave Mr. Rochester or for placing him in a situation to be married to a lunatic. She trusted that God would be her support as well as Mr. Rochester's.

God will never change. He will always be by our side, loving us and coaxing us toward righteousness. He provides a safe, healthy relationship in which we can go to Him at any time without shame or fear. He is the perfect Father.

I want you to keep all this in mind as you begin the next chapter. God did not bring torment on Mr. Rochester on purpose. But through the pain brought on by his and other people's (*his father, brother, and the Masons*) poor decisions, Mr. Rochester will learn how to be a better man. God chastens those He dearly loves and those who listen to that chastening will be His inheritance forever in heaven.

"The LORD knoweth the thoughts of man, that they are vanity. Blessed is the man whom thou chastenest [instruct, correct, reprove, admonish]*, O LORD, and teachest him out of thy law; that thou mayest give him rest from the days of adversity* [affliction, evil, exceedingly, great, grief, wickedness]*, until the pit be digged for the wicked. For the LORD will not cast off his people* [tribe, flock, nation]*, neither will he forsake his inheritance* [heritage]*. But judgment shall return* [recompense] *unto righteousness: and all the upright in heart shall follow it."* Psalm 94:11-15

Chapter XXXVII

The manor house in which Mr. Rochester is now living, was built by Mr. Rochester's father for shooting season. It was never tenanted and thus not furnished for regular living. It was somewhat decrepit and very hidden away from civilization.

Jane walks the rest of the way, having left the driver of the chaise with double the pay. She is probably a little anxious and too eager to wait in the chaise without physical action. She finds the house, after a long walk through the woods, very desolate and quiet.

"'Can there be life here?' I asked.

Yes, life of some kind there was; for I heard a movement — that narrow front-door was unclosing, and some shape was about to issue from the grange.

It opened slowly: a figure came out into the twilight and stood on the step — a man without a hat. He stretched forth his hand as if to feel whether it rained. Dusk as it was, I had recognized him — it was my master, Edward Fairfax Rochester, and no other."

She silently watches and observes. She finds that he is the same as when she left. All his features and athletic build familiar.

"But in his countenance I saw a change: that looked desperate and brooding — that reminded me of some wronged

and fettered wild beast or bird, dangerous to approach in his sullen woe. The caged eagle, whose gold-ringed eyes cruelty has extinguished, might look as looked that sightless Samson.

And, reader, do you think I feared him in his blind ferocity? — if you do, you little know me. A soft hope blent with my sorrow that soon I should dare to drop a kiss on that brow of rock, and on those lips so sternly sealed beneath it; but not yet. I would not accost him yet."

When Mr. Rochester retires back in the house, Jane knocks on the door and is recognized by the servant who answers. She is ushered in and gives a brief account of why she has come.

Mr. Rochester rings for candles and water and Jane insists that she will bring them in to him.

"'Give the tray to me; I will carry it in.'

I took it from her hand: she pointed me out the parlour door. The tray shook as I held it; the water spilt from the glass; my heart struck my ribs loud and fast."

Pilot, Mr. Rochester's dog, instantly recognizes Jane and continues to accost her in his excitement. When she tells him to sit, Mr. Rochester starts at the sound of her voice but cannot seem to pinpoint it at first.

As she continues to speak, he recognizes her and believes he is delusional; that she is only a dream.

"'Pilot knows me, and John and Mary know I am here. I came only this evening.' I answered.

'Great God! — what delusion has come over me? What sweet madness has seized me?'

'No delusion — no madness: your mind, sir, is too strong for delusion, your health too sound for frenzy.'

'And where is the speaker? Is it only a voice? Oh! I cannot see, but I must feel, or my heart will stop and my brain burst. Whatever — whoever you are — be perceptible to the touch or I cannot live!'

He groped; I arrested his wandering hand, and prisoned it in both mine."

He recognizes her fingers, her arm, shoulder, neck, and waist as he pulls her toward him. He is almost speechless as the figure in his arms matches the voice he hears.

"'My living darling! These are certainly her limbs, and these her features; but I cannot be so blest, after all my misery. It is a dream; such dreams as I have had at night when I have clasped her once more to my heart, as I do now; and kissed her, as thus — and felt that she loved me, and trusted that she would not leave me.'

'Which I never will, sir, from this day.'"

He still does not believe this is real. He has lived alone in his pain for so long that he does not believe he could be so blessed.

"'…but kiss me before you go – embrace me, Jane.'

'There, sir – and there!'

I pressed my lips to his once brilliant and now rayless eyes – I swept his hair from his brow, and kissed that too. He suddenly seemed to arouse himself: the conviction of the reality of all this seized him.

'It is you – is it, Jane? You are come back to me then?'

'I am.'"

She tells him of her independence and wealth. This seems to convince him even further that she is real as he could never make up such details on his own. Jane expresses her desire to be Mr. Rochester's neighbor, his nurse, and his housekeeper.

"He replied not: he seemed serious – abstracted; he sighed;…I felt a little embarrassed. Perhaps I had too rashly over-leaped conventionalities; and he, like St. John, saw impropriety in my inconsiderateness. I had indeed made my proposal from the idea that he wished and would ask me to be his wife: and expectation, not the less certain because unexpressed, had buoyed me up, that he would claim me at once as his own. But no hint to that effect escaping him, and his countenance becoming more overcast, I suddenly remembered that I might have been all wrong, and was perhaps playing the fool unwittingly; and I began gently to withdraw myself from his arms – but he eagerly snatched me closer.

'No – no – Jane; you must not go. No – I have touched you, heard you, felt the comfort of your presence – the sweetness of your consolation: I cannot give up these joys. I have little left in myself – I must have you. The world may laugh – may call me absurd, selfish – but it does not signify. My very soul demands you: it will be satisfied, or it will take deadly vengeance on its frame.'"

Jane reassures him that she is not leaving him and that she will nurse him as long as he needs. Mr. Rochester believes that now, in his current condition, he is no longer good enough for Jane to attach herself to. He thinks he is too broken. And yet Jane believes he has never been more precious to her.

"'On this arm, I have neither hand nor nails,' he said, drawing the mutilated limb from his breast, and showing it to me. 'It is a mere stump – a ghastly sight! Don't you think so, Jane?'

'It is a pity to see it; and a pity to see your eyes – and the scar of fire on your forehead: and the worst of it is, one is in danger of loving you too well for all this; and making too much of you.'

'I thought you would be revolted, Jane, when you saw my arm, and my cicatrized visage.'"

Jane proves her unwavering depth of love through her ability to buoy his spirits up and accept him as she has always done, no matter what.

*"My spirits were excited, and with pleasure and ease I talked
to him during supper, and for a long time after. There was
no harassing restraint, no repressing of glee and vivacity
with him; for with him I was at perfect ease, because I knew I
suited him; all I said or did seemed either to console or revive
him. Delightful consciousness! It brought to life and light
my whole nature: in his presence I thoroughly lived; and he
lived in mine. Blind as he was, smiles played over his face,
joy dawned on his forehead: his lineaments softened and
warmed."*

The contrast between St. John and Mr. Rochester becomes
more glaringly obvious. Jane can be herself around Mr.
Rochester whereas, her whole personality was stifled when
she was around St. John.

Jane and Mr. Rochester bring out the very best in each other.
They revive each other and bring joy to one another.
Throughout their conversations, he had to keep reminding
himself that Jane was still there by touching her arm or hand.
He is terrified that she will leave him again. He is afraid that
the joy he finds in her will be snatched away.

*"'And there is enchantment in the very hour I am now
spending with you. Who can tell what a dark, dreary,
hopeless life I have dragged on for months past? Doing
nothing, expecting nothing; merging night in day; feeling
but the sensation of cold when I let the fire go out, of hunger
when I forgot to eat: and then a ceaseless sorrow, and, at
times, a very delirium of desire to behold my Jane again. Yes:
for her restoration I longed, far more than for that of my lost
sight. How can it be that Jane is with me, and says she loves*

me? Will she not depart as suddenly as she came? To-morrow, I fear I shall find her no more.'"

Jane tries to draw him away from his thoughts of fear by changing the subject. She is so good at helping Mr. Rochester come out of his dark thoughts.

He asks about where Jane has been all these months. She promises to tell the story the next day, which will at least give him hope that she will return to him.

The next day…

"…I had a view of him before he discovered my presence. It was mournful, indeed, to witness the subjugation of that vigorous spirit to a corporeal infirmity. He sat in his chair — still, but not at rest: expectant evidently; the lines of now habitual sadness marking his strong features. His countenance reminded one of a lamp quenched, waiting to be re-lit; and alas! It was not himself that could now kindle the lustre of animated expression: he was dependent on another for that office! I had meant to be gay and careless, but the powerlessness of the strong man touched my heart to the quick: still I accosted him with what vivacity I could.

'It is a bright, sunny morning, sir,' I said. 'The rain is over and gone, and there is a tender shining after it: you shall have a walk soon.'

I had wakened the glow: his features beamed."

They spend the morning together outside. Jane describes to him the beauty of the world around them so that he might enjoy it alongside her. She allows him to seat her on his knee for,

"Why should I [not], when both he and I were happier near than apart?" – brackets added by me

Finally, she tells Mr. Rochester of where she has been, softening the parts she knows would cause him pain.

He responds (*repeated by Jane*):

"I should have confided in him: he would never have forced me to be his mistress. Violent as he had seemed in his despair, he, in truth, loved me far too well and too tenderly to constitute himself my tyrant: he would have given me half his fortune, without demanding so much as a kiss in return, rather than I should have flung myself friendless on the wide world. I had endured, he was certain, more than I had confessed to him."

If we ever had a poor view of Mr. Rochester and how he treated Jane the night before she left, this makes everything clearer. In his pain, he was rash, but would never have forced Jane into anything she believed was wrong. He loved her too much, too faithfully to ever force her to be anything or do anything that was against who she was.

Some envy and jealousy come over Mr. Rochester as she talks about St. John. He begins to enquire what he was like, his age, his personality, his conversation, his looks.

"Jealousy had got hold of him: she stung him; but the sting was salutary: it gave him respite from the gnawing fang of

melancholy. I would not, therefore, immediately charm the snake."

He begins questioning her and she allows it. When he finds that St. John proposed marriage to Jane, he becomes angry and tells her to go to him if she so desires. Jane refuses to leave and she tells him that St. John does not love her but only wanted her mind and servitude.

"'What, Jane! Is this true? Is such really the state of matters between you and Rivers?'

'Absolutely, sir! Oh, you need not be jealous! I wanted to tease you a little to make you less sad: I thought anger would be better than grief. But if you wish me to love you, could you but see how much I do love you, you would be proud and content. All my heart is yours, sir: it belongs to you; and with you it would remain, were fate to exile the rest of me from your presence for ever.'"

Mr. Rochester still feels that he is too broken for her to love.

"Again, as he kissed me, painful thoughts darkened his aspect.

'My seared vision! My crippled strength!' he murmured regretfully.

I caressed, in order to soothe him. I knew of what he was thinking, and wanted to speak for him, but dared not. As he turned aside his face a minute, I saw a tear slide from under the sealed eyelid, and trickle down the manly cheek. My heart swelled.

'I am no better than the old lightning-struck chestnut-tree in Thornfield orchard,' he remarked ere long. 'And what right would that ruin have to bid a budding woodbine cover its decay with freshness?'

'You are no ruin, sir – no lightning-struck tree: you are green and vigorous. Plants will grow about your roots, whether you ask them or not, because they take delight in your bountiful shadow; and as they grow they will lean towards you, and wind round you, because your strength offers them so safe a prop.'

Again he smiled: I gave him comfort."

He wants a wife. A real wife who will love him and care for him. One that he can love and care for in return.

"'Choose then, sir – her who loves you best.'

'I will at least choose – her I love best. Jane, will you marry me?'

'Yes, sir.'

'A poor blind man, whom you will have to lead about by the hand?'

'Yes, sir.'

'A crippled man, twenty years older than you, whom you will have to wait on?'

'Yes, sir.'

'Truly, Jane?'

'Most truly, sir.'

'Oh! My darling! God bless you and reward you!'

'Mr. Rochester, if ever I did a good deed in my life – if ever I thought a good thought – if every I prayed a sincere and blameless prayer – if ever I wished a righteous wish – I am rewarded now. To be your wife is, for me, to be as happy as I can be on earth.'"

From this moment on, Mr. Rochester says he will no longer hate being cared for and helped. He will find it a joy, as long as his Jane is there to perform the tasks.

"'Jane! You think me, I dare say, an irreligious dog: but my heart swells with gratitude to the beneficent God of this earth just now. He sees not as man sees, but far clearer: judges not as man judges, but far more wisely. I did wrong: I would have sullied my innocent flower – breathed guilt on its purity: the Omnipotent snatched it from me. I, in my stiff-necked rebellion, almost cursed the dispensation: instead of bending to the decree, I defied it. Divine justice pursued its course; disasters came thick on me: I was forced to pass through the valley of the shadow of death. His chastisements are might; and one smote me which has humbled me for ever. You know I was proud of my strength: but what is it now, when I must give it over to foreign guidance, as a child does its weakness? Of late, Jane – only – only of late – I began to see and acknowledge the hand of God in my doom. I began to experience remorse, repentance, the wish for reconcilement to my Maker. I began sometimes to pray: very brief prayers they were, but very sincere.

Some days since: nay, I can number them — four; it was last Monday night, a singular mood came over me: one in which grief replaced frenzy — sorrow, sullenness. I had long had the impression that since I could nowhere find you, you must be dead. Late that night — perhaps it might be between eleven and twelve o'clock — ere I retired to my dreary rest, I supplicated God, that, if it seemed good to Him, I might soon be taken from this life, and admitted to that world to come, where there was still hope of rejoining Jane…

I asked of God, at once in anguish and humility, if I had not been long enough desolate, afflicted, tormented; and might not soon taste bliss and peace once more. That I merited all I endured, I acknowledged — that I could scarcely endure more, I pleaded; and the alpha and omega of my heart's wishes broke involuntarily form my lips in the words, "Jane! Jane! Jane!""

The very time he called out in agony, is the time Jane heard her name being called in Moor House. Mr. Rochester also heard, in response to his call, "I am coming: wait for me" which is exactly what Jane called out in response.

"Reader, it was on Monday night — near midnight — that I too had received the mysterious summons: those were the very words by which I replied to it."

She did not tell him this, however, but kept it close and pondered it in her heart.

"'I thank my Maker, that, in the midst of judgment, He has remembered mercy. I humbly entreat my Redeemer to give

me strength to lead henceforth a purer life than I have done hitherto!'

Then he stretched his hand out to be led. I took that dear hand, held it a moment to my lips, then let it pass round my shoulder: being so much lower of stature than he, I served both for his prop and guide. We entered the wood, and wended homeward."

How Can You Apply This to Your Own Life?

This is such a precious chapter. It reveals so much about Mr. Rochester and how he has been fairing since Jane's departure as well as how he feels *about* himself now that he has been injured.

Mr. Rochester feels himself too broken and battered to be loved in the same way as before. More than that, he feels weakened. As a man who has always been strong and capable and independent, he is still trying to reconcile himself to the fact that he will need someone to nurse him.

Little does he know; this is Jane's utmost pleasure. She has, from the beginning of our story, said how much she desires to be useful to those around her. Not only is she loved completely for who she is, she is able to do what she loves best; serving the man she loves with a gracious heart.

You see, throughout Jane's growth, we have witnessed how she loves others. She greatly desired to be of service and that almost convinced her that going to India with St. John was her calling. But God called her to something so much more delightful.

Then we have Mr. Rochester, who has only ever desired to be the type of man that Jane deserves. During his time apart from her, he has come to a reconciliation with God. He began to pray and seek repentance. His experiences humbled him in a way that Jane never could.

He may be broken in body, but his spirit is renewed.

It is very easy to feel unworthy of love when you are struggling and in pain, whether physical or spiritual. It can make you feel inefficient or burdensome to the people around you.

What you need to understand is that in spite of all the brokenness inside you, God still loves you and will until the end of time. He desires repentance that you may be reunited in holy fellowship with Him. When that occurs, brokenness, though it may be a little sore for a time, will mend.

The more Jane believed in Mr. Rochester and showed him that he was worthy of much more than he thought, the more he believed it for himself. He believed that he was a good man because Jane showed him that he was. Her not leaving when things were difficult, showed her love for him and her steadfastness.

Jesus is the same. Jane saw Mr. Rochester's heart and knew his desires to be a good man. Jesus knows the desires of our hearts. If our desires are placed on Him and His word, what flows out of our hearts will be Christ-honoring.

"With my whole heart have I sought thee: O let me not wander from thy commandments. Thy word have I hid in mine heart, that I might not sin against thee." Psalm 119:10-11

"My son, give me thine heart, and let thine eyes observe my ways." Proverbs 23:26

"Create in me a clean heart, O God; and renew a right spirit within me." Psalm 51:10

"Examine me, O LORD, and prove me; try my reins [figuratively the mind] *and my heart."* Psalm 26:2

Only God can heal brokenness and restore you to right fellowship with Him. Seek and you will find (*Matthew 7:7*). You have the steps you need, now it is time to take action. God's arms are open and ready to receive you, His precious child.

Chapter XXXVIII

"Reader, I married him."

This line gives me chills every time. In my opinion, it is one of the greatest lines to begin a final chapter.

They had a quiet wedding. John, the long-time servant of Mr. Rochester's approved whole-heartedly and sincerely wished them joy.

Jane wrote to Mary and Diana to which Diana replied that she would come and visit as soon as their honeymoon was over.

"'She had better not wait till then, Jane,' said Mr. Rochester, when I read her letter to him; 'if she does, she will be too late, for our honeymoon will shine our life long: its beams will only fade over your grave or mine.'"

Jane also wrote to St. John but never received a reply to the letter she wrote. Instead, he wrote to her semi-regularly but never alluded to her marriage to Mr. Rochester. He expressed hope that she was not giving into worldly desires and living without God.

"You have not quite forgotten little Adèle, have you, reader? I had not; I soon asked and obtained leave of Mr. Rochester, to go and see her at the school where he had placed her. Her frantic joy at beholding me again moved me much. She looked pale and thin: she said she was not happy. I found the

rules of the establishment were too strict, its course of study too severe, for a child of her age: I took her home with me."

Jane placed Adèle in a school nearer her that cared for their students better. She became quite a docile and companionable person and Jane enjoyed it when she came to visit.

"I have now been married ten years. I know what it is to live entirely for and with what I love best on earth. I hold myself supremely blest — blest beyond what language can express; because I am my husband's life as fully as he is mine. No woman was ever nearer to her mate than I am: ever more absolutely bone of his bone and flesh of his flesh. I know no weariness of my Edward's society: he knows none of mine, any more than we each do of the pulsation of the heart that beats in our separate bosoms; consequently, we are ever together. To be together is for us to be at once as free as in solitude, as gay as in company. We talk, I believe, all day long: to talk to each other is but a more animated and an audible thinking. All my confidence is bestowed on him, all his confidence is devoted to me; we are precisely suited in character — perfect concord is the result.

Mr. Rochester continued blind the first two years of our union; perhaps it was that circumstance that drew us so very near — that knit us so very close: for I was then his vision, as I am still his right hand. Literally, I was (what he often called me) the apple of his eye. He saw nature — he saw books through me; and never did I weary of gazing for his behalf, and of putting into words the effect of field, tree, town, river, cloud, sunbeam — of the landscape before us; of the weather round us — and impressing by sound on his ear what light could no longer stamp on his eye. Never did I weary of reading to him; never did I weary of conducting him where he wished to go: of doing for him what he wished to be done. And there was a pleasure in my services, most full, most exquisite, even though sad — because he claimed these services without painful shame or damping humiliation. He loved me so truly, that he knew no reluctance in profiting by my attendance: he felt I loved him so fondly, that to yield that attendance was to indulge me sweetest wishes."

Eventually, Mr. Rochester regained his sight and was able to see enough around him to be able to find his way around and enjoy nature through his own eyes.

"When his first-born was put into his arms, he could see that the boy had inherited his own eyes, as they once were — large, brilliant, and black. On that occasion, he again, with a full heart, acknowledged that God had tempered judgment with mercy."

Jane, being the gracious and loving person she is, says that she is happier because those she loves best have also found happiness in life. Diana married an officer in the navy and Mary a clergyman. They all visited each other frequently.

"Both Captain Fitzjames and Mr. Wharton love their wives, and are loved by them."

"St. John is unmarried: he never will marry now. Himself has hitherto sufficed to the toil, and the toil draws near its

*close: his glorious sun hastens to its setting. The last letter I
received from him drew from my eyes human tears, and yet
filled my heart with divine joy: he anticipated his sure
reward, his incorruptible crown. I know that a stranger's
hand will write to me next, to say that the good and faithful
servant has been called at length into the joy of his Lord."*

How Can You Apply This to Your Own Life?

One of the greatest attributes of Jane's is that she took
personal preparation seriously. She understood that her
future was uncertain, but she had to be ready for what was to
come.

Part of this preparation was personal accountability and
responsibility for her actions, her words, and her faith. She
took the time to discover who she was as God's daughter,
establishing a solid identity.

We do not know what lies around the corner. We do not
know who God will bring into our lives, where He will place
us, or even how we will be called to serve. The key to
avoiding falling into fear is through preparation and trusting
in the Holy Spirit's guidance.

Part of that preparation is holding ourselves accountable
according to God's word. It all goes back to – where does
your heart reside?

*"But take diligent heed to do the commandment and the law,
which Moses the servant of the LORD charged you, to love
the LORD your God, and to walk in all his ways, and to keep*

his commandments, and to cleave unto him, and to serve him with all your heart and with all your soul." Joshua 22:5

"I will praise thee, O LORD, with my whole heart; I will shew forth all thy marvellous works." Psalm 9:1

Whatever you focus your efforts on, whatever you are continually thinking about, talking about, and participating in will eventually become part of you. This is why God tells us to be careful where we place our loyalties. You are to store up your treasures, not in the world, but in heaven. These will be spiritual treasures that will help provide you with a solid identity in Christ.

Love as Christ loved, choose faith over fear, read God's word, pray without ceasing, and go to God when things get difficult or when you feel weak. Remember, God will never leave your side. He is waiting for you to recognize Him and call on Him. He will be your strength. He will be your peace.

"A good man out of the good treasure of his heart bringeth forth that which is good; and an evil man out of the evil treasure of his heart bringeth forth that which is evil: for of the abundance [of that which fills the heart] *of the heart his mouth speaketh."* Luke 6:45

"For where your treasure is, there will your heart be also." Luke 12:34

Only when you have established that solid identity in who God created you to be, can you be fully prepared for the future God has for you. People will begin to see Christ in you and will seek that peace, joy, contentment, and faith for themselves.

"But sanctify the Lord God in your hearts: and be ready always to give an answer to every man that asketh you a reason of the hope [expectation, faith] *that is in you with meekness and fear* [reverence]*:" 1 Peter 3:15*

Conclusion

Thank you, reader, for going on this journey with me! It has been a glorious ride! I hope that you have been comforted by what you have read and that you have been able to grow in your relationship with your Father. I also hope that you feel empowered as a warrior for the kingdom of God. It has been my greatest joy to be able to write this book for you. Know that I am here, rooting for you and praying for you.

You are an amazing person, created in the beautiful and perfect image of God! Walk in faith that He will never leave you but will continually draw you closer to Him and will fight for your heart.

Many blessings,

Amanda